Our Husband

Stephanie Bond was seven years deep into a computer programming career and pursuing her MBA when her tutor encouraged her to write. Two years later she sold her first book, a romantic comedy, and soon left the corporate world to become a full-time writer. She has since seen eleven books into print. She lives with her husband in Atlanta, Georgia.

Our Husband

STEPHANIE BOND

Macmillan

First published 2000 by St Martin's Press, New York

This edition published 2001 by Macmillan
an imprint of Macmillan Publishers Ltd
25 Eccleston Place, London SW1W 9NF
Basingstoke and Oxford
Associated companies throughout the world
www.macmillan.com

ISBN 0 333 90739 6 (hardback)
ISBN 0 333 90740 X (trade paperback)

1 3 5 7 9 8 6 4 2

A CIP catalogue record for this book is available from the British Library.

Typeset by SetSystems Ltd, Saffron Walden, Essex
Printed and bound in Great Britain by
Mackays of Chatham plc, Chatham, Kent

I dedicate this book to the teachers who
made a difference in my life,
who filled my world with
books and art and possibilities:

Ms. Alice Sue Dehart
Ms. June Ross
Ms. Stella Patton
Ms. Rosewood Napier
Ms. Janice Harris
Mr. Larry Carroll
Ms. Nancy McKenzie
Ms. Patty Carroll
Ms. Norma Cartee
Mr. Paul Webb

And to my greatest teachers of all:

Willis and Bonnie Bond

Acknowledgements

I would like to thank the people who contributed their professional and moral support to this book: Ruth Kagle, a great friend and first-class agent, along with all the folks at the Jane Rotrosen Agency; Jennifer Enderlin, a fearless editor; Chris Hauck, my dear husband; Rita Herron and Carmen Green, steadfast critique partners; Jamie and Cindy Bond, siblings extraordinaire; Teresa Fisher, my walking buddy and plotting pal; Blair Fisher, aka Mr Trivia; and Lee Herron and Jim Campbell for input from their respective fields of expertise.

A thousand thanks.

Our Husband

One

"I'LL BET THAT trinket cost Raymond an arm and a leg." Dr. Natalie Carmichael tore her gaze from the diamond solitaire pendant she fingered and glanced up as her nurse, sagging from end-of-the-day fatigue, shuffled into her cramped office carrying a stack of yellow patient folders.

At the tired reference to her husband's prosthetic limb sales job, Natalie lifted one corner of her mouth. "Ha, ha. Wait, here's a spot." She moved the phone to make room for the files, her husband's voice still fresh in her mind. God, she missed him this week!

After lightening her load, Sara leaned forward and cooed at the large stone. "If you ever get tired of that generous man of yours, I'll take him off your hands."

Her friend's words fed the guilt gnawing at Natalie's stomach. Yes, the pendant was exquisite, but something about it . . . something about her husband over these last few months . . .

Oh, *bother*, she was just feeling hormonal and lonely. She swiveled forward in her soft leather chair and smirked. "Eat your heart out, Sara. Raymond's a one-woman man."

"Dirty shame, too. That man is like a pot of warm honey, just begging to be spread around. Anniversary?"

"Uh-hmm."

"Five years?"

"Six this weekend, but he always gives me gifts early."

"The man's a gem, I tell you." Then Sara's mouth drooped. "Unlike my Joey."

Glad for Sara's gabby distraction, Natalie dropped the long-chained pendant inside her thin sweater to keep it out of the way while she finished her paperwork. "I thought you were growing rather fond of Joey."

"I was. I *am*. But . . . he cleaned my gutters last night."

"Is that some kind of lurid small-town Missouri analogy?"

Sara laughed. "No. He really cleaned my gutters."

"And?"

"And he left his extension ladder in my garage."

Natalie blinked rapidly. "And?"

"*And* a guy like Joey doesn't leave his tools just anywhere. I think he's going to propose."

She bit back a smile at the woman's rationale, especially since her nurse had demonstrated an uncanny knack for sizing up people in their six-month liaison. Sara could practically diagnose a patient's problem—psychological and physiological—by looking at their teeth and fingernails. "Are you going to say yes?"

Sara perched a generous hip on the corner of the rosewood desk. "I haven't decided. But Joey's handy at fixing things, and my house sure could use a new roof."

Natalie lifted an eyebrow. "You can't marry him for a few shingles."

"Of course not. I'll hold out for a gazebo, too."

Natalie wagged a finger. "Admit it, you like the guy."

Sara wrinkled her petite nose. "He's kind of crummy in bed."

"I don't think I want to know this. Besides, sex does not a marriage make."

"Hmm. Easy for you to say—you and Raymond are still on your honeymoon."

Longing pooled in her stomach at the mere thought of her husband's grin . . . He still moved her. "Being away from each other so much keeps things new, I suppose." She dragged the folders toward her. "How many patients today? I lost count."

"Fifty-two. Did you get to eat lunch?"

"I found a bag of sunflower seeds in a drawer."

"No wonder you're so skinny. If you want a snack, Mrs. Raglan just dropped off a plate of oatmeal Scotties because her knee feels so much better."

Natalie smiled fondly. "That wasn't necessary."

"She swears you healed her."

"Me and a syringe of cortisone. I'm afraid her relief is temporary."

Sara shrugged. "You can do no wrong in the eyes of the folks around here." She pushed away from the desk and headed toward the door. "Joey and I are taking in both shows at the dollar theater tonight—want to tag along?"

Natalie shook her head. "I've put off unpacking Raymond's book collection far too long. The moving boxes are driving me nuts. Thanks anyway." She rolled her wrist to check the time. "Why don't you take off? I'll lock up."

"Thanks, I will. See you tomorrow." Sara turned at the door. "Oh . . . your brother called again." Her eyes glowed with curiosity, but Natalie simply forged a smile and thanked her for taking the message.

Alone, she massaged a sudden pain in her right temple. In the tidy room she wanted her life to be, her brother was an upturned area rug. Tony, the family thief, had been granted an early parole from the state penitentiary and needed a place to stay once he left the halfway house—just until he got back on his feet, he'd assured her. He'd thought of his beloved sister first, he'd declared in a charming voice when he called last weekend.

Natalie suspected his thoughts ran more toward her beloved bank account, but as his closest living relative, she felt morally obligated to help him. Still, unease needled her. She resented the threat of his appearance in her well-ordered life—a private, quiet existence she'd come to guard jealously. The worshipful respect the locals lavished upon her made her feel special. What would her patients think when they discovered not only that her brother was an ex-con, but that she'd brought him to live in their midst?

Torn, she'd stalled Tony until she could discuss his "visit" with Raymond, but she'd purposely neglected to mention Tony's name when her husband had called earlier to let her know what time he'd be home Friday. He barely tolerated her brother, leaving Natalie struggling between loyalties to the two men. She tossed two aspirin to the back of her throat and swallowed them dry.

The door opened again and Sara stuck her head in. "Oops, we have a straggler—fellow with indigestion."

Natalie sighed. She'd wanted the life of a small-town doctor, but by five-thirty on Wednesday of a spring stomach-virus outbreak week, the job's romantic appeal had dimmed. A split second later she chastised herself. "Sure, I'll see him."

"I thought you might," Sara said, pulling a new yellow folder from behind her back and walking it over. "Mr. Butler is forty-three years old, no family history of heart disease, blood pressure is good. He's also deficient in vitamin A." She tapped her temple and mouthed "the eyes," in answer to Natalie's unasked question.

"Thanks, Sara. You can go on home."

Sara lowered her voice to a rolling whisper, as if the man were crouched outside the door. "He looks dangerous—maybe I'd better stick around."

Accustomed to her nurse's melodrama, Natalie simply smiled. "That's not necessary. Which room?"

"The Blue Room."

"Got it. Have a nice evening."

Natalie sat unmoving as the paneled door swung shut. In the distance, she heard the distinct clack of the heavy front door closing. Suddenly exhausted, she held the folder with both hands, and stared blindly at the man's name and address printed in caps.

Her brother was encroaching, and Raymond was withdrawing, or so it seemed. After six years of a part-time marriage due to his travel schedule, she yearned for more emotional intimacy. But she was beginning to think her happy-go-lucky husband was afraid, if not incapable, of true closeness. At least with her.

Why Raymond's indefinable retreat had converged in her mind today, she couldn't fathom. He'd sounded normal on the phone—even anxious to arrive home. To her knowledge, their basically happy marriage was no less intact today than yesterday. So why did she have this, this . . . *premonition* that crisis lurked just around the corner?

After a few minutes of numbing muse, she pushed herself to her aching feet. The man with indigestion didn't care if she was facing personal dilemmas—he probably wanted to go home and eat pork barbecue.

In the hallway, she conjured up a smile, then opened the

squeaky door to the Blue Room. Mr. Butler, a big man, sat near the door on a diminutive chair, surrounded by cloud-blue walls, his hands resting on wide knees. From his physique, one might think he was a professional athlete, but his clothing betrayed him. His tie hung loose at the collar, his shirtsleeves were rolled up to his elbows. His jacket lay folded on the padded examination table. He was darkly handsome, decidedly unkempt, and she immediately understood why Sara had described him as dangerous. A white scar extended from his hairline, running to just above his left eyebrow, hinting at an old injury severe enough to have caused a concussion—at the very least.

"Good afternoon, Mr. Butler, I'm Dr. Carmichael."

His gaze darted to her legs, then he gave her a friendly nod. "Pleasure's mine, Doc."

Ignoring his perusal, she retrieved a mechanical pencil from her pocket. Careful to keep her skirt from riding up, she lowered herself onto a stool with rollers and opened his file. A simple case, in and out. Her thoughts skipped ahead to dinner—a salad sounded good. A half-cake of goat cheese lay languishing in the fridge. "What seems to be the trouble?"

"The trouble," the man said, his voice polite but rueful, "is that your husband's luck ran out."

Natalie glanced up from the file and blinked. "Excuse me?"

He turned and with one long-armed reach, locked the door. Disbelief bolted through her, her mind reeling at the possible ramifications of her carelessness. Sara had been right. As usual. She propelled the stool and herself into the farthest corner, then scrambled to her feet. "Leave now, or I'll scream." As an afterthought, she held up her pencil like an ice pick.

Instead, the man calmly pushed himself to his feet and

wagged a large finger, his demeanor almost weary. "Lead poisoning is a serious matter, Doc. Relax, I'm not going to hurt you. Your husband owes me money, and I'm here simply to collect a late payment."

Natalie found her voice cowering in the back of her throat. "I-I don't know what you're talking about."

He smiled sadly, his dark eyes crinkling at the corners. "Sorry to be the bearer of bad news, but your husband is a gambler, among other things. And worse, he's a bad gambler." He sighed. "I need your jewelry."

Natalie shook her head slowly, her hand involuntarily moving to cover her wedding ring. "You're not serious."

"'Fraid so," he said, leaning over to reach into a bulging jacket pocket.

A gun. He had a gun. Or a blade. All thugs carried a blade. Natalie threw her head back and unleashed a shrill scream, knowing she was completely isolated in the top of the old building, but hoping he'd be spooked.

Instead, he winced, then poked a finger in his ear. "Please don't do that. God knows I hear enough screeching at home." Instead of a weapon, he withdrew a sheath of rolled-up papers, then spread them on the examining table.

Natalie stared at him, searching her mind for the location of the closest asylum. Perhaps he had wandered away during finger-painting class. "Who *are* you?"

He pointed to the patient folder lying facedown on the floor. "It says right there—Brian Butler."

"But . . . but why would my husband owe you money?"

"Because he borrowed it and didn't pay it back."

Natalie relaxed a fraction of an inch—the guy was dim. "You obviously have my husband confused with someone else."

"Raymond Carmichael, forty-two, drives a ninety-nine green Bonneville, and sells plastic legs for a living."

"Prostheses," she corrected, determined to retain some measure of control.

He shrugged. "Tomato, tom*ah*to."

Natalie swallowed hard. Could Raymond possibly be mixed up with such a shady character? "Why should I believe that my husband owes you money?"

"Because I don't lie. And," he nodded toward the table, "I have his signature on the loan papers. If you don't believe me, check them out." He smiled wryly, then extended his hand, palm up. "But first, surrender your weapon."

When she didn't move, he wiggled his fingers. "Come on, lady. I have to pick up my kids from daycare in twenty minutes."

He didn't seem intent on harming her, so Natalie relinquished her pencil and warily approached the table. The forms were numerous, but simple: the amount of the loan, the astronomical interest rate, the collateral, the signature. The numbers swam before her eyes, as did Raymond's telltale signature. A signature that pledged her appraised jewelry and—she swallowed—their property against default. Raymond couldn't have signed over the title of their home without her permission, her mind screamed. But then she remembered that he could because she'd assigned him her power of attorney when they closed on the condo in St. Louis two years ago.

She looked back to the stranger, laughing with incredulity. "There must be over a hundred thousand dollars' worth of loans here."

He made a sympathetic sound with his cheek. "Sorry, Doc. The wife is always the last to know."

Natalie frowned. "What are you, some kind of a loan shark?"

His mouth twitched down at the corners. "I own a pawn business, and I make loans to my customers. Ray's a good customer." He pulled a calculator from his back pocket, then bent over the table to scrutinize the appraisal forms. "Okay, let's get this over with. I'm looking for an emerald cocktail ring."

Outraged, she jerked her hands behind her back. "I'm not giving you anything."

He rubbed his eyes with thumb and forefinger, then said, "Work with me, here, Doc. This is *so* much better than me having to come to your house."

He was bluffing. "You don't know where we live."

"White brick, navy shutters, messy back yard."

She shoved her chin in the air. "It's an English garden."

"Yeah, whatever. I'm doing you a favor here. If I get the sheriff involved, the whole damn town will know your business."

"Oh, well, as long as you're doing me a *favor*."

He shook his head, tsk-tsking. "You're wasting time."

The entire situation was starting to seem legitimate, frighteningly so. "I need to discuss this with Raymond."

"Later," he said. "When I'm eating Happy Meals with my kids."

"H-How about if I write you a check?" she offered, gathering courage. "How much do you need?"

"About five thousand, and I don't take checks."

Natalie swallowed. "Cash," she said, gesturing toward the door. "Follow me to an ATM and I'll give you cash."

"Have you checked your balances lately, Dr. Carmichael?"

She balked. "Two days ago."

He looked sympathetic. "I've seen Raymond put down ten gees on a single dog race. In two days, he could bankrupt the national treasury." He withdrew his wallet and extracted a business card, then handed it to her.

Butler Family Pawn

Brian Butler

Owner and Manager

Gold bought and sold by the ounce

WE LOAN MONEY TO ANYONE,
AND WE MEAN ANYONE

He gave her a pointed look. "Now, for the last time, Dr. Carmichael—one emerald cocktail ring."

Feeling helpless, she removed the ring from her finger, then threw it at him, aiming for an eye.

He caught it neatly. "Thank you." Donning a jeweler's monocle, he held the ring up to the light for a few seconds, then punched in a number on the calculator, his fingers too big for the buttons. He dropped the ring onto a snowy handkerchief spread on the table. "Next, one pair of diamond stud earrings, total weight, two point five carats."

Her hands flew to her earlobes. "These were my aunt's—they're family heirlooms!"

"Lucky for Raymond, your aunt had good taste in jewelry."

Cut to the quick, Natalie bit deep into her lip to stem her tears, but failed miserably.

He winced and covered his face with his hand. "Oh, no, no, no. Stop with the tears, okay? I'm just trying to feed my family here. You married the bum, not me."

Furious, she sucked in her tears with a giant hiccup, then handed him the earrings with shaking hands. He inspected them and whistled. "Nice." Then he added them to the hanky. "And finally, one diamond solitaire pendant."

Remembering she'd dropped the piece inside her sweater, she said, "I don't have it with me."

His gaze fell to her chest, and the skin over her heart tingled. Slowly, very slowly, he moved to stand in front of her, zeroing in on the small lump of the pendant beneath her sweater—and not exactly ignoring the more sizable lumps on either side.

Her face burned as she clutched her hand to her chest.

"Come on, Doc, don't make me take it from you."

"Raymond gave this pendant to me for our anniversary."

"I know, I sold it to him. By the way, happy anniversary."

Never before had she so thoroughly despised a person. "You . . . are . . . vile."

A scowl darkened his face, illuminating the scar. "Tell you what, Doc, I'll give you a choice. The necklace—" He snatched up her left hand. She resisted, but his fingers were stronger than her entire arm. "Or your wedding ring." His voice was soft and teasing, offering a choice that was no choice at all.

Quaking, she glanced down at the thick gold band, etched with gold leaves and studded with emeralds, designed by Raymond and custom-made for her. She would never part with it. "Let go of me," she hissed. "And I'll give you the necklace."

He released her fingers so abruptly, her arm shot back. Trembling, she lifted the necklace over her head, then pitched it across the floor, sending it skidding to the door. Chest heaving, she met his gaze and injected as much bravado into her voice as she could muster. "Now get *out.*"

He stared at her for a few seconds, and when an emotion resembling pity shot through his eyes, she understood how one person could injure another in the red haze of rage. If she'd had a gun, she would've deposited a bullet in one of several areas that when compromised, according to *Gray's Anatomy*, posed a minimum threat to life while ensuring a maximum amount of pain.

Emitting a soft laugh, the man turned and ripped off a pink carbon copy of the form he'd been filling out. "Your receipt," he said, then folded it neatly and pushed it to the edge of the table. He shoved the rest of the papers back into his jacket, which he draped over his corded arm.

After gathering up the hanky, he crossed to scoop up the necklace and added it to the glittery pile. He shoved the small bundle into his pocket, then unlocked the door with a snap of his wrist. When a pained expression crossed his face, he touched a hand to his flat stomach. "Oh, by the way, Doc. I *do* have a touch of indigestion."

Seething, Natalie glared. "Lay off the Happy Meals."

Suddenly he smiled, revealing even, white teeth. Probably caps, considering his line of work. Then he gave her a mock salute, and walked out.

Two

A FULL MINUTE passed before Natalie sank to the stool, her entire body shaking as a sense of violation and betrayal broke over her. Could it be true? Was Raymond in debt to some sleazebag loan shark? Was the change she'd sensed in him over the last several months related to this financial mess instead of another woman, as she'd suspected?

Natalie yanked up the extension phone and dialed Raymond's cellular number with trembling hands, but he didn't answer. She paged him, punched in her office number, then jogged to the front door and locked herself in, in case the odious Mr. Butler decided to return. He'd had the gonads to snatch a handful of oatmeal Scotties on his way out, she noticed, frowning at the crumbs on the near-empty plate, the plastic wrap flapping. She itched to call the police on the thug, but she wanted to talk to Raymond first. Twenty, then thirty minutes passed with no return call, during which she paced and methodically rearranged the bric-a-brac on her desk.

Her mind raced with scenes from their six-year relationship—meeting Raymond at a medical conference and being swept off her feet by his charm and good looks, dating around his hectic traveling schedule, then marrying soon after on a whim during a whirlwind trip to Jamaica. They had adopted a comfortable pattern of separating during the week and reuniting on most weekends to eat homemade pasta and to share great sex.

Anger, slow and warm, swelled in her chest. Their marriage hadn't been perfect—he hadn't been too keen on leaving St. Louis for a smaller town, for instance—but she'd given Raymond no cause to withhold information so potentially devastating to their relationship. Fighting hurt and furious tears, she gave up on hearing from him and left for home.

A storm had blown in, heaping salt onto her gaping wound of misery as she made a mad dash to her car. A howling wind flipped her umbrella inside out, and rain lashed at her lab coat as she fought her way into her Jeep Cherokee. Once inside, Natalie laid her wet head back against the seat and summoned the strength to curse, but none seemed forthcoming. "What a lousy bleeping day," she muttered.

Spring had arrived in Smiley, Missouri, on a low pressure front intent on dumping a few inches of rain by morning, according to the nasal meteorologist on the radio. She glanced at the women slumped in the cars around her, and wondered which of them had been delivered a life-changing blow since embarking on their morning commute. Everyone had a cross to bear—job being phased out, in-laws moving in, teenagers having sex in the basement—but she'd wager none of them had been shaken down by a hoodlum for their husbands' gambling debts.

Natalie picked up the phone and called Raymond's number again, to no avail. She crept toward home in the gray, slanting rain, alternately worried and angry, concerned and murderous. When she pulled into the driveway, she sat and stared at their home.

Her home, actually. Her aunt had willed her the residence in Smiley, and Natalie, ready for a change from bustling St.

Louis, had relocated her family practice south to the smallish town. Raymond had grudgingly agreed because the move placed him more centrally within his sales territory. She'd been looking forward to their spending more time together, but in the six months since she'd taken possession of the house, Raymond's traveling hadn't slowed.

She loved the house—had loved it since childhood. Every summer she'd spent fourteen precious days with her father's sister, Rose Marie Blankenship. Rose Marie owned shelves of naughty novels, maintained a bowl of cookie dough in the refrigerator for emergencies, and grew the most beautiful tea roses in the region. She'd gently guided Natalie through childhood puberty, and young adulthood, compensating for her parents' indifference with magical letters and unusual gifts.

When Natalie graduated from medical school, Rose Marie had presented her with the diamond stud earrings that had belonged to Rose's own mother. "Don't save them for special occasions," she had pleaded. Right about now Rose Marie was probably twirling in her grave in the black wrinkle-free pantsuit she'd kept hanging in the closet under plastic with a sticky note on it that said, "Bury me in this."

The sprawling white-brick colonial had been built before garages were in vogue, but Rose Marie had conceded and built a carport several years ago. Natalie pulled forward and edged the Cherokee beneath the ivy-covered corrugated tin roof, loath to go in after the thug Butler's eerily accurate description of their home.

But the need to speak to Raymond overrode her fear, so she hurried through the side door and into the kitchen. She kicked off her soaked Hush Puppies and traipsed through the downstairs rooms, turning on every light in her wake, half expecting to confront a smirking Brian Butler behind every lamp. She backtracked to the kitchen and plugged in the coffeemaker and the little black and white television on which Rose Marie had kept up with her favorite soap operas while she puttered around the gas stove. The noise of canned sitcom laughter comforted Natalie, as did the cheery yellow walls.

Knowing she needed to eat, she withdrew enough vegetables from the side-by-side refrigerator to build a passable salad. She halfheartedly tore at the lettuce, then tired and sank onto a sunflower-upholstered stool in front of the bar between the kitchen and the eating area. Fighting a headache, she pulled the phone close, dialed Raymond's number again and decided the weather must be affecting his cell phone's reception. Next she called the after-hours banking line and listened as an electronic voice divulged the balance of their savings and checking accounts.

"Your . . . balance . . . is . . . twenty . . . two . . . dollars . . . and . . . seventy . . . two . . . cents."

"Your . . . balance . . . is . . . fifty . . . eight . . . dollars . . . and . . . ninety . . . nine . . . cents."

"Your . . . balance . . . is . . . one . . . hundred . . . sixteen . . . dollars . . . and . . . zero . . . cents."

"Impossible," she breathed. She didn't know how seriously Raymond might have compromised their finances, but if she lost Rose Marie's house. . . . Natalie reached over and extracted a meat cleaver from the butcher block, then whacked a cucumber in half.

With a burst of energy, she charged into the library, swept aside a stack of new country music CDs—another recent deviation for Raymond—and flipped on the computer. After a few key taps, she launched the personal finance program, only to be encountered by a flashing box requesting a password. She tried every magic word she could think of—his name, her name, their last name, their address, their anniversary, and even a few offensive words for Raymond that she typed in just for spite. She was holding the keyboard overhead, contemplating where to aim it, when the phone rang.

Certain it was Raymond, she yanked up the extension, prepared to let him know he was not welcome to come home. "Hello!"

"Is this the Carmichael residence?"

Deflated, Natalie slumped. "I don't accept calls from telemar—"

"This is Kentucky State Trooper Nolen. Raymond Carmichael has been involved in an automobile accident."

She inhaled sharply. "I-Is he . . .?"

"He's fine ma'am, but his car was totaled and he has a broken arm, so he'll be needing a ride home. He's at Dade General in Paducah."

Weak with relief, then bolstered by renewed anger, Natalie gritted her teeth. "Thank you for calling, officer, but you might want to swing by the hospital later, because I'm going to kill him when I get there!"

By the time Natalie reached Dade General, she'd had two hours to work herself into a lather. Two hours to remember all the wonderful little items Raymond had treated himself to lately—a gold watch, Italian shoes, expensive ties. He'd always been a bit materialistic, but conversely, he'd always worked hard. Now it seemed he was working hard to keep his gambling secret from her.

She had trusted him. He knew how important financial stability was to her. Gripping the steering wheel until her fingers were asleep, she blinked back a wall of angry tears, more overwhelmed by the words Butler had told her each time she replayed them in her mind. She almost hoped to find Raymond in a full-body cast—flat on his back he wouldn't be able to make wagers, and they'd have a few weeks to get back on their feet. And if somehow the bones in his fingers had survived the impact, she had a hammer in the glove compartment for his dialing hand.

A stern-faced woman in emergency room admissions directed her down two dim hallways to the waiting room, which was jam-packed with distraught patients and relatives. A vacant surface wasn't available even if she'd wanted to sit. When several faces turned and looked as if they were about to pounce, she realized she still wore her lab coat, now wrinkled beyond credibility. Avoiding eye contact, she shrugged out of her jacket and folded it over her arm, then approached a nurse.

"Excuse me, I'm Dr. Natalie Carmichael. My husband is Raymond Carmichael. He was brought here after an accident earlier this evening."

The nurse squinted. "Mr. Carmichael is in room six ten."

Her heart accelerated. "He's been admitted? I was told his injuries were minor."

"Yes, but he complained of mild chest pains and since he was so far from home, he was admitted for observation."

Natalie's anger toward Raymond diffused. "Did he sustain any injuries other than a broken arm?"

The nurse gave her a shaky smile. "I don't know. I didn't treat Mr. Carmichael."

"But you're familiar with his case?"

Another gelatinous smile. "Um, yes, ma'am."

"Can I see him?"

"Um, sure. Down this hall—the elevators are on the left."

Brushing off the odd behavior, Natalie thanked her. She passed a ladies' room, then backtracked to freshen up and give herself more time to mull over what she was going to say to Raymond. Should she ask him why he'd been acting so strange lately and see if he came clean, or simply confront him with the information that that hoodlum Butler had divulged?

Her head began to throb as she pushed on the heavy door and walked into the dingy bathroom. Gray tile and yellowed grout surrounded her. Three stalls lined the back wall, one occupied. Natalie set her navy leather tote on the fake granite counter and rummaged for a bottle of aspirin, breaking an already short nail when she popped off the lid.

She cupped her hand and filled it with warmish tap water to down the painkiller. The spotted mirror reflected the day's toll. Her blue eyes looked bloodshot and bruised underneath, her skin devoid of makeup and natural color. Her dark hair hung limp to her shoulders, flat and stick-straight. Splashing her face with cold water revived her somewhat. With hard, therapeutic strokes, she brushed her hair back from her face, reveling in the numbing rhythm. *Everything will be fine, everything will be fine . . .*

The odor of an herbal cigarette tickled her nose and she glanced in the mirror to see a wisp of smoke rising above the closed stall door. Smoking in the hospital was completely illegal, of course, but if she had one, she'd join her unseen companion in the adjacent stall. The stimulus provoked a growl from her stomach and she realized she still hadn't eaten dinner.

The toilet flushed and she heard two quick pumps of what sounded like breath spray. Natalie dropped her brush into her purse, intrigued by the identity of the girl or woman daring enough to break the rules, but apprehensive enough to cover up her little sin. The door opened and an attractive blond woman, fiftyish and wearing an expensive pantsuit, emerged. She engaged brief and wary eye contact before striding to the sink and washing her manicured hands. She appeared agitated, and her skin tone suggested an elevated blood pressure.

Natalie wondered what brought the woman to the hospital. From the tremor of her hand and the need for a few bolstering drags on a cigarette, it was probably not the arrival of a long-awaited grandchild. Had she lost a loved one, or was she preparing to? No, she didn't appear to be devastated.

She had married well, judging by the size of the diamond cluster on her left hand. Her chin looked suspiciously tight for her age, but Natalie herself had been reading plastic surgery articles with more interest of late. Her stomach chose that moment to bawl like a calf. The sound reverberated off the walls, eliciting a surprising smile from the woman.

"Have a mint," she said, extending a roll. Her laugh lines looked unused, and her teeth were perfect.

Embarrassed, Natalie accepted the offering and thanked her.

The woman gestured to the lab coat draped over Natalie's arm. "Are you a nurse?"

"I'm a doctor, but not at this hospital."

Withdrawing a twenty-dollar lipstick from a green Coach purse, the woman gestured toward the stall. "Sorry about the smoke."

"No problem." She smiled, feeling a sense of camaraderie with the stranger. "Actually, it smelled good. Cloves, right?"

The woman nodded, drawing a wine color onto her lips. "I kicked the nicotine addiction, but I still need the stick fix."

A nurse came in, silencing their talk about smoking, and washed her hands, asking Natalie for the time before leaving.

Natalie realized with a start that she'd rather stay and chat with a stranger in the bathroom than face a showdown with Raymond. Swinging her tote to her shoulder, she forced herself to walk toward the door. "Thanks again for the mint," she called before exiting into the corridor.

At least she felt a bit rejuvenated, she acknowledged as she stepped into the elevator. But as the floors dinged by, her pulse picked up and perspiration warmed the nape of her neck. Her skin tingled with anger, anxiety, and a fair amount of fear. She loved Raymond, but her love wasn't unconditional. From the onset of their marriage, they both agreed that trust was essential to their relationship. Natalie now had the burning feeling that Raymond was about to call her bluff. When the elevator doors opened to the sixth floor, she blinked back hot tears of apprehension.

The reception area seemed crowded with visitors and personnel. Natalie moved down a hallway, realized the room numbers were going in the wrong direction, and retraced her steps to the opposite wing. The door to room six ten stood slightly ajar. Light spilled into the hall, and a low rumbling of voices floated out. Natalie inhaled deeply and pushed open the door, still unsure what lay ahead.

But she hadn't quite prepared herself for the sight of Raymond in a hospital gown, propped with pillows, a cast on one arm . . . and sharing a deep kiss with a red-haired woman leaning over his bedrail.

Disbelief shot through her, leadening her limbs. She

gasped and sucked down the breath mint, then clung to the doorknob behind her for support while she coughed. The sound disengaged the couple, who turned questioning faces her way. Raymond's eyes bulged and his good arm flailed. The redhead, garbed in what resembled a long ruffled gunny-sack, and who looked young enough to be his daughter, simply stared, a crinkle on her pretty brow.

"Natalie!" Ray shouted, his Adam's apple bobbing, his face scarlet.

"Natalie?" the woman asked, straightening. "What's *she* doing here, Ray?"

Fury, hurt, and other less identifiable emotions flooded Natalie's chest. Her knees threatened to give way. "Raymond, what is going on?" The door bumped her from behind, propelling her into the room.

"Excuse me," uttered a female voice. When Natalie jerked around, the woman she'd met in the bathroom stood holding open the door. "You," the older woman said, her voice a mixture of question and friendliness. "Did you come to check on my husband?"

Natalie was speechless with confusion.

The woman stepped into the room, her gaze resting on Raymond and the redhead who now draped her arm around his shoulder possessively. Surprise registered on the older woman's face, distorting her smooth features. "Raymond," she snapped. "What the devil is going on?"

"Beatrix?" Raymond croaked out the name. Admittedly, even he appeared to be disoriented—not to mention a bit gray. He swallowed and swayed as if he were going to pass out, then clutched his chest, emitting mewling noises.

Beatrix, Raymond's first wife? Natalie barely had time to

process the thought before her medical training kicked in. Recalling that Raymond had been complaining of chest pains, she pressed the nurse call button. His head lolled to the side and his good arm fell limp. She shouted his name as she lowered the head of his bed, fearful he'd already lost consciousness.

The red-haired woman began screaming like a banshee. Natalie was vaguely aware of telling her to remain calm as she searched for Raymond's pulse. No response, and he wasn't breathing, either. A nurse burst into the room, took one look at Raymond, dashed back to the door and called for a crash cart, then added, "All of you—out!"

"I'm a doctor," Natalie said, readying Ray for CPR, not looking at his face, trying to remove herself from the reality that the man under her ministrations was her husband. Her philandering, cheating, deceitful husband.

The nurse shooed the other women—one silent, one blubbering—from the room. A crash cart team arrived within seconds, and shoved Natalie aside as they attempted to shock Raymond's motionless heart back to life. She shrank to a corner of the cluttered room, gasping for air as if her own heart were failing. For all she knew, it might be. Her knees sagged and an attendant ushered her into the corridor, urging her to breathe deeply.

Only after she assured the man she was okay and he returned to Raymond's room did she realize the two women stood a few feet away, leaning against opposite walls. The older woman maintained an iron grip on her purse, as the younger woman sobbed uncontrollably. Natalie glanced toward the redhead with disdain—she had no sympathy for Raymond's mistress.

"How is he?" asked the woman she'd met in the bathroom. The mistress choked into silence, staring at Natalie expectantly.

"They're still trying to revive him." She wiped at her eyes, then extended her hand to Beatrix, determined to make the best of meeting Raymond's ex-wife. "I'm Natalie. It's nice to meet you, even under these circumstances."

But Beatrix ignored her hand and straightened. "You *knew* about me?"

"Of course," Natalie said quietly. "Raymond mentioned you many times."

"Mighty big of him. Before or after you slept with him?"

Natalie angled her head. "Excuse me?"

"Did he mention me before or after you slept with my husband?"

"B-Before," Natalie replied, puzzled. "Raymond was up front about the fact that he was a divorced man."

Beatrix gaped. "Divorced?"

Alarm embraced Natalie, then she recalled Raymond saying his first wife suffered from depression and other disorders. "Yes," she said calmly. "Two years before I met Raymond."

"Really? And when was that?"

Natalie began to grow angry herself. "Six years ago. We were married shortly thereafter."

Beatrix flushed. "M-Married? But that's impossible."

The redhead chose that moment to chime in. "Then he divorced her last year." She addressed Beatrix, jerking a thumb toward Natalie. "Two out of every three marriages in the United States end in divorce," she added matter-of-factly.

Natalie wheeled toward her husband's girlfriend. "Divorced?"

The young woman nodded, then hiccuped. "So that Ray and I could be married."

"And you are . . .?" Beatrix asked.

"Ruby Lynn Carmichael." She tossed her long hair, which, from the wild roll of her eyes, made her dizzy.

Feeling faint again, Natalie touched her head, trying to keep pace with the conversation. "Did you say 'married'?"

Ruby Lynn nodded and thrust out her left hand, flaunting a huge diamond, paired with a slim band. "Six weeks ago. Ain't it a beaut?"

"He married you too?" Beatrix cut in. Her mouth opened and closed. "Ladies, I have a news bulletin. Raymond and I are *not* divorced."

Horror washed over Natalie. After a long pause of her vital signs, she whispered, "Raymond and I aren't divorced either."

Ruby narrowed her eyes and stared back and forth between them. "You mean that we're all *three* married to Ray?"

"That lying son of a bitch," Beatrix muttered.

"That cheating, no-good, three-timer," Natalie murmured.

"Ray didn't tell me he was Mormon," Ruby declared.

The door to Raymond's room swung open and the doctor emerged. "Mrs. Carmichael?"

As if choreographed, the three of them turned toward the man. "Yes?" they replied in unison.

Three

FIGHTING THE IMPULSE to turn and run, Beatrix Carmichael stepped forward. "*I* am Mrs. Raymond Carmichael." An ambiguous title, apparently. Her voice sounded less than confident even to her own ears. "Is my husband going to be all right?" If the bastard died before she had a chance to confront him, she'd never forgive him.

"Mrs. Carmichael, I'm Dr. Everly." He removed his glasses and stuck an end in his mouth. "Your husband is stabilized, but he suffered a serious heart attack. Without tests, I can't predict the damage sustained. He's in critical condition. We're preparing to move him to the cardiac intensive care unit."

The woman named Natalie angled her body closer and exchanged medical mumbo-jumbo with the doctor. The red-haired coed resumed her boo-hooing at top decibels. Twenty-one years of devotion to a man, and this was her thanks—vying for position at his deathbed. A red glaze descended over her eyes.

Throwing her arms in the air, she shouted, "Enough!" and was rewarded with a few seconds of stunned silence. She moistened her lips, tasting Raisin Wine No. 3, and used her hands to punctuate her calm words. "I need . . . to speak . . . to my husband."

"Mrs. Carmichael," the doctor said gently. "Your husband is unconscious."

Beatrix gave him a tight smile. "Raymond usually dozes off when I talk to him, Doctor. Step aside."

"I'd also like to see him," Natalie said.

"Me, too," piped up the other one.

Beatrix wanted to scream. Dr. Everly's eyes darted around the group. "Are all of you immediate family members?"

"No," she declared.

"Yes," Natalie and Ruby chorused a half-beat later, and stared at her with defiance.

The doctor's eyebrows climbed, but at that moment, the door to Raymond's room opened and the foot of his bed emerged. "Sorry, ladies," he said. "You have from here to the elevator to say your piece."

When Raymond's ashen face appeared, Beatrix crowded in next to a nurse and trotted to keep up as the bed barreled down the hall. "Raymond! Raymond, can you hear me?"

From the other side of the bed, Natalie and the other one took up the refrain, each trying to elicit a response from Raymond. He lay completely still, and for a spiteful second, Beatrix wondered if he were faking it—the man hated confrontation.

"Raymond, I'm here for you," Natalie said over and over.

"I love you, Ray!" sobbed the other one.

People recoiled in their wake as they approached the elevator like a big, noisy centipede. Beatrix hated Raymond for forcing her to take part in the embarrassing spectacle. Barely able to hear herself over the din, she shouted, "Wake up, you coward! Wake up and face your problems like a man!" She could have sworn she saw him flinch.

Someone pried her hands from the rail as they slid the bed into the elevator. The baffled-looking doctor blocked the door to keep the trio from boarding. "Next elevator, ladies. It'll take us a while to get him settled in. There's a waiting room on the eleventh floor." He raised his finger in warning. "But you'll have to keep it down."

The door slid closed, nearly pinching the toes of Beatrix's Gucci loafers. She stared at her reflection in the stainless steel doors, appalled at the thought of turning around and facing the two women her husband had . . . She couldn't bear to even *think* the word. More than anyone, she knew Raymond was a playboy. But if these women were telling the truth, what he'd done to her—to all of them—was not only unconscionable, but criminal.

The young one was still caterwauling, now with a noticeable twang. Her patience exhausted, Beatrix swung around. "Will you *please* shut up!"

The girl straightened with an abrupt hiccup, covering her mouth with her beringed left hand. Natalie stood a few inches away, hugging her thin self. Gone was the confident medical persona. The woman looked as terrified as Beatrix felt.

Natalie caught her gaze. "What on earth do we do now?"

Beatrix closed her eyes and pinched the bridge of her nose. Natalie was easily young enough to be her own daughter, and the other one could squeak by as a granddaughter. What could Raymond have been thinking? Her anger boiled. After a nurse called her about the car accident and she realized Raymond was okay, she'd made the three-hour drive wearing a smirk. On the return trip, her husband would be forced to converse with her, uninterrupted, for one hundred and eighty minutes—a special occasion for which she'd skipped her evening sleeping pill. As a result, she was stone-cold sober for this little rendezvous.

She opened her eyes, still at a loss for protocol. "I don't know about anyone else, but I'm going to find a coffee machine."

"Did you know that the average coffee drinker consumes three and a half cups a day?" Ruby asked behind her.

Beatrix turned and pointed at the girl. "*You* are a kook. If you know what's good for you, you'll keep your distance."

An orderly gave her directions and they traipsed to a vending room in loose single file, maintaining silence by mutual consent. Walking as if a shield encircled her, Beatrix distanced herself emotionally by staying a few feet ahead of the other women. She punched in her selection of black coffee and watched numbly while the dark liquid bubbled out. Natalie diluted hers with non-dairy creamer. Ruby bummed fifty cents from Natalie and opted for hot chocolate with little marshmallows—surprise, surprise.

Minutes later, they boarded an elevator, each claiming a far corner, and rode to the eleventh floor. Beatrix hadn't experienced a hot flush in at least two years, but her makeup was melting in anticipation of the impending discussion. Why, oh, why hadn't she brought her pills?

At a station just outside the elevator, a nurse informed them in hushed tones that Raymond remained in critical condition and they could visit him for ten minutes every odd hour if his condition allowed. Beatrix was already thinking she'd be looking for a plug to pull.

The waiting room on the eleventh floor sat virtually empty except for a young couple asleep on separate couches and a janitor vacuuming potato chips from the smelly carpet.

Taking the lead, Beatrix pulled out a wobbly chair around a square Formica table and sat down heavily, sloshing lukewarm coffee through the hole in the lid. Pale and drawn, Natalie followed suit, and the other one joined them, her eyes welling over again.

They stirred and sipped—Ruby slurped—for several long moments while Beatrix's mind reeled. Finally, Natalie set down her cup. "Why don't you start from the beginning, Beatrix?"

The beginning. That would be the first time she saw Raymond Carmichael at a fund-raiser for a hospital clinic that would eventually bear her father's name. Outrageously handsome in a charcoal tuxedo, ten years her junior, and on the arm of her best friend, Blanche Grogan, Raymond had caught her eye instantly. After the toasts were made, he'd dumped her friend and pulled Beatrix into a coat closet to share a bottle of vanilla rum until everyone else had left.

On that night, she couldn't have imagined the suffering she would bring upon herself by succumbing to Raymond's irresistible charm—and now after years of paying penance, *this*. Damn the idle selfishness bred into her by cold, wealthy parents. She'd learned to expect so little happiness out of life . . . and her expectations had been met to the letter.

Glancing up from her half-empty cup, Beatrix realized the other women were poised, nervous and waiting. "Not much to tell, really," she said with a shrug. "Raymond and I met and were married twenty-one years ago. We've lived in the same house in Northbend, Tennessee since then. Or at least *I* did. Raymond traveled so much . . ." Of course, now she knew why.

"But you were never divorced?" Natalie's voice cracked.

Beatrix managed a dry laugh. "No, we were never

divorced." This situation would provide fodder for the Northbend Country Club gossip mill for eternity.

Natalie leaned forward on her elbows, pressing her fingers to her temples. "Did Raymond have any reason to *think* the two of you were divorced?"

"None whatsoever."

If possible, the woman's deep blue eyes grew even bleaker. Sorrowful and eroded, she remained an attractive woman. A memory stirred, but Beatrix couldn't pin it down.

Natalie's mouth twitched. "Do . . . Do you and Raymond have children?"

Beatrix averted her gaze. "No." She couldn't conceive, and Raymond had refused to adopt. Just another of life's little injustices. "Do *you* have children?"

Natalie shook her head, then joined Beatrix in a heart-pounding stare at Ruby, who swallowed hard, but at last shook her empty head.

She allowed a pent-up sigh to escape. Thank God for small miracles.

"How did you find out he was here?" she asked Natalie.

"I received a call from a state trooper who handled the accident. You?"

"The hospital called me to verify medical insurance." She cast a glance toward the other one without making full eye contact. "What about you?"

"Ray called me," she said with big-eyed innocence.

Beatrix joined Natalie in swallowing a gulp of bitter coffee. It was apparent who Raymond had wanted by his side, and why he had been so surprised to see her and Natalie. She almost smiled at the irony.

"How did you meet Raymond?" Ruby asked Natalie. The young girl's mascara leaked down her cheeks. Her eyebrows were too thin and her mouth too full for her face to be truly beautiful, but she was striking. And Beatrix suspected that under the shapeless yellow dress lurked a magnificent body. *Raymond, you insufferable cad.*

Natalie, too, seemed to size up the younger woman while she contemplated her answer. Her mouth stretched into a wry smile. "I met Raymond at a medical conference seven years ago."

Ruby nodded with youthful exaggeration. "One out of three people meet their mates at work."

Beatrix squinted at the girl's nonsense, then elected to ignore her.

Natalie fingered her gold and emerald wedding band—surprisingly, the only jewelry she wore—and lifted her moist gaze. "He told me he'd been divorced for two years, and I . . . never questioned him. I never dreamed . . . I mean, he traveled so much . . ." Her face crumpled, but she bit her bottom lip to stem her tears.

"Where do you live?" Beatrix asked with as much calm as she could garner.

Natalie inhaled deeply, then exhaled slowly, puffing out thin cheeks. "We live—I mean, *I* live in Smiley, a small town outside St. Louis."

"All those years, and neither of you suspected a thing?"

They turned toward Ruby. Beatrix felt a twinge of camaraderie with Natalie—at least they both shared a history with Raymond. The little girl barely had a history, period. "How old are you?" she blurted out, her resentment unbridled.

Ruby sniffed. "Twenty-one."

Beatrix rolled her eyes. Christ, she'd probably lost her virginity to the slug. "And how did *you* meet Raymond?"

She wiped her eye, smearing blue eye shadow across her temple. "A few months ago he started coming into the place where I work, and after a while"—she shrugged prettily—"we got to be buds."

Beatrix pressed her lips together, then asked, "And when exactly did you go from being 'buds' to being married?"

A dreamy expression softened Ruby's kohled eyes. "Ray stepped in and saved me from a rowdy customer. We went to the late show that night and made out in the back row—" She stopped abruptly and cleared her throat. "After that, we went out every time he was in town."

"In town?" Beatrix asked.

"Leander, Kentucky," she explained. "About forty-five minutes east down I-64."

Three wives in three states—which explained how he'd juggled the paperwork, she presumed.

"Ray surprised me on my birthday by proposing at the steak house." Ruby held out her ring again, moving her hand to catch the light. "I'd never seen such a big diamond."

Beatrix chewed on the inside of her cheek. "Well, I hate to be the one to tell you, but you still haven't."

Ruby frowned. "Huh?"

"Cubic zirconia—it's fake."

The young woman jerked her hand to her chest. "Is not!"

Beatrix considered the wisdom of waging an "is too, is not" war. Instead, she opened her purse and withdrew a cigarette, even though she couldn't light it. "May I ask what line of work you're in?"

"I'm a dancer," Ruby informed them with pride. "Feature show at Pink Paddy's."

Beatrix traded knowing glances with Natalie, then cut back to Ruby. "You're a stripper?"

The young woman's smile faltered a bit. "Raymond prefers the term 'exotic performer.' "

Nodding slowly with her tongue poked in her cheek, Beatrix tried valiantly to tamp down the anger that surged anew. "Well, Raymond had a remarkable talent for putting a good spin on things." *Un-fucking-believable.* She snapped the brown cigarette in two.

"Has," Ruby corrected.

Growing weary of the girl's wide-eyed innocence, Beatrix sighed. "What?"

"You said 'had,' like Raymond's dead or something."

"Oh, so you're a stripper *and* an English teacher?"

Ruby frowned. "You don't have to be mean."

Beatrix regarded her for a few seconds, then leaned forward. "No, I don't have to be mean. I could simply be *amused* by the fact that my husband married two other women while still married to me!" She smacked the top of the table for punctuation.

Ruby blinked. "Well, it's not our fault that—" She broke off and lifted her cup for a nervous drink.

"That what?" Beatrix asked, pursing her lips.

Ruby squirmed.

"Not your fault that what?" Beatrix demanded, half-standing. "Not your fault that my husband wasn't satisfied with me?"

"I . . . I . . ."

"Not your fault that I couldn't keep him happy in my bed?"

Natalie closed her eyes and Ruby shrank back in her chair.

"Not your fault that my husband is a scumbag bigamist?"

"Excuse me."

Beatrix turned toward the voice. Behind the gaping janitor, the man and woman who had been sleeping on the couches stared at them. "Would you mind keeping it down? This is a hospital, you know."

"Mind your own damned business!" Beatrix barked, standing. Her chair thumped to the carpet. She strode out of the room in the direction of the nurses' station and asked for directions to the ladies' room. By the time she reached the tiled room, her jaws ached from grinding her teeth. Thank God the place was empty.

She slammed into the last stall and whipped a new cigarette from her purse, cursing the cheap lighter she'd picked up at a convenience store when she stopped to buy gas. At last the damn thing lit, and she turned an inch of the brown cigarette into ash with the first drag. Tears and the pungent smoke burned her eyes. "How could you, Raymond?" she murmured. "How *could* you?"

The door to the bathroom opened, admitting one set of feet. Beatrix cupped her hand over the cigarette and held her breath. The person entered the stall next to her and closed the door. She dropped ash into the toilet and watched it dissolve and sink to the rusty bottom.

"Beatrix, it's Natalie." The sterile walls magnified the woman's voice tenfold.

Beatrix crooked her neck and confirmed the sensible suede Hush Puppies she'd noticed earlier. The woman had good taste in clothing—too bad she couldn't say the same about her taste in men.

"Do you have an extra cigarette?"

Surprised, Beatrix took a quick drag and exhaled straight into the air. "Do you smoke?"

"No."

Beatrix smiled wryly, then reached into her purse hanging on a metal hook and extracted another smoke. Stooping, she handed the slim cigarette and the lighter underneath the divider. "The lighter sucks."

"Thanks."

The lighter sputtered, then she heard Natalie exhale and a thin ribbon of bluish smoke appeared over the stall. Beatrix leaned against the tiled wall and considered the unseen woman thoughtfully. Perhaps if they'd met another time, in another place, under different cicumstances, she and Natalie might have become friends. Something about her . . .

A jolt of realization slammed into Beatrix. No wonder she felt drawn to the woman—aside from her dark hair, she bore a striking resemblance in her looks and demeanor to Blanche, her estranged friend . . . the woman from whom she'd stolen Raymond eons ago.

The bathroom door opened, and Beatrix frowned as she recognized the annoying shuffle of wooden clogs.

"It's me—um, Ruby." The framework of the stalls shook, announcing she'd claimed the final cubicle. Beatrix didn't feel inclined to acknowledge her, and apparently Natalie shared her regard.

"That hot chocolate went straight through me," she sang, and proceeded to empty her tight little bladder. The flushing toilet sent a shudder through the fixtures. "Anybody got an extra cigarette?"

Beatrix blew three perfect smoke rings. "Does your mommy let you smoke?"

"She lets her strip," Natalie offered.

"Good point." Beatrix withdrew another cigarette and handed it to Natalie under the stall.

She must have passed it on, since Ruby mumbled, "Thanks," and the snap of the weak lighter reached her ears.

"Good thing there's no smoke detector," Natalie said.

"One third of all smoke detectors contain dead batteries anyway," Ruby said. "Will we be in trouble it they catch us smoking?"

"All we'd have to do is explain the situation," Beatrix assured her in a dry tone. "I'm sure the police would ignore three firebugs in lieu of snaring a bona fide bigamist."

"You mean Ray could go to jail?" Ruby's voice rose in alarm.

"Prison," Natalie corrected.

"Where the women are scarce and the men are frustrated," Beatrix added.

"What if we don't press charges?" Ruby asked.

"Speak for yourself," Beatrix muttered.

"It doesn't matter." Natalie said. "The state will file charges."

"Which state?" Ruby asked.

Between a series of little puffs, Beatrix smiled. "Hopefully, all of them."

They smoked in silence for several minutes. Beatrix reached the end of her cigarette and begrudgingly dropped the butt into the commode. But instead of exiting, she lowered the cover and sat down. Slipping off her shoes, she took an inordinate amount of pleasure in the coolness of the tile against her stockinged feet. Perhaps she would have her dressing room tiled. "What do you think his chances are, Doctor?" she asked finally, twining her fingers together.

Natalie sighed. "Well, he has no history of heart disease."

Beatrix nodded for her own benefit and squinted at faint

initials scratched in the door. "He had a physical three months ago, and told me everything was fine. Of course, now we know truthfulness is not his strong point."

"No, he was telling the truth," Natalie said. "I gave him the physical."

"Ah."

"Heart disease is the number one killer in America," Ruby offered.

"What gives with the public service announcements?" Natalie demanded.

"I like trivia," Ruby said simply. "I have a knack for it."

"Well, knock it off," Natalie retorted. "Beatrix, do you know if either of Raymond's parents had heart problems?"

"They both died of cancer when he was a child," Beatrix said.

"I thought it was a boating accident," Ruby said.

"He told me they were sightseeing in a helicopter," Natalie added, clearly perturbed.

Beatrix snorted. "They probably disowned him for lying."

"But is Ray going to make it?" Ruby asked.

"The fact that he's alive at all is a good sign," Natalie said, sounding weary. "The chances of survival go up with each passing hour."

"What caused his heart attack?" Ruby asked.

Beatrix rolled her eyes toward the ceiling. "Perhaps the man's body was taxed beyond his sexual capacity."

"He was still having sex with *you*?"

"Yes," she answered through clenched teeth.

"We all need to be tested for sexually transmitted diseases," Natalie informed them.

Beatrix blinked. "Excuse me?"

"Don't take offence. Raymond might have been sleeping with other women we don't even know about."

"I caught the crabs once from a toilet seat at work," Ruby announced.

Beatrix immediately began to itch. "Great," she muttered, throwing up her hands. "That's just what I needed to hear!"

"But I got rid of them before I knew Ray," Ruby insisted. "The little boogers drove me crazy—I had to shave and everything."

"That is *so* much more than I wanted to know," Beatrix declared.

"I think the shock of seeing all of us together provoked his heart attack," Natalie said.

"I'm sure the pompous ass never even considered the possibility of being caught," Beatrix asserted, then laughed. "I have to admit, the whole sordid episode has a poetic ring to it."

"What are we going to do if he dies?" Ruby whined.

Beatrix harrumphed. "Even worse, what are we going to do if he lives?"

"Speaking of which," Natalie said, "we'd better get back. It's almost time for visitation."

Heaving a labored sigh, Beatrix stood and stepped back into her shoes, then reached for the toilet handle. They flushed away their cigarette butts in perfect synchronization, triggering a crooked smile on her face. *A fitting tribute to our husband.*

Four

RUBY WATCHED THE swirling water in the toilet and pictured her dreams disappearing with the soggy brown cigarette. Just a few hours ago, she was newly wed to the most handsome, thoughtful, successful man she'd ever known. Now she was playing third fiddle to a bitter old woman and a skinny lady doctor, both of whom, in her opinion, were not exhibiting a very sharing spirit.

Glad the fragrant cigarette had calmed her queasy stomach, she smoothed the skirt of her yellow gauze dress. Ray liked for her to wear feminine, frilly clothes—when she wore clothes. His call from the hospital had interrupted preparations for a special homecoming. She'd Velcroed together ruffled calico curtains for their bedroom, and planted pink begonias around the base of the mobile home Ray had presented to her the week after they were married. Double-wide, with wall-to-wall carpet—Ruby still marveled at his generosity.

Swinging open the stall door, she lifted her chin and joined the other women at the counter, each claiming a sink, each avoiding eye contact. Ruby moistened a paper towel and dabbed at her wayward makeup. She felt flashy in her bright outfit next to the prim, subdued clothing of her counterparts. No matter—Ray had told her he liked her style, that a woman should flaunt her good taste.

She checked her teeth, flicking out a speck of barbecued chicken, then blew her nose thoroughly. And to prove that she, too, had manners, she washed her hands carefully, removing gunk under her pink acrylic nails for good measure.

"I saw on a soap the other day where a man had a heart attack and woke up with amnesia," she offered into the booming silence.

Beatrix stopped drying her hands and stared, then tossed the paper towel into an overflowing trash can. "Raymond should be so lucky."

Ruby dried her hands and ventured a smile at Natalie as she walked through the door that Ray's second wife held open. The dark-haired woman didn't respond, but at least she maintained an expression more friendly than Beatrix's, who looked as if she were sucking on a Triple Ripple Sour Ball. In fact, Natalie was sort of pretty, like a "before" picture in a *Seventeen* makeover. With a little eyeliner and some strawberry lip gloss, she'd probably be dynamite.

Once in the hall, Ruby hung back, half because she didn't want to get in Beatrix's way, half because she'd forgotten from which direction they'd come. As expected, Beatrix marched ahead like she was the Queen of New England or something. Natalie quietly fell in behind her, and Ruby brought up the rear, limping. Her new clogs were rubbing her toe ring. "Do you think we'll give him another shock if we go in at the same time?"

"That's the plan," Beatrix tossed over her shoulder.

Ruby stopped in her tracks. "You're not serious."

Natalie turned and gave her a flat little smile. "No she's not serious. They probably won't let all of us go in at the same time."

Experiencing a surge of sisterhood, Ruby clambered up

next to Natalie and whispered, "Do you think she'll even let us look through the window?"

"You can't really blame her for being so upset," the doctor said in a low voice. "I'm numb—I can't imagine how this must be affecting her."

"Well, between me and you and the fence post," Ruby whispered emphatically, "if she's this witchy all the time, I can see why Ray went shopping for another wife."

Natalie's face paled. "I guess that doesn't say much for me, either, does it?"

Too late, she realized she'd stuck her size-nine-and-a-half foot in her mouth. "But I— "

"Just be quiet," Natalie said, her deep blue eyes watering. "This is hard enough for all of us without you calling even more attention to yourself."

Heat rose in Ruby's cheeks as Natalie wheeled and lengthened her stride to catch up with Beatrix. Choking back a sob, Ruby followed them, but tears clouded her vision. She accidentally stepped on a licked-down piece of hard candy, turning her ankle painfully. She yelped, then kicked off the clogs and scooped them up before hobbling ahead in her bare feet.

When she rounded the corner, both women were being led by a nurse through a glass door at the end of the hall marked INTENSIVE CARE—AUTHORIZED PERSONNEL ONLY.

She hurried forward, stumbled, then recovered. "Wait!"

The nurse glanced her way, but the other women disappeared through the door without hesitation.

"I want to see Ray, too!" she gasped as she skidded to a halt on the waxed floor.

The sweet-faced nurse glanced at the clogs in her hands and smiled, but shook her head as she closed the door. "Only two visitors per patient at a time—intensive care is extremely crowded, ma'am. We have rules."

"But I'm his wi— " She halted as the nurse's head snapped around. She didn't want to get Ray in trouble with Johnny Law. "Daughter," Ruby amended quickly. "I'm Ray's daughter."

"I'm very sorry," the nurse murmured. "Perhaps his other visitors will come out a few minutes early and let you go in."

Her shoulders slumped. "I doubt it. We don't exactly get along."

The woman touched her arm. "I'll try to get you in next time."

Ruby nodded miserably, then turned at the sound of the door reopening. Beatrix and Natalie, both red-faced and tight-lipped, emerged and bumped past her without so much as a howdy-hoo.

"What's wrong?" she called after them. "Ray's all right, isn't he?" They didn't answer, so she pled with the nurse. "Can I go in now? Just for a few minutes?"

The nurse held up her finger, then disappeared behind the door, only to reappear a few seconds later wearing a sorrowful expression that Ruby decided was mandatory for graduating from nurse and doctor school. "Apparently, Mr. Carmichael's heart rate accelerated past a safe range during visitation. No other visitors are allowed until a specialist sees him. I'm sorry."

Tears clogged her throat as she trotted down the hall toward the waiting room.

Beatrix and Natalie stood at opposite ends of the small room, their backs to each other, their arms crossed.

"What did you say to Ray?" she demanded. When they refused to acknowledge her presence, she sent a wooden clog bouncing off a wall, denting the plaster, but getting their attention. "Answer me!"

Beatrix's mouth twisted. "Nothing."

But Natalie's eyes narrowed as she turned on Beatrix. "Nothing? You told him if he died, you'd serve Dom Perignon at the funeral!"

Ruby shook her head to clear it. The situation was beginning to resemble an episode of *Columbo*, with strangers popping up at every turn. Who the heck was this Dom fellow?

Beatrix spun toward Natalie, her eyes blazing. "And what exactly did you expect me to say? 'Hello, Raymond, I'm here with wives number two and three and we're all praying for a speedy recovery'?"

"You don't honestly want him to die, do you?" Ruby asked.

"Only if it's slow and painful."

"She doesn't mean that," Natalie said, shaking her head.

"Oh, don't I?" Beatrix laughed, a bitter sound. "You're telling me the man deserves better after what he's done?"

Natalie jammed her hand through her limp dark hair that cried out for a permanent wave and said, "Stop acting as if you're the only person involved here. If Raymond dies, we'll *all* be left with the mess he created. If he lives, at least he can help set things right."

Worry began niggling at the back of Ruby's brain. If Ray died, she *would* be left standing in a heap of debt. With her expanding waistline, she wouldn't remain the featured performer at Paddy's much longer—she doubted her boss Mac would even let her drop back to waitressing. Ruby nibbled on the skin around her thumbnail. How would she make the trailer payment? And what about the big-screen TV? *Oh, fudge.*

Beatrix faced Natalie, her eyes blazing. "What could Raymond do to set things straight?" Then her face lit up. "Oh, I know—he can divorce *me* to marry *you*, then divorce *you* to marry *her*!" She jerked her head toward Ruby, who brightened, thinking that when Ray was well enough, that was exactly what he would do.

Cheered, Ruby lifted her chin, snatched up her shoe, then claimed the chair in the farthest corner of the waiting room. She drew her knees up to her chin, and concentrated on the episode of *Laverne & Shirley* playing low on the TV, sending happy thoughts to her unborn baby. She hadn't really lied when they asked if she and Ray had children. They didn't—yet.

Ray's other wives staked out opposite sides of the room, the skinny one crying softly, the old bag twirling a cigarette like a baton from pinkie to thumb across the top of her hand. Ruby was impressed with the trick, but not about to let on. Instead she crossed her fingers on both hands into four sets of good luck charms and repeated prayers for Ray's recovery until her mind wandered.

She dozed through the late news, the late show, the later show, and the late late show, jerking awake each time the door to the ICU opened to accommodate the flow of medical personnel in and out. Around three in the morning, she awoke to find Beatrix coming out of the ICU, alone, a smug look on her face. Furious, Ruby sprang to her feet and hobbled across the room on sleep-numbed legs to confront the woman. "Why didn't you let me go in to see him?"

Beatrix barely looked in her direction as she settled into a chair. "Because."

Ruby frowned. "Because why?"

The woman rolled her eyes upward. "Because he's *my* husband and we had unfinished business. Don't you have a curfew or something?"

Ruby made a face at her, then scooted to the nurses' station and asked to see her hus—*father* the next time he was allowed visitors. The woman gave her hand a sympathetic pat and whispered, "I don't get along with my mother either."

Beatrix shot a scathing glance toward them. "I'm *not* her mother." Ruby slunk back to her chair.

Natalie had fallen asleep, she noticed, her slim, tear-streaked face milky and drawn next to the dark fabric of the chair she leaned against. The lab coat was really cool, though, Ruby acknowledged with a sigh. She'd always wanted a job that required a smart-looking lab coat—doctor, nurse . . . hairdresser.

She picked up an old copy of *Good Housekeeping* and read an article on removing stains from upholstery. Her Shih Tzu, Miss Mame, had peed on the new couch, and although an afghan covered the spot just fine, the cushion was beginning to smell. Ray liked a clean house—he rinsed the sink after he shaved and everything. He was a dreamboat, always doing nice things for her, like bringing supplies to help control her diabetes, and setting the VCR to tape *Jeopardy* every evening so she could watch it when she got off work. The first time through she simply enjoyed the show, but the second time through she memorized the answer to every question. Even Ray didn't know she hadn't finished the tenth grade, and no one would if she crammed her head full of smart-sounding stuff she read in magazines and heard on television. She wanted to make her husband proud.

While the other women were sleeping, she was able to talk a nurse into sneaking her in to see him for one minute. Ray was so pale, with so many tubes everywhere, it gave her the heebie-jeebies. He looked old. But they wouldn't even let her speak to him before they ushered her back outside. She must have dozed for another couple of hours, then was jarred awake by a flurry of motion in and out of the ICU door. When Ray's doctor swept by, she shook Natalie's shoulder. "I think something's wrong," she whispered, needing the reassurance of a doctor.

Natalie bolted up and fired questions at the nurse, but was told they would have to wait for the doctor. Thankfully, Dr. Everly emerged, but the look on his face sent a stone to the bottom of Ruby's stomach.

"Family of Raymond Carmichael?" he asked, his gaze darting among them.

Beatrix rose and pushed past them, the witch. "Yes?"

The man braced his feet wide and spoke to the floor in a gentle tone. "Mr. Carmichael lapsed into cardiac arrest again and we tried to resuscitate him for twenty minutes, but despite our best efforts . . . I'm afraid he didn't make it."

The room exploded into little dots of color that reminded Ruby of the strobe light Mac used for special numbers at the club. "What . . . are you saying?"

"He died," the doctor said.

Ruby swallowed hard, her ears clicking from released pressure. *He died.* At least this doctor was nicer than most. When she was little and her drunkard grandfather had croaked in the shack they lived in, the doctor hadn't bothered to hide his disgust when he announced he had choked on his own body fluids. And when her mother's boyfriend had checked out in a recliner and rigor mortis had set in, the coroner had spared no detail in describing what he'd have to do to get the body into a casket.

He passed away, kicked the bucket, bit the dust, bought the farm. Overall, the words "he died" were the best, she decided. Sensitive, but to the point. Still, her heart reeled at the awful finality of the phrase. *He died.*

The doctor glanced around, as if he expected them to storm him. "I know this is very sudden," he continued, "so when you've had a chance to think about burial arrangements—"

"Oh my God," Natalie said behind her hand. "Oh my God." Her blue eyes watered.

"You can bet Raymond's not anywhere near God right now," Beatrix muttered.

"Shut up," Natalie choked out. "This is not the time!"

Ruby blocked out the rest of their angry exchange. When she'd passed the early home pregnancy test, she'd known in her heart that she'd give birth to a baby girl with curly hair, blue eyes, and dimples. She'd dress her in pink ruffles and teach the toddler to walk properly with a book on her little head. Then she'd enter her in the Little Miss Leander pageant and show those women who ignored her in the grocery store that her child could upstage their fat brats. And Ray would be at her side, handsome and bursting with pride, further proof that Ruby Lynn Hicks had acquired a genuine, upstanding family.

Only now, her baby would be branded as she'd been: the dirty-faced product of a white trash mother, with questionable paternity. "One-third of all babies in the United States are born to single mothers," she whispered, for her ears only. Ruby watched the just-vacuumed carpet rise to meet her with considerable amazement—she'd never fainted before in her life.

Five

"DID YOU KNOW?" Natalie demanded, her jaw hurting from days of clenched teeth. "The truth, Lowell. Did you know?"

Attorney Lowell Masterson averted his gaze to his Tumi briefcase. "No." Then he raised sheepish eyes and fanned his hands wide against the pecan-colored boardroom table. "But I . . . suspected something wasn't quite right. Raymond was a little vague about some areas of his life, but I never imagined— "

The door burst open, admitting a glassy-eyed Beatrix in a classic black pantsuit, and a white-suited man who looked as if he'd just swaggered off the set of *Dallas*.

"Mornin'," Whitey boomed, then dropped a black alligator-skin briefcase on the table with a *thwack*, and thumbed open the brass closures. "Name is Gaylord Gilliam, representing Mrs. Raymond Carmichael." He paused and, from beneath the brim of his absurd white hat, scanned the room—even the empty chairs—for effect. "*The* Mrs. Raymond Carmichael."

Natalie sat numbly, but next to her, Masterson pushed himself to his feet and shook hands with the man across the table, murmuring, "Ma'am," in Beatrix's direction. Natalie nodded to her, um . . . counterpart, as Beatrix lowered herself into the chair her lawyer held out. Tight-lipped and steady-handed, the woman seemed remarkably calm. *The* Mrs. Raymond Carmichael must have gotten more sleep in the past two days than she, Mrs. Raymond Carmichael, The Impostor.

"Well now," Mr. Gilliam shouted. "Who're we waiting for?"

"The other one," Beatrix muttered, shooting a look of veiled loathing toward Natalie, effectively lumping her into the same category as absent wife number three. The dig should have hurt, but it didn't. Nothing hurt. The doctor in her knew her body had kicked into a phase of self-preservation, so she didn't fight the cottony insulation. She did, however, have her wits about her enough to dread the inevitable awakening.

After a quick rap on the door, the receptionist from the Paducah law office, which had made their boardroom available to Masterson out of professional courtesy, stuck her head into the contentious room. "Coffee or tea, anyone?"

Natalie and Beatrix declined, the lawyers accepted—in anticipation of a long meeting, she guessed. The two men made small talk about traffic, Masterson mumbling, Gilliam hollering. The man had to be hard of hearing. Natalie chewed on the one fingernail she had left and studied the intricate carving on the edge of the enormous table that reached all the way to her breastbone. How many lives had been made and broken over this table as negotiations were hacked out—prenuptial agreements, divorces, custody battles, wills, trusts?

She'd bet, however, that the faux grey marble walls had never heard the likes of a predicament such as this one.

Beatrix drummed her long fingers on the table top, keeping an irregular beat punctuated with elaborate sighs as she shifted her gaze to the four corners of the room. The woman had a regal presence about her, an aura of entitlement and indifference that Natalie envied—how did one graduate past caring about what other people thought? Rose Marie had mastered it, though with considerably more outward grace than Beatrix exhibited. Her aunt might have liked Beatrix, Natalie realized suddenly, save for the fact that she was married to Raymond.

Her tears welled involuntarily, increasingly harder to blink away because her eyelids were raw and leaky. She was able to stem the flow with a sharp pinch to her palm with blunt-tipped fingers. Funny, she hadn't bitten her nails since leaving home for college. Her mother had tried everything to get her to stop—foul tasting creams, cotton gloves, even Band-Aids, but the cure had been stepping onto the bus that carried her away from fractious parents and a hell-raising brother. Surely, though, if her mother were alive to witness this unbelievable humiliation, she wouldn't begrudge her a comforting bout of gnawing.

She, along with everyone else, heard Ruby coming before they saw her. Her unmistakable high-pitched voice, the *clomp-clomp* of . . .

Natalie swallowed as the door swung open. Of white vinyl go-go boots.

The young woman pranced in, pale but glowing, shadowed by a gum-popping slick-haired man wearing a short-sleeve plaid shirt and carrying a Mead binder.

"How y'all doing today?" he asked, grinning and popping.

"Who are you?" Gilliam yelled.

"Billy Wayne Lewis, Attorney-*at*-Law," the man

announced, then jerked his thumb toward Ruby. "Her cousin, twice removed."

Gilliam smirked. "Speaking of remove—lose the gum, Billy Bob."

The man stopped midchew. "Billy *Wayne*." He glared at Gilliam while he removed the pink wad with one finger and stuck it underneath the table. "And this is my client, Ruby Lynn Carmichael."

Ruby smiled, adorably pitiful. "Hi-do."

Masterson and Gilliam both nodded cordially, maintaining stoic expressions, but Natalie didn't miss their heightened color. They took in Ruby's head of splendid red hair, white halter top, short yellow skirt and, of course, the boots. On the outside, the men seemed neutral, but inside she knew they were thinking, *Damn, Raymond, how'd you do it?*

How did you do it, Raymond? Juggle all of us? Lead a triple life? Sleep at night?

While the men introduced themselves, Natalie smoothed a hand over her khaki skirt, then crossed her arms over her pale blue button-down. Between Beatrix's sophistication and Ruby's flamboyance, she felt mousy and . . . beige.

"Won't you have a seat?" Masterson said to Ruby, gesturing vaguely, as if he didn't want to be responsible for a seating arrangement that might lead to injuries.

"Hi, Natalie," she chirped, dropping into the seat at the head of the table between the two women. "Beatrix," she added coolly.

While Beatrix's eyes rolled back in her head, Natalie managed a noncommittal grimace in Ruby's direction, still torn between hating the young woman and feeling sorry for her. Ruby probably assumed they were friends because she had helped bring the girl around at the hospital when she'd fainted at the pronouncement of Raymond's death. In truth, she'd simply assisted the doctor by elevating Ruby's legs.

Long, slender legs that had been wrapped around Raymond's waist God only knew how many times.

Natalie closed her eyes and forced her mind back to the legal matters at hand. After all, the sleepless nights ahead would provide sufficient time to torment herself.

The receptionist wheeled in a tray of coffee and tea in deference to the late arrivals, cast a nervous smile over the motley group, which had fallen silent, then exited, pronto. The men poured coffee into Styrofoam cups and passed them around the table with sugar packets.

"Coffee beans have to be picked one at a time," Ruby announced to the group.

Beatrix cut her eyes toward the young woman. "Don't. Start."

Natalie stared at her own unwanted cup, her stomach roiling from the strong aroma, thinking how absurd that they were indulging in morning routines while her husband lay in the morgue across town, waiting for them to reach some kind of consensus.

"Can we *please* get on with this?" she asked, her strident voice surprising even herself.

The attorneys respectively scurried, swaggered, and strolled to their seats, then Gilliam and Masterson seemingly competed to see who could remove the most paperwork from their crammed briefcases to stack on the table. Billy Wayne joined the race, emptying his binder down to a plastic protractor, while Natalie wondered if sheer frustration could be the elusive scientific root of spontaneous combustion. She shot Masterson an exasperated look, spurring him to his feet.

"We are gathered here today—" He flushed, then coughed. "I mean, we're here this morning to discuss the ramifications of the events which have recently come to light in the wake of Raymond Carmichael's untimely, um . . . passing."

Natalie glanced toward the door, still holding onto a thread of hope that Raymond would burst into the room guffawing, admitting that one of his practical jokes had gone too far, announcing he was whisking her off to Rome for their anniversary. Six years ago today they had exchanged vows. *Forsaking all others, until death do us part.* She willed the hulking door to open, but it sat still, separating her from the sane world.

Masterson squirmed. "According to my initial research, it appears that Mr. Carmichael, whether intentionally or inadvertently, married my client, Natalie Marie Blankenship six years ago without securing a divorce from his first wife, Beatrix Lenore Richardson."

She didn't belong here, Natalie thought, looking around the table at people she didn't want to know. These kinds of squalid things happened to naïve housewives in Peoria whose husbands were pilots. Whose waistlines had vanished. Whose marriages were deplorable.

"It further appears that Mr. Carmichael, whether intentionally or inadvertently, married—" he referred to a legal pad "—Ruby Lynn Hicks six weeks ago without securing a divorce either from his first wife or from his, um, second wife."

Women whose tongues were sharp. Whose demands were many. Whose eyes or hearts strayed.

"Inadvertently?" Beatrix asked. "Raymond knew exactly what he was doing—he simply hadn't planned on getting caught."

"Or on dying," Ruby added, nodding as if she were making a significant contribution.

Natalie hadn't yet divulged Raymond's betrayal to anyone other than Masterson, but not because of the pact of silence Beatrix had extracted from them in the surreal aftermath of the doctor's pronouncement at the hospital. She simply needed time to come to grips with the situation herself before deciding how much information, if any, to reveal to friends and family.

"I'm only trying to make the best of a very difficult situation," Masterson said to Beatrix, mopping his neck with a handkerchief.

She'd given Sara just enough details about Raymond's death to satisfy a few shocked questions, then asked her nurse to arrange for a retired physician to fill in for a couple of weeks.

Gilliam waved in the air. "Let's cut through the crap, Masterson. As Raymond's legitimate wife and sole heir, my client is entitled to all of his assets, and to half of his jointly owned assets, including homes, cars, jewelry, et cetera, et cetera."

She hadn't even had time to call her brother Tony. Actually, she'd had time, but not the strength to deal with him.

"Sole heir?" Masterson fished through the papers on the table, then held up a substantial-looking document. "I have a copy of Mr. Carmichael's will, dated January of this year, where he names Natalie as his heir."

So much to do. She still hadn't unpacked Raymond's

book collection. And Rose Marie's flower garden in the back yard was getting out of hand.

"May I see the will?" Gilliam asked, pushing reading glasses on his face.

Plus Raymond's den was a disaster. His desk hadn't yielded documents easily—one locked drawer had required a chisel before revealing expense reports and travel logs that showed he'd spent every other weekend of the last year with her or Beatrix, but most weekdays in the vicinity of Ruby.

"Ah," Gilliam said, triumphant. "This will specifies 'Natalie, my wife' as Mr. Carmichael's heir. But since we've already determined that she isn't his wife, the point is moot."

No wonder he'd been so exhausted on Friday nights.

"Even without a valid marriage license, Natalie and Raymond were practically common-law man and wife according to the state statute," Masterson said.

She'd refused to live with Raymond despite his numerous requests. Blame it on her strict Pentecostal upbringing, but she'd held out for a commitment. And now she'd discovered she'd been fornicating with another woman's husband for nearly seven years. If she were to die of humiliation, she would go straight to hell.

"'Practically' isn't a legal term," Gilliam snapped. "And if the man is already married, he can't very well be the common-law husband of someone else. Did you get your law degree through the mail, counselor?"

The town of Smiley would crucify her if the facts surrounding her marriage were released, guilt be damned. The gossip alone would destroy her practice, her reputation, her sanctity, everything she held dear. The events unfolded in her head as if on a movie screen, with the absence of a happy ending.

"What's wrong with getting a law degree through the mail?" Billy Wayne asked.

Masterson had already warned her they were on shaky legal ground. Raymond had left her in a precarious situation, pledging her to his debts, but none of his assets, at least not legitimately. Short of negotiation and good will, her financial outlook was bleak.

Gilliam withdrew two forms from his impressive pile, then slid one in front of her, and one in front of Ruby. She tried to focus on the print, but her head was still sore from the last headache, and another one was descending. Mercifully, Masterson took the paper from her.

"The law is clearly on Mrs. Carmichael's side," Gilliam continued with a cordial smile. "But in lieu of this unusual situation, my client has graciously agreed to forego her claim to the assets Mr. Carmichael owned in conjunction with Ms. Blankenship and Ms. Hicks."

Blankenship. Indeed, she had no real claim to Raymond's name. By all rights, she should change her name back. New driver's license . . . new credit cards . . . new name on her office door.

"In return for their silence," Masterson said, then read from the paper. "The undersigned hereby agrees not to discuss the nature or details of their relationship with Raymond A. Carmichael with any living person, and will take steps to expunge all connections to his name from theirs."

Six years of her life, negated. Erased. Highlighted and deleted.

Gilliam adopted an accommodating stance, his fleshy mouth curling. "Mrs. Carmichael enjoys a reputable standing within her community—I'm sure you understand how the stigma of bigamy would cast a shadow over her position and her way of life. This agreement simply assures her of the cooperation of the other two women involved to keep the details of Raymond's indiscretion confidential."

DEAD MAN LEAVES BEHIND THREE WIVES. VOTE FOR YOUR FAVORITE BY PRESSING 1 FOR THE SOCIALITE, 2 FOR THE SAINT, OR 3 FOR THE SIREN.

Next to her, Masterson scribbled a note on the legal pad for her eyes only. *You should consider signing the form to protect your assets.*

Nausea rolled in her stomach, and she pushed away the tablet. "Right now, I simply want to know how and where my hus—Raymond will be . . . buried."

Beatrix fingered the double strand of pearls at her neck, a faint smile of authority on her lips—not exactly the picture of the grieving widow. "After a memorial service in Northbend, *my* husband will be buried in my family plot."

Natalie ached to scream. Instead, she gripped a fisful of skirt in her lap. "Raymond told me many times he wanted to be cremated."

Ruby raised her hand. When everyone looked her way, she slung her hair over her shoulders, exposing her remarkable cleavage bound up in the white halter top. "Ray and I had a long talk about freeze-drying his body when he died and bringing him back to life later on."

Beatrix let out a sharp burst of humorless laughter. "Oh, that's rich. The only reason I'd want to bring the bastard back to life would be to kill him again."

Natalie's hands twitched to slap her, but she didn't have the energy. Besides, Ruby beat her to the punch. The redhead lunged across the table at Beatrix with a shriek, swinging wildly. When Billy Wayne and Gilliam dragged her off, she came away with more than a few blond hairs in her fists.

Ruby strained against the men's hands. spitting and kicking. Gilliam's hat went flying.

Beatrix's eyes bulged, and she held on to her mussed hair with both hands, her body shaking and her face scarlet. "How *dare* you assault me, you, you . . . *bimbo*! Gaylord, I want her arrested immediately!"

Natalie sat perfectly still, entertaining the thought that if the two women were allowed to fight to the death, her situation would improve by fifty percent. And despite Ruby's youth and energy, she'd put five dollars on Beatrix.

"Calm down, Beatrix," Gilliam advised in a soothing tone while Billy Wayne cajoled Ruby back into her chair, now moved safely out of striking distance.

"Don't even *think* about coming to the memorial service," Beatrix warned, shaking a finger at both of them, smoothing her hair with her other hand. "I'll have you both hauled away."

Natalie shook her head, surprisingly calm although her heart jerked frantically at the woman's words. "You can't deny me—us—the opportunity to say good-bye to Raymond."

"Watch me."

Ruby lunged again, but Masterson and Gilliam were ready this time, finally situating their chairs between the two women.

"Remember, we still have a lot of issues to work through," Gilliam murmured close to Beatrix's ear. "Let's get back to the agreement, shall we?"

Natalie squared her shoulders. "I won't sign anything unless I'm allowed to attend the memorial service."

"Yeah," Ruby seconded.

Beatrix's mouth tightened, but her eyes seemed to soften as their gazes locked.

"Why would you even want to come?"

Why indeed? Natalie wet her lips, but her voice failed her. *Because I loved him*, she finally mouthed. For a split second, she experienced a connection with Beatrix, and she suspected that the woman wasn't nearly as crusty as she let on.

Billy Wayne, apparently a slow reader, flicked his finger against the two-paragraph agreement. "This ain't gonna fly."

"And why is that?" Gilliam asked, a model of patience.

"'Cause," Billy Wayne said with a tight smile. "Raymond's first wife ain't his only heir."

Beatrix's face drained of color. "What are you saying?"

Ruby grinned and touched her flat, exposed midriff. "I'm pregnant with Ray's baby."

Natalie nearly swallowed her tongue. And this time Beatrix did the lunging, her manicured hands aiming for Ruby's throat.

Six

NATALIE CONSIDERED SHOPPING for a new black dress just to pass the unbearable hours until the memorial service Beatrix had begrudgingly agreed to hold the next day in Paducah, on neutral soil. But, she decided, staring blankly into her tidy closet, the crepe suit she'd bought for Rose Marie's wake would suffice, with the addition of an Hermes scarf Raymond had given her. She fingered the scrap of colorful silk, trying to recall the occasion for the gift. She couldn't, and now questioned how many of the extravagant presents he'd brought home were by-products of guilt.

Slowly, she opened the other side of the closet. Raymond's impeccable suits, slacks, and shirts hung benignly under dry-cleaner's plastic, waiting for his return. Natalie knelt to straighten one of his shoes, wondering if he'd kept full closets at Beatrix's and Ruby's.

She sat down hard on the floor, then pulled her knees up to her chin. Of course he had. A man who thought nothing of maintaining three wives would've certainly thought nothing of maintaining three wardrobes.

"Oh, Raymond," she moaned, lowering her head on her crossed arms. "Why?"

She sat for the longest time, breathing through the musky

fibers of her thin wool sweater sleeve. She would never be warm again. Two other women . . . a baby.

A *baby*. She squeezed her eyes shut, eking out a lone tear. She'd never pined to be a mother—she suspected her maternal instincts had gone undeveloped because her own mother had been no model of parental warmth. Raymond had said he was relieved she didn't want children because he opposed bringing children into such a corrupt world, but had it been his own corrupt conscience speaking?

The man she'd immersed herself and her life into was a stranger. She had nothing now. Even the good memories were sullied. And worst of all, how pathetic was she that she hadn't suspected a thing?

Not true, her mind whispered. She'd suspected—she'd simply underestimated the depth of his betrayal.

A distant ringing penetrated the fog of her misery. The doorbell, she realized finally, and pushed herself up when the visitor became persistent. Neighbors and acquaintances had dropped off containers of food all afternoon—Sara had effectively spread the word of Raymond's death, and apparently salads were the official comfort food of the small town. As much as she didn't want to see or talk to anyone, she wanted to sit on the floor and talk to herself even less. Besides, most of the visitors had scurried off rather quickly once they got a look at her puffy eyes and peeling nose.

Every part of her ached as she moved in slow motion down the stairs. Since that horrid night in the hospital—had it been only two nights ago?—she'd slept on the blue velvet loveseat in the library. The loveseat itself wasn't so uncomfortable, but the fall she'd taken during a nightmare had left her with bruises down her right side.

"Mrs. Ratchet," she murmured when she opened the

heavy door. Her heart picked up a couple of beats because the sweet little old woman, in addition to being her incredibly nosy next-door neighbor, was the feature writer for the *Smiley Tribune*, a weekly paper that could easily pass for a newsletter, and consisted mostly of church news.

Eileen Ratchet wore a sorrowful expression on her bird-like face and carried an orange plastic bowl covered with aluminum foil. "*Mrs.* Carmichael, I'm *so* sorry to hear about your *husband*."

"Thank you."

The bony woman looked past her into the house, hinting for an invitation inside. Receiving none, she extended the bowl. "Pea salad."

Natalie pasted on a smile as she accepted the offering. "How kind of you to come by to check on me."

Mrs. Ratchet rocked forward and whispered, "I heard he was killed instantly in a car crash."

She blinked. "Um, no, Raymond suffered a heart attack after the accident."

"Oh." Her thin shoulders sagged—she'd apparently just missed out on a headline. "Well, if you want, my dear, I'll write the obituary myself for the *Tribune*."

"I would like that, Mrs. Ratchet."

Her neighbor shot another glimpse inside the house. "Do you have a photo you'd like for me to use?"

"No, not really."

Her neighbor whipped out a little pocket-size notebook and Natalie expected her to lick the end of her pencil. She did. "I called around the local funeral homes, but none of them knew anything about the funeral."

"My hus . . . Raymond will be buried out of state."

"Where?"

She swallowed. "His family hasn't yet decided. Please keep the obituary simple—Raymond was forty-two, he worked in medical sales, he died of a heart attack."

"How long were the two of you married?"

A lump the size of Raymond's ego lodged in her esophagus. *Never.*

"Mrs. Carmichael?"

Natalie's throat convulsed. "Six . . . years. But you don't need to print that."

The woman's pencil stopped. "Whyever not?"

"Because . . . I think Raymond's obituary should be about his life, not his . . . relationship to . . . me." *Liar, liar, pants on fire.*

"Er, as you wish. What—"

"Mrs. Ratchet, I really must go."

"But can I do something to help, dear? Weed your flower garden, perhaps? I noticed it was looking a bit wild."

"I appreciate the offer, but no." She started to close the door. "And thank you for the potato salad."

"*Pea* salad."

"Yes. Lovely." Natalie retreated, nodding and smiling as she shut the door. Inside, she leaned her head against the worn slab of mahogany, wondering if anyone would miss her if she never left the house again. Maybe she'd just turn the deadbolt and founder herself on pea salad, potato salad, Waldorf salad, macaroni salad, Jell-O salad, three-bean salad, pasta salad, fruit salad, and the more puzzling "Watergate" salad. She trudged to the kitchen—now a veritable Tupperware Rubik's Cube—and began to rearrange shelves of containers to make room for Mrs. Ratchet's contribution.

Looking for items to remove, her hand fell upon a half-empty jar of anchovies—Raymond's favorite midnight snack.

Despite her disgust of the nasty little things, she'd faithfully stocked the premium brand he preferred. Natalie blinked back a fresh wave of tears and replaced the tall jar that wasn't taking up so much room after all.

The doorbell rang again—Mrs. Ratchet had probably thought of some ingenious angle to extract more details. As she retraced her steps, Natalie pushed her hair back from her face and sighed, reminding herself to be grateful that someone cared.

She tried on a patient smile as she opened the door, but sobered at the sight of Brian Butler standing on her stoop. Natalie sucked in a sharp breath. "How *dare* you come to my home—"

"I came to offer my condolences, Dr. Carmichael," he rushed to say. His dark eyes were hooded, and he didn't seem to know what to do with his big hands. "I just heard about Raymond."

"Thank you. Now leave."

"And I want to apologize."

She closed her eyes briefly. "I'm listening."

He pulled at the knot in his tie—another hard day of shaking down innocent women, obviously. "I realize how much of a shock I gave you last week. On hindsight, I could've handled the situation differently."

"Yes, you could have."

"Uncle Brian!"

Natalie glanced in the direction of the shout. A grey van with BUTLER FAMILY PAWN and the phone number painted on the side in garish colors sat in her driveway. A little girl with sagging blond pigtails practically hung out of the driver side window.

"Jeanie hit me!"

A dark head appeared. "Ally hit me first!"

His sigh was weary. "Nobody hit anybody, okay? Sit down and don't *touch* each other." The man looked back at her. "Sorry."

Natalie frowned, momentarily off-kilter.

"Anyway—" he began.

"Uncle Brian! Jeanie keeps playing with the radio!"

"Ally won't be quiet so I can hear the music!"

"Both of you—quiet! And sit on your hands." He turned back with a little smile. "Sorry again."

His brown eyes were bloodshot, the scar on his forehead stood out in relief, and his five o'clock shadow had a bad sense of timing—the man was exhausted.

"Anyway, I brought you something." He leaned over to fetch a wrinkled brown shopping bag.

"Let me guess—salad?"

He looked confused. "Hmm?"

But the bag was too light for foodstuff. She removed a small jeweler's box and opened it, her breath catching at the sight of her aunt's diamond stud earrings. She lifted a questioning gaze because her voice had fled.

His wide shoulders lifted in a shrug. "I couldn't live with myself knowing they meant so much to you."

She inclined her head in thanks, blinking rapidly.

"I'm sorry for your loss. I didn't know Raymond very well, but he seemed like a nice fellow."

She hadn't known him very well either, and as it turned out, he wasn't so nice.

"Uncle Brian, I'm hungry!"

"Me too!"

He gave her a tight smile. "Don't worry about the loan right now—we'll work out something."

When he turned and walked away, Natalie clutched the earrings to her chest, thankful for the man's latent conscience.

"Dr. Carmichael?"

He stood at the end of her sidewalk, leaning toward her as if he were reluctant to leave. His hair lifted and fell in the cool breeze.

"It doesn't feel like it now, but believe me, time does heal all wounds."

Simple, trite words she'd heard at least a dozen times today alone. Yet something in his expression touched her—was he speaking from experience of losing a spouse?

"Uncle Brian!"

"Coming." He climbed into the van, then yanked on a pigtail and tweaked a cheek before starting the engine and driving off.

Believe me, time does heal all wounds.

Natalie wanted to believe the man, but she couldn't imagine a day when she would ever feel happy again, or even normal.

The one shining spot was the knowledge that her life couldn't possibly get any more confusing.

As she turned to retreat into the house, a streak of yellow by the street caught her attention. She watched as a cab came to a halt and a man alighted carrying an athletic bag. The taxi pulled away, leaving the man at the curb. Natalie frowned because something about his tall frame seemed familiar . . .

"Natalie!" The man waved, striding toward her through the yard.

She froze—she hadn't recognized her brother without the government-issue orange jumpsuit.

"Hey, sis!" Tony's grin was magnanimous. "Hope I didn't arrive at a bad time."

Seven

"THE MONARCH IS our top-of-the-line model."

Mr. Rueben of Rueben's Memorial Chapel spoke in a soothing, too-practiced voice that grated on Beatrix's nerves. The stiff, suited man swept his arm over the casket as if it were a goddamned radar range.

"Twenty-gauge steel, with two-point brushed copper blended bronze finish."

She squinted. Was he wearing lipstick?

He opened the lid with a flourish. "The interior is royal purple velvet, hand-quilted and hand-smocked. The hardware—"

"How much?" The place stank of formaldehyde—or maybe it was Mr. Rueben.

The man cleared his throat. "Six thousand."

"Dollars?"

He nodded. "I'm sure you want a casket representative of the devotion between you and your dearly departed husband."

Beatrix glanced around the morbid showroom. "Where are your pine boxes?"

"Pardon me?"

She sighed, then ran her hand over the purple velvet. The bastard didn't deserve to rest in comfort for eternity, but she did feel obligated to uphold a certain image. A few regulars from the Northbend Country Club would make the drive to Paducah out of idle curiosity alone. Her challenge would be to play the grieving widow while keeping wives number two and three out of sight. She'd agreed they could attend the service as long as they came alone and kept their mouths shut. Natalie would behave herself, but that other one drove her batty. Too bad Gaylord hadn't let her strangle the knocked-up tart this morning—they'd all be better off, including the baby, from the looks of the girl.

The fact that Raymond had fathered a child still stunned her. She was the one who'd pined for children; Raymond had simply humored her. They'd tried for years before giving up. Even then, she'd been more than willing to adopt, but he wouldn't hear of it. He'd been obsessed with the notion of ending up with a child who had a mental disorder. She shook her head—if that wasn't the pot calling the kettle black.

"Mrs. Carmichael?"

"Hmm?"

He licked his red lips. "Would you like to see something else?"

The bottom of a bottle of vodka. "No. This model will do."

"A thoughtful choice, madam."

The injustice of being denied a child topped with his seemingly casual impregnation of that slut was akin to having her acrylic nails pulled off one at a time. Was she so undeserving of a bit of happiness?

Mr. Rueben led her toward a rolltop desk studded with brochures and stationery samples. "Now, there's the matter of the service itself, the eulogy programs, the thank-you notes, the complimentary cards and envelopes in case visitors want to send you condolences—"

"No music, no minister, no priest. Use this style of program, I have my own thank-you notes, and if anyone wants to send me a card of condolence, they can damn well trot their ass down to Hallmark."

"Er, yes, ma'am." He scribbled on an order form.

"What else?"

"We invite the family to come early tomorrow, to have private time with the deceased before the public viewing."

The deceased. Funeral director vernacular. "I'm the only family Raymond has." According to Gaylord's research, Raymond had been truthful in that respect thank goodness.

"Perhaps you'd like to bring a close friend?"

The names and faces of dozens of acquaintances revolved in her head, not one of them intimate enough to be considered family. And except for a few distant cousins, she'd outlived her own family members. "I'll be alone." She preferred her own company to most anyway.

He nodded. "I'll need to provide the name of the final resting place to the hearse driver."

"Oak Gardens Cemetery in Northbend, Tennessee."

His eyes widened. "That's a two-hour drive."

"And?"

"And . . . no problem, Mrs. Carmichael."

"Is there anything else, or may I leave this dreadful place?"

"Sign here," he said, handing her a pen. "Then you may leave this dr—then you may leave, ma'am."

After signing, Beatrix stalked out, gulping fresh air on the open street. A wave of nausea overcame her but she made it to her Mercedes without humiliating herself. She opened the door and started to lower herself into the leather seat when a building caught her attention. Trying to ignore the pull, she swung into her seat, but was compelled to look up again before she started the engine. Beatrix swallowed, then sighed in resignation. "Might as well get it over with."

She estimated the distance to the building to be about two blocks. Comparing the inviting weather with the stagnant interior of her car, she opted to walk.

Yellow pennants reading "Welcome to Paducah" waved atop old-fashioned lampposts. Lacy white-blossomed trees—dogwoods, maybe—lined the streets, their falling blooms carpeting the sidewalks and the grubby curbs. Not an unpleasant town, this Paducah, as good as any for a memorial service. And in truth, having the funeral away from Northbend afforded her emotional distance from the sordid details of Raymond's life, and his death. As she walked, she fingered the cross of solid gold she always wore next to her skin. Damn hypocritical, she knew, but old habits died hard.

Nearly two blocks later, her footsteps slowed. She leaned her head back to take in the ancient bell tower, and the virtual wall of stained-glass windows above the soaring curved wood doors. Apprehension gripped her, twisting her intestines. Breathing deeply, Beatrix removed a silk scarf from her purse, then placed it loosely over her hair before entering the cathedral.

The interior was cavernous, solemn, and empty. She jumped when the door thumped closed behind her, the acoustics returning echoes back and again. Dim lighting set off the glowing stained-glass windows along the sides, the scenes representing the Stations of the Cross. At the front of the sanctuary, a statue of the Holy Mother raised her hands toward her, across the rows of mahogany pews.

Her eyes were accusing . . . knowing.

Beatrix swallowed hard, then approached the water basin just inside the entrance. She dipped in her shaking fingers, poised for the electric jolt—real or imagined—that she always experienced when she touched holy water. She quickly crossed herself, then moved to a table on the side of the church where candles of varying heights flickered in the gloom. Fishing in her wallet, she extracted a one-hundred-dollar bill and stuffed it into the offering box, then selected a long wick and lit a candle with the flame from another.

After crossing herself again, she lowered herself gingerly to the kneeling bench—her knees had deteriorated a bit since her last visit to church. Her heart pounded as she crossed herself again. She pulled out her beloved cross pendant, kissed it, then folded her hands around the precious gold piece and bowed her head.

Father, please bless the soul of my husband, who so recently left this earth. You alone know how much I loved him, despite his many flaws. In your boundless mercy, bestow an extra measure of forgiveness on his sins, and on mine, which are great. Amen.

She made the sign of the cross and pushed herself to her feet, wiping her cheeks and feeling somewhat less burdened. Retracing her steps, she walked past a row of confession cubicles, hastening her step to ignore the fingers of guilt that plucked at her.

At the last booth, however, she slowed, taunted by the flame of the burning candle that signified a priest was standing by to take confession. Yielding to the gnawing in her stomach, she stepped into the booth and pulled the curtain closed behind her. The odor of old material and mothballs enveloped her as she knelt on the low bench, resurrecting a flood of memories from her days at Sacred Heart Catholic School for Girls. A shiver seized her and her shoulders jerked in spasms. The screen slid open with a *thwack*, and she nearly bolted.

"Peace be with you, my child," the priest said. He sounded very young.

"And also w-with you," she said automatically, then her tongue froze.

"Do you wish to confess?"

"Yes, father." She inhaled deeply, sucking stale but consecrated air into her lungs. "It's been eighteen years since my last confession."

"Go on."

"I smoke too much, I drink too much, and I swear too much."

"All is forgivable in the eyes of God. Go on."

"I don't like people, I don't like animals, and I don't like most children."

"Er, go on."

"Father, has the law changed regarding pastoral confidentiality?"

"No."

She exhaled noisily. "Then hold on to your rosary."

Eight

FOR A DEAD man, Ray looked pretty good, Ruby decided, wiping her eyes. She'd seen her fair share of corpses, and none of them had been smiling like that. She'd once dated a mortician who let her in on all the tricks, like Super Gluing the eyelids down and sewing the mouth closed so nothing happened during the viewing to freak everyone out. And he always tried to make the person look as if they were at peace with their Maker—a little rouge, a pink light over the casket. It was an art, the man had told her. Well, whoever had fixed up Ray was a master because he looked downright gorgeous.

She wanted to take a picture of him with the disposable camera in her purse, but Beatrix still stood at the head of the casket, her mouth set in a straight line, her eyes dry. The witch had agreed to let her and Natalie come in to look at Ray before everyone else, and she didn't want to push it by blinding her with a flash. Natalie hadn't yet arrived, but they still had fifteen minutes until the doors opened. Beatrix had invited people from Northbend who knew Ray, and some people who worked with him in the arms and legs business. Ruby had wanted to invite a couple of stripper friends who knew Ray, but Beatrix had nearly popped a cork when she mentioned it.

Ruby stepped closer to the casket, enjoying the silky slide

of her new red satin dress against her legs. She'd added the rhinestones on the skirt herself to save money, and her friend Plenty had loaned her the pointy-toed white ankle boots from her Victorian Virgin act to complete the special outfit. Ray would have been proud.

She belched into her hand, muttering, "Excuse me," when Beatrix glared at her. The baby was making her stomach upset, and all the stress had kept her from eating her regular bowl of Kix this morning. Even without being a legit wife, Billy Wayne had assured her she was in a good spot for money, what with being pregnant and all. But she'd have to wait until the baby was born to prove that Raymond was the father unless she wanted them to stick a needle the size of a crochet hook into her navel to withdraw fluid.

She'd decided to wait, even if the tanning bed in the guest bedroom was repossessed, because her boss, Mac, wouldn't be happy if she asked for time off for a paternity test. Especially since he didn't even know about the baby. With creative costumes, she figured she could make it to four, maybe five months before anyone at work noticed.

"Did you pick out the coffin?" she asked Beatrix.

Ray's wife nodded.

"It's nice. Since Ray's a 'winter,' the purple is a great color for him. Brings out the silver in his hair."

Beatrix pushed out her cheek with her tongue. "Thank you."

"Don't mention it."

"Going straight to work from here?" Beatrix smirked at her new dress.

Jealous hag. "I pulled a double shift last night so I could spend the day with Ray."

The older woman puckered up her mouth. "Spend the day with Ray?"

"Yeah. Did you know that in ancient times, the Aztecs kept their dead relatives in the house with them forever? Dressed them up, talked to them, even brought them to the supper table." She'd seen that on a TBS special, so there.

Beatrix touched her hand to her temple. "Don't talk."

"Do you have a headache? I have some Kmart aspirin. It's just as good as the expensive stuff."

"Just. Don't. Talk."

"Even when the visitors arrive?"

"*Especially* when the visitors arrive." Beatrix shook a bony finger at her. "In fact, if I see you talking to *anyone*, I'll boot you out on your moneymaker before you can say 'pole dance.'"

Ruby bit into her lower lip. "But what if someone talks to *me*?"

"Pretend you're mute."

"You're a mean lady."

"Yeah, well don't forget it."

At a noise behind them, they turned to see Natalie walk in, white and trembly. She looked past them to the casket, and her knees buckled. Ruby rushed to her side and she was surprised to see that Beatrix was on the other side, although she was frowning. They led her forward one shaky step at a time. At the edge of the casket, Natalie clutched the side and burst into tears. Ruby stroked her back and handed her a wad of toilet paper she'd gotten from the ritzy bathroom down the hall. Natalie blew her nose, whimpering like a puppy being weaned. When Natalie quieted, they seated her in a padded folding chair near the front of the room.

The stinky funeral director appeared with a box of Kleenex—was he wearing *lipstick*?

"Are you ladies related to Mr. Carmichael?" he asked, his voice soft and lispy. Definitely gay, she thought. Flame-o-rama.

Ruby and Natalie looked at Beatrix, who squirmed. "Um . . . no. This is Natalie Blankenship and—" She raised her eyebrows at Ruby.

"Ruby Hicks," Ruby provided.

"Yes," Beatrix said, her mouth turned down. "They're . . . they're . . . my sisters."

Ruby coughed away her smile. Sisters? Natalie seemed equally surprised.

"How nice to meet you," the man said, pumping both of their hands with his cushiony paw. "And how wonderful for you to come to provide comfort to Mrs. Carmichael in her time of grief."

"That's what *sisters* are for," Ruby said with a smile, settling one arm around Beatrix's shoulders, just for spite. The woman stiffened, but didn't belt her. "Sir, would you take a picture of us?"

He blinked, but agreed.

She dug in her purse, winding up having to remove her makeup kit and her curling iron before she found the camera.

"This is highly improper," Beatrix said out of the side of her mouth.

Natalie didn't protest, but didn't smile as the man snapped the picture. Ruby took advantage of the moment to nab a few photos of Ray. Other than two blurry Polaroids from their wedding, she didn't have a single picture of him for her scrapbook.

Beatrix appeared at her side and hissed, "What the devil are you doing, taking pictures?"

Ruby blinked. "My baby will never know her daddy—I want to be able to show her photos."

Beatrix's mouth tightened, then she spoke through gritted teeth. "Get rid of the camera and I'll get you a picture of Raymond."

She brightened. "Really?"

"Really."

"Cross your heart and hope to die?"

"Enough," Beatrix said, raising her hand. She looked toward the entrance, where two suited men and a woman stood, looking forlorn. "There's Raymond's boss and coworkers, so leave. *Now.*"

Beatrix brushed by her to greet the strangers. Ruby watched as they patted Beatrix's arm and talked amongst themselves. Envy gripped her—she'd wanted the world to recognize *her* as Ray's wife. She glanced back to the casket, her eyes watering. *Why did you lie to me, Ray? Because I wasn't good enough to be your wife? Because I was a low-life, white-trash stripper? I've got news for you, Ray. Low-life, white-trash strippers have feelings, too.*

Ruby swallowed, then walked to Natalie's chair. "Come on," she whispered. "Let's get something to drink."

At first Natalie appeared not to have heard her, but finally nodded and stood. Ruby shortened her stride to match Natalie's as they walked down the hall, suddenly feeling protective of the thin woman.

"Whew," Ruby said once she deposited Natalie at a little table in the vending room. "I could use a snack. How about you?" When Natalie didn't answer, she pulled out her change purse, heavy with tip money, and inserted enough coins to buy two bags of Doritos and two diet sodas. "I owe you money from the night at the hospital," Ruby said, setting the food on the table. "You bought me hot chocolate, remember?"

Natalie was looking at her, but her blue eyes weren't focused. Ruby thought again of how attractive the woman could be with a new hairstyle and a little makeup.

"Doc," she said, reaching forward to squeeze her small hand. "Are you okay?"

Slowly, Natalie came around, nodding. "How . . . how can you be so calm?"

Ruby ripped open the Doritos and cracked open the colas. "What do you mean?"

"You were married to him, too. How are you dealing with this?"

She took a sip of the drink. "The whole situation really stinks, but what's a person to do?"

"Hate him?" Natalie asked, kind of like she wanted permission to do just that.

"I can't hate him. He's the father of my child."

"But look what he did to us . . . to you."

Ruby frowned. "I know Ray was wrong, but he's dead now, so he's sort of been punished, don't you think?"

"What goes around, comes around," Natalie murmured.

Ruby smiled. "I always wondered what that saying meant."

The corners of Natalie's mouth lifted the tiniest bit. "Have you seen a doctor yet? About the baby, I mean?"

Ruby shook her head. "I took a home pregnancy test. Two of them, in fact. Saw a blue plus-sign both times. Do you think that means I'm having a boy?"

Natalie shook her head. "No."

"Good, because I want a girl. So did Ray."

The woman was shredding the wad of toilet paper she'd given her. "So you and Raymond talked about having a child?"

"Oh, sure. Ray said he wanted four, two boys and two girls." She patted her stomach. "This little one came along earlier than we'd planned, but Ray was thrilled. Insisted that we be married right away."

Natalie stared at her hands, then descended back into a funk.

Famished, Ruby polished off both bags of chips and both colas, then followed up with a banana moon pie, also from the vending machine. She tried to make small talk with Natalie over the next hour, sharing little tidbits she thought the other woman would find interesting:

"Did you know that they put menthol in Noxzema during World War II so it wouldn't be taxed as a cosmetic?"

"No, I didn't."

"Did you know that a duck can't float in soapy water?"

"No, I didn't."

"Did you know that the nail on your middle finger grows faster than the rest?"

"No, I didn't."

The lipstick-wearing funeral director came in about then and announced the viewing of Raymond A. Carmichael would end in approximately ten minutes. If the viewing had taken place in Leander, the family would have spent the night and the viewing would have gone on for two days. But this was the city, and everything moved faster, even funerals. She wanted one last look, and so did Natalie. They returned to the viewing room and stood among the potted palm trees until only Beatrix remained at the casket.

To Ruby's surprise, the woman bent and placed a kiss on Ray's forehead, then removed her wedding ring and slipped it on his left hand, next to his own wedding ring. He'd told Natalie and her both the same story—that the ring was his grandfather's—but Beatrix confirmed she'd given it to him when they were married ages ago.

The funeral director closed the double doors to the room as he exited, sealing them from prying eyes. She and Natalie walked side by side up the aisle to say their final good-byes. Natalie kissed Ray's cheek, sobbing now.

"I'd like to bury my wedding ring with Raymond, too," Natalie said.

"And me," Ruby added.

Beatrix turned ten shades of red. "Absolutely, positively *not*."

"But we accepted these rings in good faith," Natalie said. "We thought we were married to him."

Beatrix crossed her arms over her chest. "But you weren't married to him—*I* was. If I were you two, I'd hock those trinkets for whatever they're worth. Judging by the fake engagement ring he gave to Red here, that probably isn't much."

The door squeaked open and the gay funeral director poked his head into the room. "Mrs. Carmichael, the hearse and the limousine are outside whenever you ladies are ready."

"We ladies?" Beatrix asked, frowning.

The man nodded. "I told the driver your sisters might be riding with you to the cemetery."

"Oh, but they—"

"Yes," Natalie cut in hoarsely, lifting her chin. "We *will* ride with Beatrix to the cemetery, won't we, Ruby?"

Suspecting she might never know where Ray was buried otherwise, Ruby nodded. "After all, that's what sisters are for."

Nine

NATALIE LAID HER head back on the cool dark leather of the headrest, reflecting on the irony that not only was her first ride in a limousine on the occasion of her husband's funeral, but that she was sharing the experience with his two other wives. *Wives.* The fact that the word "wife" could even take on a plural form should be a warning to women everywhere.

Funny how a person's perception of what was acceptable changed in the light of new realities. At moments, she could almost convince herself that she was overreacting. Polygamy was not only permissible, but encouraged in early times when men were in short supply. A practicality, according to history books. Harems still existed in some cultures, and in others, married men maintaining mistresses was simply a way of life. Indeed, many women she'd met in the course of her career had admitted to looking the other way when their partner strayed. Now those women would ask her, "My dear, did you think you were special?"

No. Not until I met Raymond.

"I don't feel so good," Ruby said, sprawling in the bench seat directly behind the tinted window that separated them from the driver. Natalie sat on the side bench, facing the jiggling bar decanters. Beatrix had commandeered the back bench and hadn't uttered a word in the thirty minutes since they'd left the funeral home.

"What's wrong?" Natalie asked.

"Feel like I'm going to puke," she said, rubbing her stomach.

Beatrix smirked. "That dress is making me nauseous, too."

"It's probably all that junk you ate," Natalie said. "Do you want me to ask the driver to stop?"

"Yeah," Ruby said, holding her hand up to her mouth.

"Oh, good grief," Beatrix muttered.

Experiencing a pang of sympathy for the green-faced woman, Natalie pressed a button to lower the window and asked the driver to pull over, quickly. They were in a rural area, with little traffic other than the hearse they followed. The car slowed and eased off the shoulder.

Ruby slid from her seat and crawled toward the back door on her knees. Her cheeks ballooned and she cried, "I ain't gonna make it."

Beatrix jerked her legs out of the way just as the contents of Ruby's stomach landed on the plush black carpet.

"Jesus Christ," Beatrix shouted, clambering next to Natalie.

Natalie looked away, and shoved her nose into the crook of her arm lest she be sick herself. When she felt composed, she dragged a handkerchief from her purse and knelt to help Ruby, whose shoulders still shook from heaving. Holding her breath, she held back the girl's hair and wiped her slack mouth. "Open a bottle of water from the bar," she ordered Beatrix, then wiped Ruby's whitewashed face with a wet handkerchief while Beatrix glared.

"I'm sorry," Ruby murmured. "I'm sorry."

Remembering the girl's gentle touch when she herself had been sobbing over Raymond's casket, she gave her a little smile. "It's not your fault—it's the baby. Can you sit up?"

Ruby nodded and allowed Natalie to help her to the seat. Natalie handed the ice bucket to the grimacing driver and told him to look for sand or something absorbent.

"I can't believe I agreed to let the two of you come," Beatrix hissed. "You've ruined everything."

Natalie sat back on her heels. "I'd like to know how the day our husband is buried could be further ruined."

Beatrix's mouth tightened and she looked away. "Just hurry the hell up."

Within a few minutes, Ruby was passably clean, and her color restored. The driver returned with dirty hands and the ice bucket full of sandy soil, which Natalie dumped over the mess.

"Do you feel well enough to continue?" she asked Ruby.

The girl nodded, shoving her hand into her long hair and leaning back in the seat.

"Hallelujah," Beatrix said, moving as far away from them as possible. "Let's go already."

When they were underway again, Natalie studied the limp Ruby, obsessed with the thought that her husband's baby was inside the pitiful young woman. "Have you had a lot of morning sickness?"

Ruby shook her head.

"You should see your obstetrician for a full prenatal checkup."

The girl nodded unconvincingly—Natalie bet she'd never seen the inside of an OB/GYN's office. She swallowed a lecture, telling herself that Ruby and her baby were none of her business. Soon they would bury Raymond, and the three of them would probably never see each other again.

Beatrix snorted. "Don't guess you considered birth control."

"We tried to be careful," Ruby said softly. "But we couldn't keep our hands off each other."

Natalie closed her eyes at the wistful note in her voice, giving in to a stab of jealousy. Raymond probably couldn't wait to get to Ruby's bed every week, where the skin was tight, the boobs high, and the novelty keen.

"I'm so sorry I asked," Beatrix said.

"How come the two of you never had children?" Ruby asked Beatrix.

Natalie waited, equally interested.

"I couldn't," the woman said, her gaze trained on the window.

Her heart squeezed for Beatrix—how incredibly hard this must be for her. To find out on top of the double betrayal that Raymond had fathered a child with someone young enough to be his own offspring. She must hate him . . . and them. No wonder she was so bitter. The ill feelings Natalie held against the dour woman dissipated a few degrees.

"Oh," Ruby said softly. "What about you, Natalie?"

What about her? She was the only one of them who had no legitimate tie to Raymond—Beatrix had a valid marriage license, and Ruby had his progeny. "I . . . I never wanted children."

"Why not?" Ruby asked, a little crease rumpling her beautiful brow.

Why not? Natalie's defences soared. "Because I would've had to give up more than a career of striptease."

"Oooh, good one," Beatrix said from the corner.

Ruby sniffed noisily, then swallowed. "I read somewhere that most women fantasize about stripping. I feel lucky because I'm good at it and I make decent money."

"Well, I certainly never fantasized about it," Beatrix informed them.

Natalie squirmed—after splitting a bottle of particularly good wine, she'd once performed a striptease for Raymond, but had been so mortified the next morning that she refused to even talk about it. Her cheeks flamed at the thought of him comparing her clumsy technique to Ruby's. On the heels of that disturbing thought came the question of what Ruby would do when she became too pregnant to perform. Was the woman's financial situation as dire as her own?

The dividing window buzzed down and the driver announced they were approaching the cemetery. Silence fell among them as the vehicle bumped its way over an uneven asphalt road. Through the windshield, she saw their surroundings were green and lush, the arch above the entrance gate gnarled with vines and rust. Oak Gardens. "It's lovely," she murmured.

"Raymond and I always thought so," Beatrix offered, her mind seemingly a thousand miles away.

The hearse drove nearly to the end of the cemetery before pulling off onto a wide shoulder. A green canopy had been erected over an open grave and a row of three folding chairs sat waiting. Natalie's insides knotted at the knowledge of what lay ahead.

Silent and teary-eyed, they waited in the limousine until the coffin was drawn from the hearse. The limousine driver alighted to help carry the casket, and a handful of dirty city workers who apparently had done the digging filled in as impromptu pallbearers. They shouldered the casket to the gravesite, then the funeral director returned to the limo to retrieve the women.

They climbed out, noiseless and, in Natalie's case, numb, then picked their way among gravestones and pitted ground to the grave, above which sat Raymond's shiny coffin, supported by lengths of lumber laid across the opening. A spray of red roses covered the curved top. His favorite.

Natalie allowed herself to be led to one of the chairs, but she couldn't tear her gaze from the gaping hole beneath the coffin. Her husband would be lowered into that cold, deep cavern and covered over with dirt as carelessly as the roots of a shrub.

Ruby dropped into the seat next to her, crying softly and reeking of throw-up. Beatrix sat closest to the head of the casket. As the funeral director delivered a generic send-off, Natalie tried to imagine Raymond's face, terrified that bits of his features were already fuzzy in her mind. Tears leaked down her chapped cheeks, burning in the brisk spring chill.

She realized the funeral director had stopped talking when the pallbearers circled the casket. As they lowered the casket gingerly into the grave, red roses were passed to all three of them. Ruby was sobbing so loudly, she had developed the hiccups. Natalie assumed some of the girl's weight, even though Ruby towered over her. Beatrix tossed in her rose first. Ruby went next and very nearly threw herself in as well, but was saved by a quick jerk from Natalie. When the commotion subsided, Natalie finally opened her own hand to let the third flower drop into the grave. It bounced off the coffin, red petals exploding, then disappeared down the side.

The funeral director led a quick prayer, rushing to "amen," which everyone repeated, including the sweaty gravediggers. The director shook their hands again, gently steering them away from the tent, obviously eager to return to Paducah. Natalie kept looking back at the grave, biting deep into her lip as the first shovels of dirt were tossed on top of the coffin. She stumbled and tried to focus on something other than the fact that the man she loved was being buried.

She straightened her shoulders, and walked toward the road. She and Ruby would be riding back together after they dropped Beatrix at her home. Natalie massaged the bridge of her nose, longing for a dry, clean handkerchief. Considering the stench of the interior of the vehicle, she hoped they could trade for another limo. She sighed in relief when she realized that another long car was already sitting behind the limo, but squinted when a second, then a third car arrived.

A heavyset graying man climbed out of one of the cars. He wore a sport coat, no tie, and stood in a wide-legged stance, waiting for them. From the puzzlement on Beatrix's face, she didn't know the man. Natalie's heart lurched—was he a bill collector? An IRS agent? Had Raymond's debt caught up to them already?

When they neared the limo, the man stepped forward and read from a small card. "Mrs. Beatrix Carmichael?"

"Yes," Beatrix replied after a split-second hesitation.

"My name is Detective Aldrich, from the Kentucky State Police."

"Whatever this concerns, Detective, it can wait," Beatrix said in a queenly voice that Natalie admired "I just buried my husband."

The man scratched his temple, seemingly unmoved. "Mrs. Carmichael, your husband is the reason I'm here. The medical examiner received the autopsy results a few hours ago."

Beatrix frowned. "I didn't order an autopsy."

"Well, you got one anyway," the man said, adopting a flat smile. "The report shows that your husband died of a massive heart attack."

"Tell me something I don't know, Detective."

"Okay. Your husband was murdered."

Natalie swayed, but caught herself, trying to make sense of the man's words. It was ludicrous. Who on earth would murder Raymond? At the sound of streaming water, she turned and stared at the growing dark stain on Ruby's shiny red dress.

"Oh, my God," the young woman whispered. "I just peed my pants."

Ten

TONY SCOFFED. "YOU'RE shitting me. *Three* wives?"

Wrapped in a holey chenille robe, Natalie stood at the kitchen sink with her back to her brother, holding a cup of coffee that had grown cold. God, how she'd hoped she wouldn't have to tell Tony the sordid truth. "No, I'm not."

"Where are the other two? I mean, what do they do?"

"His real wife lives in her family mansion in northern Tennessee." She'd been in a stupor when they'd dropped Beatrix at her home, but later Ruby said it looked like "a freaking public library." "I got the impression that she doesn't do much except complain. The other woman he duped lives in Kentucky outside Paducah. She's . . . a stripper."

He grunted. "A rich bitch, a doctor, and a stripper?"

She was glad she couldn't see his face. "Raymond was nothing if not magnanimous."

"Damn, sis. No wonder you look like hell."

"I've missed you, too."

"Now I know why you didn't want me at the funeral. I just thought you were ashamed of me."

She was. But at the time she'd been thinking only of her own shame.

"Christ," he said with his mouth full. "I knew Raymond

was a player, but I never dreamed he'd go and do something that stupid."

She set her jaw at Tony's assessment—not criminal and unconscionable, just stupid. Mrs. Ratchet was right, she conceded as she looked across the dewy back yard; Rose Marie's flower garden was growing wild. Just another in the long list of things she'd neglected, apparently. Her husband, her finances, her brother, her garden. She wheeled, already regretting her decision to allow Tony to stay for a while. "What do you mean, you knew Raymond was a player?"

Tony shrugged and licked the mixing spoon he was using to consume an enormous bowl of pasta salad. Her parents had been hard pressed to keep enough food on hand when he was growing up—she remembered because her mother had made her do the shopping. On hindsight, Tony had needed his strength to pull off his many heists.

He looked toward the ceiling. Tony was so handsome, with dusky skin and aquiline features. And she should be so lucky as to have those long black eyelashes. Prison had given him hard, lean angles, but he was still a striking man.

Tony made a rueful sound with his cheek. "Raymond had the look, you know? Something in the eyes."

Her pulse spiked. As if he, the delinquent, had been savvy enough to see Raymond's flaws, but she, the physician, hadn't. "Coming from a professional player's point of view, of course," she added, not nicely.

His shoulders sagged, and he resumed eating with somewhat less gusto. "I suppose."

She closed her eyes. How did he do that? Her brother had been a screw-up his entire life, yet was able to make her feel bad for pointing out that she didn't trust his opinion. Was she so easily manipulated? Had Raymond been attracted to a weakness in her that made him feel powerful? Was what she'd deemed a cheerful disposition actually him laughing at her the duration of their counterfeit marriage?

Regardless, her brother wasn't accountable for Raymond's sins. "I shouldn't have said that," she murmured.

"It's okay, sis. What Raymond did was pretty lousy. I know you were crazy about him."

Crazy—how fitting. She turned back to the window because she didn't want him to see her choke up. She was the strong one. If she broke down, the laws of nature would be set on end.

"Sis, you're still young, you're a doctor, you still got your face and figure. I know it sucks right now, but—"

"There's more." A spider was spinning a web in the branches of an overgrown shrub outside the window.

He scoffed. "What, does he have a bunch of kids running around or something?"

She poured the coffee down the drain of the porcelain sink. "As a matter of fact, the, um, other woman is pregnant."

"The stripper?"

She nodded.

"Wow, good thing you don't need Raymond's money because it sounds like you'd have to stand in line."

"As it turns out," Natalie said, thinking she really should take down the café curtains and wash them, "Raymond also had a gambling problem I didn't know about. He depleted our accounts."

Behind her, Tony's spoon clattered against the table. "Are you saying you're broke?"

From the outrage in his voice, she surmised he had indeed been hoping for a handout. "It appears so."

"But we still have Rose Marie's house," he said, his tone elevated. "This place has to be worth a bundle."

We—how typical. "I'll do all I can to keep Rose Marie's house."

"So you're behind on a few bills—you have your own practice, for heaven's sake."

An unfortunate bug flew into the web, and the spider made short work of the insect. "Not for long. The town will blame me when word gets around that my husband was a bigamist."

"Well, technically, he was a trigamist, but have you told anyone?"

"Just you." Had the windowpane always been cracked? She must be the most unobservant person breathing.

"Then you don't have anything to worry about. The funeral was in Kentucky, and he's buried in Tennessee. As long as the two other broads keep quiet, why does anyone here in little old Smiley, Missouri, have to know Raymond pulled a fast one on you?"

Natalie set down her cup and turned back to face him, holding on to the counter. "Because it's possible that Raymond's death wasn't from natural causes."

"I'll say—having all three of his wives show up at once is damned unnatural."

"Tony, the medical examiner thinks Raymond might have been . . . murdered."

He came out of his seat, spewing pasta. "What? How?"

She lifted her hands. "The Kentucky State Police showed up in Tennessee yesterday after the funeral, but all they would say is they suspect Raymond was given something to trigger the heart attack."

Tony frowned. "Who'd want to kill— " His eyes bulged. He crossed to the sink and clasped her shoulders. "Natalie, they'll go easier on you if you confess. Just tell them the mailbox told you to do it."

Natalie shrugged off his hands. "Are you insane?" She covered her mouth with her hand and talked through her fingers. "How could you even think such a thing?"

"Well . . . you're a doctor, and besides, who could blame you if you did kill the bastard?"

"But I didn't."

He held up his hands. "Okay. So, do you think one of the other wives could have offed him?"

She pressed her hands to her temples. "I'm not thinking, period. It hasn't sunk in."

"So what now?"

"The police want to question me. I'm meeting my lawyer in Paducah in a few hours."

"Do the police know about the bigamy thing?"

She nodded. "They linked him to the woman in Kentucky first, but the funeral home led them to his wife in Tennessee and to the gravesite. They knew we were all connected to him somehow, they just didn't know the specifics."

"Have they already questioned the other two women?"

"No, they're supposed to be questioned today, too."

"Who's going first?"

She frowned. "What does it matter?"

"The person they interview first has the advantage."

"I don't care who is interviewed first, because I don't believe Raymond was murdered. I was there, I saw him have a heart attack."

"They must have some kind of evidence. You shouldn't take this lightly."

"Take what lightly? Even if Raymond *was* m-murdered, which he wasn't, I don't have anything to worry about because *I* certainly didn't kill him."

Tony frowned. "The prisons are full of innocent people, Nat."

"Oh, right."

"I'm serious. Some people break under the pressure and look guilty even if they aren't. All it takes is a motive, circumstantial evidence, and a persuasive prosecuting attorney."

"Now you're an expert in criminal law?"

"The lockup had a great legal library." He suddenly looked sheepish. "Thought I might even give law school a try if I could scrape together the cash."

She bit her tongue. Tony had tried his hand at everything from pyramid marketing schemes to raising Christmas trees, but burglary was the only occupation at which he'd truly excelled. "And as usual, the conversation revolves back to you," she said, pushing past him. "I could've sworn we were talking about my husband being murdered."

"But you just said he *wasn't* murdered."

She kept walking, dismissing him with a wave.

"I was trying to help," he said behind her.

"I don't need your help," she flung over her shoulder as she jogged up the stairs.

"No, you never needed anyone, did you, Nat?"

She stopped at the landing and considered sending a massive clay vase down to oblige his long-suffering expression. "No one was there if I *had* needed someone."

"I'm here now. And I want to be here for you, Nat."

Clutching the banister, she stared down at the man who had consistently proved that he didn't care about anyone but himself. Men. What made them feel so entitled to use the women who loved them most? Her handsome brother disappeared through a blur of tears. She was drained, exhausted . . . and done trying. Natalie turned and resumed climbing. "Just don't steal anything from the house while I'm gone."

Eleven

"DON'T TELL THESE yahoos any more than you have to," Gaylord Gilliam mumbled as he held open the door of the Kentucky State Police Paducah post.

Beatrix pressed a finger against her eyebrow to ease a relentless tic. "When this mess is over, I never want to see the inside of this state again."

"Relax," her lawyer drawled. "We'll be in and out of here in no time. I wouldn't be surprised if they roll in and say it was all a big fat mistake."

She'd thought the same thing when the limo had dropped her off at her home yesterday afternoon. Around two this morning, however, she began to worry that the police did indeed have something—else, why would that detective Aldrich have looked at her as if he'd already spent the raise he would get for locking her up? "You know, Gaylord, Raymond was no saint—the fact that his death is suspicious could look bad on me."

He stopped, pushed his hat back on his bald head and considered her for the longest time. Finally, he clasped her elbow and led her forward. "Like I said, don't tell them any more than you have to. Don't worry, Bea, I'll be with you and I'll stop the questioning if it appears you're about to incriminate yourself."

"Gaylord, I—"

"Bea, Kentucky has the death penalty." He squeezed her arm just short of pain. "Now. You will go into this interview and tell them the truth—that Raymond was a bad boy who made enemies, but you, his loving wife, was not one of them."

She was paying him too much money not to listen to him, so she remained silent as they approached a glassed-in window, her heart thumping wildly. Damn Raymond—he couldn't even die without a production. Always the center of attention. Always in control.

The female officer behind the window directed them down a hallway into a bullpen of activity. Phones rang, mouths moved, pencils scribbled. Detective Aldrich sat at a desk the size of a card table, the phone pinched between his ear and shoulder. When he spotted them, he banged down the phone and pushed himself to his feet.

"Mrs. Carmichael," he said, his voice just as unfriendly as yesterday. Beatrix introduced the men and exchanged a frown with Gaylord as they were led to a small room.

"Something to drink?" the detective asked, sweeping his arm toward four plain metal folding chairs arranged around a white table. They declined, but he disappeared anyway, presumably to fetch something for himself.

Gaylord held out a chair for her, but his Southern manners couldn't take the edge off the stark surroundings: faded indoor-outdoor carpeting, scuffed walls, a single overhead dome light hanging over the table. Two walls were darkly mirrored from waist to ceiling, leaving her to wonder who might be watching her from the other side. She craved a Valium, but she needed to keep her wits about her. *Breathe*, she told herself. *Breathe, and this will all be over soon.*

Aldrich returned, holding three bottles of water. "In case you change your minds," he said, plunking them down.

"No Evian?" Beatrix asked sweetly, then reached for a bottle to keep from imagining what might have caused the reddish stain on the table top. She opened the bottle with a twist, marveling at the irony—the last time she'd drunk straight from a bottle, she and Raymond had been sequestered in a closet together at a fund-raiser over twenty-one years ago. It was his risqué behavior that had so appealed to her, the naïve white-gloved debutante. Her friend Blanche had forgiven her for capturing Raymond's eye and heart, but the women had never again been close. By the time Beatrix realized she'd sacrificed the better relationship, Blanche had snared an anesthesiologist and moved to West Palm Beach. She herself had been the pretty one, but Blanche had been the smart one.

Aware the detective was watching her, Beatrix lifted the bottle for a quick drink so he wouldn't notice the tremor in her hands. The water was tepid, but soothing on her dry throat.

The police officer shrugged out of his jacket and draped it over the back of his chair, then grunted into his seat. From a black bag he removed a tape recorder and set it on the table. Beatrix shot an alarmed look toward Gaylord.

"No tape recorder," he chirped.

Aldrich appeared baffled. "We're just going to ask a few questions about Mrs. Carmichael's husband."

"Mrs. Carmichael has not yet recovered from her husband's passing. Taping her conversation will only add to her stress."

Aldrich adopted a pleasant smile. "You know it's as much for Mrs. Carmichael's protection as ours, counselor.

You can stop the recorder any time you want, and you can take a copy of the tape with you."

Gaylord looked to her for permission. She swallowed a second mouthful of water and, deciding that Aldrich would only be more difficult if she resisted, nodded.

The detective grunted approval, then pushed a button and recited the date, the place, the names of those present, and the fact that Beatrix was not under arrest, but had come to the station at his request. "Mrs. Carmichael, do I have your permission to tape this conversation regarding your husband—" he consulted a pad of paper, "—Mr. Raymond A. Carmichael?"

"Yes," she whispered.

"Louder, if you please."

She cleared her throat. "Yes."

He started by verifying their address, years of marriage, Raymond's last three positions that spanned a decade, and other generic tidbits. Aldrich fidgeted, a warning he was changing tack. "Mrs. Carmichael, when did you first uncover the fact that your husband had illegally married two other women, a Dr. Natalie Marie Blankenship and a Ms. Ruby Lynn Hicks?"

"L-last Wednesday night."

"Tell me everything that happened, to the best of your recollection."

Her left hand looked naked without her wedding band. She twisted the single ring that remained, a diamond cluster. When Raymond had proposed and presented her with the ring, a small solitary stone had graced the slim gold band, and she'd been ecstatic. Her parents, however, had been appalled at the puny diamond. Her father had promptly added stones to either side, both larger than the original, as a "wedding gift." Raymond hadn't objected, but on hindsight, his pride must have been horribly wounded.

"Mrs. Carmichael?"

She straightened, curling her hand in her lap. "I . . . I received a call from a nurse at Dade General around nine P.M. The woman told me that Raymond had been involved in an accident."

"What kind of an accident?"

"A car accident. He'd only suffered minor injuries, but he couldn't drive home. I said I'd come right away." A lump formed in her throat when she remembered how giddy she'd felt at the thought of having him home for a few weeks while he recuperated.

"What was the nurse's name?"

"I don't . . . No, wait—Moberly, I think."

"Are you sure?"

"Yes, Moberly. I wrote it down on a pad by the phone."

"Did Nurse Moberly say that Mr. Carmichael asked her to phone you?"

She frowned, trying to recall. "She didn't say, but she verified our insurance."

Aldrich lifted an eyebrow. "Perhaps. You didn't talk to Mr. Carmichael yourself?"

"No."

"Why not?"

Because she was afraid he wouldn't want her to come. That he'd call a friend, take a taxi—anything to avoid prolonged contact with her. "I assumed he was still being tended to."

"What happened when you got to the hospital?"

"I was told he'd been admitted because of chest pains, and I was given directions to his room."

"And?"

She closed her eyes briefly, replaying the scene in her head for the thousandth time. "I walked into his room and found both Natalie and the other one—"

"Ruby."

"—standing in his room. It looked as if Natalie had just arrived."

"Then what happened?"

"Raymond clutched his chest and slumped over. Natalie called a nurse, then administered CPR."

"Natalie, she's the doctor?"

"Yes. They sent me and the other one—"

"Ruby."

"—out of the room while they worked on him. Natalie emerged a few minutes later and that's when we discovered what Raymond had done."

"What had he done?"

Beatrix frowned. "What you said earlier. The bastard—" She stopped when Gaylord nudged her knee. "Or rather," she continued more mildly, "Raymond had apparently married both of them illegally."

"You and Raymond were never divorced?"

"No."

"Were divorce papers ever drawn up?"

"Absolutely not."

"Did he ever bring it up?"

"No."

"Because he didn't want to lose his meal ticket?"

Anger shot through her. "What do you mean, Detective?"

"Didn't Raymond marry you for your money?"

Again, Gaylord's knee prodded hers in warning. She

pursed her mouth, then said, "You would have to ask Raymond."

"I would, but someone murdered him."

Tears were good—after all, this dolt couldn't tell the difference between angry tears and sorrowful tears, so she blinked up a few. "Are you going to tell me why you think my husband was murdered?"

Aldrich sat back in his chair, playing with the pencil he held. "The medical examiner found something suspicious on a battery of toxicology tests."

"Which raises a good question," Gaylord interjected. "Mr. Carmichael died of natural causes—who ordered an autopsy?"

A frown pulled at the detective's mouth. "A mistake, really. An autopsy was requested on a body that was next to Mr. Carmichael's in the hospital morgue. Some stupid orderly didn't check the toe tags."

Beatrix looked away.

"Show some respect," Gaylord snapped.

"Sorry—bottom line, someone switched the bodies. The M.E. had already started the autopsy when he realized the error, but said that when he double-checked the records and discovered the body he'd gotten by mistake was supposed to have died of a heart attack, he knew something was wrong."

"Why?" Gaylord asked.

Aldrich slid a paper across the table. "This is a copy of the M.E.'s report. There's a lot of medical mumbo-jumbo, but basically, the heart muscles didn't show the type of damage consistent with a heart attack. He ordered a toxicology spec, and came back with 'ouabain poisoning.'"

"Never heard of the stuff," Gaylord said.

She had. Beatrix lifted the water bottle to her mouth for another drink.

"How about you, Mrs. Carmichael?"

She swallowed and squinted at the ceiling. "I don't think so, although living with Raymond was like living with a medical dictionary—he was always tossing around the name of some drug or treatment." Injecting as much innocence into her voice as was possible at her age, she asked, "What is it?"

The detective stared at her, stroking his chin. "An old heart medication that's no longer in use in the United States. Did Mr. Carmichael ever mention it?"

"I honestly couldn't say."

"So you don't know if he was taking the medicine on his own?"

"No, I don't. But then, apparently, I didn't know a lot of things about my husband."

Aldrich had the good grace to cough.

"This is an outrage!" Gaylord pounded the tabletop. "If the medication is something Mr. Carmichael could have taken on his own, how dare you go off half-cocked and say the man was murdered!"

"Except," the detective said carefully, "the concentration was too large and, according to the doc, too close to the time of death for him to have given it to himself, considering he was unconscious and all." He turned back to Beatrix. "Did you see Mr. Carmichael from the time he was taken to the ICU until the time he died?"

She hesitated.

"Mrs. Carmichael, the hospital keeps records of ICU visitors."

"Yes, I went in to see Raymond, but we all did."

" 'We' being who?"

"Me, Natalie, and the other one."

"Ruby."

"Yes."

"Together?"

"Natalie and I went in together once, and . . . Natalie went in alone once."

"Were the three of you in the general vicinity from the time he was taken to the ICU until he was pronounced dead?"

"Yes, in the waiting room. And I made a couple of trips to the rest room."

"Did you make any phone calls?"

"Yes. To my housekeeper, Rachel Shirek, to tell her Raymond was ill."

"Does she live with you?"

"No."

"Does anyone else live with you?"

"No." Alone in a house big enough for a dozen people.

"Mrs. Carmichael, can you think of anyone who might want to kill your husband?"

"No, but as I said, I didn't know that Raymond was leading a double life."

"A triple life," Gaylord amended.

"When you found out he'd married two other women, were you angry?"

Beatrix sighed. "Yes, Detective, I was angry."

"Angry enough to kill him?"

"Yes," she said softly, ignoring Gaylord's sputter. "But I didn't."

"How much insurance did you carry on Mr. Carmichael's life?"

She wet her lips. "I don't know the exact amount."

"Ballpark."

"Maybe . . . fifty thousand? I'm not sure."

"How about five hundred thousand?"

Beatrix shrugged. "I really couldn't say for certain."

"Mrs. Carmichael, do you think either Dr. Blankenship or Ms. Hicks could have killed him?"

"I don't know. Anything's possible, I suppose."

"Did you notice anything suspicious about their behavior?"

"The young one is a nut, everything she does is suspicious. Did you know she's pregnant?"

She'd succeeded in surprising him. "Is Mr. Carmichael the father?"

"Allegedly."

"How far along?"

"Two or three months, I think, although I tried to tune her out."

"How did you feel when you heard about the baby?"

She gave him a withering glance. "Just peachy."

"But Beatrix didn't know about the baby until after Mr. Carmichael had expired," Gaylord added. "The woman's condition was revealed when the women met to discuss the burial arrangements. Which," he added, "my client did not have to do."

Aldrich wasn't bowled over by her generosity. "Was Dr. Blankenship angry when she heard about the baby?"

"I wouldn't say angry—upset, maybe."

"As a doctor, she would have the knowledge and the means to administer the ouabain."

She smiled. "You said it, not me."

Aldrich squirmed, then recovered. "Did you see anyone else at the hospital acting strange? Anyone going into the ICU who didn't seem to belong?"

Beatrix shook her head.

"I need for you to speak for the recorder."

"No. But the place was busy, and I slept some of the time."

Aldrich made a clicking sound with his big cheek. "You're familiar with the workings of a hospital, aren't you, Mrs. Carmichael?"

She blinked.

"Weren't you a volunteer at Royal Memorial until two years ago?"

Until the charitable activity she began as a project for club wives thrust her into a position of actually being involved with the patients. "I . . . volunteered mostly at the hospital clinic." Trauma patients, uninsured old people, neglected children. Unbearable.

"The clinic that was named for your father, Dr. Neil Richardson?"

"Yes."

"Mrs. Carmichael, what kind of doctor was your father?"

"He was a . . . a cardiologist."

The detective nodded—he'd already known. "Your father is deceased now."

"Yes."

"Did he travel abroad when he was alive?"

"Yes, he and my mother traveled often."

"And have you traveled widely?"

"I suppose."

"Europe?"

She nodded. "All over, really."

"Where is this going?" Gaylord cut in.

Aldrich splayed his hands. "Ouabain isn't widely available in the U.S., but my sources tell me you can buy the stuff over the counter in most European countries. I'm just trying to determine if Mrs. Carmichael had access to the drug, either on her own, or through her father."

"Interview over," Gaylord chirped, standing. "Come on, Bea."

"I'm not finished," Aldrich protested.

"We are." Gaylord pressed a button to stop the recorder. "We'll wait outside while you make a copy of the tape."

The detective sighed, but lumbered to his feet. "Okay. But you have to admit that from where I stand, Mr. Gilliam, your client looks pretty darn suspicious."

Gaylord drew himself up. "Detective Aldrich, your alleged victim was a bigamist, which is a class-A felony. Dig deeper—I'm sure you'll find the man pissed off his share of people, probably a few in the medical field in which he worked. If you have a case against my client beyond reasonable doubt, arrest her. Otherwise, I suggest you stop picking on Mrs. Carmichael, who has been dealt a double blow in the past few days."

Beatrix followed Gaylord to the door, her back and neck moist. *Breathe*, she reminded herself. *Breathe, and this will all be over soon. No one will find out.*

"Mrs. Carmichael."

She glanced back to Aldrich.

"This isn't over."

Twelve

"OUABAIN?" RUBY BRIGHTENED and gave Detective Aldrich her best smile. "Sure, I've heard of it. Some West African tribes use it on the pointy end of their arrows. It can kill a person."

She had impressed him, she could tell. Billy Wayne pursed his lips and nodded—she'd impressed him, too.

"And do you have access to ouabain, Ms. Hicks?"

"Do I have to go back to using my old name?" She hated it. Always had. *Those Hicks are such hicks. Ruby Lynn Hicks has a hickey, the hick.*

"Would you prefer 'Mrs. Carmichael'?"

"I sure would."

"Okay. Do you have access to ouabain, Mrs. Carmichael?"

She frowned. "I've been to West Virginia, but not to West Africa."

The detective smiled. "Since you know so much about ouabain, if you wanted some without going to West Africa, where would you go?"

Ruby smiled in relief—she knew the answer to that one, too. "The Internet." Whew—between thinking about the funeral and knowing she'd be questioned by the police today, she'd nearly worn a path in the kitchen linoleum last night from pacing. Now she realized she'd been worried for nothing. Detective Aldrich was a real sweetie.

"And do you have a computer?"

"Oh, yeah. Ray set one up in the corner of the living room. Had an extra phone line installed, too, so he could make business calls while I visited chat rooms and shopped. I ordered Mame the most adorable little Easter bonnet."

"Mame?"

"My Shih Tzu."

"Ah. Mrs. Carmichael, have you ever purchased ouabain over the Internet?"

"Wait a minute, Ruby," Billy Wayne cut in, his eyes narrowed. "This guy's saying that's what killed Raymond. If you tell him yes, he's going to lock you up."

She swallowed her gum. "No, I didn't purchase ouabain over the Internet."

"Mrs. Carmichael, I just want you to tell the truth," the detective said.

"I am."

"Did Mr. Carmichael keep medical supplies at your mobile home?"

"Like what?"

"Like samples, medications, things like that."

"Ray sold arms and legs and elbows and stuff—there was always some spare part laying around." She laughed. "One time I found a hand in the bathtub. Scared the crap out of me, but Ray was just testing its float—said a leg he sold once saved a guy from drowning."

"That's nice."

"Ray was a nice guy." She teared up and Billy Wayne lent her his red bandanna for a good blow.

"Did he keep other things at your place? Syringes?"

She nodded. "I'm diabetic, and I give my own insulin shots. In the thigh." She poked her leg below her pink micromini. "I'm not supposed to have sweets," she confessed, "but sometimes I do and shoot up extra insulin."

"Did you have syringes with you at the hospital the night that Mr. Carmichael died?"

"Yeah, I carry them in my purse. Ray always brought me supplies. He saved me tons of money."

"Did anyone else have access to your purse at the hospital?"

She shrugged. "I dozed off a few times in the waiting room, so maybe."

"Mrs. Carmichael, did you know Raymond was already married when you married him?"

"No."

"When did you find out?"

"At the hospital, when Natalie and Beatrix came into his room. Ray keeled over, then out in the hall Beatrix said they'd never gotten a divorce. I thought Natalie was going to croak, then she said that she and Ray had never gotten a divorce either."

"Were you angry when you found out what Mr Carmichael had done?"

She chewed on her lip. "A little. I loved Ray, and I was counting on him being around to help with the baby."

"Is Mr. Carmichael the father of your baby?"

"Oh, yes, sir."

"How far along is your pregnancy?"

She smiled. "Three months."

"And how did the other Mrs. Carmichaels react to news of the baby?"

"They didn't like it one little bit. Beatrix couldn't have kids, and Natalie didn't want them."

"Do you think that either Natalie or Beatrix could have killed Mr. Carmichael while he was in the hospital?"

She frowned. "Beatrix is a real meanie—I wouldn't be surprised if she did it. On the other hand, Natalie is a doctor and knows how to kill people, I guess."

"Was Natalie ever alone with Mr. Carmichael?"

"She was in the ICU once, I think, with Beatrix. I don't know about the rest of the time."

"Was Beatrix ever alone with Mr. Carmichael?"

She frowned, trying to remember, then pointed her index finger. "Yeah! I woke up and saw her coming out of the ICU alone. I was mad because I didn't get to go in to see him."

"You didn't go into the ICU at all?"

Ruby wanted to lie, but Detective Aldrich seemed too darn smart, firing questions one right after another. "Just for a minute. The nurse snuck me in so I could look at him, but I didn't get to talk to him or anything."

"When was that?"

"I don't remember."

"Did the nurse stay with you while you were in the ICU?"

"Uh-huh."

"Do you remember the nurse's name?"

"No, but she looked like Ma Ingalls on *Little House on the Prairie*. I told her that."

"Okay."

"Hey," Billy Wayne said to Aldrich, looking as if an idea had whomped him upside the head. "Ruby's baby is entitled to Raymond's estate, isn't it?"

Aldrich nodded. "If she can prove paternity, she'll probably be granted some portion of the estate in the form of a trust. Most likely the bulk of Raymond's holdings will revert to Beatrix, his real wife."

Billy Wayne frowned. "But what if that old bag killed him?"

"No one can profit from a murder. If she killed her husband, his assets and life insurance would probably go to Raymond's offspring."

"Ruby's baby?"

"Er, yes."

"How much dough are we talking about here?"

Aldrich frowned. "About half a million loaves."

Her lawyer gaped. "You don't say."

Ruby swallowed. Five hundred thousand dollars? She made eye contact with Billy Wayne, who gave her a thumbs-up, then tapped his Timex. He had to get back to Leander to play in a softball game this afternoon.

"Are we almost finished?" she asked Aldrich.

The detective set down his pencil. "Mrs. Carmichael, we need to talk about a Mr. Hammond Jackson."

She felt the blood drain from her cheeks. "Ham . . . Ham's dead."

"Around five years ago, according to my sources."

She nodded.

"He was your mother's boyfriend?"

"For a while." Then hers—not by choice.

"He beat her?"

"Whoever was handy," she said. Hate bubbled in her stomach.

"How did Mr. Jackson die, Mrs. Carmichael?"

She glanced at Billy Wayne, who was cleaning his nails with a pocket knife and humming to himself, probably thinking about the money. "He, uh . . . drank rat poison by mistake. He couldn't read, and thought it was booze."

"He drank the poison, or someone injected him with it?"

Uh-oh. "I don't know."

"You were the last person who saw him alive."

Her armpits were sticky. "So?"

"So you must know what happened to him."

She stared at him, begging him not to ask more questions. "Can I go now? I have to be at work in a couple of hours, and I'm the feature act tonight."

Ruby hated the pity in his eyes, the condemnation (doing the daily crossword was paying off), and the doubt. "That's all for now," he agreed with a nod.

Standing so quickly she almost twisted her ankle in her platform shoes, she said, "Come on, Billy Wayne."

Her lawyer jumped up, saluted Aldrich, and followed her out of the room at a trot. "Five hundred thou," he whispered, his eyes wide. "Ruby, I know I told you I'd represent you for free passes to the club, but if you hit the jackpot, I could use a new set of tires."

"The money won't be mine unless they find out that Beatrix killed Ray," she murmured, her head pounding with confusion. The gossip surrounding Ham Jackson's death was just starting to die down in her hometown. Would they start saying she'd killed Ray, too? On TV, innocent people got thrown in jail all the time. She clutched her tummy—she couldn't have this baby behind bars. Terri, her own mother, had given birth to *her* in the clink, cursing her for life. "Better hold off on those tires for now, Billy Wayne."

"Why? I'll bet she did him in, the bat."

Maybe Beatrix did kill Ray, Ruby conceded as she shoved

open the front door and walked out into a surprising spring chill. But God would get her good if she herself profited from Ray's murder, because she wasn't totally, completely, absolutely, one hundred percent innocent herself.

Thirteen

NATALIE SQUINTED. "OF course I've heard of ouabain. Is that your theory behind Raymond's death? Ouabain poisoning?"

Detective Aldrich nodded. "Yes."

She touched her forehead. "I don't believe this. Did anyone tell you, Detective, that ouabain occurs naturally in humans?" Weak with relief, she slumped in the metal folding chair. It was all a ghastly mistake.

"This much?" He slid a paper across the table in front of her and Masterson. "For the purposes of the tape, I just provided a copy of the medical examiner's report."

Natalie scanned the autopsy results and the M.E.'s comments, then shook her head. "This report must be in error."

"Like the original autopsy order," Masterson chimed in, tossing back the paper. "Raymond Carmichael's body was not even supposed to be autopsied, yet you come back with a murder allegation. Sounds like the medical examiner's office is trying to avoid a lawsuit, Detective."

Aldrich sat back in his seat and folded his hands behind his head. "I feel pretty safe with this one, counselor, since murderers typically don't draw attention to a case by filing a suit."

"My client is not a murderer."

"I'd rather hear that from your client," Aldrich said, making eye contact with Natalie.

"I'm not a murderer."

He regarded her for a long minute. "Before you go on, Doctor, I feel obligated to inform you that one of my own men overheard you threatening to kill Mr. Carmichael."

"What?" She laughed, her voice cracking. "That's absurd."

"Do you recall State Trooper Nolen calling to tell you Mr. Carmichael had been in an accident?"

"I remember that an officer called, but not his name."

"Do you remember telling the officer to stop by the hospital later because you were going to kill your husband?"

She opened her mouth to say that he and his man Nolen were both insane. Then she remembered that when the phone rang, she'd been cursing Raymond for losing their life savings. No, make that *her* life savings. "I was angry. I'd just found out something he'd done," she stammered.

"That he was already married?"

"*No.* That he had amassed a great deal of debt without telling me."

"I see. And how did you find out about the debt?"

"A local pawnbroker named Brian Butler came to see me, to tell me that Raymond owed him money."

"How much?"

She swallowed hard. "Over a hundred thousand dollars."

Aldrich lifted an eyebrow. "Good thing you're the beneficiary of a life insurance policy for *two* hundred thousand that you took out on Raymond less than six months ago."

"Stop the recorder," her attorney said.

"No." Natalie held up her hand. "I have nothing to hide. The insurance was Raymond's idea. I didn't kill my husband for the money, or for any other reason. But I *was* angry with Raymond when I received the phone call. I just didn't expect the officer to take me seriously."

Aldrich leaned forward. "Dr. Carmichael, we're taking this case very seriously. Let's review the facts: You discover your husband has wrecked your finances, then you threaten to kill him, then on top of everything else, you find out that he's a bigamist who has two other wives, then he winds up dead from a lethal dose of an obscure poison."

All it takes is a motive, circumstantial evidence, and a persuasive prosecuting attorney. Tony had tried to warn her. "This is ridiculous," Natalie murmured.

"From my point of view," the detective said, "it makes perfect sense. You're a doctor with plenty enough know-how and opportunity to do him in. Plus you have a motive and the means."

Masterson scoffed. "What motive?"

"Money, revenge."

Her lawyer's mouth flattened, but he attempted nonchalance. "Buying life insurance is no crime."

"No, but inducing a heart attack to collect on the policy is."

Natalie wanted to scream, but if she forced herself to remain calm, perhaps the world would right itself. "Detective Aldrich, Raymond was having chest pains *before* I arrived at the hospital."

The man shrugged. "Maybe it gave you the idea to finish him off."

She inhaled deeply and swallowed her tears—she had to remain sharp, focused. "I didn't know he was even having chest pains until I walked into Dade General and found out he'd been admitted."

"Maybe you had the stuff with you. The M.E. says that low doses of the ouabain would trigger chest pains. Maybe you'd been giving Raymond ouabain without him knowing."

She fisted her hands. "I only saw my husband every other weekend. And don't you think he'd have been suspicious if I'd given him injections?"

"You don't have to inject the stuff. But then, you knew that, didn't you, Dr. Carmichael?"

She looked away.

"Please speak for the tape. Were you aware that the poison ouabain can be absorbed through the skin or ingested?"

"Yes."

"And if we were to search your office and your home, would we find ouabain?"

Panic ballooned in her stomach. She'd never gotten around to cleaning out the previous doctor's stash of samples and accumulated junk at the office. For all she knew, Jimmy Hoffa could be buried in the storeroom. And she didn't have a clue what Raymond kept in the metal lockers that lined the interior of the garage—could he have been taking the drug without telling her in an attempt to disguise a heart problem?

"How about it, Dr. Carmichael? Got any ouabain lying around?"

"No . . . not to my knowledge."

Masterson snorted. "This is crazy, Detective. Dr. Carmichael is a dedicated physician with an excellent personal and professional reputation."

"Which will be tanked when word gets out that she married a bigamist and he died from a lethal dose of cardiac poison."

True. So true. She sat back in the cold chair, overwhelmed. Where had her life gone? How could her entire identity be so tenuous as to disappear in a matter of a few days?

Her lawyer's hand on her arm was meant to comfort, but she could only stare at his soft white fingers. "If you're convinced that Raymond Carmichael was poisoned," Masterson said, his voice a bit shrill, "may I point out that there are at least two other women who might have wanted him dead."

"And I've already talked to both of them," Aldrich said.

The person they interview first has the advantage. She sprang up, her legs tingling from the adrenaline surge. "They told you that I killed Raymond? That elitist snob and that empty-headed juvenile?" Was it not enough that they both had a piece of Raymond that she didn't? Were they out to annihilate her? Did they actually think she was capable of *killing* him?

Natalie swallowed. Was she? The few hours she'd been able to sleep these past few days, hadn't her dreams been awash with fantasies of confrontation and revenge?

"Both his wife and the woman who's carrying his baby have more to gain from Raymond's death than Natalie," Masterson said quickly. "She doesn't even have a solid claim on his estate."

"So if Raymond lived, she got nothing. This way, she takes home two hundred grand."

"And maybe Raymond stiffed someone else—a coworker or a business associate who decided to get even," her lawyer pointed out.

"Or someone he owed money," Natalie ventured, leaning on the table. An image of Brian Butler exploded into her head. Could that thug have hired someone to kill Raymond?

"Who just happened to be at the hospital the night he was admitted, with a syringe full of ouabain," Aldrich said with a fair amount of sarcasm.

She exhaled. Right—how would Butler have known Raymond was in the hospital? Her brain hurt from too many connections and too few conclusions.

"On the other hand," Aldrich said, "Dr. Carmichael here could have called someone to bring her the poison."

"Like who?" Masterson demanded.

"Like her brother who just got out of the Missouri State Pen. Maybe he graduated from robbery to murder. Or accessory to murder."

Natalie clenched her jaw, close to tears again. "Look, Detective. I came in to talk to you with the hope I could find out what happened to my hus— " She covered her hand with her mouth and choked back a sob. She just wanted her life back, and to be far, far away from this, this . . . seediness . . . that manipulated other people, not her. "Lowell, I have to go. Now."

Masterson was already standing, wielding his briefcase. "Yes, it's past time to leave."

Aldrich smiled and slowly unfolded his broad body. "Would you agree to take a polygraph test, Dr. Carmichael?"

"Yes," she said.

"No," Masterson said a heartbeat later. He leaned close to her ear. "You're too emotional right now. The polygraph could misinterpret your anxiety."

Natalie set her jaw, recognizing the sanity of his observation, especially in light of a sudden revelation about herself.

"Dr. Carmichael?" the detective prodded.

Maybe she hadn't killed Raymond. But oh, God, how she'd wanted to.

Fourteen

MASTERSON HAD TOLD her not to worry—if the police had enough evidence to finger her, they would have arrested her. Still, Natalie couldn't help but jump every time the phone rang and the doorbell sounded. Even now, while pruning the neglected beauty bush, she found herself looking over her shoulder down the stone garden path, expecting Detective Aldrich to appear at the black wrought-iron gate, lift the rusty latch, and march into her overgrown sanctuary swinging a pair of handcuffs.

She'd decided she'd be better off not checking the supply room at the office for ouabain. Not that she'd know exactly what to look for, since the drug could be obtained in several forms—crystals, crystalline powder, pills, water-soluble solutions. Besides, even if the storeroom were lined with the stuff, the layers of dust on the contents would speak for themselves.

She had, however, pried open the white lockers in the garage to find financial records for Raymond Carmichael of Northbend, Tennessee, and for Raymond Carmichael of Smiley, Missouri, and for Raymond Carmichael of Leander, Kentucky. Tax returns, originals of his "loan" papers to Brian Butler, copies of forms for different driver's licenses, and other papers she simply didn't have the strength to sort through.

But no ouabain.

Natalie tossed the brittle branches onto one of the piles she'd accumulated, crushing a stand of grapefruit mint beneath the soles of her lace-up boots. They were Rose Marie's boots, actually. And her hat. The aggressive mint was a nuisance, her aunt had said, but smelled nice when trod upon. Natalie was content to blame her occasional tearing and sniffling on the fresh, stinging aroma. At a clinking sound, her heart quickened and she turned to stare at the gate. Only a spring breeze, taunting her. She knelt back to the cool earth and grabbed a handful of dead honeysuckle vine.

To his credit, Tony had been subdued. Pouting, probably, but she didn't care. As soon as he saw she was planning to work in the back yard all day, he'd mumbled something about checking in with his parole officer and hightailed it out of there on foot to ward off an invitation to help. After the degrading interrogation yesterday, she'd considered taking a short trip herself to sort through the mess that was her life, but she could barely afford gas for the lawnmower, much less a ticket to paradise. Besides, she couldn't risk leaving Tony with the keys to the house.

"Dr. Carmichael, how *lovely* to see you out and about."

She peered up from under the brim of her hat to see her neighbor smiling over the whitewashed side fence. "Good morning, Mrs. Ratchet."

"I see you're thinning the garden—Rose Marie would be pleased."

"Yes."

"How are you *doing*, my dear?"

"Just trying to stay busy."

"Gardening is *so* therapeutic. When my Pauly died, I threw myself into a pond."

"Excuse me?"

"The goldfish pond in my back yard. I'd always wanted one, but Pauly said it would draw mosquitoes."

Self-centered brute. "I'm glad you finally got your pond."

"Me too. But the mosquitoes are murder."

Natalie started at her neighbor's word choice—had the woman heard something? Was she fishing for a headline?

"Listen, dear, if you don't know what something is or how to take care of it, just holler. Your aunt often sought my advice on some of her more finicky varieties."

Not true. Her aunt had an innate way with plants.

Natalie surveyed the twenty-by-twenty-foot plot, encouraged by the splotches of bright green against the brown of old growth that promised restoration. She gestured to the dozens of metal plaques staked in the rich, dark soil. "Thanks, Mrs. Ratchet, but Rose Marie labeled everything faithfully."

"You know, your aunt was considered a bit of a healer herself. Many a time she brought me feverfew tea for my headaches."

Natalie stood and wiped her gloved hands against her work jeans. "Sounds like Rose Marie all right."

"And there's plenty of rhubarb over there for pies and conserves."

"I'm not much of a pastry chef. Raymond doesn't— " She stopped, shaken by how quickly she could forget that he was gone. Blinking back scalding tears, she said, "I mean, I guess I'll have to go through my aunt's recipe books."

"Nothing against your dear aunt, God rest her soul, but my recipe for rhubarb pie is the best in these parts. I'll fetch it for you directly."

"I'd like that."

"Dr. Carmichael— "

"Please call me Natalie."

"Natalie, then. The man I saw leaving your house this morning—is he a relative?"

Start spreadin' the news. "Yes. My brother."

"I don't remember your aunt mentioning a nephew."

"They weren't as close as she and I. Mrs. Ratchet, I'd love to chat, but— "

"Is that your brother over there?"

She followed her neighbor's gaze to the creaky gate. Brian Butler lifted his hand in a wave, but his broad face wore a serious expression. Natalie closed her eyes. What now?

"He doesn't look like you," Mrs. Ratchet said, her voice dubious.

"He's not my brother," Natalie murmured.

"Who then?" Her neighbor craned her neck and grew three inches—tiptoeing, no doubt.

"Just a . . . patient. I'd better go see what he needs."

"He looks familiar . . ."

"Good-bye, Mrs. Ratchet." Natalie removed her gloves as she approached the man, wondering why he even bothered to don a tie if the knot was already hanging low by midmorning.

"Hello," he said. He'd gotten a haircut since she'd seen him last. A rooster tail had sprung up in the back.

"Did you come to take back the earrings?" she asked, her mood compromised.

He looked sheepish. "No." After a few seconds of shifting his feet, he gestured to a stone bench inside the gate. "Mind if I come in?"

"Yes, I do."

"Your neighbor is staring."

"An even better reason for you to stay out there."

She'd stumped him—the man was obviously used to having his way. He scratched his temple, then leaned both hands on the rickety gate. "The police came to see me."

Her stomach lurched, but she refused to react. "In your line of work, I'm not surprised."

He pursed his mouth, then said, "The *Kentucky* State Police. A guy named Aldrich asked me a lot of questions about Raymond. And about you." His voice was low, his gaze intent.

Natalie tilted her hat back. If she didn't know better, she might think the man was concerned. "When was this?"

"They left my shop a few minutes ago. I called to warn you, but no one answered."

Aldrich was here, in Smiley? She stumbled backward to drop onto the cold stone bench. The corroded clink of the gate sounded, and she sensed rather than saw that Butler had followed her. She pulled her hands down over her face, relieved at least to see that Mrs. Ratchet had disappeared.

Butler stood in front of her, hands on hips, his fingers jumping. The braided leather belt around his khaki pants struck her as oddly comforting—worn, but solid. It was one of those bizarre details that one notices to postpone realization of bad news. The police still considered her a suspect in Raymond's murder, were perhaps planning to arrest her at this very moment.

He cleared his throat. "The detective told me about the other . . . women."

"Oh, goody."

"I'm . . . sorry," he said in a low voice, as if apologizing for his entire gender. "Just so you know—we're not all jerks."

A newly emerged vindictive part of her wanted to

extinguish that pitying I'll-be-your-friend-when-I'm-not-taking-your-jewelry light in his boyish eyes. "You're all jerks, you simply take turns."

"I'm worried about what will happen to you."

His contrite expression caught her off guard, but she covered with a wry smile. "I guess that means the detective told you he believes Raymond was murdered?"

He nodded.

"And that he thinks I killed him?"

Butler dropped onto the bench next to her, resting elbows on knees, steepling his fingers. "He insinuated as much."

She laughed with no humor, then tilted her head back. The air was crystal clear, the sky, a surreal blue with a high, luminous sun. The kind of weather one would expect in a town called Smiley. She didn't belong here. In fact, any minute now, a black cloud would single her out, fix itself over her straw hat, and discharge a torrent of rain. And if she were lucky, perhaps she would be struck by lightning.

"What kinds of things did he want to know?"

"How long I'd known Raymond, how much money he owed me, what I knew about you."

"And what do you know about me?"

He picked up an ornamental white quartz stone and studied it. "Besides where you work and where you live, not very much."

"So why are you here?"

He shrugged. "I don't know. I guess I feel responsible for setting things in motion last week."

She turned toward him. "Setting things in motion? You think I was so angry at Raymond for his dealings with you that I killed him?"

"I didn't say that."

"Is that what you told the police?"

"No." He dropped the stone and held up both hands as if to ward off a blow. "I told them you seemed like a nice lady whose husband had taken her to the cleaners."

"Oh, well, thank you very much for handing them a gift-wrapped motive."

"I didn't—" He sighed. "I told them you didn't strike me as the kind of woman who could kill her husband."

Last night in her dreams, she'd dismembered Raymond with a dull hacksaw. She gave the pawnbroker a tight smile. "But like you said, you don't know much about me."

"Maybe I'd like to."

Natalie stared, then guffawed. "You don't have to brownnose me, Mr. Butler. You'll get your money—unless, of course, they put me on death row."

"A distinct possibility, Dr. Carmichael."

She jerked her head around, her heart plunging at the sight of Detective Aldrich standing at her gate, just as she'd imagined, chest puffed and stance wide. She sprang to her feet so quickly, she lost her hat. "What do you want?"

He shook a green sheet of paper, a form of some kind with a sprawling signature across the bottom. "I have a warrant to search your residence, property, and vehicle." He turned and waved, summoning a team of a half-dozen plain-clothes and uniformed officers who streamed through the gate.

The ground shook when Butler vaulted up. "Search for what?"

"For a drug called ouabain," the man said. "On the chance we got here before you could tip her off."

The big man clenched his fists. "What the hell are you saying?"

"That if I find out you're mixed up in this with the doc here, you'll go down with her."

"You're insane," Butler said.

"Welcome to my world," Natalie murmured, turning toward the back door. "I'm calling my lawyer."

"Use my cell phone," Aldrich said, extending the slim unit. "It would be best, Dr. Carmichael, if you remain outside and within sight."

She snatched the phone, her mind whirling as she punched in Masterson's number. The uniformed officers went inside, the other two swept to opposite ends of her back yard. Did they now think she was a serial killer who buried her victims in the garden?

"By the way," Aldrich said. "We already searched the offices of your medical practice."

Her nurse Sara was probably frantic. "And did you find what you were looking for?" Her lawyer answered before Aldrich could, but from the set of the man's mouth, she presumed he hadn't found anything. Her heart pounded as she told Lowell what was happening. Cooperate, he said.

A bombshell hit her as she disconnected the call—Tony. He'd been a bit of a pothead when they were growing up; had he gotten deeper into drugs? Had he stashed anything in his room or elsewhere in the house that would jeopardize his parole, or make things look worse for her?

"Don't worry," Butler said close to her ear. "Once they realize they're barking up the wrong tree, they'll leave."

She pulled back. "Why are you still here?"

His eyebrows shot up. "I just thought you might need—"

"I don't." At one time his bruised expression would have elicited a response, but hadn't she decided just yesterday that she was through accommodating interference in her life, especially from male types?

"Aldrich," one of the men in her yard shouted. "Over here!"

Puzzled, she was one step behind Aldrich, vaguely aware of Butler on her heels, like a persistent puppy. One officer was snapping pictures of a climbing hedge next to the fence, while the other appeared to study the foliage. The name of the plant escaped her, if indeed she'd ever known, but a memory of orange flowers against the greenery stirred in the recesses of her mind. Pumpkin posy? She couldn't see the metal name plaque from where she stood.

"Why are you so interested in my garden?"

Aldrich smirked. "You must think we're morons, Dr. Carmichael."

Oh, but it was so much more than a thought. "Okay, Detective, I'll play along—why would I think you were morons?"

He crouched and turned the little sign in her direction. Her aunt's bold hand-lettering was unmistakable: *Strophanthus*. The facts unfolded in her head like a flowchart. *Strophanthus* was an attractive plant whose seeds just happened to be the source for ouabain. Extracting the drug would be no easy task, especially enough for a lethal dose. But a determined chemist could do it. Or a determined doctor.

"Got some foxglove over there." One of the officers pointed.

Foxglove. *Digitalis*. Distant relative of ouabain.

Detective Aldrich pursed his mouth. "You're a regular corner drugstore, aren't you, Doc?"

She wanted to run, but the ground seemed to be crumbling, falling away from her feet. The sheer absurdity of the spiraling situation left her faint.

"Natalie!" Mrs. Ratchet appeared at the fence, waving an index card. "Here's the recipe you—" She stared at the crowd assembled. "What's going on here?"

If nothing else, the woman would have her headline for the week.

Fifteen

FROM HER BURGUNDY leather club chair, Beatrix sipped a powerful gin and tonic, then used the remote control to ease up the volume of the television. The happy-looking spokeswoman, Julie, leaned closer to the camera. "If you've been looking for a rewarding pastime to bring out the creativity that you know is hiding within, this deluxe cookware set is the perfect start to becoming a gourmet chef right in your own kitchen."

Her first home-cooked meal for Raymond after they were married had been a plate of spaghetti. No meatballs, no sauce, just spaghetti. On hindsight, she'd been horribly inept at fulfilling her wifely duties, but Raymond had handled her ignorance with good humor. They'd poured a quarter pound of butter and a shaker of salt over the spaghetti and he'd taught her how to twirl it properly—her father forbade twirling at his dinner table. Raymond was ten years her junior, yet so much more worldly, so much more exciting than she. She had landed a part-time job in a delightful bookstore, and they'd made love at every opportunity so she could become pregnant without delay. Their shabby little apartment had been the center of her world. For a while.

She swallowed another icy mouthful of her drink, reveling in the progressive numbness the alcohol provided.

Then her mother, chronically fragile and possessing a wicked sense of timing, had suffered a nervous breakdown. Her father had cajoled her to return home to help, offering a suite of rooms in the house to her and Raymond as enticement. Gone were her "little job" and their quaint apartment and her fledgling cooking skills. Gradually they'd both been swept back into the elitist lifestyle from which she'd hoped to escape. But Raymond had loved the clout and acceptance her family name afforded him, and in the end, she was happiest when he was happy. So, at her family homestead they had remained.

"The cookware is sturdy stainless steel," Julie promised, "with a nonstick surface guaranteed for a lifetime."

A nonstick *heart*, now there was a marketing concept. Emotional Teflon. Because as the years passed and children eluded them and passion eroded and arguments multiplied, she'd never stopped loving him. Faking indifference had simply saved her sanity. As his interest in their marriage waned, the odometer on his company car ticked higher. Hopes they would become close again when her parents were gone were dashed when he left her father's wake early to "close a critical sale."

Had he been closing Natalie? The timing seemed right.

"The heating coils imbedded in the bottom of each pot ensure even heat distribution. The matching lids are vented—don't you just hate it when you can't find a lid to fit?"

Damn her. Damn him, but damn her, too, dammit. Attractive, intelligent, educated—didn't Natalie have enough going for her without capturing Raymond's heart? Marrying that idiot Ruby was obviously a poor attempt at gallantry after he got her with child, but Natalie . . . he must have loved Natalie.

A wife could overlook a foolish encounter here and there, but falling in love with someone else? Unforgivable.

Beatrix drank until the ice at the bottom of her glass slid down to clink against the porcelain veneers on her teeth. "Rachel!" If she were out of gin, she'd have to send her housekeeper out for more.

"On the line we have Jo Ann from Oklahoma, who purchased a set of the deluxe stainless steel nonstick gourmet cookware two months ago. She's calling back to let us know how happy she is with her purchase. Jo Ann, are you there?"

"Yes, Julie, I'm here."

"Jo Ann, how do you like your deluxe stainless steel nonstick gourmet cookware?"

"Julie, these pots and pans have changed my *life*. I used to be so introverted and bored. Now I love to cook and entertain, and I have more friends than I can shake a stick at."

Beatrix squinted at the TV. What the hell did that mean, shake a stick at? If someone were fortunate enough to have a true friend, why would they shake a stick at them? And if Jo Ann had so many friends, why the devil was she calling the home shopping show host to chat? Pathetic.

Admittedly, she herself had ordered a few things from the show, but strictly for the convenience of having a VitaMaster Juicer or a Primo Pasta Maker delivered right to the door. One of these days, when the cooking muse struck her, she would open the boxes. Meanwhile, the deluxe stainless steel nonstick gourmet cookware set would be a nice addition to her store. Beatrix picked up the phone, then hit the number seven button ("S" for shopping) to recall a programmed number. As the phone rang, her arms and hands tingled from a familiar rush of adrenaline. Referring to the item number listed on the bottom of the screen, she gave her order to the operator.

"Good choice, ma'am."

"Yes, well, I'm a gourmet cook," Beatrix said smoothly. If Raymond could tell a boatload of whoppers, she was entitled to one uplifting fib.

"I'm sorry, Mrs. Carmichael, but the charge on the card you gave me was declined."

Beatrix frowned into the phone. "That's impossible."

"Probably a computer glitch," the woman assured her. "Do you have another form of payment?"

"Of course," she snapped. But another of her charge cards was turned down before a third was accepted. After confirming the order, she banged down the phone. Raymond had taken care of their household finances outside of her trust fund. She supposed she'd have to get her accountant Fiske to pick up the slack since it appeared they were already behind on a payment or two. She sighed—another detail to take care of. Fiske and Gaylord were still pounding out the monetary ramifications of Raymond having an illegitimate child. She, on the other hand, didn't even want to think about it.

"Rachel!" She cursed and set her glass down on the leather-topped table at her elbow. Forget it, she'd get the damn gin herself.

When she stood, she grabbed the back of the chair until the den righted, then made her way across one of her mother's precious hand-tied Persian rugs. Hers now, she supposed. Funny how she still thought of the house and its contents as belonging to her parents. She bumped her hip against the cherry desk that had been sitting in the same spot since she was a child, inadvertently dragging off a stack of mail Rachel had set on the desk for her to read.

Dozens of envelopes tumbled down and fanned out across the rug. Sympathy cards. Notes of condolence. Obligatory well wishes. Delivered in soothing, pastel hues—woeful white, grieving green, pitiful pink, I'm-sorry ivory.

She scoffed. Politeness dictated that people send a card, just as politeness dictated that a handful of them come to the funeral home and murmur nice things. But not one of her co-country clubbers was a confidante with whom she could unburden herself of the weight that her husband had not kept himself solely unto her so long as they both had lived. They could never know, the vultures, else they would peck her to death. News of the bastard child would act as a rallying call among the gossipers, and rumors of a murder would send them into a feeding frenzy.

She walked on top of the envelopes, grinding the heels of her pumps for spite. As she walked toward the kitchen, she heard the hum of a vacuum cleaner from the dining room—at least Rachel hadn't been ignoring her. In fact, she conceded with a sigh, her housekeeper had fielded phone calls and otherwise covered for her beautifully the past few days. Even better, the woman kept her distance, did her job, and rarely spoke unless spoken to.

As she passed through the mouth of the marbled foyer, the stench of live flowers filled her nostrils—cheap carnations and that dreadful baby's breath florists seemed so fond of. Rachel had situated the vases of arrangements on the sideboard and bench in the entryway. Beatrix plucked the card from a particularly smelly bouquet.

Raymond will never be replaced in our hearts. Monty and Delia Piccoli.

Raymond had been the beau of the ball, the life of the party. She would spend weeks organizing auctions and golf tournaments, and he would steal the credit in an hour of emceeing. More than once she'd stood in a dark corner and watched her husband perform, accepting compliments on his wit and charm, wondering how welcome she'd be at the Northbend Country Club without Raymond. She would soon find out, she supposed.

She flicked the card to the floor, then nudged the vase with her finger before she turned, immensely gratified by the domino effect of crashing glass sounding as she walked away. All of them should have saved the lousy fifty bucks they'd spent and contributed to her father's clinic, as she'd requested, in lieu of flowers.

The ostentatious marble flooring gave way to satiny dark wood in the hallway and in the butler's pantry that flanked the ornate dining room. Lined with mahogany cabinets, the dark pantry held bittersweet memories. As a child, she had sneaked into the lower cabinets during her parents' dinner parties to eavesdrop. She'd loved hearing the delicious bits of scandal and the bawdy jokes, most of which she hadn't understood. The fun had ended one night, however, when through the one-inch opening from her hiding place, she spied her father giving Mrs. Crenshaw a rather tonguey kiss while clutching one of her mammoth breasts. Inside the cabinet, she'd accidentally knocked over a box of candles. Thankfully the noise was enough to break up the grappling couple, but not enough to betray her hiding place. Still, she'd gone to bed with a stomachache.

The huge cabinets now held extra liquor, the more valuable pieces of silver, and an odd crystal vase or two. During one of her mother's stints of paranoia, she'd had locks installed on the doors to keep the help from stealing. Out of habit, the doors remained locked, although a key hung from a gold tassel around one of the knobs for the convenience of any thief around.

Unsure what was where, she unlocked a bottom cabinet, on the lookout for a green bottle with a Tanqueray label. Instead she found an enormous silver platter, one that had graced their holiday table for eons . . . and nothing else. No matching bowls, coffee urn, chafing dishes, bread baskets, chargers, or water pitchers. No matching candelabra, compote dishes, cake plate, finger bowls, carafes, or tea service. Alarmed she yanked open the drawers that housed the extensive collection of Richardson silverware—two sixteen-place settings of patterns so old a jeweler in Nashville fashioned replacement pieces when necessary.

She swallowed. But at the jeweler's fantastic prices, she doubted if she could afford to replace the three hundred and fifty pieces that were absent from the goddamned drawer.

A quick check of the other shelves revealed the gin she'd come in search of, but no silver. Leaning heavily on the counter, she took a deep, calming breath. Rachel was simply cleaning the silver, that was all. She walked a little unsteadily to the kitchen where her housekeeper was vacuuming in high spirits, her back turned, and her wide hips moving to some lively beat in her head.

"Rachel. Rachel!"

Beatrix leaned over and pulled the plug from the outlet at her knee, reducing the vacuum cleaner to a fading whine. Rachel whirled, her eyes wide. "Mrs. Carmichael, I didn't hear you! Do you need something?"

"Rachel, are you cleaning the silver?"

"No, ma'am."

She refused to give in to the panic rolling in her stomach. "When was the last time you did clean the silver?"

"Um . . . well, I guess it was in February, when you gave the tea for Mrs. Piccoli's daughter."

"And have you seen the silver in the three months since?"

"No, ma'am. Is something wrong?"

"It's missing."

"What's missing?"

Beatrix massaged the bridge of her nose. "The silver, Rachel. It's not in the pantry. Did you move it?"

The woman's eyes widened. "No, ma'am, of course not."

"Then call the police because we've been robbed."

Rachel gasped and was halfway to the telephone before she turned back. "Mrs. Carmichael, I didn't think anything of it before, but I do recall Mr. Carmichael looking in the silver cabinet a few weeks ago. I asked if I could help him, but he said he was checking the patterns to buy a special piece for your birthday. A new picture frame, I think he said, for your wedding portrait."

Beatrix felt nauseous. He'd sent her a damned bonsai plant for her birthday—said it would give her something to do while he was on the road. When he hadn't even come home to help her blow out the candles, she'd used them to start a bonsai bonfire.

"Never mind about calling the police," she murmured. "Perhaps Mr. Carmichael moved the pieces to another room, maybe to the library with the other collections."

"Would you like for me to check, ma'am?"

"No. No, I'll look into it."

"Ma'am?"

"Yes?"

"I . . . would be glad to spend the night for a while . . . if you'd like."

At the pitying look on the woman's wrinkled face, Beatrix squared her shoulders. "Whatever for?"

"I . . . thought maybe you . . . might like to have another body in the house."

"You thought wrong."

"Yes, ma'am."

She turned to go, then added over her shoulder, "But thank you, Rachel."

Ignoring her complaining knees, she climbed the stairs with record speed and threw open the doors to the library, her least favorite room in the house. No matter how many times she'd had the place cleaned, it still stank of her father's cigars. He'd entertained hordes of physicians and hospital board members in this room, requiring only the slightest provocation to pull out his prized coin collection. He and Raymond had bonded in this room, squirreling themselves away until the wee hours of the morning while she waited in their bed, staring at the ceiling, her ears perked for her mother's plaintive call.

She stalked to the huge cabinets that contained her father's collections, her heart thumping. The heavily carved doors were locked, but she unearthed a thick ring of miscellaneous keys from the depths of a desk drawer. By the time she found the right one, her head ached and she knew perfectly well what lay behind the doors.

She was right. The cabinets yawned, empty.

Beatrix backed away, shaking her head. What had Raymond done? And what else would she discover was missing?

Rushing from room to room in the gigantic house, some of which she hadn't entered in months, even years, she mentally catalogued valuables that were absent: a bauble here, a trinket here. A blow—the bronze Umbro sculpture

Raymond himself had bought for her when they were in Vienna. And other items, small, portable, costly. The earlier credit card refusal now took on a menacing light. Raymond had robbed her of her heart and her dignity. Had he also compromised the single element of life on which she'd always been able to depend—financial security?

Leaning against the upper level banister, she stared down into the two-and-a-half-story foyer at the heap of flowers, pottery, and water seeping across the marble floor. She might have been tempted to dive over the rail and add herself to the mess, except everyone would say that Raymond's death had done her in, and she wasn't about to give the bastard the satisfaction. And she wasn't yet ready to go to hell.

The doorbell rang, sending a three-note chime through the house. She inhaled deeply, wondering if Detective Aldrich had come to take her away. Rachel's footsteps echoed in the hallway, as well as her gasp when she saw the debris. Oblivious to Beatrix standing at the top of the stairs, she stepped over and around the glass, then swung open the door.

"Hello, Mrs. Piccoli," Rachel said, smiling and nodding. "Mrs. Lombardi."

Beatrix gripped the smooth, flowing wood beneath her fingers. Let the games begin.

"I'm not sure if Mrs. Carmichael is up to seeing visitors just yet."

"Show them in," Beatrix called. She descended the stairs, more slowly this time in deference to her knees. By the time she reached the foyer, Delia Piccoli and Eve Lombardi stood staring at the broken mess on the floor.

"Hello," Beatrix said. "How nice of you to come by."

The women gave her tentative smiles, then Delia, the braver one, lowered her voice to a conspiratorial level.

"When we heard the latest news, Bea, we simply had to check on you."

"News?" she asked, thinking an aneurysm was imminent. "What news?" The bigamy? The illegitimate child? The thievery?

"You don't know?" Delia's buggy eyes bugged even further. "A woman doctor in Missouri was just arrested for Raymond's murder."

Sixteen

". . . THREE HUNDRED FIVE, three hundred six—" Ruby smoothed down the last bill with a satisfied smile. "Three hundred seven dollars in tips." She leaned over to press her face against the mug of her Shih Tzu puppy. "And that, Miss Mame, is a four-hour record for your mommy. Yes it is."

Ruby padded to the refrigerator and in a square on the calendar wrote: "Black and silver bikini, white boots, four hours, three zero seven." She tried to track which outfits seemed to prompt the most response from the men who came to watch her take off her clothes. She reviewed the other days of the month and noted that the red stiletto heels were a common denominator for good tip nights, then made a mental note to pair the red heels with the black and silver bikini tonight. Fridays were always hopping, and she didn't have many Friday nights left before her stomach swelled up.

Wiping a tear for her fatherless baby, she caressed the back of the real wood kitchen chairs. She'd found a red vinyl gingham-checked tablecloth to match the curtains that came with the furnished trailer, and decorated the nooks and crannies with strawberry canisters, strawberry plaques, and the platter from her new six-place setting of Strawberry Fields stoneware that was microwave safe.

She should have known that things were too good to last.

She missed Ray like the dickens. She hated that he was dead, but he'd done a bad thing. Like Ham had done a bad thing. Why did people have to do bad things that made other people do bad things? Billy Wayne told her she'd be in good shape if they nailed Beatrix for the murder, but she couldn't feel anything but sad because she'd still rather have her Ray alive and all to herself than all the money in Beatrix's piggy bank.

She traced the pattern in the Fresh Taupe Swirl linoleum with the tip of her plush pink and grey elephant houseshoes, then gasped in horror at the dozens of black marks left on the floor from the thick soles of her costume boots and shoes. She wet a dishcloth and dropped to her hands and knees to remove the marks just as the *Your New Mobile Home Manual* suggested—no harsh abrasives. Once the surface had been restored, she removed a chocolate soda pop from the fridge, wiped at a smudge on the faux granite countertop, then headed back to the living room to stretch out on the sectional that still crackled with newness. She didn't have to be at work until six, so she had the entire afternoon to herself. Maybe she'd have a good cry. After *Jeopardy*.

Her dog snuggled in beside her as Ruby rewound a tape in the VCR, then pressed PLAY. When the fuzz cleared and the opening credits for the game show flashed on the screen, she clapped her hands, triggering a spasm of high-pitched barks from Mame. On the big screen TV, Alex Trebek looked as if he were standing in her living room, smack in the middle of her Soft Fawn Stain Resister carpet.

"Oh, look, Miss Mame, it's the college competition—I bet I'll get some of the questions right."

At the knock on the door, she paused the recorder and took another swig of pop. She hoped it wasn't that yucky shirtless Dudley Mays who lived two trailers down and always wanted to borrow something that had her reaching or bending.

She peeked through the simulated lead glass window running alongside the door, squinting because she didn't know the suited man who stood outside, nor the man behind him who held a big honking camera on his shoulder. Hmm.

When she opened the door a few inches, Mame sniffed at the pair and barked. "Yeah?" Ruby asked.

"Are you Ruby Lynn Hicks?"

She was way too smart to fall for that one. "Who wants to know?"

A red light flashed on the camera and the guy without the camera said, "I'm Mitch Lykins, reporter for Channel Two news. I'd like to talk to you about the man you were married to, Raymond Carmichael."

Still suspicious, Ruby twirled a lock of hair around her finger. "What do you want to know?"

"May we come in?"

She glanced down at her cotton-candy-pink chiffon peek-aboo nightie. "Um, I don't think so."

"Was Raymond Carmichael already married to two other women, one in Tennessee, and one in Missouri, when he married you?"

She concentrated so her brain would work faster than normal. "Maybe."

"It's a matter of public record, ma'am."

"So why are you asking me?"

"I'd like to hear your side. Did you know about his other wives when you married him?"

"Yes." Then she winced. "I mean, no. I mean, yes, I knew he had two other wives, but I didn't know he was still married to them."

"How did you meet Raymond Carmichael?"

She chewed on her lip, not sure if she should keep talking.

"At your stripping job?" he prompted.

Mame bared her little teeth at the man, and that was enough for Ruby. "I don't want to talk anymore." She slammed the door, and Mame jumped back with a yelp.

"I'm sorry," Ruby murmured, then scooped up the little dog and settled back onto the couch, cross-legged. Her stomach felt like the Tilt-a-Whirl, but she wasn't sure if it was the baby or the bad feelings the men dredged up. All week she'd tried not to think about the look on Detective Aldrich's face when he questioned her. It was like he could read her mind or something. She shivered. Creepy.

When she hit the VCR PLAY button, Alex reappeared and introduced the players, all of them freshfaced and smiling, chatting about their college and what they were studying. Cal State, Mathematics; Harrah Women's College, Economics; Notre Dame, Biosomething or other. Wow. Those smart kids didn't know how lucky they were, going to smart colleges, studying smart things, going on a TV show for smart people.

"Victoria, how old are you?" Alex asked the woman studying economics—and not the home kind either.

"Twenty-one," Victoria said, then pushed up her smart-looking glasses.

Ruby's jaw dropped. "I'm twenty-one," she whispered, and Mame yapped her acknowledgment. High school seemed so long ago, she'd never considered the fact that she was now college-aged. She felt old, at least twenty-six. It was the mileage, she guessed. After all, college girls didn't stay out until two in the morning. Or squeeze themselves into too-tight clothes. Or strip for guys who drank too much. Or get knocked up.

No, Victoria looked too smart to do any of those things. Which was why Victoria was attending Harrah Women's college and *she* was perfecting her Chinese split. Ruby sighed and laid her head back on the couch. Ray had promised she wouldn't have to work when she started showing. Not even waitressing? she'd asked. Not even, he'd said. Not even ticket-taking? she'd asked. Not even, he'd said. She missed Ray—he'd made her feel happy about getting up in the mornings. Of course, if she didn't get up in the mornings, Mame would pee all over her Spring Meadow double tufted comforter.

The phone rang, and she considered letting it go. At this rate, she'd never get through *Jeopardy*. But the caller ID showed it was Billy Wayne on the other end, so she paused the VCR again and picked up the phone.

"Hey, Billy Wayne."

"Yo. Big news. They arrested the lady doc yesterday for murdering Raymond."

Ruby's stomach dropped. "Natalie? But she didn't kill Ray."

"What makes you so sure?"

"Well, I . . . she just didn't strike me as the murdering type, that's all."

"Yeah, well most murderers don't have a brand on their forehead."

That was true. Although she herself had a mole on her right boob. "Is she still in jail?"

"No, she was out on bail real quick like—didn't even spend the night."

She sighed in relief. Natalie seemed too delicate to survive a night in a cell with big hairy women trying to cop a feel.

"Anyway, I was calling to let you know now that the media has wind of the story, they might be looking you up."

"They already did. Channel Two news."

"No shit? What did they ask? What did you say?"

"I'm still wearing pj's, so I didn't let them in, and I didn't say anything."

"Well, get off your cute butt and put on something black. The next time a camera shows up, you got to play the part of a grieving widow. A pregnant grieving widow."

"Billy Wayne, if Mac at the club finds out I'm pregnant, he'll fire me."

"It's just a matter of time, sweetheart. Meanwhile, you got to milk the public sympathy. It'll help our case when we sue for half of Raymond's assets."

"But that could be a long time, and I need money coming in now."

"Ruby Lynn, which one of us has a law degree?"

"You do."

"And which one of us passed the bar?"

"Well, it took you a few times."

"That don't matter. Which one of us got it?"

"You did."

"Aren't you paying me for my good advice?"

"In Babe Bucks."

"They spend!"

"Okay, okay," she relented. "I'll do what you say."

"I'll call Channel Two and tell them to get back to your place for an interview. Try to work up a few tears, would you?"

"I'll try, Billy Wayne."

"Thatta girl. Later."

Ruby hung up the phone. Alex was frozen on the TV

screen with his mouth open. She gave him a wistful look, then trudged to the bedroom and opened the folding doors to her closet.

The sight of her closet never failed to cheer her up. All those poles and shelves and racks for her hats and jackets and minis and shoes. A far cry from the cardboard box that held the dingy jeans and hand-me-down T-shirts she'd worn as a teenager. Her wardrobe was now dazzling—shiny, sparkly, spangly, shimmery. More clothes than she'd ever dreamed of owning.

Then she frowned. Billy Wayne said black. Did she have anything black? Walking her fingers through the hangers, she finally found a black dress she hadn't worn in forever. Mac said it was a bad stage getup—too many zippers. She pulled the hanger over her head and held the dress against her as she pivoted in front of the white reproduction antique dresser mirror.

It mostly covered her, and leather was a nice, expensive fabric. And it would match her black knee boots. She tossed the dress on the bed, then wound her hair in a topknot as she walked toward the shower.

"I'm sorry, Raymond," she murmured. "But my daughter is going to have the chance to go to Harrah Women's College and major in bio-something or other."

Seventeen

WHEN SHE WAS little, Natalie had believed nothing was beyond the healing power of the bay window seat in Rose Marie's bedroom. *Her* bedroom now. Swathed in pale blue and yellow fabrics, and heaped with feather pillows, the little nook had seemed like an island of possibilities, optimism, and refuge. Apparently, however, Rose Marie had taken the magic with her.

She sighed and watched her breath fog the window, then disappear. Fog, disappear. Fog, disappear. The pane of glass beneath her cheek was cold, but not as cold as her skin. Or her heart. Or, according to the police, her blood.

The media had gleefully taken up the gauntlet. A cold-blooded female doctor living in a town called Smiley poisoning her bigamist husband with an herb from her garden? A news producer couldn't have scripted a more perfect tale. She'd been spared national headlines only because a young rock icon had overdosed in Miami, and a prominent politician's son had been arrested in a raid on a gay bathhouse in San Diego. In the tri-state area, however, her arrest was the story of the year, perhaps the story of the decade. And for the *Smiley Tribune*, circulation three thousand one hundred, it was the story of the century.

It helped, of course, that the newspaper's star reporter

lived next to the perp, able to provide photos of the front of the house, the side of the house, the back of the house, the neglected garden, and even the "homicide herb" as the *Strophanthus* had been dubbed. Nurseries reported a run on the homicide herb, and a state drug agency had launched an investigation into the safety of the obscure plant.

Since her arrest the day after the search, she'd learned three things. One, that she knew next to nothing about the legal system. She'd been reduced to soliciting advice from Tony, of all souls. Her hopes they might someday have a common interest hadn't included being Mirandized.

Two, that she was even less photogenic than she had imagined. Based on the wild-eyed, stern-faced pictures of her in the papers Masterson had gathered for his files, even she would be hard-pressed to acquit herself.

And three, she would never again tempt fate by questioning whether her life could possibly get worse. Raymond's secret debt, then his bigamy, then his death, now the murder charge . . . devastation was relative to a person's perspective. The threat of bankruptcy paled miserably in comparison to the threat of the electric chair.

Her shoulders jerked with a hysterical little laugh—this simply could not be happening. Not to her. Not after playing by the rules her entire life. The injustice was incomprehensible.

A knock on the door sounded, but she couldn't summon the energy to answer Tony.

"Nat. Nat?"

The door squeaked open and she lifted her head. She'd never before seen her brother so tentative.

"You want something to eat?"

She couldn't imagine ever regaining her appetite. "No, thanks."

"Jesus, Nat, you're a bone rack. How about some coffee? I just made a pot."

And he wore half of it down the front of his white V-neck T-shirt. She smiled. "Maybe a cup."

"I'll be right back."

"No, I'll come down." She slowly unfolded her boneless body. "I need to leave this room sooner or later."

"You outwaited the reporters. They're finally gone."

"For good, I hope," she said, limping on numb feet.

"They'll lose interest as soon as Masterson gets the charge dismissed."

She allowed him to assume some of her weight on the way down the stairs. "I don't suppose he's called with that little nugget of good news, has he?"

"Not yet. But Sara called again."

Natalie sighed. "Poor thing. I'm calling her right now."

"Call her from the den," he said. "I'll bring your coffee."

She stared after him as he disappeared into the kitchen. The transformation was nothing less than amazing.

"We're out of almost everything," he called. "I thought I'd go shopping if you're feeling better."

Shopping? Well, well. Perhaps her brother just needed . . . to be needed.

She picked up the phone and chased down the cord—Tony must have tired of its endless ringing. After securing the plug, she dialed her office number. Sara answered, breathless. "Drs. Carmichael and Skinner, can you please hold?"

"Sara, this is Natalie. Why are you answering the phone?"

"Dr. Carmichael! I've been worried sick about you! Gloria went down to chase off the reporters blocking the doors, so I'm manning the phone. How *are* you?"

"I'm fine," she lied.

"But the papers—"

"Don't believe everything you read and hear."

"The police were here, turning your office upside down, asking all kinds of questions."

"This is all a huge misunderstanding."

"But Raymond, was he . . .?"

"Murdered?" She sighed and pulled a hand down her face. "The autopsy results were reviewed and the results were the same—ouabain poisoning. All I know is I had nothing to do with it."

"But was Raymond . . .?"

"What, Sara?"

"M-married already?"

Natalie swallowed. "And since."

Her nurse burst into tears. "Oh, Dr. Carmichael, how *could* he?"

"I'm still trying to sort through things myself."

"Is there anything I can do to help? Anything at all?"

A rush of affection clogged her throat. "Just hold down the fort for Dr. Skinner until I can work through this mess." Getting back to her office to unimpact earwax for cookie-bearing patients was her sliver of light at the end of the tunnel.

"Dr. Carmichael . . ." Sara cried harder. "Dr. Skinner and I, we don't see eye to eye—he wants to bring back Mrs. Skye to assist him. And I . . . my sister called me about an opening at the new hospital in Riley."

The light flickered, then vanished. Natalie's shoulders fell. She couldn't blame Sara, though, with a child to support. She might not get back to her practice for weeks. If ever.

Sara sobbed. "The pay is good, and the benefits, well . . .

I don't want to move, but I need the security. Please understand."

She cleared her throat, and tried to sound normal. "What about Joey?"

"Your situation was a wake-up call for me, Dr. Carmichael. I'm doing fine all by myself, just me and my boy."

She wanted to tell Sara that all men weren't untrustworthy, but at the moment, few came to mind. And she conceded that her nurse was only being her practical self where her job was concerned. If she did reopen the practice, it seemed likely that the locals would stay away in droves. She suspected Kevorkian had cornered the market on patients who preferred an M.D. with a rap sheet.

Sara sniffed mightily. "I'm so sorry."

She closed her eyes. "Don't be. You're right to think about your family, and you have my blessing, Sara."

"Oh, thank you, thank you. I'll talk to Dr. Skinner right away."

"He can call me if he has questions about patients after you leave."

"Oh, wait—I knew there was something I needed to ask you. Brian Butler."

Natalie frowned. "What about him?"

"I found his file, but you didn't fill out his encounter sheet. He was the gentleman who came in late the last day you were here, complaining of—"

"Indigestion. I remember. Turns out I didn't have to treat him after all."

"Okay, I'll make a note of it. His was the only file outstanding. Do you need anything from your office? I'd be glad to drop by."

"Um, no, but thank you. It's been a little crazy over

here." She tried to laugh, but she wanted to cry out for yet another familiar piece of her life slipping away. "Call me before you leave town?"

"Sure thing—we'll have lunch."

"Sure thing."

"Natalie, I'll miss you. Everything's going to work out, you'll see."

Of course things would work out . . . just not for everyone. "Good-bye, Sara." She hung up the phone, resisting the temptation to drop into the nearest chair, afraid she'd never get up again. She wobbled into the kitchen, desperate for that coffee. Tony was stirring in cream, overflowing the mug.

"I'm not very good at this."

"Looks good to me." She brought the cup to her dry lips and sipped. "Hey, not bad."

"How's your nurse?"

"She got a better job offer."

"Ah, I'm sorry." One side of his mouth drew back. "You'll find someone else to work for you."

"Assuming my practice is still an ongoing concern once this mess is over."

"Smiley isn't the only town that needs a doctor."

She sipped the weak coffee. "I know, but I really love it here. Rose Marie's house, the neighborhood atmosphere. I was starting to feel . . ."

"Starting to feel what?"

Her face warmed. "Like I belonged."

"What? Since when have *you* not belonged?"

Poor Tony, she thought, studying his incredulous expression. She had always felt like the alien in the family, not once thinking that Tony had felt just as lost in their dysfunctional little household. She'd mistaken his antics for confidence. "Never mind," she murmured, shaken. "You're right . . . Smiley isn't the only place on the map." Just the only place she wanted to be.

"Do you need anything while I'm out?" he asked, scribbling on what appeared to be a list.

Money, aisle two, halfway down. Sanity, aisle eight, between justification and resignation. Strength, aisle one hundred twenty-six, top shelf—gotta work for that one. "Um . . . no."

"Are you sure it's okay for me to leave?"

"I'll be fine by myself."

Tony scratched his head. "Well, you won't be alone, exactly."

Natalie's heart blipped with panic at the thought of Tony bringing home a derelict stranger. "Is someone else here?"

He jerked his thumb toward the back yard and she became aware of a faint but rhythmic thud.

Puzzled, she walked to the back door and unlocked the deadbolt. The pounding grew louder. but through the screen door the source remained hidden. The sight of the trampled garden was enough to bring fresh tears to her eyes. What plants the police hadn't compromised, trespassing reporters and curiosity seekers had. Rose Marie would be heartbroken. Suddenly, a man came into view, wearing work clothes and carrying a sledgehammer propped on his wide shoulder. She squinted, then froze. Brian Butler?

She whirled to face her brother. "Why is he here?"

Tony shrugged. "He said he wanted to help. I told him to go for it. I thought he was a friend of yours."

"Well, he isn't."

"He was here when I came home the other day and found the police swarming the place."

"Not at my invitation. The man is a menace."

"Then why did he offer to post bond for your bail?"

She gaped. "What? That's absurd."

"It's true. Masterson told him it would look bad since he had a stake in whether you collected on Raymond's life insurance."

"Lowell didn't tell me anything about it."

"He probably figured you had enough on your mind."

"I *don't* need to be protected." She glanced back to the door. The pounding had resumed, and her ire rose with each strike. Who did Brian Butler think he was, barging into her life?

"I'll tell the guy to leave, sis, if you don't want him here."

She gritted her teeth. "I'll take care of this. Let me get you money for the grocery." Another worry—converging creditors. With her accounts depleted of ready cash, Masterson had arranged for a short-term loan of ten grand on her Cherokee while her broker scrambled to liquidate the few stocks that remained in her individual account. Their joint brokerage account, of course, was frozen, a moot point since Raymond had nearly bankrupted it without her knowledge over the last few months.

Five thousand of the ten went to cover the premium for her fifty-thousand-dollar bail. *Bail.* Funny, but when she'd met with her financial planner, she'd been thinking IRA, disability insurance, long-term care coverage. Not once had she thought to tuck away a few dollars in case she ever needed to make bail.

"Don't worry," Tony said, waving her off. "I have a few bucks."

She was instantly suspicious. "You don't even have a job."

He grinned. “I start tomorrow.” He grabbed his jacket and headed toward the front door.

“Where?” He was in too big of a hurry. “Where do you start work tomorrow, Tony?”

He stopped and turned. “Butler Family Pawn.”

She scoffed. “This is crazy. You can’t work for that loan shark.”

“The man’s a pawnbroker, sis.”

“Don’t split hairs.”

“Nat, I was looking for work, and he had an opening. There aren’t many folks around here who are going to gamble on an ex-con.”

Which proved what she’d suspected all along—that Butler himself was shady. How perfectly perfect that her brother would get tangled up with him. She could just picture Tony shaking down patients of hers when they were behind on loan payments.

What patients? her mind whispered. Where Tony punched a clock was the very least of her problems.

“I’ll be back,” he said, taking advantage of her silence and slipping out the front door.

At the sound of a mysterious boom from the back yard, Natalie marched through the kitchen, stuffed her bare feet into her gardening boots, and flung the screen door wide. It banged shut behind her as she flapped down the steps descending from the ancient stoop. Butler tossed another chunk of concrete into a wheelbarrow already piled high, then stopped and wiped his hands on grimy navy work pants. “Hello there.”

Her feet faltered at his sudden smile, white teeth against dark, dusty skin, but she quickly recovered “Mr. Butler, once again, you’re intruding.”

"Call me Brian, Doc." He stole a glance at her legs extending from baggy drawstring shorts.

She resisted the urge to stoop and cross her arms over her scrawny knees. "*Don't* call me 'Doc,' Mr Butler."

He grinned wider and retrieved a blue bandanna from his back pocket to mop at the moisture on his neck. His grey T-shirt was saturated and clung to his wide torso.

His presence struck her as . . . domestic. And too familiar. She frowned hard.

He nodded toward the wasteland behind him. "I thought you could use a hand here, considering those thickheads demolished your garden."

Indeed, the yard was forlorn—the sagging trellises, the brown of old stalks, the black of broken earth. Even the white board fence, which had girdled the overflowing garden for eons, looked violated by the remnants of yellow tape that had previously identified the area as a police scene. A picture of disgrace. Still, it was her disgrace, and none of his damn business.

"You might have asked before you pulverized my sidewalk."

"It was beyond repair. I spoke to your brother."

"You might have asked before you pulverized *my* sidewalk."

He gave her a wry smile and leaned on the sledgehammer. "I figured I'd be better off asking for forgiveness rather than permission."

The man was so . . . problematic. "And if you receive neither?"

He shrugged. "I'll still sleep better tonight."

"Oh, *you'll* sleep better tonight." She crossed her arms.

"I didn't realize the goal here was to relieve your latent machismo guilt. And now that I know, I still don't care."

"I do believe that's the most you've ever said to me." His smile rebounded. "We're making progress, Doc."

"Leave."

He acted as if he hadn't heard her. "I've been worried. Did they treat you well?"

"Oh, you mean in jail? It was lovely."

"I'm serious."

She chewed on the inside of her cheek for a few seconds. "It was dreadful. Fortunately, I was only there for a few hours." Natalie blinked and lifted her chin. "I hear you offered to post bond for my bail—was that also out of guilt?"

"Can't I just be a hell of a nice guy?"

"You already blew that one."

"Oh. Well, then I guess guilt it is." He flashed another grin, and this one made her want to, to, to . . . run. "You're only making things worse by being here." She gestured wildly in the air. "P-People are liable to think we know each other."

He cocked his head at her. "Then my devious plan is working."

She squinted and shook her head at the man's nonsense. The source of that scar on his noggin must have severed a connection or two. "What do you want from me?" Other than a hundred thousand dollars she didn't have.

He leaned toward her, rocking on the head of the sledgehammer. "You got a glass of cold water in there?"

She pursed her mouth, and considered him for a few seconds. "Yes."

"Think we could go in and talk for a minute or two?"

"No. It wouldn't look good."

"It doesn't look good now."

She weighed his motivation for dogging her, deciding that he was only protecting his investment. "Give me one good reason why I shouldn't call the police and have you hauled away for trespassing."

"Dr. Carmichael!" She turned her head in time to see the light of a TV camera flash on. At the gate stood a woman holding a microphone, waving while her partner filmed. "Did you kill your husband because he was married to two other women?"

"Get off my property," Natalie said as calmly as she could.

"Were the three of you wives in it together for revenge?"

Butler was closer to the pair, and reached the gate in a couple of strides.

"Who are you?" the reporter asked, shoving the microphone in his face.

"Dr. Carmichael's pest control service. You're trespassing, and you have two seconds to turn off that camera and leave."

"But—"

"One, two." He plucked the microphone out of the woman's hand and hurled it in the direction they'd come. Both the reporter and the cameraman stared openmouthed. "And I've got a rock for that lens if you're still here when I turn around." He walked toward the wheelbarrow, but he didn't have to bother selecting a chunk of concrete—the people had fled, presumably in search of the microphone.

He turned a smile toward Natalie. "Now, where were we?"

"Wipe your feet before you come in."

Eighteen

"NICE PLACE," BUTLER said as he emerged from the utility room, drying his face and arms on a green towel. "Lots of personality."

Natalie set two glasses of ice water in front of adjacent chairs at the white tile-topped kitchen table. When she noticed how much his appearance had improved with a quick wash-up, she realized how dreadful she must look—shapeless clothes, no makeup, hair yanked back into a ponytail. Not that she cared what he thought. Or that she thought he cared. Or that she even cared if he cared. "This was my aunt's house. She had quite a personality."

"Your aunt planted the garden?"

She nodded and settled into one of the cane-bottomed chairs that imbedded the backs of her thighs with an attractive waffle-y print. Not that it mattered. "My contribution to the garden over the last year has been utter neglect."

He sank into a chair gingerly, as if he were afraid it wouldn't support him. "Why would she have that plant *Stro—Stropha—?*"

"*Strophanthus?*" She sighed. "Rose Marie fancied herself a bit of an herb healer. She was always making sachets and poultices and teas. I sincerely doubt she could have extracted ouabain on her own—more likely she ran across the plant in her research and wanted it for the novelty. Perhaps she was planning to experiment on herself—she died of a heart attack. Anyway, the police confiscated her herb library and dehydrator."

"But if you haven't used them, then they won't find your fingerprints on them."

"Except I must have shuffled them around a half-dozen times to make room for other things."

He grunted. "How does your lawyer feel about your case?"

She clasped her hands in front of her on the table, hesitant to confide in him, but compelled to talk to someone. "He's hoping the charges will be dropped, but he's interviewing defense attorneys just in case."

He drained the glass in three swallows, then gave her a studied once-over, all the way down to her bare feet. "You look . . . little. And pale."

"More water?"

"I'll help myself."

Which saved her from exposing her waffle-y thighs. Not that it mattered.

He refilled the glass from the tap, drained it, then filled it again and glanced all around the eclectic yellow room before reclaiming his seat. He moved as if he were comfortable in a kitchen, although granted, this large space suited his athletic frame. He was probably checking out the inside of the house in the event he decided to foreclose upon the title he held. Natalie frowned. "Why aren't you working today?"

"I don't work weekends so I can spend time with the girls, but they had a birthday party sleepover today." His brown eyes shone with affection.

"You must be very close to your nieces to see them every weekend."

"They live with me. Jeanie and Ally are my sister's kids. She and her husband were killed in a small-engine plane crash a couple of years ago."

"I'm very sorry," she murmured, struck by the reminder that she hadn't been singled out for tragedy.

A weary smile materialized. "Things are better now, although the girls are still quite a handful."

Natalie tried to reconcile the image of the large man before her with fatherhood. Tea parties. Pink back packs. Uncontrollable giggling. Her opinion of him shifted again to incorporate the paradox. "How selfless of you and your wife to bring the children into your home."

"I'm not married. It's just the three of us."

"Oh." Shifting, shifting. "I . . . can't imagine how you juggle it all."

"No kids of your own?"

She shook her head. "A good decision, as it turns out."

He shrugged. "Maybe. But kids have a healing way about them."

The personal turn of the conversation made her edgy. Tapping a twitchy finger against her glass, she tried to steer the topic back to neutral ground. "Mr. Butler, you wanted to discuss something?"

"Actually, I just wanted to see for myself if you were doing okay since the arrest. So—" He gestured toward her. "How are you feeling?"

She blinked. "Why do you care?"

He blinked. "Because you're in a bad spot, that's why."

"The understatement of the year, wouldn't you say?"

"So, what are you doing about it?"

She bristled. "What can I do?"

"Well, assuming you didn't kill your husband—"

"I didn't."

"—you're in the best position to find out who did. You knew Raymond as well as anyone."

"That's supposed to be funny, right?"

"And you certainly have more incentive to clear your name than the police does."

"That's true. Detective Aldrich seems quite content to see me hang."

He leaned forward and rested his elbows on the table. "How much do you know about the other, um—"

"Wives?" Was it her imagination, or was it getting easier to say? "Basic things—how they met Raymond, where they live. The younger one is pregnant, you know."

"I read it in the papers, but I wasn't sure if it was true."

She pressed her lips together, nodding. "And both women are primarily alone, I think, like I am." Which was probably why Raymond picked them, now that she thought about it. And perhaps why he discouraged her from having a relationship with Tony?

"You have your brother."

"Only recently. But then you know that, too, don't you?"

"Tony told you I offered him a job?"

She attempted to keep the disapproval out of her voice. "Yes." It didn't work.

"I thought you'd be glad for him to be working."

"I was hoping he'd find something—" She stopped and took a quick drink of water.

His eyebrows shot up. "Something more noble? You're quite the little snob, aren't you, Doc?"

She set her glass down hard. "Don't be ridiculous. My brother is a convicted thief—surely you understand the temptation of him working in a pawnshop, having contact with people who might have even stolen whatever they're pawning!"

"Like Raymond?"

Her heart lurched. "Raymond? He pawned things?"

He reached into his back pocket and withdrew a thick wallet. When he flipped it open, a plastic sleeve unfolded, revealing picture after picture of the little girls. Receipts stuck out at all angles. He removed a piece of paper and crammed the rest of it back into place. "I gave this list to the police. Raymond told me he was always running across some super deal while he was on the road. Now I'm not so sure. Do you recognize anything?"

Natalie scanned the long list, her mind reeling. *One Tiffany desk lamp, one antique silver tea service, two antique silver candelabra, one Rolex watch, three antique silver chafing dishes, two lead crystal decanters, one Umbro bronze statue, two sixteen-place settings of antique silverware, fifty-two gold coins . . .*

The list of treasures stretched on and on. She held her breath, expecting any second to see something precious of hers or her aunt's that she hadn't yet missed. At the end, however, she exhaled. "No, I'm not familiar with any of these items. But I bet Beatrix would be. My attorney said she's from old money, and these pieces sound like heirlooms."

He winced. "Some I've already sold, but I'll hold whatever's left in case it's hers and she wants it back."

She rubbed her temples, feeling as if she were on a roller-coaster ride and each time she slowed to approach the terminal, the attendant shouted, "One more time!" and threw the lever again. "I can't believe a man would steal from his own—" she swallowed, "—wife."

"A *man* wouldn't," he said, then downed the third glass of water.

Funny, but most of the newspaper accounts had managed to reduce Raymond's bigamy to the level of a fraternity prank, intimating that boys will be boys. In the ugly swirl of misplaced sympathies, Butler's comment was a gift. She contemplated the man in her kitchen and acknowledged that some women might consider him to be good-looking. But with an abundance of available and willing females, why would he bring his sledgehammer to *her* garden? Sara's assertion that a man bearing tools meant something . . . intimate . . . leapt into her mind, but she dismissed the thought with a private scoff. Surely the man realized that the last thing on her mind right now was . . . Of course he did. He was, just as she assumed earlier, only keeping tabs on his investment.

"If you need anything at all," he said softly. "Just call."

She shifted in her chair, interrupting the waffle-y pattern. "Mr. Butler, I do appreciate you giving my brother a chance."

"I sense a 'but' coming on."

"But the police and the media could misinterpret your involvement—employing my brother, being at my home."

He shrugged. "*But* you and I know we're not in cahoots."

"But how do I know that *you* aren't involved somehow?" After all, he probably had all kinds of underground contacts and know-how. Broken limbs and severed horse heads came to mind.

One side of his mouth pulled back. "Until you get to know me better, I guess you'll have to trust me."

She studied his serious brown eyes, then slowly shook her head. "I'm fresh out of trust, Butler."

His gaze dropped, then he rose and carried his glass to the sink. "Pardon me for saying so, but it seems to me like you need all the friends you can get right now."

She stood—thighs be damned. "Since my reputation and my freedom are on the line, I'll choose my own friends, thank you."

He gave her a patient smile. "You really should be nicer to the man who's helping to restore your gaden."

"I don't need your help."

"I know." Butler pushed himself off the counter he was leaning on and headed for the back door. "I'd better get back to that sidewalk. Thanks for the cold water, Doc."

With a well-defined arm, he casually pushed open the screen door, allowing it to flap back in place. She walked to the sink to empty her glass. Through the window she watched him retrieve the shovel and resume transferring broken concrete into a wheelbarrow, creating clouds of gray dust. Rose Marie had wanted to replace that sunken sidewalk for ages. Natalie worked her mouth from side to side. Despite her resentment of Butler's interference, some part of her responded to his optimism.

Of course, it was easy for a person to be optimistic when someone else's world was crashing down around them.

Her stomach clutched in a spasm, rumbling like thunder. She opened the refrigerator and peered inside, wincing at the smell of ripe salads. With one quick shove, she closed the door and waved the air clear of the odor, hoping Tony would return from the grocery soon.

She was suddenly starving.

Nineteen

"I'M JULIE HARPY, host of Home Shoppers, and on the line we have Beatrix from Tennessee. Hi, Beatrix!"

"Hello, Julie," she said, then sneaked a quick sip of her requisite gin and tonic.

"Which of our fine products did you choose today, Beatrix?"

"The stainless steel nonstick gourmet eight-quart pressure cooker with the extra lid and fry basket."

"Oh, *good* choice, Beatrix. Do you have any other pieces of our gourmet cookware?" Julie smiled at her over the television set—her mouth moving a few seconds behind her voice sounding over the phone. The operator had directed Beatrix to turn down the volume during the conversation so the delayed transmission wouldn't disorient her.

Julie looked like such a nice person. Beatrix felt a rush of affection for her—doing such a good thing by bringing products that people needed right into their homes. "Yes, I ordered the deluxe set of gourmet cookware a few days ago."

"Wonderful! You must entertain a great deal."

"Oh, yes." Beatrix's voice echoed in the big, empty den. "My house is always full of happy people."

A chiming melody sounded in her ear. Julie squealed, and five seconds later on the TV screen, she jumped up and down.

"Beatrix, this is your lucky day! The music means you have the chance to win fifty bonus dollars to spend with Home Shoppers. If you know the answer to the question, you're a winner. Are you ready?"

Beatrix wet her lips and sat up straighter in her leather chair. "Yes."

"Okay, here we go. If you tune in at one P.M. every day, which of our daily specials would you see—the Afternooner, the Bonus Bonanza, or the Super Saver?"

She smiled in relief. "The Afternooner."

"You're right, Beatrix! If you tune in at one P.M. every day, you'll be able to save even more money with our Afternooner special. Beatrix from Tennessee, your Home Shoppers account will be credited with fifty dollars! You might want to use your free money on the *most* beautiful blender coming up in the next half-hour."

Beatrix smiled, immensely buoyed. "Thank you, I will." She hung up and sighed with satisfaction. After discovering that Raymond had run up her multitude of credit cards on cash withdrawals and expensive gift items she'd never received, she did the only sensible thing—she applied for a Home Shoppers credit card over the phone and was rewarded for her longtime patronage with a twelve-thousand-dollar limit. She swallowed another mouthful of the cold, cold drink. Three thousand down, nine to go.

She turned at the sound of timid footsteps. Rachel gripped her purse and offered a miniature smile from the doorway. "Mrs. Carmichael, I'm going home now."

"Yes, Rachel." She pointed to a large paper shopping bag. "Please take those items home to your husband and sons."

Her housekeeper reached into the bag and lifted a two-hundred-dollar dress shirt with the tags still dangling. "These are Mr. Carmichael's things."

"Some of his things, yes." Giving in to her fermenting anger over his careless disposal of her family antiques, she had torn into his closet, determined to destroy everything that reminded her of him. But she'd stopped short at the sight of his worn flannel robe, the ugly brown and yellow plaid one she'd given him their first Christmas, their only Christmas in the apartment. Despite thin elbows and permanently stained lapels, he'd kept it on a hook in his closet and had worn it every morning he was home. Desperate to prove something to herself, no matter how minute, she'd chosen a few newer, less personal items to discard. "Toss whatever your family can't use, Rachel."

"Th-thank you. Remember I won't be coming tomorrow, ma'am."

Beatrix frowned. "Remind me."

"My granddaughter Danielle is being christened."

"Oh." She and Rachel were the same age—fifty-two. "A family affair?"

"Yes, ma'am." Rachel's smile faded slightly. "You're welcome to come, too, Mrs. Carmichael. We're having the reception at the church, nothing fancy, just white cake and ice cream punch."

She vaguely remembered receiving the invitation. Remorse leaked through her buzz. She rose slowly to maintain her balance, then crossed the room and stopped in front of her devoted housekeeper. Beatrix smiled to hide her jealousy—after all, the woman deserved the love of a warm, extended family. She lifted her gold cross pendant from around her neck, kissed it, then pressed it into Rachel's hand. "My gift to your granddaughter."

Rachel's eyes widened at the sight of the elegant chain and the exquisitely carved cross. "No, Mrs. Carmichael, it's too much."

"Nonsense. It shall be Danielle's first fine piece of jewelry. I want her to have it."

Rachel's eyes turned glassy. "You are too kind, Mrs. Carmichael."

She cleared her throat lest the moment become too intense. "Have a wonderful day with your new granddaughter."

"Bless you, ma'am. Have a nice weekend."

"I will."

But her smile slipped as soon as the heavy door closed behind Rachel. Saturday night, and everyone had somewhere to be and something to do and someone who cared about them . . . well, almost everyone.

Behind her, Julie's voice came from the television. "Hey, Beatrix from Tennessee, if you're still watching, that beautiful blender I promised you is coming up right after our break."

She tilted her head and smiled. There was always Julie.

On her way to and from the pantry to fetch more gin, she flipped on all the lights the conscientious Rachel had extinguished. From the street she knew the house probably looked like a luminary, but she didn't care. She hated sleeping in the big house alone, and with Raymond gone for good, the rooms seemed exponentially more depressing. She grabbed her glass and carried the liquor and the tonic water with her to the master bedroom suite on the second floor, illuminating her trail as she went.

In the jewel-toned bedroom, she set the glass and bottles on the nightstand, kicked off her Vaneely pumps, and crawled onto the king-sized teakwood bed. After pounding the stiff decorator pillows into submission, she leaned back against the headboard and used one remote control to retrieve her friend Julie on the thirty-six-inch television, another to close the vertical blinds that led to the verandah, and another to adjust the ceiling fan to medium speed. She and Raymond would never again argue about the temperature in the room. Or about his snoring. Or about his bizarre nightmares that had kept both of them awake.

At least now she knew the root of his nightmares—the man had been preoccupied.

She made herself a fresh G&T, going heavy on the G and light on the T.

Now *she* was having the nightmares, and as usual, Raymond wasn't around when she needed him. Of course she knew the root of her own nightmares: Natalie.

The woman couldn't have killed Raymond. Beatrix had lied when she told the police that Natalie had been alone with Raymond in the ICU—she'd given Natalie's name to the nurse instead of her own when she'd gone into the ICU by herself.

Perhaps Natalie had had the *ability* to kill him, perhaps she'd even wanted to kill him, but she hadn't had the opportunity. Besides, the woman didn't have it in her, she was certain. And if she didn't have it in her to kill a man who so richly deserved their wrath, she'd never survive incarceration, maybe not even the trial. Not unless the woman was a hell of a lot stronger than she let on.

She held a mouthful of the drink until her tongue tingled, then swallowed slowly.

Still, she had to admit that some not-small part of her felt a wicked sense of vindication that the woman who had stolen Raymond's affection, who had so swept him off his feet that she'd driven him to commit bigamy, would be arrested for his murder. Symbolic, really, since Natalie had killed what she and Raymond might have had together. It wasn't her own fault that her parents had been ill, that the pressure of dealing with them and their obligations she'd assumed at the club had left her feeling jealous of Raymond's time, that she and he had spent most of the last decade arguing the few waking hours he'd been home.

She smoothed a hand over his side of the bed. Regardless of the emotional chasm between them, their passion for each other had remained strong until the end. Her mother had once told her at an uncharacteristically uninhibited moment (she'd been soused) that her best chance of keeping Raymond from straying was to keep him sexually sated at home.

And so she had. She'd donned dark glasses to purchase a couple of naughty how-to books, and initiated marathon lovemaking sessions. When exercise and strict diet was no longer enough to maintain her youthful figure, she'd flown to Brentwood to go under the talented scalpel of a doctor who serviced the country music celebrity crowd. When the threat of her parents interrupting them or hearing them was removed, she'd bought outrageously sexy lingerie and costumes to entice him. A few times, she'd dared to remove her clothing to music. Now she burned with shame at her pathetic attempts to keep a rein on his cock.

How could she possibly compete with Natalie's natural beauty, or Ruby's spectacular body? She was fifty-two, dammit, and married to him for twenty-one years—she shouldn't have *had* to compete with other women for his attention when he was alive. And she shouldn't have to endure this kind of scandal upon his death.

"Bea, *tell* us the rumors aren't true," Delia Piccoli had gasped in the foyer the day she and Eve Lombardi had stopped by. "Was Raymond *married* to *two* other *women*?"

"It appears so," she'd said, at the time still too stunned by the revelation that her husband was also a thief to put up a fight against Northbend Country Club's dastardly duo.

"How perfectly horrific!" Eve had said, her eyes shining with delight.

They'd murmured a few more shocked and thinly veiled sympathies before Beatrix had grabbed them by the elbows, shepherded them out the door, and slammed it behind them. She was quite sure she was the topic of discussion at this very hour in the little room where the board of directors congregated as necessary to determine if a particular member's conduct or reputation had become a detriment to the club as a whole. She wondered if they would send up a smoke signal once her fate had been decided.

As for Natalie . . . well, hell, the woman probably had a cushy support system around her—loving parents, siblings, friends, and neighbors who were probably holding bake sales and raffling off quilts to raise money for her defence. Natalie didn't need her help, and *she* didn't need the trouble. Besides, if she were seen fraternizing with the woman, people would talk. More.

The phone next to the bed trilled, spooking her. She reached for the cord to rip it from the back of the phone, then froze when she glanced at the caller I.D. screen.

RAYMOND CARMICHAEL.

Her heart vaulted to her throat. Impossible. Before reason could steal the moment, she yanked up the receiver. "Raymond? My God, is that you?"

First silence, then a female voice asked, "Beatrix?"

The disappointment was so fierce, she could only choke back a sob.

"Beatrix, it's Natalie Car—it's Natalie."

The explanation hit her like a thunderbolt. Natalie's phone was in Raymond's name, of course. Feeling foolish, she tried to recover. "What do you want?" The words came out more violently than she'd intended, although she wasn't so sure a husband-share protocol existed for her to violate.

"I had a visit today from a local pawnshop owner whom Raymond owes—owed—a great deal of money." Her voice sounded diluted with fatigue.

Beatrix frowned. "If you're looking for money, forget it." According to her accountant, she had none.

"What? I'm not looking for money." Her tone grew stronger, more strident. "The man showed me a list of items that Raymond sold him over the past year. He thought Raymond might have taken them from our—from my home without my knowledge. I didn't recognize any of the items, but if you're interested, I'll send it to you."

Was Natalie trying to get on her good side in preparation for the trial? "You think that Raymond could have stolen things from this house and I wouldn't have noticed?"

"He had two other wives and you didn't notice."

So much for the "good side" theory. She smirked. "Tell me, dear, are you calling from jail?"

"Sorry to have bothered you."

"Wait!" Beatrix bit down on the inside of her cheek, the chance to know the truth about her belongings, the chance to retrieve the Umbro bronze sculpture too irresistible. "I'd like to see the list just to know . . . just to know."

"Where can I send it?"

"I'll have to look up the fax number." She stood, swayed, then carried the portable phone toward Raymond's study. They exchanged impatient sighs during the silence. "What happens next?" she finally asked Natalie.

"The trial—I . . . shouldn't discuss it."

Fair enough. Beatrix opened the door to his home office and turned on a floor lamp. The tastefully decorated room was the picture of luxury and efficiency. After he died, she'd ventured past the locked drawers in the wee hours of a desperate morning, looking for more details of his double life. What she'd found was an absence of any documentation, work or otherwise. The drawers were bare, the elaborate desktop filing system filled with empty manila folders, his Rolodex blank. Whatever he'd been doing in this room, it hadn't been work.

She had frequented the room to use the fax machine when organizing events for the club, but she'd never pried. She'd never felt the need. And this was the thanks she got for trusting Raymond—a phone call from his other wife wanting to fax over a list of items he might have stolen and pawned. Good God.

"The fax number is 901–555–1302."

"Shall I send it now?"

"Now is fine."

"Then I'll send the list when I hang up. The telephone number for the pawnshop is on the letterhead."

"All right." Beatrix inhaled deeply. "Thank you."

"Good-bye."

"Natalie?"

"Yes?"

Would she be this calm if she were in Natalie's shoes? This noble, this generous? Hell no. "Nothing. Good-bye."

After disconnecting the call, she leaned on the desk by the fax machine until it rang and kicked on. The paper inched out of the machine, revealing a letterhead for Butler Family Pawn in Smiley, Missouri. Smiley? Jesus Christ, it sounded like a village of leprechauns.

If possible, her heart sank lower and lower as the list printed. The lamp, the silver pieces, the crystal, the bronze statue, the gold coins . . . her vision blurred. She grabbed the list to her chest and stumbled back to her bedroom. When she bumped into the bed, she threw herself down and screamed. She pounded the covers and kicked her feet and flailed about like a child. It wasn't supposed to be this way. Everyone—her father, her mother, her husband, Natalie, and that other one—had taken a little piece of her life and she was left with nothing. She clawed at the list, then lunged for Raymond's closet door.

The plaid robe hung there, benign and domestic and mocking. She yanked it from the hook and violently ripped it wherever she could get a handhold. The worn fabric gave easily, issuing gratifying tearing sounds amidst her guttural noises that escalated with each relenting seam. With a final cry, she flung the fabric to the floor, but seeing the robe destroyed and lying in pieces was too graphic. She sank to the floor, sobbing, furious with Raymond for living, more furious with him for dying. Dying before she was through with him.

She sat there for a long while, crying softly, listening to Julie on the television in the next room.

"Home Shoppers, if you *don't* have a set of our stainless steel gourmet cutlery, your cookware collection simply is *not* complete."

"I have it, Julie," she whispered. "The parer, the boner, the utility, the bread, the cleaver, and the shears."

She leaned her head back against the wall. Oh, damn it all to hell, Natalie was a nice person. The problem with nice people was that you had to be nice back to them, dammit, no matter how annoying they were. The truth of the matter was, Natalie wouldn't be in this position if her own plan had gone more smoothly.

"You know, Home Shoppers, the kitchen shears are the single *most* underrated piece of cutlery, and I don't know *why*. Try them—I guarantee these shears will cut anything in your kitchen, *anything*, including metal, or return them for a *full* refund."

Instead of trying to be clever, maybe she should have just cut out his black heart with the stainless steel gourmet kitchen shears. If it hadn't worked, she could have gotten a full refund. Beatrix sighed. Only *she* could botch a murder.

She dragged herself to her feet, then located the phone and dialed her lawyer's number.

"Gaylord, this is Beatrix. Set up an appointment with the Paducah D.A. and that loathsome Detective Aldrich for tomorrow morning . . . Yes, I know tomorrow is Sunday—what better day to get something off my chest?"

Twenty

Ruby wasn't much of a churchgoer (although she knew the books of the New Testament thanks to a song she'd learned in vacation Bible school), but stripping on Sunday just didn't seem proper. Mac got around the blue laws that prevented him from selling liquor on the Lord's day by hosting "private parties" on Sunday for about a hundred select customers instead of opening to the public.

As much as pulling the Sunday shift bothered her, she had to admit that the clientele was a bit more upscale than during the rest of the week. Some of the customers came directly from church, still wearing their fancy suits and smelling nice. One straight-up guy had slipped in a few weeks ago, though, and interrupted her friend Plenty's number with a screeching sermon, so now Mac patted everyone down for Bibles as they came in.

Taking advantage of the smaller, quieter crowd, she'd worn the most decent costume in her wardrobe—a long white shimmery vest over black leather panties and bra, and thigh-high black boots she'd shined up with Vaseline. If she were lucky, she'd be able to leave on the vest to help cover her tiny tummy bulge. Depending on the crowd though, sometimes, Mac would give a hand signal from the back that meant "take it down to the jewelry," and then you had no choice but to get buck naked. But since he knew about the baby—who could've guessed he watched Channel Two news?—maybe he'd go easy on her.

The music started, her cue to hit the stage. "You Sexy Thing" by Hot Chocolate—her favorite. She snapped her fingers to get the beat, made a false start, then got her footing right the second time. When she'd first started stripping, the taking off her clothes part had been easy—it was the dancing that gave her problems. Mac said she was completely tone deaf, but Plenty had pulled her aside and told her instead of trying all those tricky moves, just skip around the stage until she got the hang of it.

Skipping, now there was something she could do. And after a few months she'd worked her way up to some fancy steps—it was sort of like cheerleading, she finally figured out, and she'd always wanted to be a cheerleader. The music would be blaring all around her, and inside she'd be chanting, "We got the spirit, yes we do, we got the spirit, how about you?"

The men shouted and applauded when Mac announced her name. Her stage name was Ruby Red—or Red Ruby, she could never keep it straight. She grinned and stuck out her chest as she skipped by the guys. It seemed really packed today. The music was loud, but it wasn't too smoky yet, which was good. Even though Plenty said it wouldn't hurt the baby, she still worried. She remembered the concern on Natalie's face when she told her she hadn't seen a doctor yet, and tripped, almost falling into the lap of a big blond-haired guy up front. The crowd thought it was part of her act, so she played along, then forced herself to concentrate on the beat. *We got the spirit, yes we do . . .*

By the second verse, she had to start taking off her

clothes. She unhooked the front closure of her bra and shimmied her shoulders. The men went nuts—they were so easy to entertain. For the thousandth time, she thanked her lucky stars. Where else could a girl make so much money with so little talent and so few smarts?

She tried to take off her bra without taking off the vest, but got it tangled somehow around her armhole, and she had to stop jumping around for a minute to fuss with it. After a while, though, she gave up and shrugged. In the back of the room, Mac looked a little irritated, so she covered by yanking off her Velcroed panties, and the guys forgot all about the bra knot hanging under her arm. She danced around the stage again, swinging her panties back and forth and letting the tippers stick bills in a pink garter around her thigh. She smiled a lot and tossed her head in circles, careful not to make herself too dizzy. Near the end of the song, she counted to three, then wowed them with her signature move—a Chinese split, no easy task in clunky boots. They loved it, and gave her a standing ovation. She skipped backstage, then headed for the dressing room to count her tips and freshen up before hitting the floor for table dances.

The dressing room was crowded with dancers, some of them rouging their nipples and oiling their bodies, some of them trading clothes and shoes, all of them yakking about their kids and their boyfriends.

Suddenly sad and missing Ray, she found a vacant spot to sit. She'd met him one night while doing table dances. He'd bounced a guy who was bothering her, then told her she was pretty. She'd offered to strip or to let him drink a test tube shot of whiskey from her cleavage, but he'd just patted the spot on the couch beside him and paid her table dance rates to talk to him all evening long. He made her feel so special, and so smart.

"Ruby."

She turned her head and saw her friend Plenty had stuck her head inside the bustling dressing room.

"Mac wants to see you, pronto."

"Just counting my tips," she said with a sigh. "He's probably going to fire me."

"Are you kidding? The place is packed today because of your interview on the news—you gave Mac a great plug."

That danged interview. They made Natalie out to be some kind of monster, when all she could think of was Natalie wiping her face after she'd tossed her cookies in the limo on the way to Ray's burial.

Plenty winked. "And you were great out there just now, kiddo. The guys love you."

Ruby smiled at her friend and handed her a ten. "Here. Add it to your fund." Thirty-nine-year-old Plenty was saving for a boob job, and Ruby admired people who tried to better themselves.

"Thanks, Ruby."

After righting her clothes, she scrunched and sprayed her curly red hair, then touched up her bright pink lipstick. Maybe, she thought on her way out to find Mac, he would let her waitress until the baby was born. The money wasn't nearly as good, but it might help hold her place until she could dance again, and help her meet some of the monthly bills. She had lots of them, she suspected.

A stab of pain deep inside her brought tears to her eyes. She doubled over until it subsided, then tried to walk again. A few steps later, the same pain stopped her, and it took longer to go away. Her vision dimmed. Something was wrong with the baby. Natalie had been right—she should have gone to the doctor. Now she'd really done it. When she could walk again, she made it to the bar and told Jocko to hand her the phone, quick. Leaning against a stool, she pressed zero, then said, "Operator, can you give me the number for Dr. Natalie Carmichael in Smiley, Missouri?"

"Her office number?"

She frowned, breathing hard. Natalie probably wouldn't be working on a Sunday, if she were still working at all. "Is there a home number?"

"I have a residential listing for a Raymond and Natalie Carmichael on Cobb Street."

She fought another wave of dizziness. "That's the one I want."

"Hold, please."

Ruby motioned for Jocko to hand her a pen. She scribbled the number on the back of a napkin and hung up. She used the pen to punch in the number, surprised when a man answered, "Hello?"

Ruby groaned as another pain hit her. "Is Natalie there?"

"Can I take a message?"

"I need to talk to her. Tell her it's Ruby and that I think something's wrong with my baby."

He put down the phone. Ruby clasped her stomach, afraid to look down, afraid she'd be bleeding. She closed her eyes. "Please God, take care of my baby and I'll set everything right with the police. I promise."

A scraping noise sounded over the phone. "Ruby? What's wrong?"

"I don't know. My stomach hurts something awful and I'm real woozy."

"What were you doing when your stomach started hurting?"

"Just walking across the bar."

"You're *working* today? I mean, have you been . . . dancing?"

"Yeah, I just finished my first number." She moaned when the pain struck her again. "Am I going to lose my baby?"

"Ruby, calm down and have someone call an ambulance, right now."

"I'm scared, Natalie. Will you come?"

"To the hospital?"

"There's no one . . . else." Except Plenty, and she couldn't afford to miss work. Billy Wayne would be of no use whatsoever. And Mac wasn't exactly the comforting type. Into the silence, Ruby added, "Please, Natalie?"

Twenty-one

TONY SWUNG INTO the driver's seat of the Cherokee and closed the door with an inconvenienced exhale.

Natalie gave him a sideways glance. "I told you, you don't have to go. I can drive myself."

"All I'm saying is that this is a little weird, you visiting your husband's pregnant wife in the hospital. The same hospital where he died, no less."

"Do you think I asked for this? Any of this?"

He started the engine. "Duck so the cameras won't get you."

"I'm not going to duck leaving my own home."

Tony backed the vehicle down the driveway, frowning in the rear-view mirror at the reporters staked out at the edge of the street. "I oughtta take out a dozen of those clowns."

"Oh, yes, let's give them another feature story."

He grunted. "At least they're staying out of the yard."

"That's because Butler tossed a microphone and threatened to break a camera."

She felt his curious gaze on her, but she concentrated on maintaining a noncommittal expression for the cameras to capture. If she smiled, she'd look too happy to be in mourning, if she frowned, she'd look murderous. They crowded close, mouths flapping, arms raised. Tony goosed the gas to scatter the group. Once the car cleared and he accelerated, she lay her head back on the headrest.

"So what's up with that?" he asked.

"With what?"

"With you and Butler?"

"Don't use our names in the same sentence, please."

"I think he likes you."

She scoffed. "No offence, big brother, but thinking has never been one of your strong suits."

Tony shrugged. "I'm just saying he seems like a nice guy."

"Well, in case you haven't noticed, looks can be deceiving."

"Not everyone is a schmuck like Raymond."

Natalie closed her eyes. Among the list of words that described Raymond, "schmuck" was downright kind.

"Butler got a good start on cleaning up your garden. I noticed he left his tools, so I guess he's planning to come back."

"Can we change the subject, please?"

"He feels bad about the way the two of you met."

"Good."

"He's trying to make it up to you."

"What are you, his messenger boy?"

Tony rubbed the back of his neck. "When did you get so sensitive?"

"Last Wednesday." The day the entire world went insane.

"Sis, you're going through a rough time, and Butler is trying to help. We both are."

"He's making things look worse by hanging around, and you're making things look worse by working for him. You two are a regular cavalry, all right."

"We both believe you're innocent. That has to count for something."

She bit her tongue in concession. After all, Tony had been on his best behavior since arriving on her doorstep. And when the house snapped, crackled, and popped at night, she was comforted by his presence in the bedroom down the hall. A sudden swell of affection crowded her chest. She marveled that the tables had turned, that she was the troubled one and he the composed one. A simple truth hit her—in a world where she could be arrested for murder, Tony could certainly make it through law school.

"When will you see Masterson again?" he asked.

"He and I are meeting Thursday morning so I can take a polygraph test."

"Damned unpredictable machines."

She nodded against the headrest. "Masterson tried to talk me out of it, but I insisted."

"By the way, did you let him know you were making this little trip?"

"I didn't think it was necessary."

He grunted, signaling that she'd made yet another mistake in her new role as an outlaw.

She lifted her head. "I still can call him."

"And if he told you not to go?"

Natalie sighed. "I'd go anyway."

"Then don't call."

She lay her head back again, content to obey, loath to converse. But when the Cherokee weaved across the centerline, eliciting a staccato honk from an oncoming car, she grabbed the armrest. "Do I need to drive?"

"Sorry," he said, his face sheepish. "My license was

reinstated while I was in the halfway house, but I'm still adjusting."

Of course—he hadn't driven in two years. She stared at the inky black cross on his left forearm, trying to imagine a place where the days were long enough to provoke self-tattooing. "What did you miss most?"

He grinned. "Besides women? A private bathroom. And Big Macs."

"Well, that explains all the take-out bags."

"And I thought of you pretty often. The care packages were always the highlight of my month."

She swallowed hard, concentrating on the dashboard. Paltry snacks and toiletries and magazines—why hadn't she sent them every week?

He laughed. "My cellmate Coolie wanted to marry you."

Her own laugh was hollow. "Little did we all know, I was single." Then she sobered. "Was it terrible?" A practical question, considering she might be cooling her heels in a similar facility soon.

"Ah, most of the time it wasn't too bad," he said, his voice philosophic. "Cooke would freak out occasionally—Granada invasion flashbacks—and when the weather was bad, we missed rec time in the yard. But I got caught up on my reading, and I taught myself Spanish."

"Really?"

"*Si, señorita.*" He grinned, and she decided that with his dark good looks, the language would suit him. And serve him well if he someday practiced law. *When* he someday practiced law. She had allowed Raymond to convince her that Tony was a lost cause. Remorse coursed through her, binding her chest. "I'm sorry I didn't visit, Tony."

His mouth twitched. "I'm sorry I missed Rose Marie's funeral, although I have a feeling she would have somehow channeled one last reprimand through the minister."

"She wanted more for you. So did I."

"You always could see only the best in people."

"To a fault, obviously."

"Were things bad between you and Raymond?"

She sat up. "Not bad, a little stale maybe. That's what makes this whole thing so hard to swallow. I sensed he was becoming more distant, but I never imagined . . ." Natalie studied her wedding ring. It had become a band of fiery lead on her finger, but she hadn't been able to bring herself to take it off. A form of denial, she knew. Denial that the man she'd fallen in love with was an elaborate illusion. An illusion that she had bought into because it was easier to believe than to get close enough to him to discover his demons.

Easier at first. When his breezy charm and superficial small talk had begun to wear thin and she'd pushed for more intimacy and depth in their marriage, he had retreated. Retreated to Ruby, she realized now, whose demands were undoubtedly less complicated. Determined not to cry, she inhaled deeply. "He should have just told me he wanted a divorce."

Tony hummed his agreement. "But a bigamist gets off on the thrill of deceit. I knew a guy in lockup who had eleven wives scattered all over the country. Swore he loved them all, said he got jazzed by the thought of all those women waiting for him to come home."

Her stomach rolled. "That's absolutely prehistoric."

"Yep." His laugh surprised her. "He had as much sex as he could handle, but the guy also had high blood pressure, ulcers, insomnia, and migraines. Said prison was an absolute relief."

She had to smile. "He's in prison for bigamy?" Masterson told her that offenders were almost never prosecuted, an appalling statistic.

"No, the guy was running an auto theft ring. And he's in no hurry to get out, since all his women found out about each other. Hell hath no fury and all that jazz."

Women could be just as vengeful as men, she agreed. Perhaps more so, when their hearts had been compromised. Which was why she made such a likely suspect. Beatrix was too harsh, Ruby was too naïve. To Detective Aldrich, she must seem like the just-right candidate.

Natalie turned to the window and watched the landscape slide by, the burgeoning foliage a blur of lime green and pale yellow. Birds swooped in multiples, some invisible radar system allowing them to remain in perfect synchronization. Clouds shifted, forming tomorrow's weather. Time marched on, just as if her life hadn't been ripped at the seams.

"What are you thinking?" Tony asked.

She spun the ring on her finger. "I'm wondering what would have happened if Raymond had lived."

"You'll make yourself crazy if you play that game."

Natalie chewed on the inside of her cheek, wondering when her brother had gotten so smart.

He reached over to squeeze her hand, surprising her. "Don't worry, sis. Things will work out."

Ah, the optimism of an unindicted person. But she squeezed back.

"So tell me about this girl Ruby," he said, sounding very lawyerlike.

Gorgeous, pregnant, gorgeous. "The newspaper said enough, I believe."

"Yeah, but do you think she killed Raymond?"

"I don't think Ruby could kill anything but time."

"Well, if you didn't do it, and she didn't do it, that only leaves the old broad—what's her name?"

"Beatrix."

"Yeah. Think *she* killed him?"

Natalie lifted her head. "She was certainly bitter enough throughout the funeral to warrant suspicion, but when I called her last night with the list that Butler gave me—"

"Of the stuff that Raymond hocked?"

She nodded. "It was strange. She seemed almost protective of Raymond, as if she didn't believe he would steal from her, even after . . . even after."

"So?"

"Well, I'm no J. D. Fletcher, but she didn't react like a murderess."

"And how would that be?"

"Well, I don't know—cynical . . . vengeful. She sounded embarrassed."

"Maybe she's a good actress."

Natalie bit her lip. "Maybe."

"She had a shitload of motive—she found out her husband had married two other women."

"Not to mention the life insurance money."

"Even better," he said, his enthusiasm growing. "Why not arrest *her*?"

"Maybe because I had a shitload of motive, too. Being angry that he married two other women could also apply to me, plus I'm the beneficiary of a life insurance policy on

Raymond. And the ICU log incorrectly reflects me being alone with Raymond—Masterson is working on that angle—and don't forget the ouabain."

"Okay, the drug thing." He scratched his head. "Well, hell, if Rose Marie can grow it, can't other people?"

"Trust me, Beatrix isn't the gardening type. Besides, she only found out about me and Ruby when she got to the hospital. She would've had to be carrying the poison with her to kill him at the hospital."

"Maybe she already knew about the two of you and was only waiting for an opportunity to bump off Raymond."

Interesting theory. "But she seemed as surprised by the bigamy as Ruby and I were."

"Like I said, maybe she's a good actress."

"Maybe." She pressed on her temples. Why was she having to perform these mental gymnastics? Weren't the *police* supposed to pursue justice?

"Headache?"

"Yeah."

"Hungry?"

"Not really."

"Oh, come on. I see golden arches up ahead. Let's get something for the drive."

She laughed. "Okay, maybe a milkshake."

When they left the drive-through, Tony abandoned the subjects of Raymond and the other wives and the charges against her to reminisce about their childhood.

"Remember the tree house we built?"

"Sure I do." Their daytime play dwelling and nighttime hiding place when their father drank and their parents fought. At puberty, Tony had tired of the child's hiding game and hit the streets looking for trouble, leaving Natalie to huddle alone in the tree house beneath a moldy quilt, reading Judy Blume books by flashlight.

"Wonder if it's still standing?" he asked, his voice almost wistful.

Neither one of them had returned to their childhood homestead in the distant suffocating Missouri town in years, not since the death of their mother. "Probably, if the tree is still standing."

"Wow, that seems like a lifetime ago."

"It was." And adulthood was supposed to be better than this. "I took white poinsettias to the cemetery last Christmas."

"How was the grass? You know how Dad was about his lawn."

"No bare spots."

"That's nice." Tony swallowed a mouthful of hamburger, then shifted in his seat. "I've never told you, Nat, but I really admire what you've done with your life."

She stared at him. "My life is a train wreck."

"No. *My* life is a train wreck. Did a lot of thinking in the joint. You threw yourself into your books, and I threw myself into the gutter."

"Neither of us wanted to be at home," she murmured.

"I know. You knocked yourself out trying to please them, and I knocked myself out trying to make them angry."

"And neither one of us succeeded," she said, fighting a bittersweet pang.

His laugh was humorless. "They were too wrapped up in their own misery to notice us."

"I was fortunate to have Aunt Rose Marie," she said.

"Yeah, she was a good old gal. Did you know she wanted you to go live with her?"

Natalie blinked. "No."

"When you were thirteen. I heard Mom and Dad fighting about it. Dad thought it was a good idea, but Mom had a fit. Said she needed you at home."

Needed her. Not loved her and wouldn't consider letting her daughter live elsewhere. Needed her to do chores and keep the house running smoothly. "Mom had problems."

"Yeah—Dad."

"Although she did seem to have more energy after he passed away." Which must have been too much of a shock to her lethargic system, considering she'd succumbed to a stroke mere months later. Natalie drew deeply on the straw in her milkshake to counter the moisture gathering in her eyes.

"Damn shame the way they wasted their lives," he said. That's why I decided to get my ass back in school. I already finished nine college credit hours."

"That's great, Tony." She turned what felt like her first genuine smile in ages in his direction. "If I get out of this mess, I'll help you all I can."

He shook his head. "*When* you get out of this mess, all I want is your moral support."

A stab at being a sister again was a surprising silver lining in the dark cloud hovering over her. For the rest of the drive, she asked questions about his goals, trying to distract herself from the memory of driving this route only days ago, poised to confront Raymond with knowledge of his debt, only to walk into an emotional ambush.

But the gray and navy hospital loomed innocuously. Early

Sunday afternoon traffic consisted of families visiting loved ones and new mothers going home, bouquets and balloons abundant. She stared at one pink-checked mother, her arms full of a blanketed baby, and Natalie's mind fast-forwarded to Ruby holding Raymond's daughter or son. She wanted to hate the unborn baby, but the infant couldn't very well be responsible for the stain surrounding its conception.

Her eyes burned as she and Tony walked into the emergency waiting room. So familiar. So nauseating. The strawberry milkshake was getting its second shaking for the day within the walls of her stomach.

As luck would have it, the admissions nurse was the same woman who'd given her directions to Raymond's room a few nights ago. Of course, now she realized the woman had been acting so strangely because she'd already given directions to two other women who claimed to be his wife. Now, as she approached the woman, heat rushed to her face.

"May I help you?" the nurse said automatically, then squinted, as if she recognized Natalie. Two seconds later, she did recognize her, no doubt boosted by the media coverage. "You're that doctor—"

"Was Ruby Carmichael brought here a while ago?" Natalie cut in.

The woman floundered for a few seconds before confirming that Ruby had been brought to the hospital.

"Is she still here?"

"Let me check," the nurse said, then yanked up the phone, stabbed in a number, and turned her back for a hurried, hushed exchange. When she hung up, she said, "Ms. Carmichael is still here."

"Are she and the baby all right?"

The nurse swallowed, her eyes bouncing around the room

as she fumbled beneath the counter. "Have a seat. Someone will be with you shortly."

"I need to see her," Natalie said, now imagining the worst. Ruby hemorrhaging, scared, alone. How could she even have hesitated to come to the girl's aid? "I need to see her *now*."

"Er, right this way."

Twenty-two

AGAINST THE WHITE sheets, Ruby looked like Sleeping Beauty, pale and ethereal, waiting to be resurrected from semiconsciousness. She'd been crying and Natalie wouldn't have been a bit surprised if she'd found her sucking her thumb. Natalie's eyes inadvertently filled with tears of helplessness. God damn Raymond for the impossible position he'd left them all in!

As if she felt Natalie's presence, Ruby's eyelids fluttered open. She squinted, then focused on Natalie standing at the end of the curtain, and smiled. "I knew you'd come," she whispered.

The quiet despair in her voice tore at Natalie, but she put on her best doctor's face. "It took me a while, but I'm here."

"My baby—"

"Is fine," Natalie said quickly, moving to the side of the bed. "You didn't tell me you were diabetic."

Ruby touched the gauze taped across the back of her left hand. "I didn't know it was so important."

"But now you do?"

Ruby nodded, looking like a contrite child, then held up a brochure. "Diabetes is a leading cause of death and disability in the U.S."

"Didn't your family doctor tell you those things when you were first diagnosed?"

She shrugged. "That was a few years ago, and he mostly talked to Mom. I just remembered that I had to watch my sweets and take my insulin every day."

"How many times a day do you inject?"

"Four, sometimes five."

"You should talk to your doctor about having a small pump installed in your stomach to regulate your insulin."

"That's what Raymond said."

Well, at least the bastard was dispensing good medical advice along with romance. "You were very lucky this time."

Ruby teared up, her blue eyes swimming. "I've never been lucky before. Maybe this baby is my good luck charm."

Natalie smiled. "Maybe. Is there anyone I can call for you? Family? Friends?"

"No." She sat up and pushed her hand through her red hair. Dazzling, even in the shapeless, faded hospital gown. "When can I go home?"

"The nurse told me you're free to go if you have a ride home."

"I don't. My Camaro is at the club."

In for a penny, in for a pound. "My brother and I will see you home."

Ruby brightened instantly. "Thank you, Nat. Can I call you Nat?"

"Um, sure."

"Oh, and you can meet Miss Mame!" Just as quickly. her face fell and her lower lip began to tremble.

"Are you in pain?"

"No. But I feel just awful about that television interview

I did. That reporter twisted my words and made you sound really bad."

"I didn't see it." But she could imagine.

"And I'm sorry you were arrested, Nat. I know you didn't kill Ray."

Natalie swallowed. Did Ruby know she hadn't killed Raymond because she'd killed him herself? She obviously had access to syringes, and knew how to use them. Was her little-girl facade an act to conceal street-smart cynicism? What was it Tony had said? *You always could see only the best in people.* She spoke carefully. "My lawyer is certain the charges will be dropped."

"Oh, good. Do you see my clothes anywhere?"

Another act, or was her attention span really as short as her skirts? "Here," Natalie said, retrieving a plastic draw-string bag from a sterile chair. She opened the bag and withdrew a black leather bra, minuscule panties, and a sheer white vest. "This is all you have?"

"Uh-huh."

"What about shoes?"

Ruby frowned. "I had boots. Tall ones."

Natalie found them under the bed. They weighed at least twenty pounds. Each.

"I'm feeling much better," Ruby said, sitting on the edge, swinging her legs. She stood and disrobed in one motion.

In an instant, Natalie's medical sensibilities fled. Pure feminine envy clutched her as she took in the long, lean limbs, the narrow waist, the incredibly full and high breasts reserved for youth. In comparison, Natalie felt like a tall prune with thin hair, and she suspected the tightness in her chest was the precursor to her own breasts caving in in protest.

"I'll see if I can find you a robe or something," Natalie said, then escaped to the hall, her heart pounding. But Ruby's body was branded in her mind, and all she could think of was Raymond's hands on Ruby's breasts . . . Raymond lying with Ruby . . . Raymond impregnating Ruby. Natalie pushed the heels of her hands against her eyes. Why had she come? To honor her Hippocratic oath, as she'd pretended, or to satisfy some perverse curiosity about her husband's young lover?

Tony stood when she returned to the emergency waiting room. "Bring the Cherokee around," she said, then informed the nurse that they would take Ruby home. After managing to wangle a disposable sheet from the woman to cover Ruby, she returned to her scantily dressed charge and convinced her to drape the sheet around her shoulders to ward off a chill in her weakened state. The nurse eyed them warily as Ruby signed release papers.

Her brother's expression, on the other hand, was something other than wary when Natalie introduced them. Appreciative. Masculine. Traitorous.

Since Tony was driving, and since the patient was relegated to the comfy bucket passenger seat, Natalie found herself tucked in the back seat, her knees to her chin, feeling very unnecessary. Ruby and Tony chatted like old friends, and although Natalie couldn't hear what they were saying, assumed they were getting along famously from the occasional fit of giggles that erupted from Ruby.

She frowned at the back of her brother's head—an hour ago he'd been ready to lay Raymond's murder at Ruby's feet. Judging from the cocky angle of his chin, he now wanted to kiss them. After he told what appeared to be a particularly hilarious story, Natalie reached forward and discreetly flicked him on the back of the ear. He straightened, then shot her a sheepish glance in the rearview mirror.

He followed Ruby's gesturing directions, and a few minutes later they pulled into the parking lot of Pink Paddy's Dancing Palace, which wasn't a palace, and was surprisingly busy for a Sunday afternoon in the Bible Belt. Tony offered to drive the Camaro and follow Natalie and Ruby to Ruby's home. When Natalie agreed, she told herself she wanted to make sure Ruby didn't return to work before resting, but in reality, she was burning with curiosity over where and how the girl lived.

But she hadn't expected a shabby trailer park. Granted, the double-wide red and white trailer Ruby called home was the nicest of the lot, but the desolate surroundings were enough to have Natalie looking over her shoulder as Tony helped Ruby up a set of wooden steps to the front door.

"Ray built and painted the steps," Ruby said proudly, then pointed to a stack of wood lattice sheets lying near the corner of the trailer. "He was planning to put lattice around the bottom to hide the wheels, but didn't get to it."

Natalie pursed her mouth. Raymond—the same man who once hired someone to come to their condo in St. Louis to hang pictures? She tried to imagine him in a tool belt, lovingly building a set of steps and handrail while his young new wife planted pink begonias in the red clay mud. The image simply wouldn't materialize.

The door swung open to the sound of hysterical yapping. Ruby knelt and swept up a little dog that resembled a dust mop wearing a perky yellow ribbon. "Miss Mame, meet my new friends, Tony and Nat."

Natalie had never been introduced to a dog before, so she allowed Tony to extend their mutual greeting with a quick scratch to the mop's head. Ruby invited them in with an excited wave. "Want some iced tea?"

"Sure," Tony said.

"No." Natalie shot him a sharp glance. "You need to rest, Ruby. I want to check your vitals and your blood sugar level before we go." The interior of the trailer was warm, uncomfortably so, and although the furniture was neat, and the beige carpet showed signs of recent vacuuming, the faint odor of urine—Miss Mame?—emanated from the cramped living room. "We'll wait here while you change into something comfortable. And warm," she added, lest the girl emerge in lingerie.

Ruby pouted, but kissed the mop on the nose and lowered it to the floor. "Y'all have a seat, and I'll be back in a sec. The clicker's on the table," she added, flashing a grin at Tony.

He grinned back, and Natalie elbowed him in the ribs. Ruby disappeared down a carpeted hallway, and while Tony inspected the television that was big enough to tip the mobile home to one side, she scoured the walls and shelves for pictures, knickknacks, anything to prove that Raymond had actually lived there. Her head knew he had, but her heart, stubborn organ, needed some bit of tangible evidence to further torture itself.

The living room featured mass-produced landscape prints in drab colors that complemented the furniture, and a large wall hanging of brass-colored metal leaves with matching sconces. The whatnots around the room consisted of bean bag animals, sea shells, and a Bride Barbie doll on a stand.

Nothing of Raymond there. No favorite magazines or videos, no photos, no shoes. The computer, not a brand she recognized, sat silent on an end table.

The kitchen, visible through wooden rails that topped a half wall, had sprouted strawberries on every conceivable surface. No pasta cookbooks, no copperbottomed pans that Raymond preferred, no gourmet spices he liked to keep handy on the countertop.

Before she could stop herself, she stepped onto the linoleum and opened the refrigerator door. Lots of lunchmeat, plenty of diet soda . . . and a half-full jar of the premium brand anchovies that Raymond fancied. She inhaled sharply against the quick pain.

"Did you change your mind about the tea?" Ruby asked behind her.

Natalie whirled. "I, uh . . . yes."

Ruby smiled. "Good."

She was dressed in a familiar navy sweatsuit featuring the University of Virginia's insignia—Raymond's alma mater. A rip on the left sleeve. Natalie tried to swallow. She'd worn the same sweatsuit herself to lounge around in, although not to the same voluptuous effect.

"I, um . . . no, thank you," Natalie said, closing the refrigerator door. "I changed my mind again." She inhaled deeply to clear her thoughts. "Did you test your blood sugar level?"

Ruby bobbed her head. "It's in normal range."

"Are you sure?"

"Uh-huh."

"Do you need test strips for your blood glucose meter?"

"Nope." She had pulled her riotous hair into pigtails, shaving another couple of years from her appearance.

And in six months this child would give birth to a child. "Sit down so I can take your pulse and blood pressure."

Ruby obeyed, sitting in a kitchen chair and pushing up her sleeve. Her skin was cool and baby soft, and her vital signs registered normal. Satisfied, Natalie suddenly couldn't get away fast enough. Her own skin crawled, as if she were the unwilling partner in a ménage à trois. Her conscience rebelled, spurring her. She stood and stuffed the blood pressure cuff into the small emergency bag she kept in the Cherokee, her hands flying, her feet moving toward the door.

"Would you like to see the nursery Ray and I worked on for the baby?"

Natalie jerked her head up in synch with her heart dropping to her stomach. What she would like was to break the speed barrier going home, but Ruby's hands were clasped beneath her chin and her eyes shone like a child's on show-and-tell day.

No, no, NO! I don't want to see the nursery that my husband and you created for your child! But once again she was consumed with raging curiosity. "Of course."

Twenty-three

DETECTIVE ALDRICH SMIRKED. "I didn't realize you smoked, Mrs. Carmichael."

Beatrix leaned back in the metal folding chair and exhaled three smoke rings that twirled to form perfect figure-eights. "I don't. Where the *hell* is my lawyer?"

"He must be caught up in that snag out on Bridges Highway," the assistant district attorney, Peter Keane, offered. "Tractor-trailer jackknifed. Want to call him?"

Her cellular phone service had been cut off for non-payment, and she didn't want to use a phone that half the hillbilly cops in western Kentucky had handled. "No." God, this unfiltered Camel tasted better than any morsel she'd ever put in her mouth. "But I suppose I don't need Gaylord here for this."

Aldrich stabbed a button on the recorder at her elbow and spouted the preliminary info, time, place, purpose, then smiled. "A confession, Mrs. Carmichael?"

She laughed and stubbed out the butt in a battered ashtray. "A clarification, Detective, that's all."

"The tape is running."

Beatrix cleared her throat. "Over the weekend, I remembered something I said in my earlier statement that might have been misleading."

"Misleading how?"

"By making the doctor look bad."

"Which doctor, Mrs. Carmichael?" Keane asked.

"The second woman that Raymond married, Dr. Natalie Blankenship."

"Yes, go on."

She cleared her throat again and drank from a plastic cup of water, trying not to touch her lips to the rim that was probably crawling with germs. "I would like to see the statement I made last week."

Aldrich pulled three sheets of paper stapled together from a bulging accordion file folder.

She scanned the pages, stopping when she got to the part about seeing Natalie go into the ICU by herself. "Here. I recalled that I did not see Natalie go in alone."

"The visitor log for the ICU says different."

She shrugged. "I'm not saying that she didn't go in alone, all I'm saying is that I didn't see her."

"And what am I supposed to do with this information?" Aldrich asked.

"I don't give a monkey's ass what you do with it, I just didn't want to be responsible for incriminating the woman, that's all."

"Natalie Blankenship incriminated herself," Keane said. "She was growing the plant the drug comes from in her back yard."

"I read that in the paper," Beatrix said. "She seems smarter than that, don't you think?"

Keane shifted forward in his seat. "You're not angry with the woman accused of killing your husband?"

She shifted forward in her seat, mocking him. "One woman on the jury, and it's hung, Mr. Keane. Raymond Carmichael was a three-timing bigamist bastard."

"Who deserved to die?" he pressed.

She sat back in the chair and withdrew another cigarette. "Don't put words in my mouth."

"Are you saying we should let her go with a slap on the wrist?"

"Turn up your hearing aid, counselor. I'm saying I didn't see her go into the ICU alone."

Keane cracked a couple of knuckles—a weak attempt at intimidation? "And maybe you're covering for her."

Beatrix laughed. "What?"

"Maybe you and the good doctor are in on this together. What do you think, Detective? Think we have a conspiracy on our hands?"

"Maybe."

"A conspiracy? I don't even know those women!"

"Yet you're coming to the doctor's rescue. Curious, don't you think, Keane?"

"Very curious."

Beatrix scowled. "I don't even *like* those women."

"Yet you allowed them to attend your husband's funeral, even ride in the limousine with you to the gravesite."

"I had no choice. They promised to keep their mouths shut—" She stopped, thinking perhaps she should wait for Gaylord after all.

"Go on, Mrs. Carmichael," Keane urged. "They promised to keep their mouths shut about what?"

"About the murder?" Aldrich goaded.

Beatrix gritted her teeth. "No. About their involvement with my husband. I was trying to keep all of this as quiet as possible. I'm certain even you blockheads understand why."

The detective narrowed his eyes. "It's your statement that

you had no knowledge of Natalie Blankenship and Ruby Hicks until you met them in Raymond's hospital room?"

"That's correct."

"That's strange, because we have a witness who says she saw you and Natalie in the ladies' john chatting. She knew the time because she asked the doctor for it. Turns out, it was before Raymond even *had* his heart attack."

She'd completely forgotten about their chance meeting prior to the scene in Raymond's room. "I gave Natalie a breath mint—I had no idea who she was."

Aldrich grunted. "If you say so." He studied a gnawed-down number two pencil as if he were a bored student. "Did Natalie and Ruby know each other before that night in the hospital?"

"I couldn't say for sure, although they seemed as surprised as I was."

He bounced the eraser end of a pencil against the table, tripping on her nerves. "Have you talked to either of the two women since Natalie was arrested?"

"No."

Tap-tap-tap. Tap-a-tap-tap. "We can check phone records, Mrs. Carmichael."

Beatrix sighed. "Natalie called me last night to give me a list of items Raymond pawned in the city where she lives. She thought some of the things might belong to me."

Tap-a, tap-a, tap-a-tap-tap. "Mighty nice of her, being a stranger and all. Did you discuss the statement either of you had made to the police?"

With a smack of her hand, she captured the pencil against the table. "No."

He conceded the pencil with a hateful little smile. "Did you discuss your mutual husband at all?"

"Only as it pertained to the items he pawned."

"And did some of those items belong to you?"

"Yes, many were family heirlooms."

"Raymond took them without your permission?"

She hesitated, realizing she was handing him motivation for her participation on a platter.

Aldrich leaned closer. "Did Raymond steal and pawn your family heirlooms, Mrs. Carmichael?"

Beatrix tried to smile. "'Steal' is a very strong word. Perhaps he was planning to buy the things back, thinking I would be none the wiser."

"Did your husband think you were stupid, Mrs. Carmichael?"

She looked away from the detective to collect herself, trying to remember why she'd come in the first place.

Keane cleared his throat. "Mrs. Carmichael, do you have the list with you?"

She did because she'd planned a drive to Smiley to pick up as much as she could afford with the scant cash she was able to scrape together. With a trembling hand, she withdrew the list from her handbag and slid it across the table to the district attorney, the lesser of the two evils, but Aldrich picked it up.

"Ah, our old friend, Mr. Butler."

"You know this man?" she asked.

He returned the list, nodding. "He's been hanging around Natalie Blankenship. We believe they're involved."

She frowned. "An affair?"

"Looks like it. Her ex-con brother is working for him."

"I . . . I didn't realize Natalie had a brother. What was he in prison for?"

"Armed robbery," Keane piped in. "He was paroled about a month ago. Interesting timing, eh?"

Her mind spun. "Are you saying that Natalie's brother might have killed Raymond? Or this, this Butler person?"

He shrugged. "We're still investigating."

"Then why did you arrest Natalie?"

"Because we're pretty sure she has knowledge of the murder, even if she didn't commit it herself. And sometimes an arrest causes others to come forward—like yourself."

She simply couldn't reconcile the image of Natalie with a cold-blooded murderer, but maybe her judgment was slipping, like everything else . . .

"Did you know that Ruby Hicks was a suspect in the death of her mother's boyfriend when she was sixteen years old?"

That little idiot—a murderer? She swallowed a smile. Things were definitely looking up. "No, I didn't."

"The man was injected with rat poison."

"Injected?"

"Yep. Just so happens that Ruby is a diabetic, handy with a syringe. But maybe you already knew that."

He was studying her for a reaction. She quickly transformed her jubilation into a shocked expression. "No, I didn't." Beatrix lifted a hand to her chest for effect. "Was she convicted of the murder?"

"Nope, not even arrested. She had a watery alibi. Everyone thought she did it, but the guy was such a bad seed, there wasn't much of a public outcry for justice."

She wet her lips. "You think that . . . other woman killed Raymond?"

Keane shrugged. "Maybe. Or maybe she and Natalie pulled it off together."

"What? Why?"

Another shrug. "Maybe Natalie found out about the

bigamy, and knew that without a child, she had no claim to any of Raymond's money. Maybe she and Ruby conspired to get rid of Raymond so they could split the life insurance and estate money."

She arched an eyebrow. "And next they'll try to get rid of me, is that what you're saying?"

Aldrich pursed his mouth, then said, "Not if they had your cooperation."

Keane's demeanor changed—his head tilted, his eyes softened. "Mrs. Carmichael, if the three of you were in on this together, I'll do my best to arrange a deal for you . . . *if* you tell us everything that happened."

Words of denial exploded in her head, but she couldn't speak. Everything was going wrong.

The door opened and relief flooded her that Gaylord had arrived. But instead of her comforting, arrogant lawyer, an officer stood in the doorway, gesturing to speak with Aldrich. The detective obliged, and after a muttered exchange, turned back.

"I'm afraid I'll have to cut this little meeting short. I just received word that Ms. Hicks was admitted to the hospital this afternoon."

Beatrix's heart quickened. The baby?

"She was released in good condition," he continued, giving his waistband a yank. "But the real interesting part is that Natalie Blankenship and her brother drove all the way up here to take Ruby home." He eyed Beatrix. "Funny how the whole bunch of you alleged *strangers* have gotten so chummy now that your husband is out of the way."

Beatrix curled her fist, digging her nails into her palm. Could Natalie and that other one be in cahoots? She pressed her lips together, mindful that between the cigarettes and the constant licking, she'd worn off her lipstick, dammit. To think she'd believed their acts of grief and innocence—had even come to this pedestrian place to try to help Natalie. Were they planning to turn on her next? Or maybe they were going to set her up. The *bitches*.

The stout detective walked to the door and stopped, his hand on the knob. "Mrs. Carmichael, if I were you, I'd seriously consider Mr. Keane's generous offer. The first birdie who sings gets the prize. I'll let you think on that while I collect the other two Mrs. Carmichaels."

"I was just leaving," she said, half standing.

"I don't think so," he said with a nasty little smile. "It's high time we talked to all three of you wives in the same room."

Her mouth opened as she searched for the words to profess her innocence without protesting so much that she looked even more guilty than the picture of collaboration all three of them had unwittingly painted.

She scowled at Keane and sat down with a sniff. "Where the *hell* is my lawyer?"

Twenty-four

RUBY HUGGED HERSELF. Every time she walked into the nursery, happiness bubbled so high inside her, she had to raise onto her tippy-toes to keep from getting a head rush. "It's bunnies," she announced to Natalie, then pulled her inside the small, yellow room because she seemed hesitant to enter.

"I see," Natalie said, tilting her head, probably so she could take it all in.

Ruby knew just how she felt—from the bunny-covered wallpaper and bunny border, to the bunny bed linens and curtains, she'd never seen a more beautiful room, not even in a magazine. "How do you like it?"

"It's very . . . stimulating," Natalie said, nodding. "Lots of bunnies."

Pointing to the ceiling fan, Ruby said, "I cut bunnies out of the wallpaper border and pasted them on the blades." With a flip of a switch she turned on the fan. "See, it looks like they're running."

"Backward," Natalie said.

"Oh, that was a little mistake, but Ray said it was 'unexpected.' Just don't stare too long 'cause it might make you dizzy."

"Okay."

"Isn't the furniture to die for?" Crib, chest of drawers, and changing table, all white, with decoupage bunnies, except for the bottom drawer because she'd gotten a blister from the scissors and had to stop.

"It's very nice," Natalie said. "Very . . . coordinating."

"You don't think it's too girly, do you, in case I have a boy?"

"Well, babies are babies. Gender decorating is more for the parents."

Ruby grinned. "Ray said the same thing!"

"He probably heard me say it."

"Oh. You look really pale, Nat. Want to go for a couple of minutes in my tanning bed?"

"You have a tanning bed?"

"In the guest room. State of the art."

"Er, no, thanks. Tanning isn't good for your skin, you know. Especially for someone with your fair coloring."

"Oh, I don't use it that much. It was Ray's idea—he loved being brown."

"I thought his tan was natural. He said he was playing lots of golf with clients."

Ruby smiled. "I didn't know he was an athlete. Ray was a talented man, wasn't he?"

"You could say that."

A strange tickle inside her stomach stopped her, a bubble dancing behind her navel. Gas?

"Is something wrong?" Natalie asked.

"I don't know. I felt something." She frowned and rubbed her tummy through the loose sweatshirt.

"There it is again." Realization dawned and she gasped. "The baby moved!"

Natalie's tongue moved over her thin lips, then she

nodded. "It's a little early, but you might be further along than you think."

"She's okay, then." Ruby cupped her stomach. "Oh, Nat, she's okay!"

Natalie was slow in responding—thinking heavy doctor stuff probably, because she was leaning against the bunny-covered bookcase and staring at her sensible shoes. "Of course the baby is okay," she said. "But you'll need to take your vitamins every day, and monitor your blood sugar level."

"Oh, I will," she sang, overjoyed. "I promise." She felt a rush of affection for Ray's second wife, for coming to her rescue and making her feel better. She wished they could be girlfriends—go shopping, see matinees, swap clothes. "Nat, can I show you something else?"

Natalie looked up. "What?"

"Curtains I made for the master bedroom. Ray never got to see them."

Natalie looked as if she might say no, but finally she nodded. Bursting with pride, Ruby led her to their master bedroom where she discreetly kicked last night's costume beneath the bed and smoothed the floral comforter where Mame had put a dent in it.

"They're very nice," Natalie said of the ruffled calico valances that topped the miniblinds, but her eyes darted all around the room. "Do you like to sew?"

"I don't have a sewing machine," Ruby admitted. "But I can use a glue gun and Velcro."

Natalie was staring at the two Polaroids of her and Ray's wedding that she'd put in one frame on their dresser.

"The pictures aren't very good," she said. "The old

justice of the peace took them, and his hands shook something awful."

Natalie picked up the frame and ran her finger over Ray's blurry face. Suddenly she thrust the gold frame back into Ruby's hands. "I have to go."

"Already?" Ruby said, fighting her disappointment. It seemed like everyone else had somewhere to be, something important to do. Everyone except her.

Natalie practically ran down the hall, so she trotted to keep up. "How about some lunch?" she asked, wanting to prolong their visit. "I can make grilled cheese sandwiches."

Before Natalie could answer, the doorbell rang, setting off Mame. Ruby grinned—she loved having a doorbell. Delighted at the prospect of a house full of company, she scooped up Mame, then swept by Natalie and flung open the door. But at the sight of the man standing on her stoop, she banged it closed again.

"Who is it?" Natalie asked, her brow wrinkled.

"Nobody," Ruby croaked.

"Open up, Ms. Hicks," Detective Aldrich boomed, pounding on the door. "We know Dr. Blankenship is with you. We need to talk."

Across the room, Natalie's eyes widened and she glanced at her brother, for comfort, no doubt. Tony was a religious man, judging from the tattoo on his arm. She had once considered being a nun. Before Ham, that is. Ham had changed everything. "What do I do?" she whispered loudly.

"*Now*, Ms. Hicks," Aldrich said, rattling the doorknob so hard, the wall shook.

"Let him in," Natalie said, her voice dull.

Recalling her promise to God that she'd come clean with

the police if she survived the sick spell, she wondered if the detective was psychic. Puffing out her cheeks with a sigh, she opened the door again.

Detective Aldrich gave her a little salute. “Afternoon, Ms. Hicks. Feeling better?”

She swallowed—he *was* psychic. “Y-Yes.”

“May I come in?”

She shrugged, but stepped aside. Mame went nuts, snapping in the air in the direction of the man who smelled like cheeseburgers. He ignored her pet, and instead, nodded at Natalie and Tony.

“Dr. Blankenship, Mr. Blankenship. Nice day for a drive, eh?”

“What do you want?” Natalie asked, clutching her medical bag. She didn’t look scared at all, but then again, *she* wasn’t a murderer.

The detective unfurled a sheet of colored paper with important-looking signatures at the bottom.

“I know why you’re here,” Ruby blurted out. She felt everyone’s eyes on her. *Ruby Hicks, such a little hick.*

“You do?” Aldrich asked.

“Yes,” she said, then released a squirming Mame and took a deep breath. “And I’m ready to come clean.”

Twenty-five

"SO I KILLED HIM," Ruby said with a shrug.

Natalie stared at the young girl sitting across the table. They'd graduated to a larger room at the Paducah State Police post to accommodate the three of them and their hastily summoned lawyers, not to mention Assistant D.A. Keane, and the perpetual Detective Aldrich. Tony waited for her somewhere.

No one moved for a good thirty seconds. Finally Aldrich cleared his throat. "You're admitting to the murder of Hammond Jackson five years ago?"

Next to her, Masterson stirred, and she knew what he was thinking—that Ruby's lawyer *wasn't*, else he'd never let her confess to murder in the presence of so many witnesses. Indeed, Billy Wayne seemed morbidly fascinated by Ruby's tale of repeated sexual abuse at the hand of her mother's boyfriend.

"Yep," Ruby said with wide-eyed conviction.

"How did you do it?" Billy Wayne asked, evoking a strangled noise from Masterson.

Ruby was undaunted. "Mom was working, and Ham was drunk, like always. It was just the two of us. He held me down and when he finished, he zipped his pants and staggered over to the recliner, then conked out. I was getting dizzy because I hadn't taken my insulin, so I went to the bathroom for a syringe. I had to throw up and saw a bottle of rat poison next to the toilet that my mom had bought at the hardware store. And I couldn't think of a bigger rat than Ham."

Natalie's heart squeezed for the girl. To his credit, even the D.A. looked queasy.

"So I loaded up the syringe with poison and stuck it in his big stomach. Then I set the poison next to the empty beer bottles beside him and went to a movie."

Keane wet his lips. "A movie?"

"*The Lion King*."

Natalie swallowed hard. Masterson looked away.

"Ms. Hicks," Keane asked, looking none too comfortable himself, "why are you coming forward with this information now?"

"I promised."

"Promised whom?"

"God," she said solemnly. "I got real sick today and promised if the baby were okay that I'd come clean about what I did to Ham. He deserved to die, but I shouldn't have lied about it."

The D.A. appeared to be at a loss. He glanced at her attorney, who seemed mesmerized. "You understand, Mr. Lewis, that I'll have to place your client under arrest?"

Billy Wayne finally came around. "But you heard her—it was self-defence."

"The man was asleep," Keane said quietly. "And drunk."

"Not too drunk to rape her," Masterson said, obviously unable to remain silent. Natalie silently cheered.

"Am I going to prison?" Ruby asked, her eyes filling.

Keane squirmed when every eye in the room landed on

him. "I'll see what I can do. You were a juvenile . . . the victim was abusing you . . . you've stayed out of trouble—"

"Whoa," Aldrich broke in. "Believe me, I won't be losing sleep over the death of some scumbag who liked little girls, but it seems a little too coincidental that Raymond Carmichael went out in a similar manner." He aimed a dark look toward Natalie. "And it seems a little too coincidental that the two of you are so darned friendly." He motioned for a uniformed cop to enter the room. "Add that to the fact that the girl was alone with Mr. Carmichael in the ICU, and my job is pretty clear. You can sort out the charges, Keane. Stand up, Ms. Hicks." He addressed the cop. "Place this woman under arrest."

Natalie sprang up. "But she was in the hospital only a few hours ago from insulin shock—she needs to rest." Masterson laid a hand on her arm and pressed her back into her seat.

"She'll be under medical supervision," Keane assured her.

Ruby cast a tearful glance at Natalie while being led out, which only made them look more guilty, she realized.

"Now what the hell am *I* supposed to do?" Billy Wayne demanded.

Masterson glared at him. "Arrange bail for your client."

"Oh."

With a look of disgust, Gaylord Gilliam extended a business card toward Lewis. "Here's the name of a bondsman. Scram."

Billy Wayne beat a hasty exit, probably hurrying home to reread the laws of arrest.

Natalie glanced at Beatrix, but the woman stared straight ahead. Was that *guilt* in her eyes? Why?

"Well, we're through here," Beatrix's lawyer said, standing.

"Not exactly," said Aldrich, strolling the perimeter of the room. "You see, while we've been socializing all afternoon, a search warrant was exercised at Mrs. Carmichael's home in Tennessee."

Beatrix shot up. "What? How dare you?"

"And guess what we found?"

Gilliam sputtered like a car. "I forbid you to discuss evidence that might be used against my client in front of the woman who has already been arrested for the crime."

Keane held up his hand. "Sit down, Mr. Gilliam. From my point of view, I have three women, all with motive, knowledge, and opportunity to execute the murder individually, and a conspiracy between two, or even all three of them seemingly more probable every day. I think it's important for each of them to know how strong our case is, in the event one of them wants to break their silence."

Cold fear flooded Natalie—they were serious. Dead serious.

"What could you possibly have against my client?" Gilliam railed.

Aldrich smiled and whipped out a plastic sleeve that contained what appeared to be a handwritten list.

Beatrix gasped.

"A checklist for murder, under your client's mattress." The detective read from the protected sheet. "Step number one: Increase life insurance." He lifted his gaze. "Shall I go on, Mrs. Carmichael?"

Stunned, Natalie watched the blood drain from the woman's perfectly made-up face.

"I can explain," Beatrix said, her voice breaking.

"I'm looking forward to it," Aldrich said, motioning for the uniformed cop to return to the room. "Stand up, Mrs. Carmichael. Officer, place this woman under arrest, too."

Twenty-six

"WHICH DO YOU prefer?" Tony read a morning newspaper at the kitchen table. " 'Femme Fatales,' 'Vengeful Vixens,' or 'Homicidal Housewives'?"

Natalie winced into her yogurt. "Is that the best they could come up with?"

"Personally, I give Mrs. Ratchet ten points for her headline 'Surplus Spouses.' "

"Has she called this morning?"

"Oh, yeah. Left a message. She still wants to tell your side of the story."

She licked her spoon slowly. "No one wants to hear my side of the story—the truth is much too anticlimactic."

He folded the paper across his empty plate. "So now that you've had a few days to think about it which of them do you think did it?"

The sixty-four-thousand-dollar question—literally. When Tony last checked, a bookie in St. Louis reported the odds were running 4–1, 3–1, and 3–1 on the guilt of Beatrix, herself, and Ruby, respectively, and even money that they would all be convicted. She idly wondered if Raymond were alive which bet he'd put her money on.

"I go back and forth," she said. "It's hard to think that either one of them is capable of killing Raymond."

"Well, according to what you said, Ruby is definitely capable of killing."

"That's different." Despite the charges, she felt sorry for the young woman whose childhood must have been wretched. "Of the three of us, I suppose Beatrix would feel the most betrayed, and the most vengeful."

Tony narrowed his eyes. "Aren't you afraid that Ruby or Beatrix will make up something about you to save their own skin?"

Terrified. "I can't worry about that."

"Are you still supposed to take the polygraph tomorrow?"

She nodded.

"Have the other women taken one?"

"I don't know. Keane wants to observe the test, so I'm hoping Masterson and I will get an update."

"Butler had to fax copies of the loan papers Raymond signed to the D.A.'s office."

Natalie scraped the fruit-on-the-bottom from the crevices of the yogurt cup. "I'm sure they had to twist his arm." She was aggravated at the man for invading her dreams. Dreams that, by all rights, should be dark and anguished instead of . . . arousing and anguished.

"As a matter of fact, they did threaten to send a state trooper to 'help' him before he finally gave in."

"Now he knows how it feels to be intimidated."

"He asks about you every day."

"Gee, business must be slow."

"Nope. Business is great."

"It's a good thing—he has two kids to provide for."

"I know." Tony grinned. "Jeanie and Ally spent the afternoon at the store yesterday. They're regular little dolls."

Natalie frowned. "Why weren't they in school?"

He shrugged. "Teacher in-service day or something."

"A pawnshop hardly seems like a safe place for little girls."

"Butler keeps all the dangerous goods locked up. The kids love it there. Entertained themselves for hours."

"So he ignored them?"

"No." Tony scratched his head. "Why are you determined to dislike this guy?"

"You're mistaken—I don't care enough to dislike him." She turned to put away the carton of orange juice.

"Since when do you keep the orange juice in the freezer?" Tony asked.

Dismayed by her distraction, she jammed her hands on her hips. "Maybe I'll have a frozen juice shake later, okay?"

"Okay."

"Aren't you going to be late?"

He hesitated, then checked his watch and grabbed his coffee mug. "You're sure it's okay that I take the Cherokee?"

She nodded. "I'm just going to straighten up around here today." The police had left things in such disarray.

"How about I bring you home a salad for lunch?"

"That would be nice."

"Okay, later. Be sure to lock the door behind me."

"Bye."

As promised, she locked the door, thankful that in the swirl of this staggering scandal, she and Tony had reclaimed some of the camaraderie they'd enjoyed when they were eight and ten. After pouring herself a half-cup of coffee, she cleared the breakfast clutter and climbed the stairs, her feet and legs moving automatically. She'd decided that the danger of shutting down, especially while she was alone, was rooted in thinking. If she took the time to ponder her circumstances, she would come up with too many reasons to wallow. Or cry. Or sleep. Or succumb.

For now she would concentrate on things she could control, like taking a shower. At least the bruises she'd sustained from falling off the loveseat had faded, she noted when she shed her clothing. She turned on the shower and while the hot water traveled at a snail's pace from the basement water heater, she gave her body a critical once-over.

Always thin, she had a few more bones protruding than even she was used to. She should start drinking whole milk again, and real cola. Exercise, not to mention fresh air, might improve the color of her skin. Perhaps she should skip the housework today in favor of working in the garden, reporters be damned. A chill brought her modest breasts to a point, triggering unwanted comparisons that she squashed in favor of stepping beneath the warm water.

They'd always taken showers together, she and Raymond. In Jamaica they had stumbled upon a private waterfall within walking distance of their resort and slipped out every night to make it their own. Water had been his favorite venue for lovemaking, both of them slick with suds and body oils. Just the scent of musky soap resurrected memories that made her ache for him. Splendidly handsome with water streaming from his toned body and his lion's mane of salt-and-pepper hair. He would massage shampoo into her hair, rub her neck and shoulders, wrap her legs around his waist and rock her until . . .

A sluice of icy spray jarred her back to reality. A reminder from the temperamental hot water heater that Raymond's lovemaking, and his love, had been a twisted joke. What to her had been the essence of life, to him had been part of an intricate game he'd played to amuse himself. Shivering violently, she escaped the glass stall and rubbed her skin with a rough towel until she felt halfway warm.

Driven to cover up the body that couldn't satisfy her husband, she dressed quickly in a long-sleeve T-shirt and faded jeans. Then she gave her overgrown hair a hasty blast with a weak blow-dryer and pulled it back into a ponytail. A glance in the mirror confirmed that she looked almost as plain as she felt.

Yes, Brian Butler, with all his promising smiles and playful words, was simply toying with her. He'd already admitted that he felt guilty for his role in her dilemma. And she conceded that he probably felt sorry for her. But, she thought as she laced up her work boots, she wasn't about to let Butler convince her that he acted out of anything close to affection. *Burn me once, shame on you; burn me twice, shame on me.*

At the sight of her desolate garden, she entertained second thoughts about spending her day outdoors. But on the heels of her hesitancy came the thought that she was tired of being powerless in every facet of her life. The investigation into Raymond's murder had taken on a life of its own and while the media's tendency to inflate every detail gave the appearance of momentum, in truth the police had exerted little effort into looking into Raymond's business dealings and associations outside of his marriages. Her status as a suspect ensured the swift dismissal of her suggestions by investigators. Masterson urged her to be patient with the grinding wheels of justice, but this was her life.

Or rather, the remnants of her life.

So, today she couldn't control the media, she couldn't control the investigation, and she couldn't control the weather, but she *could* control the state of her garden. From the hall closet she retrieved the old wooden toolbox that held trowels and gloves and stakes. On the way out the door, the phone rang, but she ignored it. Natalie grabbed her hat—the day promised to be sunny and clear—just as if everything were right with the world. And she could pretend.

With the first breath of moss-fragrant air, she knew she'd made the right decision to pass the day in the neglected garden. Perhaps Rose Marie would be close by, imparting silent words of wisdom. From the old cabinet her aunt had turned into a miniature tool shed, she withdrew a rake, shovel, pick, and several other tools of what purpose she wasn't entirely certain, and picked up where Butler had left off.

The man really had made quite a bit of progress, she conceded. A new concrete sidewalk leading from the wrought-iron gate, which no longer hung crooked. The stepping stones had been leveled, and mounds of black, pungent compost lay at the roots of surviving plants. She tackled the Dropmore Scarlet honeysuckle first because its burgeoning blooms were in danger of being choked out by last year's growth. One project led to another, and she found the act of pruning and trimming therapeutic. After whacking a particularly stubborn outgrowth from a lavender shrub rose, she stopped to wipe her brow.

"Yoo-hoo!"

Natalie cringed at the sound of Mrs. Ratchet's voice.

"Yoo-hoo, Dr. Carmichael!"

There was little use in ignoring the woman, and if she

grew louder, she might tip off any reporters lingering at the front of the house. "Hello, Mrs. Ratchet." But she kept working in a flimsy attempt to dissuade further conversation.

"I just made a pot of tea, dear. Why don't I bring it over?"

Sneaky old bird. "No, thank you. It's such a pretty day, I want to get as much done here as I can."

"But it's almost lunchtime, dear. You'll have to stop for a bite to eat. I'll make sandwiches."

She hadn't realized so much time had slipped away. "Thanks anyway. My brother is bringing me a salad. Now if you don't mind—"

"One of my articles about your case was picked up by the Associated Press."

She sighed.

"They said it was 'folksy and fair.' And that's how I would treat an exclusive interview with you, my dear—fair. Fair, fair, fair."

Frustration tightened her chest. "Mrs. Ratchet, my lawyer advised me not to speak to the press."

"But I'm your *neighbor*, a family friend."

She amputated an offending rose branch with pent-up energy. "Good *day*, Mrs. Ratchet."

From the twist of the woman's beak, Natalie had just made another enemy. Probably a mistake, since her neighbor could very well invite the cameras onto her property for the best view of Natalie's comings and goings.

The telltale sound of the Cherokee pulling under the carport was a welcome distraction. She was thirsty, and immensely satisfied that she'd managed to while away the morning with few thoughts of the ugly predicament she had been thrust into. She gave Mrs. Ratchet a conciliatory wave as she pulled off her gloves and headed to the back door.

Tony was knocking on the side door as she entered the kitchen. She stepped out of her boots and left them on a mat, then unlocked the door. "Am I glad to see you," she said, then stopped.

Brian Butler smiled. "Likewise."

She looked past him to the parked Cherokee. "Where is Tony?"

"He took my van for a pickup in Riley. When he said he promised you lunch, I offered to fill in." He held up a white paper bag transparent with grease.

"That doesn't look like a salad."

"That's because it's a hot dog."

"A turkey hot dog?" she asked hopefully.

"Chili and cheese."

She wrinkled her nose.

His eyes danced. "You really should try something coarse once in a while. You might be surprised."

Natalie plucked the bag from his hand. "Thank you. Good-bye."

"Oh, didn't I tell you? My lunch is in there, too. I was hoping we could eat together."

"Why?"

"Because when that hot dog gives me indigestion, I'll have a doctor nearby."

She contemplated the unnerving meddler. His earthiness reminded her of the baseness of men, but his proportions gave her an odd sense of protection. Her fingers tingled. Good or bad, the man made her feel seriously female.

And that, at least, was no crime.

He flashed a tempting smile. "What do you say, Doc?"

She managed not to frown. "Wipe your feet before you come in."

He did. "I see you've been working in the garden."

"I'm making headway." She set the bag on the table then walked to the sink to wash her hands, glad to have her back to him when she added, "Thanks to your contribution."

His footsteps vibrated across the wood floor and traveled through her sock feet as he came up to stand beside her. "That wasn't so difficult, was it?"

She turned to find his eyes dancing and pumped more soap into her hands. "What do you mean?"

"Acknowledging that it's nice to have a little help once in a while."

She narrowed her eyes. "I told you—"

"I know—you don't need my help. Or anyone's. But you don't have to be a martyr, Natalie."

A retort sat ready on her tongue—until he said her name. Deliberate. Gentle. Possessive. She squeezed her sudsy hands together so hard, her wedding ring popped off to ricochet around the porcelain sink, heading in slow motion for the gaping drain. Natalie's heart lodged in her throat. They both lunged forward, and after an eternity, Butler came up with it in the palm of his large hand.

She stared at the foam-covered lump of gold for long seconds, trying to remember the joy she'd felt when Raymond had slipped it on her finger, waiting for relief to overcome her. But the good memory was tainted by his betrayal, and the relief diffused by Butler's presence. As the bubbles dissolved in his hand and the ring became clearer, so did her course of action. Natalie lifted her chin to meet his gaze. "How much?"

"How much what?"

"How much is my wedding ring worth?" She dried her hands on a checkered dish towel in the ensuing silence. Thoroughly. Twice.

"To whom?" he asked quietly.

"To a pawnshop dealer."

His lips parted. "To this pawnshop dealer, it's worth a great deal."

She swallowed, rehashing this morning's discussion with herself. "G-Good. Then just apply it toward my d-debt."

"Are you sure you want to do this?"

"Yes."

His fingers curled, covering the ring. "I'll make sure you get top dollar."

Since to her the value of the ring was running into negative numbers, she wasn't about to dicker. She trusted him.

Her pulse skipped. Not trust. Trust wasn't the word a woman used with a man she barely knew when she was still reeling over the death of her cheating husband. Desperation—now *there* was a word. She was desperate for a sympathetic ear, that was all. An *ear*—other body parts need not apply.

"How about that hot dog?" he asked, slipping the ring into his pocket as if nothing of great import had transpired. Of course, he wouldn't have realized otherwise unless the confusion and uncertainty galloping through her chest was evident on her face.

"Your face," he said, tilting his head, his dark eyes shining.

Oh my God.

He reached out and swept a finger across her cheek. She blinked, but was frozen in place. "You're wearing some of your morning's labor," he said with a grin, then held up his finger, smudged with the proof.

"Excuse me for a moment," she murmured, then skedaddled to the utility room to survey her dirty face, now red with embarrassment. Mud striped her cheek and chin. The hat had compromised her ponytail, leaving her hair in disarray. Scary. Glad for the excuse to collect herself, she bent over the deep sink and flushed her face and neck with cool water. Refreshed, she loosened the ponytail and finger-combed her hair into some semblance of order. Her hands shook for no discernible reason, except that she wanted this . . . this, this little non-rendezvous to end quickly. Why Brian Butler made her nervous, she couldn't fathom, but she was determined he would never know. A deep inhale strengthened her resolve.

By the time she returned to the kitchen, he had spread their lunch on the tile-topped table.

"I found tea in the refrigerator," he said. He'd also found paper plates and a radio station, not to mention her sore spot. The man acted as if he belonged there, in her life.

Moving cautiously, she claimed a chair, then stared at the hot dog bulging out of its bun, with orangey mystery meat sauce spilling everywhere. "You actually eat these things?"

He lowered himself into an adjacent chair. "As often as I can," he said, then bit into the mess with a practiced technique and chewed with gusto. On the radio, Billy Joel was trying to convince Virginia that he might as well be the one, because only the good die young. Oh yeah, baby.

Natalie used both hands to lift the so-called food for a sniff. "No wonder you have indigestion problems."

"Ah, come on. Live a little."

Billy and Brian were a persuasive pair. Natalie tasted the hot dog gingerly, conceding defeat when the rich flavors exploded on her tongue. Cheese, grease, and salt. Wickedly delicious. She could visualize free radicals somersaulting toward her vital organs. Oh, well, prison food was sure to have state-approved levels of roughage and antioxidants—she'd catch up. Natalie took two more bites before chasing the dog with a swallow of tea.

"Isn't that better than a salad?" he asked.

"Not bad," she said, nodding. "But ask me again in an hour."

He laughed, a pleasing rumble. "You look . . . better . . . today."

"Gee, thanks."

"Less stressed, I mean. I heard the two other women were arrested."

"Yes."

"Does that mean the charges against you will be dropped?"

She sighed. "Don't you read the papers? The popular theory is that the three of us wives are in cahoots."

"No, I hadn't heard."

"The good news is they no longer think the two of us are an item."

He made a funny face. "I was kind of enjoying it."

"The notoriety?"

"The two of us being an item."

She swallowed an unchewed bite and forced it down by dragging her fist over her breastbone. "Look, Mr. Butler—"

"Brian."

"—this boyish charm of yours is wasted on me. My husband was just buried, for heaven's sake." Her words sounded perfectly logical to her own ears. So why didn't her feelings follow suit?

"Did you love him?" he asked.

"Of course I did."

"Then why did you just hock your wedding ring?"

Good question. She cast about for a good answer. "I don't have to explain myself to you."

"No, you don't." He turned his attention back to his lunch and took another healthy bite.

As she watched him eat calmly, Natalie frowned in exasperation. Did nothing faze the man? She was torn—part of her wanted to toss him out of her kitchen on his sympathetic ear, and part of her yearned to draw upon his unshakable composure. A revelation that only fed her nervousness. "The truth is, right now I don't feel anything for Raymond except anger."

"Anger is good," he said casually. "Makes a person want to get on with life."

She mulled his words as she took another bite and decided that, yes, of all things she could be feeling at the moment, anger was the most productive. Of course, from Detective Aldrich's point of view, anger was also the best motivation for murder.

Butler wiped his mouth with a paper napkin. While she wrestled with her emotions, he had made short work of the rest of the hot dog and emptied the glass of tea. He pushed to his feet, and scooted the chair back under the table. "Seeing as how I've worn out my welcome," he said with a tight smile, "I guess I'd better be going."

Natalie glanced up midchew, suddenly embarrassed by her behavior. The man hadn't done anything to make her think he was interested in anything other than his investment. And how cynical had she become to suspect ulterior motives behind every good deed? She swallowed thickly and stood to face him, although she had to look up. "I'm sorry I was rude

. . . Brian." Her cheeks flamed. "I had no right to jump to conclusions. I'm not ungrateful for your . . . company."

He studied her face, allowing her to do the same. Had he been a smaller man, he would have been almost pretty. Instead, his handsome features were broad and rugged and pleasingly placed. His jawline sharp, his cheekbones defined, his eyes framed with untanned crows' feet. His dark eyes were extraordinary, fluid and seemingly incapable of dishonesty. Suddenly, she knew that about him. He was genuine.

"Natalie," he said softly. "You jumped to all the right conclusions. I was hooked the first time I saw you. I think I behaved so badly in your office because I knew I couldn't have you, and that Raymond didn't deserve you."

Her throat convulsed.

He slowly curved his hand around the back of her neck, poised for her retreat. She didn't move. She didn't think. She didn't breathe.

"I know my timing is lousy," he whispered, "but I'm impatient for you."

As she was for him. Her heart pounded in anticipation. His fingers burned into her neck as he pulled her mouth up to meet his. His kiss was urgent and jealous and guttural. Natalie went boneless, absorbing his comforting energy, allowing him to assume her weight. He wrapped his other arm around her waist and drew her against his solid body, his legs wide to cradle hers. Everything about him emanated strength—his hands, his mouth, his ragged breathing. Enveloped in his embrace, the pain and ambiguity of the past several days drained away. Gone was the rejection. Gone was the anxiety. Gone was the anger.

And in their place was a big, warm, wraparound diversion from reality.

Oh, yeah—reality. Her common sense returned with the force of a head-on collision. She froze, then tore her mouth from his, and twisted out of his arms—an impossibility without his cooperation, which he gave under protest.

"Natalie—"

She leaned on the counter, her back to him, her chest heaving. "Brian, please . . . leave." She pressed the back of her hand to her mouth. *God, what was I thinking?*

"Okay." His breathing was also compromised, his voice broken. "But whether you want to admit it or not, Doc, there's something here."

She closed her eyes. There was something here, all right—a mushrooming cloud of calamity. A dead husband, a murder charge, a reckless kiss. She sunk her teeth into her hand. Perhaps she was having a nervous breakdown—that would explain her bizarre behavior. And at the moment, crazy was preferable to just plain stupid. The floor vibrated as he walked toward her, and she stiffened. He must have sensed her withdrawal because his footsteps paused, then retreated. Behind her, coldness filled the space he vacated.

At the sound of the doorknob turning, she glanced over her shoulder. He, too, was looking back, his eyes questioning.

Natalie turned away and concentrated on the broken pane of glass in the kitchen window.

"I'm not through," he said. "I want you to know I'm not through." The door opened and closed behind her.

Twenty-seven

BEATRIX FROWNED AT the map—what kind of a town was so damned small that Rand McNally didn't even know about it? She wadded the useless piece of paper into a ball and tossed it into the back seat of her Mercedes. At the next wide spot in the road with a gas station, she pulled over and got directions to Smiley from a kid loafing in the parking lot who she tipped to pump her gas. Then, herself refueled with a cup of God-awful java and a pack of Camels, she pointed the car in the right direction and settled in for another forty-five minutes of podunk parkway.

She'd intended to make the drive to the pawnshop Sunday on her way back from Paducah, but being arrested had a way of messing up a person's plans.

Okay, at first she'd been shaken. She certainly hadn't counted on the list being found—what kind of barbarians look under a lady's mattress pad? But Gaylord, bless his overtaxed heart, had railroaded the booking process for her, and by association, for that other one. As a result, she hadn't had to spend the night in jail, although she was still trying to remove that dreadful black ink from her hands due to the fingerprinting. A humiliating experience, especially since she was processed with a queue of stray drunks from the previous night. She shivered at the memory.

Not to worry, Gaylord had promised, insisting she plead not guilty at the hurried arraignment because, after all, the list was strictly circumstantial—a prop for a murder mystery dinner party, for all the D.A. knew—and besides, two other suspects were already under arrest for the same crime.

Still, the day had been tense. When she made it home, she'd ordered a wok from Home Shoppers and downed a half-bottle of gin before passing out—er, before going to sleep.

She vacillated between being furious with the two other women for botching what could have been such an open-and-shut case, and being fearful that the circumstantial evidence against them mounted every time they were interviewed. Yet she didn't know what to do to stop the hemorrhaging situation now that a major leak had sprung.

News of her arrest hit Northbend about eleven A.M. Monday morning. At eleven-fifteen, she had received a call from the Northbend Country Club membership chairperson informing her that her membership had been placed on probation, pending outcome of the charges and a vote by the membership board. She'd bloodied her tongue from biting it, but endured the cheerful threat in silence. However, they were supreme fools if they thought anything would stop her from presenting a service award named for her father at a club gala next week.

Tuesday she'd worked the phones as calls poured in, downplaying her arrest by saying that the insurance companies were involved—a criminal trial would postpone the payment of the money she was rightfully due. Bastards.

Wednesday she declared her damage control a success when the calls took on a more sympathetic tone. Even so, Gaylord had told her last night on the phone, they weren't out of the woods. He was worried about his inexperience as a trial lawyer. She, on the other hand, was worried about her inexperience as a poor person.

Living large was expensive, dammit, and bills were pouring in from unfamiliar creditors who'd seen the notice of Raymond's death in the newspapers. At this rate, she'd be driving a bourgeois BMW by summer.

The quiet panic undulating in her stomach was diverted by her first impression of the town of Smiley, Missouri, as the car bounced over the speed bump marking the city limits. As expected, a smiley face adorned the sign, population fifty-six hundred. In the distance, a water tower against a background of ridiculously fluffy clouds carried the same silly insignia. Good grief, hadn't they filmed a sitcom about this place?

She followed the meandering main street around several blocks, cruising by a knot of people, including one man shouldering a news camera, gathered outside a narrow stoop to a refurbished building. She'd bet her last one hundred dollars the crowd had something to do with Natalie—staking out her office, perhaps? Surely she wasn't working during this mess.

Main Street gave way to a courtyard whose centerpiece fountain was flanked by white- and pink-flowered trees. At the sight of a farmer's market in a long paved lot, she pulled over and asked a grinning old man for directions to the pawnshop.

Not the wisest move, she quickly discovered.

"You new around here?" he asked, his bushy eyebrows wagging.

Oh, brother—at least he didn't recognize her. "Just visiting."

"Mighty nice addition to the scenery."

The man smelled like a horse. "Butler's Pawn, do you know where it is?"

He scratched his bald head. "On the other side of town, past the interstate. Sittin' on Spring Street, behind the truck stop. Can't miss it."

"Thank you."

"Here you go." He pulled a shiny yellow apple, still bearing leaves on the stem, from a pocket of his overalls. "A treat for a pretty lady."

"Er, no, thank you."

"On the house," he said, pressing it into her hand.

Deciding it was easier to take the fruit than to argue, she forced a smile. "Thanks." Then, on the chance she might get more out of the man than directions and a snack, she asked, "Is this the town where Dr. Natalie Carmichael lives, the one who killed her husband?"

He stuck his thumbs in his bib. "Yep. Darned shame, too. People here thought a lot of the good doc."

"So you think she's guilty?"

"Haven't you heard? Turns out the man was married to two other gals. The three of 'em did him in."

"But from what I heard, they didn't even know each other."

"Yeah, right. Hell hath no fury as a woman scorned. Can't imagine what three of 'em could do." He leaned forward and winked. "Me, I'm a single man, still waitin' for the right woman."

"Good luck." She pressed the accelerator and sped away.

Can't imagine what three of 'em could do. People actually thought they had committed the murder together? Her heart pounded as the first real possibility of serving time hit home.

She'd counted on Natalie's medical background and the other one's criminal background to swing the odds of acquittal in her favor, but would the mystique of a conspiracy snowball into a shared conviction? She would have never come forward on Natalie's behalf if she'd had the slightest notion that she herself might be arrested. The one time she'd given in to the impulse to be nice, and look where it had gotten her.

Beatrix sighed. She could *not* spend the rest of her life in prison gray. She had to make something happen.

Past more buildings outfitted in Americana colors, a new school complex, and a couple of miles of scattered residential landscape, she drove over an interstate and entered what appeared to be a boomlet of retail business for the town. Anchored by a bustling Wal-Mart, a shopping center sprawled like some sleeping farm animal she didn't want to know about. Fast food shacks, cheap shoe stores, nail salons.

Her hunt for Spring Street was hastened by the gaudy sign for the truck stop the smelly farmer had promised. She wheeled into the half-full parking lot of Butler's Family Pawn, wincing at the abundance of neon: LOANS, JEWELRY, GUNS, COINS. Suddenly she wished she'd brought a hat to pair with her dark glasses. And maybe she should have dug out that pair of Donna Karan blue jeans she bought on a whim three years ago but had never worn.

She banged her way out of her car, hitting the keyless remote twice to lock it up tight from would-be thieves. Then, carrying herself as if she frequented pawnshops, she entered the vulgar establishment.

Unfortunately, the inside was so dark, she was forced to remove her glasses. Butler's Family Pawn was crammed with inventory from the carpeted floor to the ceiling tiles: cases of jewelry, racks of musical instruments, shelves of silver, tables of stereos, cabinets of guns. Customers milled around, some selling, some buying. All in all, exceedingly tawdry.

"What can I do for you?" a man asked behind her.

She turned and eyed the tall, dark-haired fellow, taking in the crude black cross on his arm and the attitude clothing. "Are you Mr. Butler?"

"No, I'm Tony Blankenship."

Beatrix recalled snippets of her conversation with Detective Aldrich. "Natalie Blankenship's brother?"

He held up his hands. "Hey, I don't do interviews."

"I don't want an interview," she snapped. "I want to see the owner. Pronto."

He squinted at her, then his expression opened. "You're Beatrix Carmichael."

She pursed her mouth, regarding the ex-con. Had he seen pictures of her while hatching his own plot to kill Raymond? "How do you know who I am?"

The man smirked. "Let's just say I've heard a lot about you."

She smirked back. "Nice prison tattoo. Is Mr. Butler in?"

"I'll tell him you're here."

Beatrix stayed within a one-foot circle as she waited, marveling at how some people made a living. She couldn't imagine being surrounded by junk all day long. Wheeling and dealing. Ugh.

"Mrs. Carmichael?"

She turned. The man was striking—dark-headed and dangerous-looking. "Yes."

"Brian Butler. My condolences on your husband's passing."

He had enough manners—or guilt—not to mention that she'd been arrested for helping Raymond pass. She shook his extended hand, wondering what violence the large extremity had recently wrought. "Mr. Butler, I understand you have some items in your possession that might interest me."

"Right this way."

She entertained the brief thought that the giant could be leading her to a stockroom to toss her into an airtight cooler, but she decided she'd just as soon die as conduct this humiliating exercise within plain sight of others. So she followed him down a hallway to a surprisingly neat office, away from the noise of the showroom. Her gaze immediately went to an organized collection of tagged items on his desk. To her relief, the Umbro bronze statue looked to be in good condition. Her trophy.

"Coffee?" he asked.

"No, I'd like to get this over with, if you don't mind."

He nodded and walked to his desk. "These are items that your husband pawned over the last year. I understand from Natalie that some of them might be yours."

"Yes." She fingered her mother's precious silver, her father's precious coins. "All of these things have been in my family for generations."

"I had already sold a few things, but I've contacted those customers, and I'm doing my best to get the items back."

"That's . . . very nice of you."

"How about I call off the pieces and you check them against this list?" He handed her a list identical to the one Natalie had faxed. "One Tiffany desk lamp," he said, his voice sounding tired.

"Wait a minute," she said, unreasonably embarrassed in front of this stranger. "Raymond's death left me in a bit of a cash crunch. I'm not sure I can afford to buy all of this back from you today."

"No matter." His smile was indulgent. "I've been in the position of relieving people of their family heirlooms, and it didn't suit me. Now, that was one Tiffany desk lamp."

"Here," she said, stunned by his generosity. As he wrapped the lamp in bubble wrap and placed it inside a small box, she wondered if he were simply trying to unload evidence that he'd had a business relationship with Raymond.

"One antique silver tea service."

"Here." He had to have an ulterior motive, but what was it?

"One Rolex watch."

Beatrix picked up the slim watch from a white jeweler's box. Her mind raced backward for an explanation, then leaped ahead in quiet triumph. "This is a woman's watch."

"Yeah, so?"

"It's not mine," she said. "When I saw it on the list, I assumed it was Raymond's, but it must be Natalie's."

"No, it isn't hers."

She lifted one eyebrow. "I hear you're in a position to know."

"What's that supposed to mean?"

The man truly seemed to be in the dark—was he playing her? "The police detective told me that you and Natalie are having an affair."

His face darkened. "Detective Aldrich is grasping at straws to make Natalie look bad."

"You're not interested in her?"

If possible, his flush deepened. "I'm only interested in being a friend to a woman who's gone through a rough time."

"Is that why you hired her ex-con brother to work for you?"

His jaw hardened. "We're getting off track. The watch isn't Natalie's because she said none of the items belonged to her."

Diamonds circled the face—the piece was worth at least five thousand dollars.

"Could it belong to, um . . ." He coughed.

"That other one?" She didn't bother to hide her disdain. Remembering the cubic zirconia ring Raymond had given the girl, she said, "Not a chance."

"I remember when Raymond brought in the watch," he said. "I told him I'd have a hard time selling something so pricey around here."

Beatrix smoothed a finger over the gold link band that moved with the ease of liquid, then held it up to the light. She smiled at the exquisite piece. The exquisite ticket to her freedom.

Twenty-eight

Ruby tried to read the small type on the piece of yellow paper the fat guy had given her, but the words all ran together. "You can't take my TV!" Mame echoed her distress by barking like a maniac at the guy's hairy ankles.

"Take it up with the finance company," the guy said, gesturing for his scrawny partner to squat and pick up the other end. "I just do what they tell me."

Ruby focused on the sheet of paper. *Repossess.*

"Hey, doll, does that mini-mutt have an off button?"

She picked up Mame and stroked her fur to quiet her pet and to calm herself. The police had confiscated her computer during their search Sunday—without the television, she'd be left with nothing to do except—gulp—*read.*

"How much money do you need?" she asked the men. She'd stuffed last night's tips inside her strawberry cookie jar, about two hundred in cash, plus a book of stamps.

"I need about a million bucks," Hairy said with a laugh. "But we can't take money, just the merchandise we came for. Sorry, doll."

Ruby chewed on her lip. How would she keep up with *Jeopardy*? "I didn't know we were behind on the payments." If the paper the man gave her was right, Ray hadn't made *any* payments.

"The wife is always the last to know," he said. With ferocious grunts, the two men lifted the massive TV and carried it out the door to a waiting van.

"It's not fair," she whispered, jiggling Mame and shifting from foot to foot.

The man returned, wearing a sad smile, and handed her a clipboard. "I need for you to sign here to say we took the TV."

She wiped her eyes and signed her name, dotting the "i" with a little heart.

The guy stared at her signature. "I *thought* you looked familiar—you were married to that Carmichael dude who had wives everywhere."

Ruby lifted her chin. "Just three."

"Man, that's low. I don't blame you dames for taking him out."

"B-But *we* didn't."

"Sure." Hairy gave her a big wink, like in cartoons. "Well, don't worry, doll. My sister did some time in the state pen for stabbing her roommate and she said it wasn't so bad. At least you'll have a TV. And cable. See ya."

"See ya." Ruby stood in the doorway and watched the van plow through the mudhole that was her front yard. Two days of rain had chased away bothersome reporters who had trampled her pink begonias, but left six inches of muck that gooped up her shoes when she walked back and forth to her Camaro. With their finger, someone had written WASH ME on the side of the blue car.

"Hey, Ruby!"

She turned to see Dudley Mays, her neighbor who owned only half a wardrobe—the bottom half. She guessed she should be thankful it wasn't the other way around.

"I hear you're single again," he said, grinning and rubbing his white belly.

The man reminded her of Ham—big and shaggy and greasy. A bad taste backed up in her mouth. "You might want to keep your distance, Dudley. My husband was murdered, you know."

It was a really ugly thing to say, but worth it to see the scared look on Dudley's face.

Ruby slammed the door behind her, then teared up at the sight of the living room, practically bare with the computer *and* the television gone. She dropped onto the couch, still holding Mame. What a crummy week. Well, except for the baby moving—that was cool. She'd known the cops would be ticked when she admitted to lying about killing Ham, but she hadn't expected them to slap her with an additional charge of conspiring to kill *Ray*, too. Billy Wayne said that if she were convicted on both charges, she could probably serve the sentences con—. . . con—. . . at the same time, and that they were likely to go easy on a pregnant woman.

But she wasn't so sure. And the three hours she'd spent in a jail cell after being arrested Sunday was enough to convince her she didn't want to go back, cable TV or no cable TV.

It had taken her hours to straighten up after she returned home—the police had messed up the place something awful. According to the form they'd left taped to the inside door, they were conducting a search for computer files, syringes, and heart medications. They'd taken the PC, a bag of syringes, and the calendar she kept on the refrigerator.

Mame squirmed out of her arms and Ruby sighed, already bored to death. Six hours to kill before going to the club. She guessed she might as well take a look at the mail that had piled up since the week Ray had died. There was lots of it. She took her time separating the heap into four categories: catalogs, missing children flyers, bills, and other stuff.

The catalogs were always neat. Lillian Vernon was her favorite, full of all those clever little novelty items—she loved the toilet tissue with trivia printed on it; she still had two rolls left in the master bathroom. And Frederick's of Hollywood was a dancing girl's best friend. Great shoes.

She squinted at the missing children flyers, studying the face of each little person, searching her memory in case she'd seen them on the playground in the trailer park. She couldn't bear the thought of tossing the slips of paper when she might be the one to help find one of them. No luck today, though.

Bills. Yuck. But she'd developed a system to make the job as fun as possible. First, she used a steak knife to slice open the envelopes, all of them. Then she opened the envelopes, and peeked at the bottom-line figure with one eye closed. Finally, she sorted the bills into three piles: doable, hopeful, and impossible. Since most of the impossible pile was credit cards that Ray had acquired in her name, he always took care of those. At least he was *supposed* to. Now that she thought about it, she *had* been getting a lot of calls from people saying she owed them money. Each time, she'd passed the info to Ray and he'd said he'd take care of it.

She stared at the ring she'd thought was a real diamond when Ray gave it to her. He'd told her a whole pack of lies. Had he lied when he told her he loved her?

Of course he lied, Ruby Hicks. Why would a man like Ray be in love with you, a little hick?

Ruby blinked back tears and added up the bills due with a big-button calculator. The sum was so humongous, she had to add the entire pile again just to be certain. When the same number came up, she covered her mouth with her hand. She made decent money at the club, but it would take her years to pay off this amount. Clothes, dinners, concert tickets, vacations.

Her stomach churned from the pressure—she had to make sure Mac was going to let her waitress when her pregnancy was beyond hiding onstage. Dragging the phone to her lap, she kept repeating to herself that everything would be all right, as long as she could keep working at the club, as long as her baby was healthy, as long as she stayed out of prison, as long as she was allowed to collect Ray's life insurance.

Jocko answered the phone and went to find Mac. Music played in the background while she studied her acrylic nails. The pink polish had been ruined when she'd tried to remove the black fingerprinting ink. She'd have to have them polished again before the weekend.

"What's up, Ruby?"

Uh-oh. Mac sounded cranky. Maybe she'd better wait and talk to him in person. "Um, I was just checking in."

"Checking in? You've never checked in be—never mind, I needed to talk to you anyway."

"Okay."

"I hate to do this, Ruby, but I gotta let you go."

Her heart plummeted. "Why?"

"Oh, come on, Ruby—you're under arrest, for Christ's sake. The police came here and searched your locker. It's bad for business, and it has the other girls shook up. Besides, pregnant strippers aren't as much in demand as they used to be."

"I can wait on tables, Mac. That's what I called to talk to you about."

"Forget it, Ruby. You're a swell gal, and I'll give you two weeks' base pay, but that's the best I can do."

Alarm numbed her, like cough syrup. "Please, Mac, I need the work."

"Sorry, sweetheart. Put me down as a reference. Gotta run."

"But—" He'd already hung up.

Ruby replaced the handset and sat silent while cold fury stirred inside her. Men. They thought they ruled the world. Using her. Telling lies. Discarding her like a piece of trash. Well, she hadn't survived poverty as a child to settle for poverty as an adult. Hugging her tummy, she whispered, "We're going to be all right, princess. We have to be."

She would think of something, even if she had to sit there for a half-hour. After all, desperate means called for desperate measurements. Or something like that.

Twenty-nine

"HOW'D THE POLYGRAPH test go?" Tony asked before Natalie could clear the back door. He did take the time to lean out and shoot the bird at a couple of reporters who lingered by the street.

"It didn't," she said, dropping into the first vacant chair. "My luck—the polygraph examiner had a court appearance, so they rescheduled me for next week." She laughed, a bitter sound to her own ears. "I can't believe the lengths a person has to go to in the legal system to simply tell the truth."

"So, where have you been?"

She rubbed her temples, thinking it might help the morning's news to sink in. "Want a good laugh? I drove to my office on a misguided mission to offer a hand to Dr. Skinner."

"And?"

"And I braved the reporters only to have Skinner hand me a letter from the state medical board." Natalie closed her eyes. "They've suspended my license to practice, pending outcome of the charges."

"I'm sorry, sis."

"No matter. Being a doctor was only the center of my existence." She blinked back fresh tears, wondering what kinds of new trades she might learn in prison—woodworking . . . auto body . . . flag-making. A fellow med student had once remarked that the worst thing about being a doctor was being able to recognize when you were losing your mind. Sometime during the past several days, she had at the very least misplaced hers, evidenced by her concession to have lunch yesterday with Brian Butler.

The meal hadn't been wholly unpleasant, but that was, she kept telling herself, because she'd forgotten how good a chili cheese hot dog could be. Which had nothing whatsoever to do with Brian Butler's imposing company, or his unexpected kiss, or even with the hot dog, for that matter—she'd simply worked up an appetite from all that kissing, er, gardening. *Gardening.*

She realized Tony was staring at her, and straightened. "Did you come home for lunch?"

"Not exactly."

At his sheepish expression, an alarm sounded in her head. "What is it?"

"I brought a visitor to see you." He nodded toward the front of the house.

She scowled—Brian Butler's presumption was absolutely galling. "You can *tell* your boss that I have *enough* on my mind without dealing with his *inept* attempts to win me over."

"It isn't Butler."

"Oh." Her scowl deepened. "Who then?"

"Beatrix."

"Excuse me?"

"It's Beatrix. She came by the pawnshop about an hour ago, then asked if I would bring her to see you."

"Why?"

"She didn't want her car to be spotted in front of the house."

She sighed. "I meant why does she want to see me?"

"She wouldn't tell me, except to say that it was important."

"I don't think she and I are supposed to talk."

Tony shrugged. "Tell her. She's in the library."

Nothing fazed her anymore, Natalie decided as she pushed herself to her feet. Not even entertaining her husband's wife in the library.

The bookroom, as Rose Marie had always called it, was on the front of the house, a left turn from the short hallway off the foyer. A black hand-tied wool runner softened her footsteps, and well-oiled hinges silenced her arrival. Beatrix stood with her back to the doorway, a streaming cigarette in one hand, a hardback book from an open moving carton in the other. From behind, she could easily pass for a woman in her thirties, Natalie acknowledged. Black continued to be the mainstay of the woman's wardrobe, probably unrelated to the fact that she was mourning her husband. Her blond hair was a convincing shade, precision-cut just above her collar in a chic pageboy. A woman of power, a woman in control, despite her arrest. Envy knifed through Natalie.

She must have made a noise because Beatrix turned, her eyebrows raised. A flat smile crossed her lips before she took another drag. "Sorry," she said then dropped the cigarette into a Styrofoam cup, eliciting a sizzle. "I seem to have taken a liking to these things again."

"They're bad for you."

"Yeah, well, everything that feels or tastes good is bad for you." She held up the hardback volume, the green cover hand-worn. "Edgar Allan Poe. Raymond's favorite."

"I know."

"Think it should have been a warning sign?"

"Maybe, on hindsight."

Beatrix caressed the book with a glassy expression. Natalie tried to imagine her sitting down to plot out Raymond's death, and the image chilled her.

"Are you moving?" Beatrix asked, gesturing to the boxes.

"Um, no. I hadn't gotten around to unpacking them all." Ironically, so many of her aunt's gardening books had been confiscated during the search, the shelves were now empty enough to accommodate Raymond's volumes. "We only moved here from St. Louis six months ago. My aunt left the house to me when she died."

"You and she must have been very close."

"We were."

Beatrix returned the book to a carton. "You've had to deal with much loss recently."

Natalie nodded carefully, spooked by the woman's calm demeanor.

"My mother used to say that tragedy comes in threes."

She managed a little smile. "Frankly, over the past several days, I've lost count."

Beatrix's dry laugh caught her off guard. "True. Natalie, we need to talk."

"I don't think that's a good idea."

"Because I was arrested for murdering Raymond?"

"Yes."

"Well, you were arrested for murdering Raymond, what's the difference?"

"The difference is that the cops didn't find a blueprint for murder under my mattress."

Beatrix dismissed her concern with a wave. "All that proves is that I *wanted* to kill him, not that I did." She quirked a brow. “And don’t tell me the thought never crossed *your* mind.”

Natalie blinked. It had. When Butler had revealed the extent of Raymond’s indebtedness, his betrayal had stirred a passion, an anger she’d never known before. She’d wanted to hurt Raymond, and since he was emotionally aloof—why had she just now realized this truth?—her first thought had been to hurt him physically. The impulse had been short-lived, but had she been in Beatrix’s designer shoes . . .

She indicated the blue loveseat on which she’d slept during those first hideous nights alone. “Would you like to sit?”

“No.”

“Okay, I’m listening.”

Beatrix inhaled and exhaled deeply, as if this entire ordeal were extremely bothersome. “Your brother probably told you I went to the pawnshop this morning.”

“Yes.”

“Your Mr. Butler showed me all of the items Raymond pawned recently—”

“He isn’t ‘my’ Mr. Butler.”

“Whatever. But there was one item I didn’t recognize.” She pulled a white jeweler’s box from her purse, and opened it to reveal a delicate gold watch. “Is it yours?”

Shaking her head, Natalie couldn’t resist picking up the lovely piece. “No.”

“And you don’t think it could belong to—that other one?”

“Ruby? No. Even if she or Raymond could afford it, somehow I don’t believe Rolex is quite her style.”

Beatrix smirked. “It could have been a gift to her from a grateful customer.”

Natalie shrugged agreement. "But not likely." The diamonds glittered back at her. "So if the watch doesn't belong to any of us . . ." Her mouth fell open. "There's . . . *another* woman?"

"Looks like it," Beatrix said.

"But the police scanned state records for other marriage licenses."

"Maybe he hadn't gotten a chance to marry her, or maybe he used an alias."

Her mind reeled—what *else* could happen? As soon as the thought was completed, she remembered her promise not to tempt fate. "We have to tell the police right away."

Beatrix scoffed. "We're under arrest for *conspiracy*—they won't believe that the watch doesn't belong to one of us."

"But they *have* to believe us."

Beatrix's color heightened and a muscle jumped under her left eyebrow. "Natalie, put yourself in their place. What would you think?"

She sighed. "That we were trying to throw them off."

"Right. Besides, the police are so content with us as suspects, they haven't even bothered to look into Raymond's business dealings."

Natalie tried to guess where the conversation was going. She couldn't. "But our lawyers will do their own investigations before any trial."

"How long will that take? And how much money will it cost?" Beatrix paced behind a table, shaking her head, her hands jerking. "No, I think we'd be better off trying to find this woman ourselves and see if she has information to help our case."

"Cases, plural. We can hire a private investigator."

"Oh? And do you have money?"

Natalie shook her head.

"Well, neither do I. On the other hand, I do have time. And motivation."

"And I have Raymond's travel log."

Beatrix stopped. "Well, it's decided, then. You and I can take a little road trip, retrace Raymond's steps, see what we find. How about it?"

The idea was simple to the point of absurdity. And absurd to the point of stupidity. Questions poked at her: Could she trust Beatrix? "But all I have are the travel logs—I don't know whom he called upon."

"He had a black leather organizer."

"I remember it well, but I don't know where it is."

"Probably in his briefcase in the car. The police haven't yet released the car or its contents to me."

"What about Raymond's company—they might help us if one of our lawyers called the home office in Louisville."

Beatrix coughed into her hand. "I think it's best if we don't tell our lawyers what we're doing."

Natalie gaped. "What? Why not?"

"The two of us going off to play P.I.—what the hell do you think they're going to say?"

She was right.

"Besides," Beatrix continued, "if we don't find anything, no one's the wiser. If we do—we'll present the evidence to the police."

"But if we don't know the people he talked to, the whole scheme seems moot."

"Let's think on that angle while we make plans. Can you leave in the morning?"

Natalie hesitated, then sighed—she had nothing better to do. "I suppose." But she didn't have a warm, fuzzy feeling about being alone with Beatrix for an extended period of time.

From the travel log, they determined that northern Tennessee would be the best place to start. Feeling like a cross between a Girl Scout and a fugitive, Natalie agreed to meet Beatrix at a bus station an hour outside of Northbend and go from there.

"Pack for two or three days, just in case," Beatrix said, all business now that a decision had been made.

"But what if my lawyer calls? And what should I tell my brother?" Why Brian Butler's face entered her mind, she couldn't fathom. She pictured him with a big frown on his big face—but *he'd* been the one to ask what she planned to do in her own defence.

"Tell them you want to get away for a couple of days by yourself, away from the reporters."

She could give them her cell phone number if they needed to contact her. "Okay."

And with that little word, a pact was made.

Beatrix returned the watch to its box.

"Won't we need the watch for identification?"

"I'll tell your Mr. Butler that I want to check it against my mother's jewelry inventory."

"He isn't 'my' Mr. Butler."

"Whatever. See you in the morning. Don't be late."

Thoroughly dismissed, Natalie had to catch herself to keep from relinquishing the library to Beatrix. But the woman snapped up her purse and strode to the door.

"I'll walk you out."

"Don't bother."

After the door closed behind her, Natalie stared, wondering what she'd gotten herself into. Two, maybe three days in the company of that woman? She needed a buffer. Maybe they could go in separate vehicles.

Tony stuck his head into the room to ask if she was all right, and she nodded, feeling somewhat buoyed. Maybe they wouldn't find anything at all, but at least she wouldn't feel so powerless.

At the sound of a sharp honk, she peeked from the side of a window shade to see Tony clearing a path through the media. Beatrix was nowhere to be seen—lying in the back seat, perhaps? At least the reporters wouldn't suspect a clandestine meeting and start a rumor that would alert the lawyers and the police.

Just to satisfy the nagging question, however, she picked up the phone and dialed Ruby's number.

"Hello?"

The girl was crying. "Ruby, it's Natalie. What's wrong?"

"Everything! My TV was repossessed, and I just got fired. Oh, Nat, this murder charge is ruining my life."

Imagine that.

"I didn't do it, Nat. I didn't kill Ray. You believe me, don't you?"

The childlike tone tore at her—Ruby was left with a burden neither she nor Beatrix had to contend with, the possibility of giving birth to a child in prison, an illegitimate child. "I want to believe you, Ruby. Tell me, have you ever owned a Rolex watch?"

"What kind of watch is that?"

"An expensive one, with gold and diamonds."

"No. I had a Betty Boop watch, but I lost it."

From the mouths of babes.

"I know this sounds awful, Nat, but sometimes I wish I'd never met Ray."

She knew the feeling. His life, and death, had been a catalyst in all of their lives, and not for the best, as it turned out. She felt deceitful that she and Beatrix were about to undertake a trip whose outcome could rightly affect Ruby just as much as it affected them. The girl sounded desperate—maybe she needed a distraction. Not to mention supervision. Since the girl had been fired, she wouldn't be missed at work. And frankly, as daft as Ruby could be sometimes, Natalie almost preferred her company to Beatrix's.

Except Beatrix would never go for it, not unless she could convince her that Ruby could contribute to the search in some way.

"Ruby, did Raymond tell you the names of anyone he saw or spoke to the week he died?"

"You mean like customers?"

"Yes, or acquaintances."

"No, but hold on a minute and I'll tell you."

Natalie frowned into the phone, wondering if Ruby had misunderstood the question. What was she doing?

"Nat? Do you want his schedule for the whole week, or just for that day?"

She wet her lips. "Ruby, how do you know Raymond's schedule?"

"It's right here," she said. "In his black organizer. He gave it to me in the hospital to put in my purse before you got there. I've been using it to prop up the TV 'cause the trailer leans a little, but I don't need it anymore."

Never one to ignore a celestial sign, Natalie asked, "Ruby, do you have plans for the next couple of days?"

Thirty

NATALIE EASED HER Cherokee into the parking lot of the appointed bus station, peering side to side for Beatrix's or Ruby's car. With a shaking hand, she pushed her hair behind one ear, and slowed to a crawl. She could still back out. Simply turn around and drive back to Smiley, or find a little resort hotel somewhere to spend a meditative weekend, like she'd told Tony she was going to do. She'd hated lying, but she didn't want to implicate him in their ruse in case they all went down.

In case they all went down? Good grief, she was starting to *sound* like a crook.

The sight of the silver Mercedes tucked between two mini-vans sent her heart rate skyward. What kind of masochist would embark on a road trip with her husband's two other wives?

A masochist desperate for insight into the man she thought she knew, a masochist desperate for insight into the kind of person *she* was to be so easily taken in by such a man. She sighed as she pulled the SUV into the nearest empty space. She needed peace, some semblance of control. And even if this stunt seemed like a bizarre way of achieving a measure of both, at the moment, it was the best offer on the table.

She didn't see Ruby's blue Camaro, but she'd told the

young woman to come fifteen minutes later so she'd have time to break the news of her joining them to Beatrix—not a task she was looking forward to.

Beatrix alighted from the car. Her outfit of dark glasses, black slacks, and white pearls were more befitting a magazine cover shoot than a weekend on the lam. Since she herself had dressed in black jeans, tennis shoes, and a loose denim shirt, Natalie decided she would probably get the dirty jobs, if there were any.

"I wondered if you'd changed your mind," Beatrix said as Natalie approached.

"I did, a dozen times."

Beatrix's smile was fleeting. "I hate to drive. Do you mind?"

"No, I'll drive."

"You do have air conditioning?"

"Yes."

"With individual controls?"

She pursed her mouth, then nodded. The trunk of Beatrix's luxury car popped open and Natalie stared at the three matching Hartmann leather suitcases. "I thought you said to pack for two or three days."

"I did."

She inhaled deeply. "Okay. Well, at least my Cherokee has plenty of room."

"I can't believe the luck of you finding Raymond's organizer," Beatrix said as she removed the luggage. "How did the police miss it when they searched your place?"

"It was, um . . . well hidden." She glanced all around, dreading how Beatrix would take the news.

Beatrix followed her gaze. "Don't worry, I don't believe anyone here will even notice us, much less recognize us."

"Beatrix, there's something I— "

The sound of a loud car horn trumpeting interrupted her. Ruby's Camaro rolled toward them, horn singing. Every person in the parking lot turned to stare.

Beatrix slammed her trunk. "What the hell is she doing here?"

"I was about to tell you— "

"Hi, Nat!" Ruby yelled through her open driver side window. Then her smile dropped. "Hi, Beatrix."

"She is not going with us," Beatrix said, arms crossed.

"Oh, yes, I am."

"Oh, no, you're not."

"Oh, yes, I am!"

"Oh, no, you're not!"

"Wait a minute," Natalie said, waving her arms. "Beatrix, I called Ruby to see if the watch was hers, then asked her to come with us. She has as much at stake here as we do, and she might be able to help."

"How could she possibly help?"

"She has Raymond's schedule book."

Ruby lifted the black leather organizer and waved it back and forth.

Beatrix stalked over to the car and lunged for the book. Ruby shrank back and Beatrix followed through the window, twisting and kicking, her legs off the ground. Natalie scrambled over to grab Beatrix by the waist and drag her out.

"You're creating a scene," she hissed. "Both of you!" She set Beatrix aside and told a wide-eyed Ruby to park the car. Ruby stuck her tongue out at Beatrix before driving off.

Beatrix righted her clothing, then gestured wildly after the Camaro. "I'm not going if she's going. How could you even expect me to?"

Natalie sighed. "She was fired yesterday. She sounded desperate when I called to ask about the watch."

The older woman rolled her eyes.

"And when I found out she had the organizer, I thought it would be a good idea to invite her along."

"But she's unbearable! Raymond's little knocked-up mistress-stripper! At least you're—"

Natalie lifted her eyebrows. "At least I'm what?"

"Tolerable."

"Gee, thanks."

Beatrix scoffed. "You know what I mean. Jesus, she's an embarrassment."

"So none of us would have picked the other two for friends," she said with a pointed look. "But maybe between the three of us, we can find a way out of this mess. Ruby might know something that she doesn't even realize is important."

"How can you be so sure that the little slut didn't stick Raymond like she did that other man?"

Natalie swallowed. "How can I be sure that *you* didn't stick Raymond and are simply trying to lead us off on a tangent?"

"But the watch—"

"The watch could be yours. You could be lying."

"*You* could be lying," Beatrix shot back. "You were growing the damn stuff that killed Raymond right in your back yard."

"My aunt was growing the stuff. I had no idea the plant was even in the garden, and wouldn't know how to get poison out of it even if I'd wanted to."

"But you had access to the drug."

Natalie crossed her arms. "So did you—your father was a cardiologist, and you used to work in a hospital."

Beatrix gave her a wry smile. "You don't honestly believe I killed Raymond, do you?"

She considered the woman thoughtfully, trying to read those ice-blue eyes that glittered like hard, clear crystals. The eyes of an angel? The eyes of a murderer? "I honestly don't believe that any one of us knows the other two well enough to be completely sure of anything. But maybe by the end of this trip, we will."

The older woman's mouth twisted in concession, but her body language screamed aversion. Natalie opened the hatch on her Cherokee and watched with no small amount of amusement as Beatrix lifted and thrust in her suitcases, none too gently. "If that little dimwit gets diarrhea of the mouth, I swear I'll duct-tape it shut."

"I'm ready!" Ruby tottered up to them, flushed and wearing strappy super-high heels, white spandex shorts, and a skintight pink T-shirt that read, "KENTUCKY—Fast Women and Beautiful Horses." The black words stretched across her chest were distorted almost beyond recognition, and she was not wearing a bra. Her hair flowed loose and luxurious. In addition to the enormous gold vinyl purse hanging from her shoulder, she carried a bulging blue athletic bag in one hand, and some kind of plastic carrier in the other. A split second later, Natalie's unspoken question was answered when a tiny black nose appeared through the vent in the side and an annoyingly familiar yap sounded.

"Miss Mame asked to go," Ruby said, smiling like an indulgent parent.

"I don't believe this," Beatrix muttered.

Natalie hesitated. "Ruby, I'm not so sure about traveling with a dog."

Her face crumbled. "Oh, but Miss Mame is almost like a person!"

"Yeah," Beatrix said to Natalie. "Didn't you hear her?—the dog *asked* to go."

"Oh, Nat, she'll be good, I promise! She'll sleep most of the time and she'll pee only when we stop to pee. Besides, I can't leave her here."

If this was any indication of what the rest of the trip would be like, Natalie thought, they could leave *her* here. "She'll have to stay in the back."

"You're not serious," Beatrix said.

"What choice do we have?" Natalie asked, her own ire escalating. She jammed her fingers into her hair. "Look, we can call off the entire trip and my feelings won't be hurt."

Beatrix and Ruby stared at each other with belligerent eyes. "Just stay away from me," Beatrix muttered.

"Gladly," Ruby said with a toss of her head.

Natalie exhaled. "Can we please go?"

Thirty-one

BEATRIX GROUND HER teeth. After playing *Jeopardy*, the travel edition, for the past seventy-five miles, Natalie had accumulated ten thousand six hundred in winnings, and she was a distant second with a lousy three hundred bucks. She looked out the car window and considered a timely jump—going into the hereafter merged with Tennessee State Road 22 might not be such a bad mode of delivery. Very down-home. Perhaps someone would erect a white cross that would have tourists asking, "What tragic accident took someone's life in that godforsaken spot?"

"Suicide," some old geezer would answer. "Woman threw herself from a car she was riding in with her husband's two mistresses, couldn't deal with the humiliation." When in truth, she couldn't deal with the entertainment.

"The answer is," Ruby said, her empty head stuck between the front bucket seats, "This former Marine allegedly shot President John F. Kennedy in Dallas, Texas, on November 22, 1963."

"Lee Harvey Oswald," Natalie offered.

"You're right!" Ruby said, grinning. Then she wagged her finger. "But you keep forgetting to put it in the form of a question. I'll have to count it wrong the next time. The correct answer is '*Who is* Lee Harvey Oswald?' " She bounced up and down on the back seat. "Next category, American history for four hundred."

Beatrix checked the glove compartment for duct tape, but came up empty. "Okay, enough with these inane questions."

"You're just sore because you're losing," the girl admonished.

"No I'm not."

"Yes you are."

"No I'm not."

"Yes you are."

"Yes you are."

"No I'm—" The redhead frowned. "Hey, you tricked me."

Not a gargantuan feat.

Ruby waved the question-and-answer cards. "Beatrix, you should be winning since you were alive when most of this stuff happened."

Killing her would be worth a second murder charge. "Shut. Up."

"Like, where were you when JFK was shot?"

"On the grassy knoll."

"Huh?"

Beatrix sighed. "I was in tenth grade geometry. Our principal came over the intercom crying, and sent us home."

"Golly. I hated geometry."

"Raymond always thought the CIA was behind the assassination," Natalie said, a pitiful attempt to salvage the derailed conversation. The corner of her mouth twitched.

"Well, if you ask me," Beatrix said, "Jackie had it done."

Ruby's eyes bulged. "You think?"

Natalie grimaced. "That's pretty twisted."

"Not when you think about what the woman must have

been going through—mistresses revolving through the White House, Marilyn Monroe in a gown made out of rice paper singing 'Happy Birthday, Mr. President'—it would make a wife testy."

"She might not even have known he was cheating," Natalie challenged.

Beatrix scoffed. "Of course she knew. All women know—"

"I didn't," Natalie said. "Did you?"

"Did she what?" the other one asked, obviously having problems keeping up.

Natalie had more patience than she. "Did Beatrix know that Raymond had women on the side?"

They both looked at her, eyebrows lifted. She stalled by rearranging her legs. "I suspected he hadn't always been faithful."

"Why did you suspect?" Natalie asked.

She shrugged. "Stereotypical cheating-husband behavior—traveling more, increasingly vague about his whereabouts, things like that. Did *you* suspect he was getting his bread buttered elsewhere?"

Natalie stared at the road, her knuckles white around the steering wheel. "Must you be so crude?"

"Just answer the question."

"I . . . deep down, yes, I guess I suspected lately there might be another woman."

Beatrix emitted a small laugh. "And neither one of us confronted him. Why is that?"

"Well, I wasn't certain," Natalie added quickly.

"What would it have taken to convince you?"

Her mouth flattened. "I don't know."

"Meeting his other wives in his hospital room?"

She squirmed. "You made your point. I was in denial."

Beatrix sent a smirk in her direction. "We both were."

"Over half of all married men have cheated on their wives," Ruby said.

"With you?" Beatrix asked her, feeling nicotine-deprived.

From the back, the mutt-mop started yapping as if someone had stuck a hatpin in its scrawny rump. The girl turned in her seat and cooed to the pooch, but the high-pitched yelping continued.

"Is there an eject button?" she asked Natalie.

"We're almost to Quincy. I think everyone is ready for a pit stop."

In an effort to block out the commotion in the back, she picked up Raymond's schedule book. By comparing it to the travel log that Natalie had found in Raymond's desk, they'd determined Raymond had spent the last day of his sorry life in the vicinity of Quincy, Tennessee, where, Natalie remembered from previous conversations with Raymond, Glomby Medical Center was located. He'd pursued the large account vigorously, she'd said, and was hoping to close an exclusive deal very soon. It was news to her, Beatrix admitted, but then again, she and Raymond rarely discussed his job.

For more than a decade, he had attended company functions alone—she'd hated mingling with all those cheesy salespeople he worked with, who were constantly "on" and making tasteless jokes about prostheses. When they first met, Raymond had told her and everyone else that he was working toward medical school, although transcripts of classes in progress never seemed to materialize.

And so Raymond wasn't a successful financier like Delia Piccoli's husband. Or a manufacturing guru like Eve Lombardi's husband. Or a tax lawyer like Toni Knipp's husband.

But she'd never been ashamed of Raymond, only sad that he settled for the occupation of prosthetic limb salesman, a job that allowed him to live vicariously through the surgeons he called upon, and to pick up an impressive vocabulary. At the club, he'd fallen short of introducing himself as "Dr.," but didn't object if someone called him "Doc"—in tribute, he said, to the time he resuscitated Marilee Waterson when she ventured into the deep end of the club pool. Personally, she thought Marilee was a two-bit actress—with plastic tits the size of hot air balloons, how could she have sunk? But Raymond swore she wasn't breathing when he'd put his mouth over hers. And he'd been dubbed a hero, the infuriating flirt.

She opened the schedule to the last week he lived. While in Quincy, they would check out the hotel where Raymond spent his final night, and, if necessary, retrace his route for the week in reverse order, moving west to east across northern Tennessee.

The banal margin notes in his tiny, cramped handwriting unexpectedly tugged at her heart. The scribbling of a man who expected to live: *Expense report. Software upgrade. Windshield wipers. Razors.*

She blinked rapidly, refusing to cry. *Oh, Raymond. If you'd only behaved yourself you'd still be alive.*

The dog was going absolutely berserk, and so was she. Beatrix twisted in her seat. "If you don't muzzle that yaptrap, I'll tie him to the luggage rack."

"It's a her," the redhead shouted.

She gritted her teeth. "Then I'll tie a bow in the rope around *her* neck."

The dog stopped, apparently realizing there was only room enough in the vehicle for one bitch.

"Told you she was smart," the girl sang, then held up her *Jeopardy* cards. "Want to keep playing?"

Beatrix grabbed the cards, zoomed down the window, and tossed them out, immensely gratified to see them scattering over the roadside behind them.

Ruby gasped and pressed her face to the side window. "You littered! And you threw away *my* game!"

"If you can breed with my husband, I can throw away your game."

Ruby looked to Natalie, as if the woman was going to take up for her, but Natalie simply glanced in the rearview mirror and shook her head in warning. Smart lady. The girl sat back in a huff, but at least she and her hound were quiet.

"Did you find anything new?" Natalie asked, nodding toward the schedule book.

"Not yet," Beatrix said, scanning the now-familiar pages for a name or personal scribble she hadn't noticed before. "Wait, here's something the day before he died, scratched out. I thought it was a mistake, but maybe it's a separate to-do item." She held the book at arm's length to scrutinize the tiny scribble in the corner of the page—damnable farsightedness.

"*Pick up roses for B-day*," Ruby said over her shoulder, without so much as a squint.

"Thanks," she said sourly. "My birthday was in April. Was he referring to one of you?"

Natalie shook her head. "My birthday is in March."

"February 29," the other one said, grinning like a fool. "I've only had five birthdays."

The maturity level matched. "Then ladies, we just might have a clue to finding the mystery woman. I doubt if Raymond would take roses to a client. Assuming the scratch-out means he bought the flowers versus changing his mind, there has to be a receipt or something." She rifled through pockets to come up with a few paper clips, a stick of gum, and a business card with familiar lettering. Slanting a look in Natalie's direction, she said, "Here's a card for your Mr. Butler."

"Who?" Ruby asked.

Natalie's mouth turned down. "He isn't 'my' Mr. Butler. I barely know the man, and what I do know, I don't particularly like."

"Who?"

"How did you meet him?" Beatrix pressed.

"Who?"

The woman's slender throat convulsed. "He . . . came to my office under the pretence of seeking treatment, then proceeded to repossess jewelry that Raymond had put up for collateral against loans."

"Jesus," Beatrix breathed.

The girl thrust her head between them. "*Who?*"

"A man who loaned Raymond a lot of money for gambling debts," Natalie answered, her cheeks aflame.

"So maybe *he* killed Ray."

Natalie wet her lips. "Brian—I mean, *Butler* was questioned by the police. He had an alibi."

"*Brian?*" Beatrix asked. "Sounds like the two of you are chummy."

"Is he cute?" Ruby asked, bouncing.

The SUV swerved off the shoulder, spewing gravel, then found blacktop again. Natalie's chin jerked up. "I will not dignify this discussion with a response. Need I remind you my husband was buried a few days ago?"

"*Our* husband," the girl amended, still bouncing.

"Did you forget to take your Ritalin?" Beatrix snapped. "Be still."

"Quincy city limits," Natalie said, sounding relieved. She stopped at a gas station so everyone could pee (at the sight of the bathroom, however, Beatrix opted for a smoke by the Coke machine) and to ask for directions to Glomby Medical Center. They threaded through a downtown area past an obscure state university before finding the astonishingly large medical center. The place must employ half the people in the area.

Natalie maneuvered the Cherokee into a parking deck, then cut the engine and turned to Beatrix. "Okay, what's the plan?"

Beatrix blinked. "Plan?"

"Who are we supposed to be? What's our story?"

"We need a story?"

Natalie pursed her mouth. "How else are we going to get in to talk to this, this—"

"Chub Younger," Beatrix supplied from the schedule book.

"How else are we going to talk to him about Raymond without raising suspicion?"

"I don't know."

Natalie leaned her forehead on the steering wheel and laughed. "This is crazy. We should just go home and turn over Raymond's schedule and the information about the watch to the police."

"We've been through that," Beatrix said. "We're already here, so let's think of a way to check out these leads. If it doesn't work out, then we'll be back home by dinnertime and at least we know we tried."

Ruby's head appeared. "What if we pretend we're reporters doing a story on the hospital?"

"Fine," Natalie said. "Except they'd probably hand us off to public relations, and even if we did get to interview this Younger fellow, how would we get him to talk about Raymond specifically?"

"Well, what if we tell him we're from Ray's company and that we're taking over his arms and legs accounts?"

Beatrix scoffed. "And with that mastery of medical terminology, I'm sure he wouldn't suspect a thing."

"Besides," Natalie said, "his company would've already sent out a rep to pick up such a big account."

Snapping her fingers, Beatrix said, "Natalie, you're a doctor, for heaven's sake—you should be able to get in and talk to just about anyone. We'll split up, and keep our eyes peeled for a fading bouquet of roses on a woman's desk."

Natalie lifted her head. "You think the woman he gave the roses to is here?"

"According to the schedule, he was supposed to meet Chub at nine o'clock in the morning, and we know he spent the night here. It makes sense that he gave the flowers to someone in Quincy, maybe to someone at the medical center."

"*If* he bought them."

"And if he bought them," Beatrix continued, "maybe he bought them here, too. I'll see if the center has a gift or floral shop and snoop around. You try to find Chub."

She opened the door, but Natalie stopped her. "What if we get caught snooping?"

She shrugged. "Say you're lost, and don't give your real name."

"Oh, just like *Charlie's Angels*," Ruby cried, then clapped her hands.

"And Red goes with you," Beatrix said pointedly. "Do you have a lab coat?"

Natalie sighed and nodded.

Beatrix brightened. "How many?"

Thirty-two

"THAT WAS A CINCH," Ruby said as they exited the medical center. She smoothed the sleeve of her white lab coat, marveling at how smart she felt—and looked, judging from the admiring glances she'd gotten in the halls. To look busy while Natalie made inquiries, she'd listened to her own heartbeat with the stethoscope Natalie had loaned her from her doctor bag.

"We didn't get anything concrete," Natalie said. "Our luck that Mr. Younger isn't in the office today. We should have called."

"But at least we know where to find him tonight," Ruby said. She was tempted to ask if she could keep the beautiful white lab coat, but she didn't want to be rude to Nat, who had been nice enough to loan her a long black skirt and baggy blouse to look "respectable," as Beatrix had put it.

"And we might even have fun," she added, skipping ahead two steps before she remembered that doctors didn't skip. She slowed and walked beside Natalie who remained silent, her forehead crinkled, until they reached the parking deck.

Beatrix was pacing next to the SUV, smoking a cigarette that she stubbed out as they approached. "Did you talk to Mr. Younger?"

Natalie shook her head. "No, he's at an off-site meeting. But his secretary said tonight he'd be at a place called Razor's—maybe we can catch him there."

"Razor's?"

Beatrix yanked open the door to the Cherokee. Miss Mame commenced to bark her happiness that they were back, but stopped when Beatrix hollered and bounced an empty pop can off her carrier. Beatrix rummaged around the floorboard, coming up with Ray's schedule book that was still a little dented from the weight of her big-screen TV. Boy, did she miss that TV.

She flipped through the pages furiously, then stopped. "Here it is. A note on the page for the day before Raymond died. It says 'Razors.' I thought it was a shopping list, but maybe he was supposed to meet someone there."

The phantom woman they kept talking about? Ruby bit into her lip. Wives were one thing, but she was really going to be ticked off if Ray had a girlfriend on the side. "Did you find a flower shop?" she asked Beatrix.

Ray's wife looked at her for perhaps the first time without complete disgust in her expression. Ruby swallowed—the woman actually looked . . . excited.

"Yes, and I hit pay dirt. Raymond did buy the roses there—a dozen red ones. The woman couldn't remember the exact day, but she remembers he bought them late in the day and that he paid cash."

For a few seconds Natalie looked as if she might start bawling, but suddenly her chest expanded, then she exhaled. "Guess we might as well check into the hotel and see what we can find out there."

Ruby smiled—someday she wanted to be smart and strong like Nat. "Can we share a room?" she whispered as they climbed inside the SUV. "I don't have very much money."

Natalie stared, then gave her a small smile and nodded. "I don't have very much money, either."

And as it turned out, Beatrix had to stay with them too because there was only one room available, one with two double beds. Beatrix was super irritated and demanded that she at least have her own bed. And they had to put down an extra fifty-dollar deposit so Miss Mame could stay in the room with them. It was almost all the money Ruby had, but they promised she'd get it back if Mame behaved. Once they got to the room, she sat her pet on her lap and had a little talk with her, then, just to show her she was still mama's precious little lovebug, Ruby changed her hair bow to pink with white polka-dots.

Afterward, she went into the bathroom and gave herself an insulin shot, then unpacked her gym bag so the medicine could work before they left to find something to eat. The other women had already unpacked, and Beatrix's stuff was everywhere. She'd used all the hangers, and left one little drawer for her and Nat to share. As she compared their clothing, embarrassment burned in her stomach. Next to Beatrix's plain, expensive flats and Nat's comfortable-looking loafers, her white plastic high-heeled sandals looked cheap. Beatrix had brought slacks, Nat, khakis, and she, short shorts. Beatrix had hung a bag made out of soft leather on the back of the bathroom door to hold her toiletries. Natalie's cloth bag with clear pouches that held her bathroom items sat on the vanity. She, on the other hand, had crammed her stuff into a Ziploc freezer bag. How did these women know what to buy? Who taught them how to be classy? Was it something they were just born being? If so, she was sunk.

Nat appeared in the open door. "Ruby, are you feeling okay?"

She nodded. "Just unpacking."

"How is your blood sugar level?"

"Normal. I checked it a few minutes ago."

Nat tilted her head. "That skirt suits you."

"Really?" Ruby breathed. "It's nice and soft."

"Keep it."

"But I didn't get it dirty or anything."

"That's not what I meant. I want you to have it."

Her jaw dropped. "Really?"

"If you want it. Are you ready to get something to eat?"

Stunned at her generosity, Ruby could only nod. A knock sounded at their room door. "I called houskeeping for more hangers," Nat said, then disappeared.

When Ruby emerged from the bathroom, a maid was putting extra towels and hangers on the foot of a bed. Beatrix stood close by, holding a twenty-dollar bill in her hand the same way a customer at the club would hold a tip if he wanted her to see it and do something special to get it.

The woman looked all around at the three women, her eyes wide. "Did you need anything else?"

"Information," Beatrix said, unfolding her wallet to show a picture of Raymond. "Do you remember this man? His name is Raymond Carmichael."

The maid nodded. "Mr. Carmichael comes here every few weeks for a night or two. He always asks for extra towels, too."

"Is he always alone?"

The maid looked nervous. "You'll have to ask the front desk about that."

"We did, but we thought you might know more ... details." Beatrix put away the picture and waved the twenty.

"Are you the police or something? Is this man a criminal?"

"We're gathering information for the police," Beatrix said with a straight face.

Wow, she was an excellent liar.

"And, yes, Mr. Carmichael might be a criminal. If you know anything, you have to tell. But the police don't tip."

Ruby almost felt sorry for the woman, who looked as scared as a chicken the day before Thanksgiving.

"Mr. Carmichael does have company sometimes," the maid said. "That's why he needs extra towels."

Natalie covered her mouth with her hand. Beatrix looked shaken, too, but asked, "Have you ever seen his visitor?"

The maid shook her head. "No, the person is always in the bathroom when I come to his room. I just know it is a woman, I smelled the perfume."

"Did Mr. Carmichael have company the last time he stayed here, a couple of weeks ago? It would have been on a Tuesday night."

The woman licked her lips. "I was working, and I delivered extra towels. He was alone ... but he was expecting someone."

"How do you know?"

"There was a vase of red roses on the table. I made a joke about someone sending them to him, but he laughed and said it was a special occasion—he was going to propose."

Her heart squeezed painfully at the news. Nat's eyes watered. Beatrix sat down heavily on the bed, jangling the hangers. "D-Do you know if this woman arrived?"

"No. But when I came to clean the room the next day, it

was a mess. The roses were all broken up, petals everywhere. Shame, all that money wasted. But I didn't tell my boss because I didn't want to cause trouble for Mr. Carmichael."

"Was there a card with the flowers?"

"Not that I remember."

Beatrix extended the twenty-dollar bill, which shook like a leaf in December. "Thank you."

The woman vamoosed, and for a few seconds, the only sound in the room was the newscaster on the twenty-four-hour-a-day news channel that Natalie had turned on. Why anyone would want to watch news all the time was beyond her. Not when the Cartoon Network was available.

"And now to state-by-state news," the anchor said. "In Tulsa, Oklahoma, a farmer has harvested an apple that weighs in at nearly fifteen pounds. In Paducah, Kentucky, the three wives of a bigamist have been charged with his murder. In Tecumseh, Washington, a festival . . ."

Nat stabbed a button on the TV and the picture went black.

"I can't believe the bastard was going to marry again," Beatrix murmured. "The man had gonads the size of bowling balls."

Looking deathly pale, Nat hugged herself. "At least we can go home now."

Beatrix frowned. "Go home?"

"We have enough evidence to give to the police—there was another woman in Raymond's life, and something happened between them the day he died. Let Detective Aldrich sort it out, I just want the conspiracy charges dropped, so my life can get back to normal."

Beatrix's laugh was raw. "Let Detective Aldrich sort it out? I say we keep digging until we find out something concrete about this woman—a description, a name. We know she was here with Raymond, so there has to be someone in this town who saw them together. Maybe she *lives* here." She stood, a little wobbly. "Besides, I don't know about you, but I could use a drink."

"I'd like to take a shower," Nat said, heading toward the bathroom. "Suddenly I feel very dirty."

The bathroom door closed and Ruby swallowed at the prospect of spending time alone with Beatrix. The woman could strike at any time. But Beatrix sat at the table squeezed in the corner of the room and studied Ray's schedule book—it was as if she and Mame weren't even there. Which allowed her to give Ray's wife a good looky-loo.

In her younger days, she must have been a headturner, because she actually was pretty decent-looking—when she wasn't frowning.

"What?" Beatrix asked, startling her.

"What?"

Beatrix sighed. "*What* are you looking at?"

"Your hair. It's really nice—what color do you use?"

"It's natural."

"Oh, come on."

She patted her hair. "Viva Ashe, number seventeen."

"Can I feel it?"

"What?"

"Your hair."

She sighed again. "Christ, go ahead."

Ruby fingered the strands, squinting to pick up all the highlights. "Wow, no split ends, and your scalp is so nice and pink—do you use a conditioner?"

"Er, yes."

"Great texture. Have you always been blond?"

"Yes."

"Did you know that blondes have thirty percent more hairs on their heads than brunettes?"

"No."

"Well, they do. Have you had plastic surgery?"

"That is *so* none of your business."

"I wondered because you look pretty good, considering your age and all."

"Gee, thanks."

"How old are you?"

"Didn't you bring a coloring book or something to play with?"

Ruby retreated and lay on her stomach on the bed closest to the window that looked out over the parking lot of a Laundromat. Mame whined until she put her on the bed with her, and the dog snuggled next to her ribcage.

"That just became your bed," Beatrix muttered. "Keep that mutt off the other one, which is mine."

Ruby shifted to find a more comfortable spot on the mattress. The baby moved a couple of times a day now, little flutters like bubbles being blown into a glass of milk. Too bad Ray wouldn't be around to see his own little girl, but if he was planning to marry someone else anyhow, he wouldn't have had much time to spare. She sighed heavily, hurt that he would take another wife after he'd said vows with her only two months ago. She loved Ray—their wedding had been the happiest day of her life. She'd felt special in her white satin dress and with a big bow in her hair. Now she only felt . . . discarded. Like trash. Like always. She sighed again.

"Stop that," Beatrix said, not looking up.

"Stop what?"

"Stop making that pitiful little sound—Natalie isn't here to fall for it."

Ruby lifted herself on her elbows, cupping her chin in her palms. "Why do you hate me?"

Beatrix finally glanced up. And frowned, of course. "I don't hate you."

"Yes, you do."

She shrugged. "Okay, I hate you."

"But *why* do you hate me?"

Beatrix looked up, her eyebrows knitted. "Because you talk too much, you're too young, and you're not very bright."

"I know," Ruby said, then bit into her lower lip. "I'll bet you were smart when you were my age, weren't you?"

Beatrix got the strangest look on her face for the longest time, then she looked away. "No." Her voice suddenly sounded weak and a little scary. "No, I wasn't very smart when I was your age. In fact"—a small laugh escaped her—"I'm not very smart now."

Ruby stared. "How could you say that? You're rich—you live in a mansion and you drive a ritzy car. I bet you even went to college."

Beatrix nodded, but her smile was wry. "To get an M.R.S. degree."

She knew her eyes were bugging, but she couldn't help it. "That sounds really important."

But the woman only laughed. "M-R-S, as in 'Mrs.' I went to college to find a husband."

"Oh."

"But I didn't. I dated a few young men, but they all were more interested in my daddy's money and influence than in me."

"Until you met Ray?"

She nodded, then puffed up her cheeks and exhaled. "I thought he was different, but turns out he was simply a better actor."

Actor was a classier word than liar, she supposed. "Are your parents both gone, Beatrix?"

"Yes. Yours?"

"I never knew my father, but my mom is still kicking. She hasn't much cared for me, though, not since she thought I killed Ham Jackson. We don't talk, unless she needs money."

"That's . . . terrible. Does she know you're having a baby?"

"Oh, yes, I told her right away. Invited her to my wedding, too, but she didn't come."

"What kind of wedding did you have?" Beatrix asked, and really looked interested.

"We went to a justice of the peace—it was over in about six minutes. But I did wear a white dress, and Ray looked so handsome, I thought I would die." She closed her eyes, remembering. "He had this way of looking at you—"

"That made you feel like you were the most special woman on Earth."

She opened her eyes. "Right!"

"Raymond had that effect on almost every woman I know."

Wistful, Ruby said, "I'll bet you have loads of friends, don't you?"

She laughed, the way a person would laugh at a stinky joke. "Oh, sure. As we speak, all of my so-called friends at the club are gathering firewood to burn me at the stake."

"Because they think you murdered Ray?"

"No, because having a member who was married to a bigamist is too scandalous."

"But you didn't know—it wasn't your fault!" Miss Mame barked her agreement. "Gee, I thought rich people were at least nice to *each other*."

"Well, we're not. But to be fair, a conspiracy to commit murder charge isn't in keeping with the membership code of conduct."

"Belonging to this club must mean a lot to you."

She studied her perfect manicure. "I suppose."

"I wanted to be in Beta club when I was in school, but I wasn't smart enough, or popular enough."

"I figured a girl who looked like you would be plenty popular."

Ruby swallowed her surprise—she'd sounded only a tiny bit mean. "I d-didn't have the right clothes, and . . ." She couldn't very well tell her she stank beause her mother hardly ever paid the water bill. *Stinkin' hick*. "Well, you know better than anyone how important that stuff is for other people to be nice to you."

"Yes," Beatrix said, but her voice was faint and she looked to be about a million miles away.

"Don't worry. The police are bound to drop the murder charges when we tell them everything we find out. Then the people in your club will come around."

"Unless," Natalie said from the doorway, knotting the ties of her robe, "the police track down this woman and arrest her too, then say all four of us were in on it."

With the dark circles under her eyes and her wet hair slicked back, she looked like a skinny raccoon wearing terry cloth.

"Jesus, you might be right," Beatrix said.

Nat sighed. "I keep thinking this mess will get better. Instead, every day brings a new nightmare."

"Meanwhile, Raymond is probably charming the devil's daughter out of her pitchfork."

Natalie sat down on the other bed. "Why do you think he deceived us?"

Beatrix sat back in her chair. "Money and power. Wouldn't you say that most men fantasize about having a harem?"

"But why do you suppose he chose *us*?"

"You're assuming he didn't love us," Beatrix said dryly.

"I'd say that's a given," Natalie murmured, her eyes bleak.

"If you're asking if I think he picked us because he thought we'd be easy to fool, then I'd say yes."

Ruby's vision blurred. "You mean he thought we were all . . . dumb?" *Dumb Ruby Hicks, she's such a hick.*

"Dumb and willing to settle for a superficial relationship," Beatrix said.

"Our relationship wasn't superficial," Natalie whispered.

Beatrix sat forward. "Did you fall in the shower and hit your head? He lied to you, woman. He lied to all of us. He screwed around, he took our money, and he destroyed our reputations."

Nat looked positively ill. "I meant I didn't *realize* our relationship was so superficial. God, how stupid could I have been?"

"Well, we're all less stupid today," Beatrix said, pushing herself up from the chair. "Which is why we have to get ourselves out of this predicament we allowed Raymond to put us in. She moved to stand in front of Natalie. "Agreed?"

Ruby scrambled off the bed, not about to be left out of

the huddle. "Agreed," she blurted out, then put her hand palm-down in the middle of the circle.

Nat squirmed a little, then put her hand on top of Ruby's. "Agreed."

They both looked at Beatrix, who sighed and put her hand on top of theirs. "Agreed, already. Let's go—I'm thirsty."

Thirty-three

"I LOOK RIDICULOUS," Natalie said, fingering her hair self-consciously as they walked through the crammed parking lot toward Razor's Restaurant and Bar, which, according to the noise and the neon, was the happeningest spot in Quincy, Tennessee.

"You look righteous," Ruby squealed, proud of her handiwork. "A puff of mousse, a little teasing, and your hair is twice as big."

Big was right. She could feel the draft on her scalp as the warmish night air filtered through her high hair. Dread had settled in her stomach when Ruby begged to fix her up. But at the time, it seemed more expedient to acquiesce. Besides, she simply couldn't bear to extinguish the light in the young woman's eyes.

"At least no one will recognize you," Beatrix whispered.

"Gee, thanks," she lisped, unused to the slick gloss Ruby had applied to her mouth. Her skin felt a little stiff from the makeup, and her eyelashes were heavy with mascara. "You don't look much like yourself tonight, either." Beatrix had donned a pair of designer jeans that flattered her slim figure, and topped them with a blue silk blouse. Her jewelry was large and flashy, and she smelled extremely . . . *beguiling* for a woman who'd been recently widowed.

"Yeah, well, while in Rome . . ." Beatrix said unconvincingly.

Natalie marveled at the change in her. The woman was even insulting Ruby less, although she *had* threatened to strangle the dog with her pantyhose just before they left the hotel. Natalie shot a quick prayer upward that the room would be intact and odor-free when they returned.

"Beatrix, what kind of perfume are you wearing?" Ruby asked.

"Sterling. It's a custom blend I've worn for years."

"It smells dynamite—I'll have to drag the cowboys off the two of you," she said with a grin as they walked into the dim interior.

Natalie rolled her eyes and nearly slammed into someone who appeared to be waiting with dozens of others for a table.

"Oh, good Lord," Beatrix muttered. "It's a barn."

The country-western bar was indeed a barn, or at least used to be. Exposed rafters, rough-hewn board walls, sawdust on the floor. The twangy song playing over the stereo must have been a popular tune since several couples were dancing in sync in a sawdust-free area. Line dancing? One would assume.

Natalie scanned the smoky interior and tried to imagine Raymond hanging out in a place like this, but she couldn't. At least the mystery of the country music CDs was now solved—he must have spent many hours at Razor's, but was he entertaining Chub Younger in hopes of closing a deal, or was he rendezvousing with, as they'd dubbed her, the rose lady?

Maybe he'd met the rose lady while shmoozing with Chub. Her mind spun with unanswered questions and new revelations. She was most astounded that the hurt of hearing he'd been about to marry yet another woman had washed down the shower drain with what she promised herself were the last tears she would ever shed over Raymond Carmichael. Anger had settled in her heart, pushing out the anguish, and the yearning. Now she just wanted back the life she'd lost to a lie. And next time—no, wait, there would be no next time.

"Hidy," shouted a chubby woman who appeared to be the hostess. Her full-skirted red gingham dress was a questionable management choice, but she seemed resigned to it *and* the black patent leather flats. "You gals come for dinner? We're backed up about an hour, but you're welcome to wait in the bar."

They garnered quite a bit of attention as they settled themselves on stools at a tall, sticky table in the bar. Her skin prickled, and she grew warm enough to discard the thin cardigan she wore over a sleeveless blouse, but she didn't dare. Out of the blue, Brian Butler's mocking face popped into her mind, but she blamed it on being in a place a man like him would probably find appealing. Although he seemingly doted on his nieces, she would wager he was no angel, and escaped frequently to indulge in baser pursuits.

From the way he behaved when she had foolishly allowed him to stay for lunch the other day, it was clear Brian thought she was ripe for the picking. Poor pitiful Natalie needed to be rescued. She had replayed the kiss in her mind a couple of dozen times—but only to figure out how she might have circumvented the encounter. On hindsight, closing the door in his face when he first arrived would have been prudent.

Well, as Beatrix had observed, she was growing less stupid every day.

Feeling daring, she smiled at the waitress taking their drink order. "White zinfandel, please."

"We got beer and hard liquor," the girl said, her nasal voice impatient.

"I . . . rum and Coke." She'd never drunk a rum and Coke in her life, but she was having one tonight. Beatrix ordered gin and tonic, Ruby ordered a diet soda and fried cheese to munch on since dinner was another hour away.

"We're looking for a man named Chub Younger," Natalie said. "Do you know him?"

"Know him?" the waitress asked, then snorted. "The beast is married to my sister." She narrowed her eyes. "What do y'all want with Chub?"

"W-We don't know Mr. Younger. We're trying to find a friend of his, Raymond Carmichael."

Beatrix whipped out a photo, but the woman shook her head. "I don't remember seeing the guy around, but that don't mean he ain't been here. Chub will be dragging his fat ass in about nine, when the karaoke starts."

"Karaoke?" Beatrix asked.

The woman cocked out her hip. "Where've you been? It's where anybody who thinks they're a star gets on stage and sings to taped music."

"They give you the words and everything," Ruby added.

"It's cheaper than a band," the girl said. "I'll be right back with your drinks."

Natalie glanced at her watch. "So we have about an hour to kill before we're seated and before Chub gets here."

"Why don't we split up," Beatrix suggested, "and start asking if anyone knows Raymond?"

"Men only," Natalie said. "We can't run the risk of inadvertently asking the rose lady and spooking her."

"Do you really think she's here?" Ruby asked, panning the crowded room.

"I can't decide whether or not I want her to be." Natalie scanned the masses, stopping on every woman. Which one would have caught Raymond's eye? The platinum blonde two tables away, or the voluptuous raven-haired woman who sat next to her, giggling. Since he already had a blonde, a brunette, and a redhead, what was left—an international flavor? And if his pattern of choosing younger and younger wives held true, the rose lady would be too young to even be *sitting* in the bar. She sifted the information and pivoted, keeping her eyes peeled for preteen albino females, but came up empty.

"Here you go," the waitress said, plunking down their drinks. The first sip of the rum and Coke crossed her eyes, making Beatrix laugh.

"You'll get used to it," she said, taking a healthy swallow of her own drink.

Natalie didn't think so, but when they left Ruby to eat her cheese while they canvassed the room, she sipped more for courage.

The first few men she approached seemed willing enough to talk, until she told them she was looking for a man—someone other than them.

"Ah, why would you want some other man when you could have me?"

And: "I'm right here, sweetie, and he ain't."

And: "If the man stood up a purty thing like you, he don't need to be found."

Fifteen fruitless inquiries and a half-empty glass later, Natalie escaped to the bathroom, which was mercifully empty. She stripped off the cardigan and fanned herself in a futile attempt to lower her body temperature. With a moistened paper towel, she dabbed at her neck, then stopped when she caught a glimpse of herself in the cloudy mirror.

Dark blue eyes bugged back at her. That . . . that . . . *vamp* was her? No wonder those men were coming on to her—she looked as easy as a paint-by-number kit. Okay, the color in her cheeks was becoming, but the rest of her . . . well, okay the hair wasn't as horrid as she'd first imagined, but the red lip gloss . . . well, actually she didn't look half bad, dammit. And didn't she have the right to not look half bad? She wasn't married. Hell, she'd never *been* married. And she had needs, like any red-blooded woman in her mid-thirties. In fact, she had no emotional or legal strings to keep her from going out there and dancing with the next man who asked her.

The ringing of her cell phone in her purse reverberated off the tile walls so loudly, she nearly dropped her drink. Tony—she'd forgotten to check in this afternoon. By the time she fumbled the phone to her ear, it had rung five times.

"Hello?" she gasped.

"Natalie?"

"Tony?"

"No, it's Brian."

She frowned into the phone. "Brian who?"

"You're very funny, you know that?"

"How did you get this number?"

"It sounds like you're in a cave."

"Why are you calling?"

"To check on you."

"To check up on me?"

"That's not what I said."

"I'm hanging up."

"I wish you wouldn't."

"*How* did you get this number?"

"I called your house to see how you were doing, and Tony said you'd taken off for a couple of days of peace and quiet."

The bathroom door opened, ushering in a blast of music. Three women practically fell into the room, laughing and shrieking. Natalie tried to cover the receiver, but she should have known that Brian Butler's big ears would pick up on the noise.

"Gee, if you wanted music and screaming, you should've come to my house for the weekend."

In one heartbeat, dozens of taboo scenes passed through her mind.

"Jeanie and Ally would've been happy to oblige," he continued.

Natalie closed her eyes and swallowed. She was drunk. "I have to go."

"When will you be home?"

She blinked at his implied familiarity. And the fact that she . . . liked it. She took another deep drink from her glass, just as Ruby and Beatrix walked in. They stared, eyebrows up. She swallowed guiltily.

"Natalie? Are you there?"

"Yes. I'll be h-home in a couple of days." Was that squeaky voice hers?

"Can I see you when you get back?"

"What?" She tapped her finger against the mouthpiece. "My phone is breaking up, we'll finish this conversation when I return. Good-bye . . . you."

"Good-bye, Natalie."

She disconnected the call and pointed to the phone. "My brother," she said.

Beatrix squinted at her. "Our table is ready."

"Well, what are we waiting for?" Natalie asked cheerfully.

"You," Ruby said, taking her arm. "Are you all right?"

"Absolutely."

"How's Tony?"

"Tony?"

"You said you were just talking to your brother—do you have another brother?"

"Um, no. Tony's fine." She downed the rest of her drink, then tossed the ice into the sink. "Did either of you find out anything?"

They shook their heads.

"Me neither. Guess we'll have to wait for Chub."

She scrupulously avoided eye contact with Beatrix during dinner, afraid the woman would see deep into the recesses of her mind where she replayed the abbreviated conversation with Brian at least, oh, forty-three times.

Home?

"That has to be our man," Beatrix said, pointing her fork toward a hefty man who parted the crowd with handshakes and backslaps as he moved toward the bar. His head jerking around at the shout of "Chub!" confirmed the suspicion.

"Do we have a plan?" Ruby asked. She was looking a little fuzzy around the edges. Wait a minute—she hadn't even been drinking.

"I think only one of us should approach him," Beatrix said. "If he's been following the news, he might recognize us, especially if we're together." She turned to Natalie. "You go, you don't look like yourself."

"Thanks."

"You look great," she added quickly.

"Thanks again." She stood, then swayed when the alcohol rushed to her brain. "But I think I'm drunk."

Beatrix frowned. "You can't be drunk, you've had two lousy drinks."

Compared to Beatrix's . . . she'd lost count.

"Hurry before his sister-in-law tips him off."

"Okay. You can pick up the tab." Natalie grabbed her purse and made her way toward Chub, touching every table in between for stability. By the time she reached the table where he sat among mixed company, however, she identified the need to sit down before she fell down. Luckily the seat next to Chub was empty. She swung into it without warning, then smiled up at the surprised man.

"Hello," she said.

Chub recovered quickly. "Well, howdy, little lady. I haven't seen you in here before."

"First time," she admitted. Perhaps Chub Younger had once been a good-looking man, but he now had a twitchy, rawboned look about him that repelled.

"Name's Charles Younger," he shouted over the music.

"But his friends call him Chub," a man next to him yelled.

Chub elbowed him out of hearing range. "Call me Chub," he added. "What's your name?"

"Um . . . Marie. Yes, my name is definitely Marie."

"What are you drinking, Marie?" He cupped his right hand over his wedding ring.

"Rum and Coke."

Chub flagged a waitress and ordered her drink, and an extra shot of whiskey for himself. "Helps me loosen up," he explained.

"For what?"

His chest puffed out. "I'm going onstage here in a few minutes. I'm a singer."

"Really."

"Yeah. I've sung in all the best nightclubs in Nashville."

"So what are you doing here?"

He blinked. "Well . . . life on the road is tough, see, so I decided to slow down a little." He flashed a killer smile.

The waitress tossed their drinks on the table as she sashayed by. Natalie sipped hers, aware her mind was already gummed up. It was, however, amusing to realize she could still keep up with a stone-cold-sober Chub. He tossed down the whiskey, winced, then wiped his mouth with his sleeve just as the fleshy hostess appeared onstage to announce open-mike karaoke.

"Any requests?" Chub asked her. The man had incredibly small teeth.

She only knew one country music song from her youth. " 'Harper Valley PTA.' "

His eyebrows shot up. "Are you sure?"

She nodded, enjoying herself now.

"Okay. I know that one." He pushed away from the table and bounded onstage.

He was dreadful. Back-chilling, vision-blurring dreadful, although he deserved points for his enthusiastic gestures to the words, and sheer nerve, considering the song was supposed to be sung by a woman. But the crowd was either too polite or too drunk or too hungry to throw their food, and he received a respectable smattering of applause as he left the stage.

"Wha'dja think?" he asked as he dropped into his seat.

"Nashville's loss," she managed to say, still tingling with embarrassment for the clueless man. But at least the performance had sobered her enough to come up with a story. "Listen, um, Chub, I'm looking for a friend of mine and I was told you could help me out."

"I'll sure try."

"I was supposed to meet Raymond Carmichael here, but he didn't show."

His eyes widened, then he shook his head. "I hate to tell you this, little lady, but Raymond's dead."

She feigned surprise. "Dead?"

"Yep. Murdered by his three wives."

"Three wives?"

"Yep. Man was married to all three of them at the same time, can you believe it? I've got one and that's e—" He stopped, realizing he'd almost spilled the beans on his marital status. "I mean, uh—"

"Oh, that's just terrible." She made a face. "Raymond was going to introduce me to a friend of his, a lady he said could get me a job."

"What kind of work do you do?"

"I . . . make things. I'm sorry about Raymond, but I *have* to talk to this woman, and I don't know her name. Would you have seen them together? She might be a local."

"I don't know who she could be." He snapped his pudgy fingers. "Wait a minute! I saw Raymond the night before he died, right here. He'd been after me for months to sign a deal with his company—I'm the head of a big medical center in town—and I finally agreed." He frowned. "At least I think I did—we were both plenty drunk."

She gave him an encouraging smile, but her heart pounded in anticipation.

"Anyway, since I'd picked him up at the hotel, I offered him a lift back, but he said he already had a ride." He grinned. "Good thing, too, since I ended up taking a cab. But from the look Raymond gave me, he was going to get lucky."

She swallowed. "Did you see who he left with?"

"Nah. He left the bar alone, and was still standing outside when my cab came. But when my cab pulled away, I looked back and saw him getting into a car."

She tried to be calm. "What kind of car?"

"Red Ford Taurus, looked like a rental." He shrugged. "Sorry, I didn't see the face of the driver."

She wrote down her cell number on a napkin. "Will you call this number if you find out who she is? I simply have to find this woman—Raymond promised me she had the position of a lifetime."

"Okay," he said, stuffing the napkin into his pocket. He pointed his pinkie toward the stage. "Wanna sing a duet with me? Do you know 'The Woman in Me'?"

"Um, no. Thanks for the drink." She pumped his hand and grinned like a fool, hoping the man would come through for her with a name, but doubting it. She looked over his head for Beatrix and Ruby, found them, then jerked her head toward the bathroom.

"Okay," Chub said, then gave her a hopeful smile. "See you around?"

"Definitely," she said, then made a beeline for the john. Well, her bee was a little inebriated, so it took longer than she'd planned, wobbling and fending off a handful of invitations to dance and share a table. The women were waiting inside, feet tapping.

"Well?" Beatrix asked. "What did you find out?"

Natalie sighed. "Not much." She repeated Chub's bits of info as they listened.

"So," Beatrix said, "all we have to go on is a red rental car? The woman isn't from around here if she's driving a rental."

"Maybe her car's in the shop," Natalie said with a shrug.

"Or maybe she doesn't want her real car to be spotted," Ruby suggested.

"At least we have something to go on," Natalie said. "We can check out the rental places tomorrow."

Ruby looked at her watch. "It's too early to go back to the hotel, but I don't want to stay here—it's kind of creepy being where Ray was. Let's check out that dance place we passed on the way here."

"I don't dance," Beatrix said. "At least not to that freaky new music."

"Oh, come on, let's have some fun." Ruby shook her booty for encouragement.

"I said, I don't dance."

"We can drop you off at the hotel," Natalie suggested, not about to squander what might be her last weekend of freedom.

Beatrix inhaled and exhaled deeply. "All right—only because I refuse to spend the evening with a damn dog. But I *don't* dance."

"We won't laugh," Ruby said, her expression sincere.

"I don't think I should drive," Natalie said, holding the keys out to Ruby. "Can you?"

"Gee, I've never driven anything but a stick shift, but I'll try." She skipped ahead to the parking lot.

Beatrix crossed herself. Natalie laughed and pulled her in the direction of the Cherokee.

Thirty-four

When Natalie pulled under the carport Sunday in the early afternoon, her chest felt lighter and her head clearer than in ages. The weekend adventure that she'd embarked upon with such trepidation had turned into the emotional and physical release she hadn't even realized she needed. After leaving Razor's Friday night, Ruby had driven (and she used the term loosely) to the dance club, where they had partied like the loose women they weren't. Beatrix had discovered that she could dance after all. Ruby had discovered that she could dance with her clothes on. And Natalie had discovered that she could dance without a partner.

They'd fallen into their room late and laughing, she and Ruby and the pooch shared one bed, Beatrix sprawled across the other. But she and Ruby had both gotten a kick out of waking up to find Miss Mame curled snugly around Beatrix's shoulder. Still determined to track down the rose lady, they had checked with the three local car rentals, which revealed nothing. At a loss what to do next, they elected to kill the day shopping—Beatrix had sprung for makeovers at a Clinique counter—before taking in a chick flick and gorging on popcorn.

This morning they'd slept in before piling into the Cherokee and heading home. They'd passed the time exchanging stories about their courtships with Raymond, his good and bad habits, even his idiosyncrasies in bed.

"Lights on," Beatrix said.

"Water on," Natalie added.

"Toupee on," Ruby said, and Natalie had run off the road.

"I didn't know he wore a toupee," she and Beatrix had cried in unison.

"It was a good one," the young woman offered.

All in all, it had been a very . . . *satisfying* weekend. They had gathered enough evidence, in her opinion, to warrant a meeting with Aldrich and the D.A. as soon as possible. And despite their marked differences in age and personality, they'd actually, well, gotten along. Attributed, most probably, to the fact that they had more in common right now than any three women on the planet.

Tony wasn't home, although she didn't mind the quiet of the big house since she was fatigued from driving. He'd left a note on the table, though, asking her to call him at the pawnshop when she got home. Remembering that Brian didn't work on weekends, she judged it safe to call and punched in the number.

"Butler Family Pawn, Brian speaking."

She hung up. Tony was probably busy anyway.

The phone rang, and she winced, but answered. "Hello?"

"So you're home," Brian said, his voice smiling. "I thought it might be you, so I hit star sixty-nine."

"How convenient. I thought you didn't work weekends."

"I just stopped by to pick up a deposit. Are you free?"

"If you mean am I not in jail at the moment, then yes."

"Good, because I was thinking about driving to Shakerag

to check out an estate jewelry sale, and I'd like a second opinion."

"On whether you should go? Absolutely, go."

He laughed. "On the jewelry. I can pick you up in ten minutes."

"I thought you were Mr. Mom on the weekends."

"The girls went to my mother's house for a few days."

"That's nice."

"How about it? I could use the company."

"But I just walked in the door. I'm tired. And cranky."

"You can sleep on the way if you want."

"I snore."

"That's okay, I'm hard of hearing."

"You must be."

"Wear comfortable clothes." Then he hung up.

She hesitated ten seconds before bounding up the stairs.

Thirty minutes later, they were on their way to Shakerag. "My father always told me not to trust men who drove vans."

He smiled. "I'll add that to my list of things to tell Ally and Jeanie."

Their photos were taped to the dashboard of the dilapidated van, both grinning, one front-toothless. "You miss them."

"Not sure what I did before they were with me. Life has a way of forcing you into situations that make you a better person."

"Is that my pep talk for the day?"

"No. I didn't figure you'd need one after a weekend of peace and quiet."

"You're right."

"Good." He tilted his head at her. "Whatever you did, it put some color in your cheeks."

"I could be running a fever," she said, willing away the blush.

"Guess that means another kiss is out of the question."

She dragged her gaze from him and looked out the window. "I wouldn't be much of a doctor if I started an epidemic."

His laugh boomed around them. "So, what were you really doing this weekend?"

"That's none of your business."

"You're right, but I'd like to know. I might be jealous."

He was so ridiculous, she couldn't suppress her smile.

"Whatever that thought is," he said, "hold it for the rest of the day."

"I didn't realize I was such a morose person."

"Understandable, but temporary, I hope. Did you change your hair?"

"No."

"It looks good."

"Thanks."

The blush held fast for the remainder of the drive, and while they inspected the hodgepodge of jewelry at the out-of-the-way estate sale. "What do you think?" he asked.

She shrugged. "Well, I don't know much about jewelry, but the sapphire tennis bracelet is nice."

"Excellent eye." He picked it up, along with six other pieces and paid a man after some good-natured dickering. She watched him, fascinated at the easy way he had with people. They gravitated toward him. *She* gravitated toward him.

On the way back, they picked up chicken salad sandwiches from a hole-in-the-wall grocery and ate them sitting on the grass at a roadside park.

"This weekend I went to find out about someone . . . else . . . Raymond might have been involved with," she confessed.

"Does this have anything to do with the ladies' watch?"

"You knew?"

"Pretty coincidental that Mrs. Carmichael discovered the watch, asked to hang on to it for a few days, and then you disappeared. I figured you were either chasing down information or had sold the watch and both of you split." He grinned. "I was really hoping you hadn't split."

"Because I owe you so much money?"

"Because you owe it to yourself to see your name cleared."

She smiled. "Hopefully that will be sooner than later."

"You found this woman?"

"No, but enough leads, I think, to get the police off our backs."

"So both other wives went too?"

Natalie nodded.

"What a motley crew."

"As strange as it sounds, I actually enjoyed myself."

"Now that I'd like to see."

"What?"

"You enjoying yourself."

The air was summer-sweet, the sun beating down. Natalie chewed her sandwich slowly and studied the big, handsome man sitting across from her. "Then take a look at me now."

"I've been looking." His Adam's apple bobbed. "I missed you."

She tried to laugh, but failed. "I was only gone for a couple of days."

"You're habit-forming."

And to her dismay, his face had been hovering less than a split second away from her mind over the past few days, too. Natalie shook her head and looked away. "This is crazy."

"What? Being honest? I'm not very good at playing games."

She glanced back. "I mean this—" She gestured vaguely between them. "Is too soon."

"I'm getting old and wise. When I find something good, I don't keep browsing."

Natalie sighed. "Brian, you know what I've been through—what I'm still going through. I'm not exactly in the most healthy frame of mind here."

He abandoned his sandwich and leaned forward to brush her cheek with his thumb. "I figure that's the only way I have any chance at all."

She laughed, and it felt so good just knowing she *could* laugh. "I can't promise you anything," she whispered, leaning forward.

"I'm not asking for promises—yet." He touched his lips to hers, then captured her in a hard, pent-up kiss and eased her back into the soft, fragrant grass. He moved against her, slow, but resolute. He communicated his desire for her with his hands, his mouth, the desperate noises in his throat. She responded in kind, wanting, needing whatever comfort and strength and pleasure he had to offer. His body hardened against her, and they instantly remembered where they were.

"Come on," he said, pulling her to her feet, then tugging her toward the van.

As giddy as a naughty teenager, she ran with him, her body singing for a thorough release. She was single. She was aroused. And she was entitled.

He locked them in the back of the van. Amidst cardboard boxes and furniture, Brian dropped to the carpet and pulled Natalie on top of him. They kissed and rolled around with abandon, bumping knees and elbows, shedding clothes haphazardly. His physique was a magnificent master plan of rugged muscle and dark skin, powerful enough to render her weak-kneed, adept enough to make her cry out. He strummed her pliant body to a fever pitch, then lifted her to straddle him. He ran his hands over her slight curves with reverence and authority, murmuring words of appreciation and encouragement as she slowly accommodated his sex.

When at last they were joined, he breathed her name with joy. She'd never felt so thoroughly desirable, and the knowledge stripped away her inhibitions. With nothing at stake and nothing to prove, she allowed her starved instincts to take over. Fantasies took wing—she wanted an experience to savor in the dark days ahead. They locked gazes as she rode him to mutual completion, jarring and noisy and profound.

Depleted, she fell forward onto his chest, drawing the scent of their sex into her lungs. He stroked her hair and moaned as their bodies recovered. She dared not move, lest she have to leave the immunity from the world that his arms provided. But even as she reveled in the heat of his skin, the crushing weight of accountability descended on her bare back.

"My father was right," she muttered against his collarbone.

"Hmm?"

"Never trust a man with a van."

He laughed heartily, but her only consolation was that tomorrow she would be less stupid.

Thirty-five

"WE CHECKED OUT the three car rentals in Quincy," Natalie told Detective Aldrich and the rest of the group assembled, "but none of them could or would give us any information." Still, she felt almost light-headed with relief over the revelation. The police would rush off to find the mystery woman. The conspiracy charges would be dropped. Her life would return to normal. Brian's face flashed in her mind, triggering a smile. Maybe better than normal.

But the detective tossed down his pencil and leaned forward. "That's because most people won't divulge confidential customer information to anyone except *the police*!" He pushed himself up and paced the room. "I ought to have the three of you arrested for, for . . . meddling!"

"Now wait just a minute," Masterson said. "Maybe they went about it the wrong way, but you can't dismiss the information these ladies uncovered. Perhaps *you* should explain how three women were able to track down information you and your men weren't."

"Because," Aldrich said, leaning on the table, "they're lying."

She made fists under the table.

"We are not!" Ruby said, then elbowed her lawyer.

Billy Wayne jerked awake. "Yeah. We are not."

"This from a woman who lied about killing another

man?" Aldrich threw back. "You're already facing a murder charge, missy. You'd better think twice before bringing more trouble on yourself."

Natalie strove for a calm voice. "Detective, you can check out our story. You'll see we were together in Quincy over the weekend."

"And all that proves," he said, "is that the three of you were together long enough to cook up a good story. Don't you see how you're damaging your own case?"

"We brought this information to you in good faith," she said through gritted teeth. "We were trying to help."

He scoffed. "Trying to help yourselves by creating this phantom woman."

Frustration drove her to her feet. "What kind of man are you? Why are you so determined to ruin all of our lives? I swear on everything I hold sacred that we did *not* conspire to kill our husband. If your office could get their act together enough to schedule a polygraph, you'd know that."

Aldrich didn't even flinch, but at least she had managed to silence him.

District Attorney Keane cleared his throat. "Perhaps you'd better let them in on the new evidence."

"New evidence?" Gaylord asked.

Natalie tensed. What now?

Aldrich hooked his thumbs through his belt loops. "We finished analyzing Mr. Carmichael's car—the brake line had been cut, which probably contributed to his accident. *And* we found Mr. Carmichael's toiletry kit. One item contained enough ouabain to trigger those heart pains, a bottle of—" He consulted a sheet of paper. "Sterling For Men cologne"

She sucked in a sharp breath.

"*Beatrix, what kind of perfume are you wearing?*"

"*Sterling. It's a custom blend I've worn for years.*"

She looked at Beatrix, who sat rigid. A horrible suspicion washed over her. Betrayed again?

"I thought your M.E. said Mr. Carmichael was *injected* with the poison," Masterson said suspiciously.

"Secondarily. The M.E. theorizes that whoever put the ouabain in the cologne probably thought it would kill him."

"But a person can't absorb enough ouabain through their skin to kill them," Natalie murmured, still staring at Beatrix. The woman swayed.

"Right," Aldrich said. "But it would've been enough to trigger the pains that he complained of after the accident. The injection finished him off." He looked at them in turn. "Well, what do the three of you have to say for yourselves?"

Her mind raced, tossing out all the little tidbits she should have picked up on.

Beatrix had discovered the watch and convinced her it belonged to a mystery woman.

Beatrix had suggested the road trip and led them straight to Quincy.

Beatrix had deciphered clues from Raymond's schedule book, and supposedly talked to the flower shop owner.

Beatrix had sent her to ply Chub Younger, because she knew the man didn't know the rose lady.

Because *Beatrix* was the rose lady.

She stood, her throat convulsing, and nearly tripped over her chair. "You did it," she whispered. "You set us up as alibis to support this ridiculous idea of another woman."

"That's not true," Beatrix said, but her voice was small.

"She wears Sterling cologne," Ruby blurted out, standing. "She told us while we were in Quincy."

"Mrs. Carmichael, did you buy the cologne for your

husband? We've already contacted the boutique listed on the label for their sales records, but you can save us some time."

"Yes," Beatrix said, her face pasty. "I bought the cologne for Raymond. But that doesn't mean I poisoned him. And I d-don't know anything about a b-brake line."

Natalie's heart fell.

"Mrs. Carmichael," District Attorney Keane said, folding his hands. "We have a murder checklist in your handwriting, listing several ways you could kill your husband, including tampering with his car and poisoning him."

"I was angry," she said. "But I could never kill my husband. My therapist told me to write down things to get them out of my system."

Natalie ran her hand over her eyes. Not Beatrix.

"Mrs. Carmichael, we confiscated medical books from your home which listed uses and sources for ouabain."

"Th-those were my father's reference books."

Natalie choked on a lump in her throat.

"Tell me, Mrs. Carmichael—do you think we found your fingerprints on the cologne bottle?"

Beatrix fingered a strand of blond hair behind her ear. "I suspect so—I sometimes helped Raymond pack."

Say it isn't so, Beatrix.

"Mrs. Carmichael," Keane said gently. "Is there anything you'd like to tell us?"

Gaylord placed a restraining hand on her arm, but she waved him off and wiped her eyes. "You don't understand," she said, her voice strained and squeaky with emotion. "I did *plan* to kill my husband. But someone else beat me to the punch."

Her words were miserably unconvincing, evident by the look on everyone's face. Natalie closed her eyes. *Not you, Beatrix. Not you.*

Thirty-six

"It's only temporary," Beatrix lied to Rachel. "As soon as this mess is cleared up, I'll bring you back full-time."

Rachel wiped a tear and bobbed an awkward curtsy. "Yes, ma'am."

She pressed an envelope into her faithful housekeeper's hand. "Good-bye, Rachel."

"Good-bye, Mrs. Carmichael. I will pray for you."

She certainly needed all the help she could get, earthly and otherwise. "Thank you."

Rachel was almost out the door when she turned back. "I almost forgot to tell you, Mrs. Carmichael—your corsage for the club gala is in the door of the refrigerator, and your dress is on the back of the sitting room door. Have a wonderful time."

She swallowed. "I will."

When the big door closed, the hollow sound reverberated through the two-story entryway. She wasn't sure how long she stood listening for . . . something, anything. Any noise to prove that she wasn't completely alone in this monstrosity of a house, that if she fell and broke her neck right now, she wouldn't lie there until the mailman noticed an odor.

When the phone rang, she practically sprinted to answer it, hoping it was Natalie, but knowing the chance that the woman would talk to her again was slim to none. "Hello?"

"Beatrix, this is Jim Fiske."

Oh God, more financial problems? "Yes, Jim, what is it?"

"Same as before, except worse. Your debts are sky-rocketing, and your cash is nil."

"I let my housekeeper go," she snapped. "What else do you expect me to do?"

"For starters, cut up your credit cards," he said sternly. "And you might consider, um . . ." He cleared his throat.

"Consider what, Jim? Spit it out."

"You might consider getting a job."

She dropped into the club chair next to the phone. "What?"

"A job. You know, something that brings in money on a regular basis."

"Jim, things couldn't be *that* bad."

"Beatrix, you're going to have to face the facts. Your trust is almost gone. Except for the house, most of your assets are depleted, and your joint accounts are frozen. Meanwhile, there are Raymond's medical bills, his funeral bills. And Gaylord can't work for free forever. You have eight weeks before the trial starts, so I'd suggest that you look for a job. Besides," he added, his voice gentled, "if you stay busy, it'll help to keep your mind off things."

She'd never felt this disoriented without the benefit of alcohol. "But who would hire someone about to go on trial for murder?"

"Use your contacts at the club, call in a few favors."

"But it's been a long time since I worked. I mean, I don't know how to do anything." God, she sounded pathetic.

"Everyone can do something, Bea. Think about it."

So she spent the afternoon sipping gin and thinking about what she'd like to be when she grew up. Armed with pen and pencil, she came up with a short list: owner of an exclusive clothing boutique, personal assistant to the governor, or chef in a four-star restaurant.

She smiled. A chef . . . It was meant to be. For years she'd been gathering cookware and appliances, unwittingly leading up to the day when she would need them. Driven by her sudden enthusiasm, she abandoned her gin and headed to the kitchen to unpack some of her goodies. Two hours later, she was surrounded by grills, steamers, roasters, toasters, basters, broilers, cookers, pots, and pans. At first she tried to keep up with the instruction booklets, but after a while, they all ran together so she figured she'd just learn by trial and error.

Her first mistake, however, was microwaving a cup of coffee so hot that it burned her tongue when she tasted it, burned her hand when she jerked it away, then burned her foot when she dropped it. She tossed a roll of paper towels on the floor to soak up the worst of the mess, then limped upstairs to run a bath.

In the light of Fiske's call, tonight's gala would be more than a venue to show everyone she was alive and thriving. She would make discreet job inquiries of longtime acquaintances, make up something about her trust being frozen or whatnot. In fact, one of the owners of the famous Fenneck's restaurant had worked with her on a fund-raiser last year. And hadn't Sasha Cummings' father just opened a French restaurant?

Warming up to the idea of actually working, she bathed and dressed with care, glad she'd had her hair and nails done yesterday, before Fiske's call. The black and red Denali gown had been a coup on her last shopping trip to Atlanta. It would be the talk of the ladies' lounge, she was sure.

The worst moment of her lengthy preparation was the realization that she would have to drive herself. Gaylord and Fiske both had plans, and there was no money for a limo. Her arrival would be compromised, but on the other hand, she might garner even more attention and sympathy for not making a spectacle.

Yes, she decided. Driving herself in the Mercedes would be . . . demure.

So, duly preened and polished, she pinned on her own corsage, then tucked her skirt inside the car and drove herself to the Northbend Country Club.

Situated strategically on a rolling hill, the lights of the clubhouse welcomed members and teased outsiders for miles. A line of limos and luxury cars crawled up the winding driveway that rivaled Lombard Street in San Francisco.

At the bottom of the hill, Beatrix was waved down by the guardhouse attendant, smartly outfitted for the formal occasion.

"Evening, ma'am. I'm collecting invitations."

She laughed merrily. "I forgot mine, but my name is Beatrix Richardson Carmichael. If you'll check the program, you'll see I'm presenting an award named for my father, Dr. Neil Richardson."

The young man dutifully checked the program.

"I'm sorry, ma'am, but the program says Mrs. Robert Crenshaw is giving out the award."

Big-breasted Mrs. Crenshaw—the woman she watched grapple with her father years ago from her hiding place in the silver cabinet. How despicable.

She conjured up a sweet smile. "That's because I wasn't going to be here due to a death in the family, but I changed my mind."

The youth scratched his head. "I don't know, ma'am."

Beatrix narrowed her eyes. "If you don't get out of the way, I'll put a tire motif on those rental shoes, got it?"

He jumped back and she rolled through the gate, fuming. How dare they not send her an invitation! But when she pulled up to the valet, she alighted elegantly, holding her head high and bestowing gracious smiles all around. Couples stacked up outside the door, waiting their turn to be announced. She was prepared for stares and whispers, and she got them.

"Can't believe she's here, with all the trouble she's in."

"Husband barely cold in the ground."

"She put him there, you know."

Delia Piccoli and her husband stepped down to meet her, but instead of a greeting, their expressions were cold.

"Hello, Delia, Monty."

"Beatrix," Delia whispered. "You shouldn't be here."

"But I'm feeling fine. And I wouldn't miss presenting the service award named after my own father."

"No, I mean you shouldn't be here," the woman said with harshly outlined lips. "Your membership was suspended."

"Oh, and I suppose *you* had nothing to do with that." Beatrix drew her red silk wrap tighter around her shoulders and stared at Delia. "Step. Aside."

Murmurs zipped through the crowd standing behind Delia, all of them having been guests in her home at one time or another. Monty walked toward a security guard with purpose in his stride.

"Don't make a scene," Delia said quietly.

"Don't make a scene?" Beatrix shouted, gesturing to the crowd. "You hypocrites, hiding behind your drug habits and your wife-swapping. You would pass judgment on *me* before I'm even convicted?"

Delia pulled back and touched her diamond necklace with her black-gloved hand. "God, you were always so crude."

"And according to Eve's husband, Delia, you were always so *limber*."

Shocked gasps filled the entryway.

Eve Lombardi stepped up with a swish of black skirts. "Go home, Beatrix. You're not wanted here. Go home to your empty house."

Beatrix's head jerked back as if she'd been slapped. The notion that these people, any of them, had ever been her friends was laughable. Of course, she couldn't fault them totally—she'd not given as good as she'd not gotten. She stared at them, turned out in designer finery for a good cause to cover their black hearts.

Monty Piccoli returned with a security guard who said, "Mrs. Carmichael, I'm afraid I'm going to have to ask you to come with me."

Still gaping at the crowd, Beatrix threw off his hand, then stumbled backward to escape the ugly truth. She wasn't as bad as they were. She was worse.

She couldn't get away fast enough, screeching tires—and driving like a madwoman down the zigzag driveway. Her mind screamed with all the mistakes she'd made in her life, all the people she'd slighted, all the good deeds she'd turned her back on. When she was gone, would a single person say she had made a difference in their life? Tears of disappointment in herself streamed down her cheeks. She headed for the country, hoping a peaceful night drive would restore her sanity before she had to return home.

Go home to your empty house.

She rolled down the windows and pulled the skirt of her obscenely expensive gown to her knees, then lit a cigarette. She found an oldies station on the radio, and leaned her head back, her eyes open just enough to see the road. When had she made such a mess out of her life? When she'd cast her eyes in the direction of Raymond Carmichael? When she'd caved to her parents' request to move back home? When she'd drawn her first breath?

No, it would be too easy to blame her catastrophic existence on Raymond. In truth, she probably would have been just as miserable being married to any number of men. What she got was exactly what she deserved for relying on people around her to make her happy.

She wanted another chance. The priest in Paducah had absolved her for plotting to kill Raymond, and Gaylord remained optimistic that she would be acquitted. The D.A. had offered her a plea bargain, but she refused to spend one day in jail if there was a chance she would be exonerated.

A sour odor wafted up to wrinkle her nose. Gawd. Was it coming from under her seat? She held the steering wheel with her smoking hand while she bent and searched with the other hand. Her fingers met a moist, soggy ball of something. "Ugh." She yanked it out, then stared at the rotted yellow apple, stem and leaf still intact, but shriveled and oozing. Cursing, she tossed the mess out the window, then rummaged in the console for something to wipe her hand. When she came up empty, she shrugged and wiped the sticky decay on her gown. What the hell.

A car zoomed up behind her and turned on its bright

lights. She winced, then slowed down to let it pass. It didn't. Beatrix sped up, and so did the car. Her first instinct was irritation, but then she realized the rotten apple had probably bounced onto the car's windshield. The driver probably thought she'd done it on purpose.

She slowed to a less than normal speed, knowing the driver would eventually tire and go around her. Sure enough, after a mile or so of tailing her with the brights on, the car made a move to pass her. When the car pulled abreast of hers, she decided to offer a wave of apology, else she might never have seen the gun.

Funny how the brain can register so many details in a split second. The flash of gunfire, the black mask of the shooter, the color and make of a car: red Ford Taurus, probably a rental.

Thirty-seven

RUBY SQUINTED, CONCENTRATING hard on keeping the bright red fingernail polish off the cuticle of the big square hand she was working on. Finished at last, she exhaled.

Laverne pulled back her hand, studied her nails, then smiled. "You're hired."

"Really?"

"Really, doll."

"Oh, thank you!" She hugged the Amazon woman, then tilted her head, taking in the big-boned features, the heavy makeup, the elaborate hair. "Are you a man?"

Laverne laughed heartily. "Not for much longer, if I can help it. I'm scheduled to have all the plumbing rearranged this fall, but I'm still going through debriefing."

"Debriefing?"

"You can't just up and decide you want to change your sex and then go do it—you move toward trans-sexuality one step at a time. The clothes and the hair were easy. Then came the hormones, ay-ay-ay. Then I had to change my name legally to a feminine form. Like it? And now I'm in the last stage—living and working as a woman."

"Wow. I don't think I'd go to all that trouble just to be a woman."

Laverne gave her a once-over. "Looks like it comes pretty easy for you, doll."

"I'm pregnant."

Her new boss smiled. "Congratulations."

"Do you think the fumes of the polish and the remover will hurt the baby?"

"No problem." Laverne snapped her fingers. "We'll get you a surgical mask to wear. You'll be working the tanning booth, too, but it'll be in the next room. Your resume says you have experience running one?"

"Yeah, I had one in my guest room for a while, but it got repossessed the other day."

"When can you start?"

"Right now. I really need the money."

"Wish I could offer you permanent work, but I just need a fill-in until Janeece gets back from her honeymoon."

"That's fine."

Laverne looked at her hard. "You look so familiar."

"I've been in the news some lately."

"Ruby Hicks," she murmured, shaking her head.

"Not as Ruby Hicks, as Ruby Carmichael. My husband died and I found out he was married to two other women."

"Oh, honey, that's *you*?"

She nodded.

"What's going on with that now—weren't you all arrested or something?"

"Yeah. First, I'm supposed to tell you that I killed a man when I was sixteen, and I'm on probation."

"Did he deserve it?"

"Did he ever."

Laverne shrugged. "Works for me."

"They dropped the conspiracy charges against me and

the second wife for killing our husband, but I still might have to testify against the first wife when the trial starts."

"You don't look too happy about it."

"I'm not. Beatrix is . . . okay. My Shih Tzu likes her."

"Oh. But the woman killed the father of your baby—he is the father, yes?"

She nodded. "I can't explain it. It's like me and her are attached somehow, and I don't want to see anything bad happen to Beatrix."

"You're a real sweet person, Ruby. What happened to the second wife?"

"Natalie? She called me yesterday to make sure I kept my doctor's appointment. She's a doctor, too, and said she was thinking about moving to Florida to start her life over. I hope not, because then I'd never see her."

"Sounds like the three of you turned out to be friends."

Ruby bit into her lip. "Not at first, but I guess we sort of grew on each other."

"You all should go on *Oprah* or something."

She sighed, thinking about Beatrix. "Except we don't know how it's all going to turn out yet."

"Don't worry yourself too much." Laverne handed her a folded pink garment. "Now, put on your lab coat."

Ruby stared, then squealed with joy.

Thirty-eight

NATALIE SNEEZED FROM the motes she stirred with a feather duster as she moved around her office. Patients were few and far between, so she decided to take advantage of the chance to clean. Tony kept telling her things would pick up, but things hadn't, even though Mrs. Ratchet had run notice of the state medical board reinstating her license on the front page of the paper, in return for an exclusive interview at some point in the near future. Still, patients stayed away. Being an urban legend was great if someone needed a dinner guest, but not if they needed a doctor.

A buzzer sounded, alerting her to visitors. Since she couldn't afford to hire a receptionist or a nurse, she was handling all duties. When she walked into the waiting room, Brian stood between his nieces, one towheaded, and one brunette, chained together by their disproportionate hands. Both the girls had been crying, and he looked close to a breakdown himself.

She was careful not to betray her cheer at seeing him again. She'd scrupulously avoided his calls for a week, determined to disentangle herself from everyone until she could come to grips with the fact that Beatrix had murdered Raymond. On the one hand, she should have been furious, but knowing the extent of his betrayal to all of them had tempered her reaction to numbness. She simply couldn't believe the woman she'd come to know—or thought she'd come to know—could plan and execute a murder.

Which was further proof her judgment of character was enormously skewed.

"Hello," she said.

"Hi. I heard the doctor was back in."

"And this must be Ally and Jeanie."

The girls nodded and huddled closer to Brian's legs "I think they picked up a bug while they were at Mom's," he said.

"Ah." She smiled at the girls. "I'm Dr. Natalie, and I'll do my best to make you feel better."

"How come no one else is here, Uncle Brian?" Ally asked, looking around the empty waiting room.

"Because no one else is sick. Isn't that nice?"

Natalie gave him a wry smile. "Bring them back to the Blue Room—I think you know the way."

His mouth quirked to one side, then he herded them along. The girls were a wriggling, giggling, runny-nosed mess, but she was finally able to ascertain they both had mild respiratory infections.

"Are you going to give us a shot?" Ally asked, her eyes welling up.

"No." Natalie tugged on her pigtail. "Just some pink medicine you'll have to take for a few days."

"She's pretty, Uncle Brian," she whispered loudly behind her hand.

"Yes, she is," Brian said, locking gazes with her over the girls' heads.

"Why don't you bring her home sometime for spaghetti?" Jeanie suggested.

"Um, girls," he said, lifting them from the examination table to the floor. "I think I saw a bowl of lollipops in the waiting room. Why don't you each get *one* and wait for me there? And don't run," he added, his words drowned out by their tennis shoes pounding on the carpet.

Natalie squirmed, dreading the conversation.

"So how's business?"

She laughed softly. "It isn't."

"Things will pick up again."

"I'm moving."

He blinked. "You're *moving*? I hope you mean across town."

"I've been sending resumes to Florida. I'm putting my house up for sale."

"Just like that, you're leaving?"

She scowled. "Not just like that—I have given this decision some thought, you know."

His jaw hardened. "Did I imagine there was something between us?"

"Friendship," she said quickly, then busied herself with the girls' files.

His fingers curled loosely around her wrist. She lifted her gaze and swallowed. "What happened was a mistake, Brian. My life has been a roller-coaster, we were both lonely—"

"Don't give me that crap, Natalie. We're good together."

She pressed her lips together, not wanting to hurt his feelings. "We're moving in different directions. You're a family man. After everything that's happened, I need to acclimate."

"You mean you want to be alone."

"Can you blame me?"

He sighed. "No. But I don't like it."

"I'm sorry, Brian. I appreciate the way you've helped me and Tony. And I'll make sure you get the money Raymond owed you as soon as I sell the house or receive the life insurance settlement."

At the mention of the money, his mouth turned down. "Is Tony going with you?"

"I think so."

"How soon are you leaving?"

"As soon as I can sell the house. A real estate agent is coming by this weekend."

He ran his hand down over his face. "Can we at least spend time together until you have to go?"

She shook her head. "It'll only make things harder."

"For you?"

Yes. "No."

He pursed his mouth, then laughed humorlessly. "Okay, I'm hard-headed, but I think I'm getting the picture here."

Her heart squeezed. Another time, another place . . .

Suddenly his face rearranged into a smile. "But, hey, we can still be friends, right?"

Relieved, she nodded. "Absolutely."

He leaned back against the exam table and crossed his arms. "How is the case going?"

"Against Beatrix? Full speed ahead, I assume. My lawyer says I'll have to testify."

"Do you think she'll be convicted?"

"I honestly don't know. Her lawyer will bring up the fact that Ruby and I were both arrested for the murder—that's bound to create some doubt in the minds of the jurors."

"But I thought she confessed."

Natalie shook her head. "After they presented her with evidence about the poisoned cologne, she simply told the detective and the district attorney that she had planned to kill him, but someone else beat her to it."

"But no one believed her."

She sighed. "No. They dropped the charges against me and Ruby because we passed a polygraph test."

"Did Beatrix take one?"

"No." She straightened the folders, then straightened them again.

"Something's bothering you."

Natalie chewed on the inside of her cheek, wondering how crazy she would sound if she voiced her opinion. "I don't think she killed him."

"Of course she killed him. Who else is left?'

"The mystery woman."

"But you told me that Beatrix was the mystery woman."

"I thought so the day we were all talking to Aldrich and Keane, with the evidence against her piling up in my mind. But I've had time to think about our little road trip, and when that maid told us that Raymond was going to propose to someone else, I swear she was as shocked as I was."

"Maybe she's a good actress. She probably paid the maid to say all that."

"Then the maid was a good actress, too."

"But Beatrix had made some kind of murder to-do list, hadn't she?"

She nodded. "But like I said, she doesn't deny *wanting* to kill him."

"And you still think she didn't do it?"

"It's just a gut feeling."

"Have you talked to her lately?"

"I left a message yesterday, but she didn't return my call."

Brian straightened. “Mom came back with me to help with the girls. After I fill their prescriptions, let’s you and I drive to Northbend.”

She frowned. “I don’t know—”

“I tracked down a set of silver candlesticks that belonged to Beatrix but were already gone when she came by the shop. I was going to mail them, but Northbend is only an hour and a half from here.”

Natalie hesitated. The last time she and Brian had taken a drive, they’d ended up rolling around in the back of the van. “On one condition.”

“What’s that?”

“We take *my* car.”

Thirty-nine

THE BAD THING about driving, Natalie realized about a mile down the road, is that it allows the passenger free license to stare. "Do I have something on my face?"

"Yes," Brian said. "Freckles."

"I've been gardening, trying to get the back yard in shape to sell."

"Such a shame, seeing as how you love that house."

Tears on her pillow every night. "I have to be able to practice medicine, and I can't do it in Smiley."

"I think you're giving up. Too soon."

"Yeah, well you don't have to endure the stares and the whispers at the grocery store."

"Oh, I get stared at and whispered about a lot. People seem to think I'm a gangster or something."

"It's the scar," she said. "How'd you get it?"

"Brother," he said simply. "We were kids, playing war or something. He threw a half brick, and I looked up to meet it."

"You could have been killed."

He laughed. "Between me and my brother, I think my mom had a reserved seat in the emergency room."

"Where is your brother?"

"In Germany. Career military man."

"And your parents?"

"Pop died when I was a teenager. Mom remarried after I left home and moved to Key Valley."

"On the other side of St. Louis."

"That's right, your brother told me you and Raymond lived there for a while."

She swallowed.

"I'm sorry," he said. "I shouldn't have brought it up."

"His name? Don't be silly. Raymond was a big part of my life for a long time. I can't expect not to think about him, or for other people not to mention him." She glanced sideways. "What did you think about him?"

He shrugged. "Seemed like a nice enough guy, but I knew he was in a money bind. He was desperate, making crazy bets."

"Trying to win enough money to juggle three households. He was robbing Peter to pay Paul. Did you think he was a—" What were the words Tony used? "A player?"

"Oh, sure."

Her hands gripped the wheel tighter. "How?"

"I don't know. It's like you said about thinking Beatrix is innocent, just a gut feeling."

She wondered why she hadn't interpreted the stone in her stomach at the time she took her vows as uncertainty rather than nervousness. She'd been so caught up in the momentum of her husband's spirit. There was nothing casual about Raymond—no puttering in the garden, no estate sales and roadside picnics, no lovemaking on yellow shag carpet in the back of a van.

Really coarse yellow shag carpet that smelled of a citrusy cleaner and felt rather remarkable on bare skin.

"Natalie?"

"Hmm?"

"I asked if you've talked to the other wife, the young one?"

"Ruby? Yes, I called her a couple of times, to make sure she's getting prenatal care."

"How does that make you feel?"

She ignored his question. "Like a doctor."

"I mean, how does it make you feel that she's having Raymond's baby?"

She sighed. "Sorry for her, actually. She's so young, and she has no family around that seems to care. I hate Raymond for betraying me, but I don't think I'll ever forgive him for what he did to that girl. Her life will always be a struggle. She was even fired from her dancing job."

"I think Tony mentioned it."

"He has a crush on her. Anyway, I can't imagine how she's going to make ends meet *and* take care of that baby."

"Won't she get life insurance, child support, social security?"

"Since the policy was so new, the company opted to refund the premiums instead of paying the death benefit. I doubt if there will be anything left of Raymond's estate once the bills are paid, so the baby stands to inherit very little. She might get social security, though, or welfare. I wish I could help her, but I have to get my own affairs in order first."

"Did you ever want children?"

His voice was innocent enough, but his sudden preoccupation with the passing scenery betrayed his interest.

"No," she said honestly. "I never wanted children. With Raymond." Now why had she added *that* little disclaimer? "Where do I turn next?"

He consulted the map. "Two miles up, take a left onto

Willoughby, then a right onto Saddlebrook. Her address is 2525."

"I might recognize her house when I see it, although I was pretty out of it the day of the funeral." God, that horrid day seemed like a lifetime ago.

The house was relatively easy to find since it was the size of a city block. Five garages. Unbelievable landscaping. And not a sign of life anywhere.

"Maybe she still isn't home," she said as she put the Cherokee into park. She'd called before they left, but got the voice recorder again.

"The Mercedes is here," Brian said, peering through the tiny window slits on the garage door. "Parked crooked and the driver side door is open. Battery's bound to be dead if it's been like that long." He turned. "She was in a hurry when she got home."

Or drunk? Still, Natalie's pulse picked up.

Brian pointed. "Newspaper is still on the stoop."

"Something's wrong," she said. "You ring the doorbell, I'll try to call again."

She pulled out her cell phone and dialed Beatrix's number. "Beatrix, it's Natalie. Pick up. Brian Butler and I are in your driveway, and we're worried that something is wrong. Please pick up."

"No answer," Brian said, moving to a window and shading his eyes. "The windows are shuttered, can't see a thing."

Together they moved around the house, but all the windows and doors were shuttered. Morbid thoughts ran through Natalie's head. Had she committed suicide? Died in her sleep? Fallen down the stairs? Passed out?

Natalie was dialing 911 when the front door suddenly

swung open. Beatrix stood in the doorway wearing a muumuu—an expensive muumuu no doubt—and very obviously hung over. "Boy, am I glad to see you," she slurred. "Come on in. Quick."

She and Brian entered the house—a palace, really. The scent of live flowers in the foyer was overwhelming—dozens of vases, with white florists' cards springing from the arrangements. Beatrix slammed the door behind them, then turned the deadbolt.

"Natalie," Brian whispered, then nodded toward a table.

Natalie's eyes widened at the sight of a revolver. "Beatrix, what's going on?"

"Wish I knew," she said, holding her head. "Been trying to figure it out all night."

As evidenced by the empty bottle of gin next to the gun.

"Did something happen?"

In the light of day, with no makeup, she was still a beautiful woman. She winced, then appeared to be trying to concentrate, or to remember. "Yes. I distinctly recall that something did happen. And whatever it was, it scared the shit out of me."

"Beatrix, why do you have a revolver?"

Her expression lifted. "Ah, now I remember. Someone shot at me last night."

Natalie put her hand to her heart. "In this house?"

"No, I was driving."

"Maybe we'd better sit down," Brian urged.

"Oh, how rude of me," Beatrix said. "Yes, please, sit down."

Natalie sat next to Brian on the sofa, Beatrix in a chair. "Why don't you start at the beginning?"

"There was a gala at the club last night," Beatrix said in

a calm voice. Then she smiled. "They were giving away a service award named after my father. I always present the award, but last night they wouldn't even let me through thc damn doors, can you believe it?"

When she lapsed into thought, Natalie asked, "Then what happened?"

Beatrix snapped back to attention. "I left, of course. Sons of bitches. Decided to take a long drive, to clear my head." Her eyes clouded. "I found a rotted apple under my seat and tossed it out the window. A car came up behind me and turned on its bright lights. I thought perhaps the apple had hit the car and the driver was angry." A fine sheen of perspiration appeared on her brow. "But it kept tailing me, wouldn't pass. Finally I slowed way down, and the car pulled up alongside me." Her throat convulsed. "The person driving was wearing a mask and pointing a gun at me. I screamed, and luckily, the bullet went through the car without striking anything. I ran off the shoulder, and the car sped away. After I collected myself, I drove home, scared silly."

"Did you report the incident to the police?" Brian asked.

"No."

"Why not? That was a pretty insane reaction to a rotten apple."

"I didn't report the incident because I think the person driving was the rose lady."

Natalie's jaw dropped. "What?"

"They were driving a red Ford Taurus."

"All the more reason to call the police," he said.

"They wouldn't believe me," Beatrix said softly, her eyes glazed.

Brian shot Natalie a look that said, "She's gone mad."

"Beatrix," Natalie said gently. "Were you drinking when this happened?"

The woman shook her blond head. "Sober as the Pope." Then she frowned. "Why are you two here?"

"Brian brought your candlesticks he recovered, and frankly, I was worried about you."

Beatrix tilted her head and smiled. "Ah, that's sweet. But there's no need to worry about me—I got Clarence over there on the table to protect me."

"First, we're going to get some coffee and food into your stomach, then we're going to the police."

After she herded the woman into an upstairs shower, she joined Brian in the kitchen where he had one of—four?—coffeemakers going.

"Look at all this stuff," he said. Appliances lined the counters. "She's a pretty eccentric gal, you have to admit."

Natalie accepted a cup of coffee. "Do you believe her story?"

"You're the one who said she was innocent. If that's so, then the rose lady is still out there somewhere."

"But why would she be after Beatrix? If Raymond's murderer is still out there, their best chance of getting away with it is if the police think Beatrix is guilty."

"Yeah, but if Beatrix is dead . . ."

"A suicide might close the case, but a shot from a moving car? The police would know the killer was still out there." She shook her head. "I don't think it happened. Else, why wouldn't she have gone to the police?"

"Don't try to figure people out," he said, then one side of his mouth drew back. "There's one person in particular who's giving me fits."

She ignored his bait with an eye roll, then sighed. "I'm starting to believe Beatrix hallucinated this entire rose lady thing. I remember her saying her mother had mental problems, so maybe she inherited schizophrenia."

"Maybe you should suggest a psych workup."

She raised her eyebrows.

He grinned. "Oh, didn't I tell you? Psychology degree from Penn State."

Her eyes widened. "Now you're scaring me." She set down her coffee cup. "I'm going to call Masterson to get his advice."

"I'm going to find a trash bin and get rid of this smelly garbage."

She walked through the hall that was big enough to bowl in toward the massive living room. As she reached the marble foyer, the doorbell rang, scaring the bejesus out of her. Beatrix was coming down the stairs, knotting the ties of her robe. She held up a hand to stop Natalie from answering the door.

Natalie's heart pounded as Beatrix stepped to the window of the second-floor landing and peeked through a shutter. Then her shoulders sagged in relief. "It's just the florist—more goddamned flowers for Raymond."

"Do you want me to answer the door for you?"

"Yeah, but don't tip the kid, for heaven's sake. I've already given him enough for college tuition."

Noting that sobriety had restored Beatrix's good cheer, Natalie unlocked the door and opened it slowly.

Her first thought was that someone was incredibly generous to send such a huge vase of red roses. Her second thought was that she would be reunited with her beloved Aunt Rose Marie sooner than she'd planned.

Forty

IN SLOW MOTION, Beatrix watched the vase of red roses crash to the ground and a handgun appear inches from Natalie's face. The delivery person wore a loose uniform over her long curvy figure, gloves, and a snug hood pulled over her head.

But several strands of long hair had managed to escape the hood—several strands of long *red* hair.

She thought she might be sick.

"Move back," the woman ordered, then kicked the door closed.

If she remained perfectly still, perhaps she could go undetected until they moved out of the foyer. Then she could call for help. Her hungover brain chugged slowly—her revolver was on the table in the living room. Shit. If she got out of this alive, sweet Jesus, she would never drink anything but Evian.

"Beatrix," the woman growled. "Get your ass down here. Now."

So much for going undetected. The woman swung the gun back and forth to let them know she could pull the trigger at any minute. Where the hell was that good-looking behemoth when you needed him? Beatrix descended the stairs very slowly, then walked to stand next to Natalie. Perhaps together they could reason with the young woman. "Ruby, don't do this."

The woman stopped and stood fully erect. "Ruby?" She laughed, a sound that struck a memory chord in the back of Beatrix's mind. "Well, you're right about one thing. I'm going to let poor little Ruby take the rap, but I think it'll be more fun if you know the truth." She pulled off the hood in one motion, sending piles of red hair flying. A red wig.

But the face beneath the wig wasn't Ruby's, and it wasn't young. And for one long moment, it wasn't familiar. Then her heart dropped to her knees. "Blanche Grogan."

The woman grinned. "Hello, Beatrix. It's been a long time. How's that lying, cheating husband of yours? You know, the man you stole from me, then left me a laughingstock?" She put one hand to her temple. "Oh, wait—he's dead."

Natalie tried to speak past her tightened throat. "You . . . killed . . . Raymond?"

"Well, I didn't *want* to. We ran into each other at a conference several months ago, and picked right up where we left off." Her face was mean and gloating. "I always knew he loved *me*, but your daddy had all the money in the state, so he married you." Her hand began to shake, and she looked confused, far away. "Raymond told me he'd always loved me and he would divorce you so we could marry. But I got smart this time and did a little investigative work. Not only had he not divorced you, but he was married to two other losers besides."

"Wh-What did you do?" she asked, trying to find something in the woman's eyes that was reasonable, lucid.

"Did you know that I got married?" Blanche asked, lifting her chin.

"Yes, to a doctor, I recall."

"I hated him. He kept putting me in hospitals, telling people I was crazy. He took ouabain for his heart and made the mistake of telling me one day that too much of it would kill him. So I helped him along."

"What about R-Raymond?"

"Do you believe he had the nerve to propose to me?" she asked. "When I told him I knew his dirty little secret, he told me it didn't matter—that no one would believe a crazy woman like me." She laughed. "It was tricky, but this 'crazy woman' was able to get rid of him and make sure the three of you met at the hospital. I wanted you to suffer, Beatrix. Who knew things would work out this well? I've been having the time of my life watching the three of you dig yourselves deeper and deeper."

Out of the corner of her eye, Beatrix saw Brian sneaking up the hall. "Okay, Raymond's dead, and I've suffered. Why are you here?"

"Because," she said in a superior tone, "I realized that I could get rid of all of Raymond's wives this way." She whipped out a tiny plastic bag. "They'll find the two of you dead and a few of Ruby's long, red hairs. Oh, and I rented the Taurus in her name—it's just down the road. I'll make sure several people see me driving around in the wig. Ruby will go to prison and guess who has enough money and clout now to adopt Raymond's baby when she has to give it up?"

Not you, you lunatic. "You'll make a wonderful mother, Blanche. Now why don't you put down the gun and let's talk?"

"Talk?" The woman's arm straightened and she took aim with the automatic. "How about pray?"

With a whooshing sound, Brian tackled her and Natalie from the side, shoving them so hard they were lifted off the ground. Beatrix heard a bone or two crack as she fell hard on the cold, slick marble, but all she could think about was reaching her revolver. Behind her, Blanche's gun went off three times, followed by ricocheting pings. She clawed her way to the table and reached for the revolver only to realize the bones cracking must have been in her right arm, since she couldn't use it. She grabbed the gun with her left hand and ran to the foyer, horrified to see Natalie lying still. Brian, whose shirt was soaked with blood from an unseen wound, wrestled with Blanche, who was still holding the gun. She was no match for his size, but he was no match for her insanity. Beatrix took shaking aim with her left hand and pulled the trigger.

Blanche dropped to the floor and Brian went with her momentum. He rolled off the woman and dragged himself to his feet, holding his side. When he saw Natalie, his face went ashen.

"Don't pass out on me," Beatrix warned him, then stooped to find a pulse on Natalie's wrist before giving him a reassuring wink. "She must have hit her head when you tackled us." Assuming some of his weight with her left side, she helped him to the sofa, trying not to think about the bloodstain on her four-thousand-dollar couch. Or the events she'd set into motion twenty-some years ago for a woman who had once called her a friend. With her left hand she yanked up the phone and awkwardly punched in 911.

"Nice shot," Brian murmured weakly.

"Thanks to target practice. It was one of the ways I was planning to kill Raymond."

"Oh."

"Yes, operator, there is an emergency at 2525 Saddlebrook. One person is dead, one is almost dead, and one will wish she were tomorrow when she wakes up."

Forty-one

RUBY STOPPED OUTSIDE the hospital door and crossed her fingers. Then she turned the knob—hard to do with crossed fingers—and poked her head inside the room.

Beatrix's eyes flew open at the noise.

"Hi," Ruby said, and offered a smile.

To her amazement, Beatrix smiled back. "Hello, Ruby. Come in."

"I promise I won't stay too long," she said. "I brought you some cookies," she said, holding up a little plastic container. "Chocolate chip."

"My favorite."

"Mame's too." She moved closer to the bed. "Wow, cool cast. Can I be the first to sign it?"

Beatrix smiled and nodded against the pillow.

Good thing she had a Chango marker pen in her purse—it wrote two colors at once. Being real careful not to press down, she put a big swirl on the "Y" and made a smiley face in the top of the "R." "There. How are you feeling?"

"Old."

"Well, you look great."

"Have you seen Natalie and Brian?"

Ruby fell into the guest chair and nodded. "Natalie's still got a pump knot on her head, but she said she was feeling fine. Brian said he could go home in a couple of days. He's cute, don't you think?"

Beatrix nodded.

"Do you think they're in love?"

"I hope so."

She picked at a raveling at the hem of her sleeve. "I wanted to thank you, Beatrix."

Beatrix frowned. "Whatever for?"

"Detective Aldrich told me that woman who killed Raymond wanted my baby, so thank you for stopping her."

"You're welcome, but they would never let someone as nutty as Blanche Grogan adopt your baby, or any baby."

She bit into her lip. "It's funny, isn't it? You have to be rich and successful and not crazy to adopt children that no one else wants or can take care of, but any stupid person can have their own kids."

Beatrix smiled. "I never thought about it, but I suppose you're right."

"Do you think I'm smart enough to be a good mother?" The more the baby moved, the more she worried about how she was going to pull it off, this parenting thing. She didn't want to be a failure at absolutely everything in her life.

Wincing, Beatrix pushed herself up straighter. Ruby leaned forward in case she needed her.

"Ruby, I think the fact that you're worried about whether you'll be a good mother is a good sign that you *will* be a good mother."

"You mean even good mothers worry about whether they're good mothers?"

"Well, I don't have much experience in this department,

but I think that good mothers *especially* worry about whether they're good mothers."

Ruby smiled as understanding dawned. "Because bad mothers don't care."

"Precisely."

She sat back, feeling important, even without her lab coat. "When do you get to go home?"

"As soon as I can hire someone to stay with me for a few weeks until my arm heals."

"I'm sure there are lots of people who would jump at the chance."

"Actually, Ruby, I was hoping you might agree to."

Stunned, she could only mouth, "Me?"

Beatrix nodded.

"Me, live in that big fancy house and help you?"

"Well, I'll pay you, of course. But it won't be a picnic. You'll have to help me bathe and dress, and drive me around and fix meals."

She grinned. "I fix an awesome grilled cheese sandwich."

"I haven't had a good grilled cheese sandwich in a long time, although I think I have a machine that makes them."

Ruby laughed, already thinking how much she could learn from Beatrix. Then she stopped.

"What's wrong?"

"What about . . . Miss Mame?"

"Hmm. Well, she'll just have to learn her way around a new house, won't she?"

She clapped her hands. "It'll be like a vacation."

"That's another thing," Beatrix said. "We'll see how it goes, but I've been thinking about how it might work out for both of us if you consider living with me even after the baby is born."

She didn't know what to say. "I don't know what to say."

"Say you'll think about it."

"You'll think about it!" Ruby cried, so happy she couldn't imagine a more wonderful day.

Forty-two

"SO YOU'RE REALLY going through with it?" Tony asked.

Natalie sighed. "I've already *gone* through with it. The agent said I wouldn't get many offers this good. The buyer saw the pictures on the Internet, and was willing to close right away. Easy. It's over."

"I still think you should stay here and . . . see what happens. Business is picking up a little, isn't it?"

"A little, but it's mostly curiosity seekers with a manufactured cough. Yesterday a guy whipped out a camera while I was taking his blood pressure." She stopped packing books and squeezed her brother's hand. "Listen, I was fortunate to land this position with a new medical group in Pensacola. Maybe I'll be able to have a normal life in a place where I'm completely anonymous."

"Sounds like a barrel of fun, all right."

"Tony, I know you like it here. It's a sacrifice for you to come with me, and I'm grateful."

"I just don't want you to be alone."

She smiled.

"'Course, neither does Butler."

She frowned. "Tony, we've been through this. I mailed Brian a check this morning from the house proceeds to cover

Raymond's debts, and that's the end of our so-called relationship."

"It doesn't have to be the end."

"Yes, it does. Right now I need peace and quiet in my life, and Brian Butler is the equivalent of a one-man band."

Tony leaned on the desk and crossed his arms. "I don't get it—what is it about him that's so . . . noisy?"

"Stop."

"No, humor me. Please."

Natalie pushed up her sleeves. "He's just so . . . I don't know—big. He crowds me."

"And?"

"And I'm not so sure I like the kind of business he's in. It seems a little . . . suspect."

"He's an honest man who runs an honest business."

"And he's raising those two little girls. I'm not ready to be a mother."

"He wasn't ready to be a father."

"And frankly, I'm just not that attracted to the man." A bald-faced lie, but impossible to refute. "He always looks like he just got out of bed, and he doesn't exactly take pains to impress me."

"No, he's not the kind of guy who has to impress anyone, that's for sure."

She waved him off. "See—I knew you'd take everything I said and turn it around. Aren't you late for work?"

"Yep."

"Have a nice day."

He shook his head. "Why the man is so crazy about you, I'll never know."

She scowled after him as he exited the library, then threw

herself into getting as many books packed as possible. The man was not crazy about her. He was just crazy, period. Damsel-in-distress syndrome. They'd been thrown together in this whole murder investigation mess, but proximity was no basis for a relationship. And, yes, she was grateful that he'd saved both her life and Beatrix's, even though he'd given her a concussion in the process and nearly induced a secondary stroke when she woke to find him bleeding all over Beatrix's couch. If for no other reason, she hated him for the fact that she . . .

Tears spilled over her cheeks. For the fact that she could feel something stronger for a man she'd known mere weeks than for the man to whom she'd been married for six years. It scared her, dammit. What if she plowed up her life and her plans and invested in becoming a mother, only to find out years down the road that she wasn't good enough or exciting enough to keep his interest? She refused to spend the rest of her life starting over.

A sound from the back of the house caught her attention. She wiped her eyes, cursing herself, and went to see if the new bench she'd ordered had arrived. The least she owed Rose Marie was to leave the garden in better shape than it had been when she moved in.

But at the back door, she stopped, supremely irritated. Brian was pushing a wheelbarrow of white round stones over the pathway, whistling. She flung open the door and charged down the steps. "What do you think you're doing?"

He looked up. "Oh, hi. I thought I'd scatter these rocks between the stepping stones—it'll cut down on weeds."

"You're not supposed to be lifting."

Brian grinned. "Are you worried about me?"

She jammed her hands on her hips. "I'm your doctor,

remember. Besides, I happen to like the stepping stones just the way they are."

He set down the wheelbarrow. "Well, since I'll be doing the weeding, the rock is going down."

"*You'll* be doing the weeding?"

He crossed his arms and surveyed the area with a proud smile. "It's my garden."

"Have you lost your mind?"

"Nope. I just bought this house, and if memory serves, the garden goes with it." He pulled a paper she recognized as the house listing from his back pocket. "Yep, says right here: 'English garden with great hobby potential in back yard.'" He waved the paper for emphasis.

Her jaw felt loose. "But . . . but . . ."

He shoved the paper back into his pocket. "Now don't start complaining—I gave you a good price."

"But . . . but . . ."

"Of course, I did throw in a little as a bribe in case you wanted to, say . . . stay?" He gave her a hopeful, little-boy-in-a-man's-body smile.

Natalie pressed her hand to her heart, feeling its insistence on her palm. Brian's smile was for her alone. If there was such a thing as one moment of transformation in a person's life, this was hers. Her long-held illusion of an orderly, safe existence was not only arrogant, but utterly foolish. She'd married the presumably perfect man—handsome, ambitious, and charming—only to be used and humiliated. And she'd almost allowed Raymond to rob her again, by rendering her too tentative to extend herself to a man who held out the hope of real happiness.

"Natalie?"

She lunged for him.

Epilogue

NATALIE STOOD WITH Beatrix and Ruby over Raymond's grave, each holding a long-stemmed red rose. Natalie could scarcely believe the recent changes in her life—she was a bona fide wife and mother now, her days jammed with so many snatches of joy, her existence before seemed comatose by comparison.

Beatrix's broken arm had healed nicely, although Natalie suspected she had dragged out her recovery longer than necessary to keep Ruby close by. Meanwhile, the younger woman had settled into Beatrix's life with the permanence of a kudzu vine, and despite their constant arguing, it was clear they adored one another. Beatrix was taking cooking classes, of all things, and working part-time in an antique bookstore.

Ruby's stomach was well-rounded. She was due to deliver a baby girl in a couple of weeks (a relief to Natalie and Beatrix who shared nightmarish visions of Raymond Carmichael's son being unleashed on the unsuspecting women of the world). Flush with pride over her recent GED certification, Ruby chattered on and on about the possibility of taking college classes in the spring. The metamorphosis was nothing short of astounding.

Natalie's eyes brimmed. If Raymond Carmichael had

performed a single deed to warrant grace in the afterlife, it was bringing the three of them together.

They dropped their roses on the new grey marble headstone that read simply "Our Husband." As they walked away arm in arm, Ruby halted abruptly, looked down, then lifted a beaming smile. "Twenty percent of firstborn babies arrive early."